# SAILING UNCHARTED WATERS
## A Mystical Voyage into the Unknown

## Volume Two, Trilogy

## Nan Colwell Creaghan

ℰᏟᏩℭᏨ
**MacKenzie Publishing**

# Dedication

*I dedicate this second volume to my British, Irish, and Acadian*
*ancestors and any skeletons in the closet,*
*Who gave me who and what I am today.*
*To my husband, Tom; sons, Jonathan and Geoffrey*
*For their long-standing courage*
*And patience in withstanding,*
*Hopefully with some humor, my life-style,*
*To my grandchildren*
*And to Janice Buchanan for the humour and patience she*
*Exhibited in editing this volume.*

*God bless 'em all!*

# Foreword

The first volume of my trilogy has thirteen chapters. This second volume has two chapters, 14 and 15, with the third volume yet to be published. The little red sailboat, as in life, continues to sail on.

The story *Sailing Uncharted Waters, a Mystical Voyage into the Unknown* is an Allegory based on the life of a female skipper sailing in a little red sailboat, taking her she knows not where.

She is left to the mercy of the elements; winds, rains and tides, creation around her and to the fragile hurricane motions of her mind, soul, psyche, and emotions controlling her.

What is that uplifting, joyous, exciting and wondrous mystical energy she is allowed to sink into and envelop, sometimes with terrifying fear and oftentimes, resting in peace and calm; sailing along, continuing to survive the ordeals of her voyage in her little red sailboat?

I will leave you to discover the answer as you read on, after hopefully you, dear readers, have read the first volume, through this second volume, and into the third future volume when published.

Nan Colwell Creaghan
November 5, 2016

# Contents

# Chapter 14

# Burbourne Drive

Victoria, knowing she must sell her beloved Brae Na Beith, tries to blank the thoughts out of her mind as the mounting pressures of again having to find real estate agents occupies her. She tells herself the place doesn't mean anything to her anymore. She and Jack must look for another house while still managing this one. Her day-to-day routine must continue in spite of the disruptions, including dealing with Jack's attitude toward her. It soon takes a toll on her. A deep depression takes over. She is, as yet, not spiritually strong enough to handle the mounting weight upon her shoulders.

But life goes on. Jack is established in his new job in a very charming town, and they find a home just off the main street. The house has great potential even though it needs much work; this Jack always looks for in a house as he wheels and deals the price. He calls her to invite her to lunch and to co-sign the mortgage papers at the bank. She never once questions the seriousness of her signature on these papers, trusting Jack completely. Brae N Beith also sells and again, she co-signs to seal the deal.

Their new home on Burbourne Drive overlooks a small Anglican Convent sitting in a grove of trees. Another church can be seen from the back of their house, also surrounded by a grove of trees. Trees, especially oaks, seem to be the hallmark of this quaint and beautiful town.

Matt and James, their sons, have settled into a new way of life again for the umpteenth time: Matt in his first year of high school and James in a private school in Toronto, his last year. Jack is, of course, traveling two or three times a month, to Mexico and other South American countries to carry on the business for the company.

They are all moved in accept for a few odds and ends, and Jack is home this weekend, very much under the weather. He was out late the night before; she suspects a hang-over. The odds and ends of the move into this new house won't get completed this weekend.

She receives a call from her doctor to discuss her blood-work. The doctor tells Victoria she should be resting. "I will try," she tells the doctor.

Victoria thinks with discouragement, "Who could possibly get rest?"

"Anyway," the doctor, said, sounding impatient, "the blood tests are all normal so you don't have rheumatic fever after all."

"Oh, I'm so glad," Victoria exclaims, wishing to God she had so that she could find an excuse to end up in the hospital and get a good rest.

So today, she is getting that "rest" lying on her chesterfield in the living-room, blanketed in her sister's gift, a cozy comforter. Under her, in the "not so insulated from the noise" family room in the lower level, are Matthew and his friends tearing at her shattered nerves and ears with their loud, jarring hard-rock records called music. Matt, at fifteen, is certain her ears are not made like his or that she is a different creature from outer space since she can't tune into the grating of those electronic, vibrating instruments he loves so much. Now, mind you, on a better day, she can appreciate Pink Floyd like the rest of them. She can value and appreciate the artistry of these talented young musicians, but she can't seem to get it into their heads that today is not the day!

She thinks, "Why don't I go to the bedroom where it is quieter?"

Oh! Yes, a great idea until the phone rings and she has to answer it, and the doorbell rings and she has to rush, in her half-opened kimono and bare feet, to answer it. Why? Poor Jack is sleeping in the den and mustn't be disturbed.

"Tell me," a little man with pointed horns on his head screams, "Who is sick, anyway? Why don't you go and wake him up and blast him. Who is looking after whom?"

A sweet figure dances through her conscience, singing! "Oh! He should be allowed to sleep. He is under so much mental stress!"

But the little man with the pointed horns is louder. "No! What about me?" In her imagination, she goes in there and shakes the living daylights out of Jack and makes him answer the door. She doesn't do that, of course, so here she is, feeling hostility and anger because she has to lie on the living room couch to get some rest for her flu so that she can answer the door and the phone, so that Jack can get some much-needed rest.

The door and the phone having been answered, she crawls back under her blanket and prays. Guess what! Within fifteen minutes the gang leaves the family room, the music dies, Jack still snores quietly, and she hears nothing but the sounds of birds in the trees, soft rain splashing against the window-pane, and her cat purring happily and contentedly as it nestles in the curve of her legs. , the newness and color of nature, all green from the new April rains.

She can feel peace stealing over her that brings such comfort and joy. She wishes she can share this moment of aloneness with all that has been spiritually provided. There is safety and security in knowing that a Spiritual Power is near whether one is sick or well, or wherever one may be. Truly a miracle to sense His Presence in her life within minutes! One just has to believe and let Him in! Then her thoughts accuse her again: Are not the kids better off and safer here where she can keep an eye on them? That thought brings peace, too.

Their move to this beautiful community opens up more spiritual arenas in her life she had suspected but has not been prepared to receive, until, one morning she answers a knock on the door. A pretty, young woman with dark hair stands there. She is canvassing for the Heart Foundation. Victoria invites her in to make the donation when all of a sudden the conversation turns to a prayer life. She had just been through a crying jag, not knowing where to turn next. Victoria thinks the young woman cues in on her tear-streaked face and eyes and nose so red, because she begins to talk about a prayer group she belongs to.

--------------- --------------------- ---------------------

*"Unbelievably, the little red sailboat with its lone female sailor sails into calmer waters."*

--------------- --------------------- ---------------------

They talk, standing at the door, a few minutes longer with Victoria asking her the name of her group.

"Women Aglow Ministries," she says, "and our group is going to have a speaker tomorrow afternoon. Would you like to come?" She explains what the luncheon will be all about.

Victoria has no idea what to think but she was never one to turn down an invitation to a luncheon. Anyway, she is assured, as she listens to this pleasant woman, that everything is above-board.

"Yes! Thank you for asking me. I would love to come." The woman hands her a ticket. "How much," Victoria asks, only too happy to pay.

"No, no! This is on me," she offers with a smile. Victoria is astounded but accepts the ticket with joy.

By the end of the afternoon, Victoria is flying high. It is the very tonic she needs to get her over these doldrums. She does not realize it but it is a confirmation of the beginnings of a life very unfamiliar to her.

Jack is late for dinner; in a bad mood, he complains about the cold meal. Better not tell him about her plans for tomorrow. He wouldn't understand anyway. A negative response could be expected which would dampen her enthusiasm.

The next day, as she enters the hotel convention room where the luncheon is being held, she feels her heart soar as she hears the music coming from the stage. The many tables around the room are filled with women of all ages and Victoria feels at home even though Heather is the only one she knows. The talk with the women at her table, the words of the speaker, the spiritual witnessing, plants seeds of encouragement in her very depressed heart, soul and mind. No more tranquillizers, antidepressants for her; she has been given all the "highs" she requires to feel like a real person.

Up to now she knew nothing about the bible or bible studies. All she can recall is the big, ancient, leather bible her mother bought from a traveling, door-to-door book salesman. As she remembers, she can still see it on the bottom shelf of a living room table which, for some reason, never seemed to gather dust.

Still, even with nervous and unsure thoughts, she joins the bible study with the members of the Women Aglow Group in her area. It also means that she is establishing her place with people who are supposed to be such "stuffed shirts." She thoroughly enjoys the camaraderie of these good Christian women.

It opens up a world other than her husband's business world, their wives, or anything connected with business, socially or otherwise. This is her world, a world just for her, she feels, not just because she is Jack Adam's wife. On the positive side, though, she knows that the links with Jack's associates and wives proved very good too, as it gave her the opportunity to join the Elizabeth Fry Society as a volunteer to work with prison women. This has given her experience in relating with women in trouble with the law; helping her see another side of society.

The Women Aglow Ministries teaches her much about the people of the New Testament and how Jesus worked in their lives. When they begin to study about Paul in the Book of Acts, however she begins to argue with the group having a hard time accepting what is being taught. She still is not completely a believer as yet. She knows that her relationship with a Higher Power is real and she is hungry for more but she still has much fear, depression and anger. She is learning about the healings that Jesus performed but she did not believe she was worthy to receive or even believe that this could happen to her. The biblical seeds that are slowly being planted are still trying to find their way up through thorns, thistles and through hard, rocky ground.

Up until now she never stopped to think about her past life; she just knew she was always angry and depressed. Why? Was she really a "nut-case" as Jack is telling her she is? But, something is nagging at her.

One day, she invites her friend, Heather for a visit. Over a cup of tea they discuss Victoria's need to discuss the things she is being taught at the bible study get-togethers. Heather listens quietly and then without any advance discussion she asks Victoria,

"How would like to attend a Spiritual weekend in Honey Harbor with a few of our group?"

Victoria is, all of a sudden, filled with fear. What in heaven's name was she getting into? It's one thing to study the bible but to go off, heaven only knows where, with a bunch of women, to a spiritual convention boggles the mind! Anyway, what really happens at these conventions? She had heard the women talk of strange things happening and heard a strange language being loudly proclaimed at these monthly luncheons but thought nothing of it. She is not so deeply involved that she participated, just listened. She had no opinion, really, of what she read in the bible.

"I'm sure you understand, Heather, that my faith right now is as weak as a kitten."

She gives Heather a hug as the young woman leaves.

5

However, Providence has other plans for Victoria. She gets a surprise phone call from Heather the following week. Victoria is very pleased to hear from her but can't imagine why she is phoning.

Heather asks her point blank without any other discussion, "Victoria, I have a ticket to go to the Women Aglow Convention I told you about but I won't be able to go. Would you please, use the ticket?"

Victoria is so surprised she doesn't know what to say, however she senses the urgency in Heather's voice. She is hesitant to give an answer, so to make time, she asks a few questions.

"No problem, you can have it for nothing and your weekend is paid," in answering Victoria's worrisome question.

How could she possibly turn down Heather's offer? They are leaving on the bus the following weekend and so she has no time to dwell on it. She knows that being given this invitation and the way it came about, leaves her no choice. She commits herself in Faith even though she doesn't realize that is what she is doing.

They arrive Friday afternoon, amidst women from all over the province and country, pouring out of buses and cars to begin one weekend Victoria will never forget.

Early evening sees the women in the dining room enjoying their first meal of the weekend. They, then flock into the convention hall to the sounds of gospel music from a group of singers. The words of the songs are printed on a screen for all to see, so everyone joins in. It is an exuberant and joyful evening with Victoria just sitting quietly not able to move. She had never heard any of the songs before. She is used to conventions, having attended many with Jack through his business affairs but never like this. The talk of the evening stresses the weekend's schedule of activities and they then, all drift off to their rooms, chattering and chirping as they go. She can't wait until tomorrow!

Saturday morning, with coffee, tea and sweets laid out in the convention room, they all meet to the sound of music. This time there is a witnessing of a very powerful conversion which gives Victoria an idea of what this get-together is all about. All enjoy lunch and then back to the Hall.

Music fills the air and hearts. She still does not know what's happening but she didn't care. Her friends around her are so supportive that she feels comfortable, at ease and very happy.

However she is not prepared for what happens next.

As the afternoon wears on things begin to pick up. The Minister, who is a woman with long, flaming red hair knotted up to the top of her graceful head, begins to pray in this strange language. Victoria feels herself growing weak. The Minister prays even more strongly, and then she explains the process of healing through the laying on of hands with anointing oil. She asks the gathering of women,

"I am now asking those of you who need healing; physically, mentally, spiritually and emotionally to come to the stage and I will pray over you with the help of a number of chosen healers."

Victoria just sits there unable to move. She can't understand just how this healing thing would come about. Anyway, she's too weak to move. Finally a friend, who, sitting beside her gives her a nudge and suggests she walk up to the stage. Victoria hesitates just a second, lifts herself up, and feeling the strength coming back into her legs, joins the others to the stage. They are all lined up with the Minister moving gently along the line praying and touching foreheads with the anointing oil.

The Minister and another woman, when they come to her, ask her to move to the side of the stage. Victoria does so with some perplexity. The Minister then touches her forehead with the anointing oil, holds her hands and prays in that strange language.

Then, very softly she whispers, "As a child, you were sexually molested by your father,"

With those words echoing in Victoria's ears, the Minister continues to pray over her for healing. Victoria feels a tingling rush through her body and she is thrown backwards with the other woman holding her, gradually letting her fall to the floor. The words echo in her ears,

"I was sexually molested by my father!! NO! NO! NO! It can't be true!! How could this Minister have known this? I have never seen this woman before. How could she have known?"

Somehow, with the help of the woman standing over her, Victoria, still crying, with tears blinding her eyes and streaming down her face, manages to stand up and find her way to her seat. One of her friends comes half way, puts her arms around her and helps her. Her friends then crowd around her with such consolation, sympathy and love. She has never experienced this warmth of love rushing through her being before. Victoria spends the rest of the afternoon in a daze, sobbing off and on, not able to comprehend what happened. She just couldn't stop the heart-wrenching weeping.

7

In the evening the Minister prays over her again to heal those past memories. The Minister then asks her if she would like to receive Jesus into her soul. Victoria agrees and then feels, in a powerful rush within her, the infilling of the Holy Spirit. She knows, without a doubt, the healing Power of God in the Name of Jesus Christ, her Saviour, by the power of the Holy Spirit which had been given her in Baptism, as a baby, now released within her. However, right now, she is not able to understand and put all these revelations into words; perhaps in later years? As she prepares to leave she is given a small leather bible which she cherishes. Many of her friends sign their names in it for her.

She can now rest back in the caverns of her mind, this revelation, experience and trauma relating to her father where, if they surface again, she can face without pain. But she still has a long way to go.

--------------- --------------------- ---------------------

*"The skipper sits in contemplative silence as the soft breeze rocks her little red sailboat."*

--------------- --------------------- ---------------------

For the next week her whole being is immersed in peace and serenity. Nothing Jack says to her affects her. She seems to be unaware of what is happening around her. She is very happy in the bliss of this new way of life; life in the Holy Spirit. A real Spiritual High they call it. She begins to spend more time in prayerful silence. Everything is the same around her and yet nothing is the same. Heather, her friend from Women Aglow Group, who introduced her to this new world, moves away, leaving her with memories and a beautiful book inscribed with words of affection. Victoria is overwhelmed, as it seems to her, rightly or wrongly, that no one cared about her.

--------------- --------------------- ---------------------

She often goes down town and walks along the park which is situated on the banks of the lake. To get to this park she walks through the old section of town and passes a beautiful, old Catholic Church. One day she enters this church and sits in silence. All the memories of her past child-hood relationship with her Catholic Faith come flooding back. Such good memories she had of those years as a child and young adult. She wonders how she could have gotten through those years without her church life.

She has been keeping in touch with her friend from Brae na Beith who often talks about the Mass and the changes in the church today.

It did not take much persuading for Victoria to return to this inspiring, moving but still weak, branch in her life. Jack is not very impressed with her decision but he is so busy with his own life he really doesn't pay that much attention.

So she begins to attend Mass every morning at this beautiful, historic Church. She loves this routine in her day which also includes joining the other church-goers at the local coffee shop after Mass. It's a rich and fulfilling daily routine which inspires her to grow more and more in her faith.

It is a way of life she always dreamed of living but didn't believe possible. How was it possible that Victoria Adams from the backwoods of N.B. could be sitting in this historic church, rubbing shoulders with the elite and influential of this beautiful town? Quite unbelievable!

Jack's position as partner in his new company with Victoria as his wife, takes on a variety of activities including socializing with his partner and owner Gerald and his wife. Victoria guesses that's why it was so important they move there. Thankfully, with it being a small, private company the socializing does not involve the pressures that were required with the major American companies where Jack held the title of General Manager and Executive on the Boards. Those positions placed them in the realm of the very powerful and wealthy, the so-called Establishment of Canada and the United States.

They are still living in an upper class community catering to the upper echelons of society. They did not lose their position in society; if anything they climbed a little more upward. They are living the kind of life Jack wants for them, are they not? Isn't that what she wanted when she lived her growing-up years back home? She wanted to mix with the upper class and so, here she is. Of course, she did not see herself as high class but here she is. Does this life-style make her better than others? Why does she always turn back to those past years growing up, those years of not seeing herself as good as others?

Of course, there is always a downside to everything in life. As was the case with the other companies, Jack continues to do a lot of traveling; this time to South America. This means that he is away from home a couple of days or weeks every month. He is not saying much about these trips; however, he does ask her if she would like to go along.

Victoria thinks about her last trip with him; so very traumatic. She makes an appointment with her doctor for one thing or another and while there she discusses these trips with her and how they affected her.

The doctor looks at her and asks," why are you going on these trips with him?"

Victoria stares at her open-mouthed.

"Good question. Now, why didn't I think of that? Why am I going on these trips with him" she asks herself.

Then she says to the Doctor, "Jack is not someone you say no to. I'm afraid of him."

"Well, my dear, for your own sanity you are going to have to learn to say no!" The doctor states the facts clearly. Knowing Victoria's problems, she questions, "Have you ever thought of leaving him?"

"Leaving him?" The thought never enters her head. It would be unheard of in a marriage; not a good Catholic! Anyway, where would she go? She stores the thought in the back of her mind.

Things are moving along at a steady pace at her church. Father Helman, the Parish priest, has asked her to do some morning readings at the daily Masses. This truly is an honor and a big responsibility. She is very happy to do it. This makes her feel as if she truly belongs now. She has broken her ties with the Pentecostal Women Aglow Group and is more established in a Catholic religion where she was baptized as a child.

She hears about a Charismatic Group at St John's, another Catholic Church on the other end of town. One of her friends is going to the next meeting and asks her if she would like to go along. This group, Victoria finds out after a few visits, is very similar in some ways to the Pentecostal Church and the Women Aglow Group where she was anointed with Holy oil by the Power of the Holy Spirit in the Name of Jesus Christ. These events brought alive the scriptures, the first chapter of The Book of Acts in the bible when the Holy Spirit settles on the Disciples, anointing them in the Name of Jesus Christ. This also happened to Jesus when John the Baptiste baptized Him with water and the Holy Spirit in the form of a dove settling on Him, and her own awesome healing weekend in Honey Harbour with the group, Women Aglow.

One morning she is praying quietly in her room when, as she prays out loud, much to her surprise, a strange, beautiful sound spills out from her mouth. She calls a friend and asks her what is happening.

She giggles and says," Victoria, you are praying in tongues! It's proof that you have been blessed by the Power of the Holy Spirit!" This Tongues or language, you are praying is a prayer to God by the Holy Spirit within you, when we, ourselves, can't find the words to pray." She can't believe it! The sounds are so beautiful. She is so overwhelmed tears flow.

Christmas, this year takes on a very special meaning for her. To be attending this Christmas Midnight Mass in the arms of this beautiful little church for her first Christmas is more than she can handle. She breaks out in tears as she becomes immersed in the beauty of this awesome time of the year; the birth of Jesus Christ being so delightfully expressed through the Mass and the music. Jack and the boys go with her, giving the whole season a meaning she has not experienced in a very long time.

--------------- --------------------- ---------------------

*"A new year, the rivers are still open. She sits in her little red sailboat and decides to write. The little skipper is inspired to keep a record of her thoughts as a prayer form; writing how her prayers and spiritual life becomes a mystical voyage into an unexplored and unknown world."*

--------------- --------------------- ---------------------

The thirteenth of January/83, her birthday; Victoria goes to Mass and then to the coffee shop with some friends from the church. They are all chattering about something that was announced in the bulletin on Sunday; a Notice of a new form of prayer taking place at the Anglican Sisters' Convent across from her home. Everyone is excited.

Victoria arrives home, has lunch and writes:

Father Lawrence of the Benedictines Monastery in Montreal is setting up Ecumenical Meditation Groups to teach meditation in a variety of churches including the Anglican churches in Toronto and area. The talk is that this form of prayer is based on the Tradition of Saint John Cassian who taught it to Saint Benedict. Father John Main O.S.B. brought the teachings to the Benedictine Priory in Montreal.

The Catholic Women's League has decided, as a Catholic Church Parish Group, that they will join the Anglican Sisters for this momentous opportunity. She is very happy about this as she is always open to new forms of prayer that will take her deeper into her spiritual life. It will take place once a week at the Anglican Convent across the street.

"Dad would be ecstatic, being Anglican" she muses to herself as she finishes writing her thoughts.

--------------- --------------------- ---------------------

She wakes up this morning feeling a bit down. She took a tranquilizer last night that helped a bit. It's been two weeks since she took one. She didn't go to Mass; just watched a movie in bed. She tried earlier to get Jack away from his paper but no go! He really vexes her as he never seems to have any time for her. He's been sick since he returned home from his trip to Mexico. She decides to get up and take a shower. She begins to pray to Blessed Mother, Mary for help.

"Lord, I really need help," she prays.

Jack is always sick when he returns from these trips.

Yes, without her prayer life, the attendance at Mass, the receiving of the Eucharist each day and the praying of her Rosary, she would not be able to handle the next whirlwind about to hit their home on Burbourne Dr.

She notices a change in Jack's enthusiasm for his job and the trips he must take to the Latin American countries. Something is wrong; she feels it deep down in her gut.

A bright spot; the next day she receives, in the mail, an invitation to a wedding in N.B.; a sister-in-law's daughter is getting married in July.

--------------- --------------------- ---------------------

She is receiving another prompting to continue writing. So much has happened to her in the past and the future. How will she get all those many interesting, sad, traumatic and amazing things down?

"I'm not very good with words and I have so much to say. I must include my spiritual encounters, especially. They are a very important part of my life. I have now let my will be God's Will. What He has in store for me each day I will do. It is important that I now let the Lord shape my life and to do His activities as He Wills. May God help me, guide me, discipline me, give me the Graces necessary and love me through this undertaking. I place myself and this book, "Sailing Uncharted Waters" in God's Hands."

--------------- --------------------- ---------------------

*"She and her little red sailboat are trying to steady the Course but the winds are battering the sails and the fragile vessel again."*

--------------- --------------------- ---------------------

Jack walks in about 5:P.M. It certainly is early for him. He joins her, mixes drinks and then sits down. The scowl on his face is like a dark shroud. He doesn't mince any words. Victoria tries to remain calm. What did she do now? After a few more sips he drops the bomb.

"I am going to have to sue Gerald. The company has lost all our money. It's bankrupt."

She sits in astonishment, her mouth open as she holds her cocktail. "What does this mean? Is Jack going to lose his job again?" She doesn't realize she has spoken out loud.

Jack seems not to hear her. He says not another word. No explanation.

Victoria has his dinner ready and they sit down after a few more cocktails. The mood around the table is dark and very somber. Jack adds a few more tidbits and then, nothing more. He turns in early.

She keeps quiet. No point in discussing her day. It's as if it never happened. Now what? Her heart is heavy as she contemplates this new episode taking place in her life.

"Jack is going to have to sue Gerald, his partner. He has only been with the company, what is it, two years? The phones were cut off today. Jack said he might have to borrow from the bank again to help the company get back on its feet. Will there be another mortgage on the house? Jack is now going to have to look for another job, she supposes." All she can think to do is pray.

She wakes up at 7:00A.M., not feeling very well. She's been having attacks of severe pain all through her body that have gradually been getting worse all week. Her temperature was 98 yesterday. For her, normal is around 96. Jack is preparing to have a meeting with Gerald today. He says he is going to sue him. She wonders what good that would do. She said a prayer with him before he left. Surprisingly, Jack didn't argue. Didn't curse or swear either. Maybe there is hope yet.

Victoria goes to mass and did a reading. Then Father Holli said he would see her for a few minutes. She discusses with him her conversion as a Born Again Christian. He politely listens but said he didn't believe in the new approach to Faith through the Charismatic Movement in the Catholic Church. His reaction left her unhappy, but

13

she believes she was being led by the Holy Spirit to witness her conversion to him.

The pain through her body is excruciating!!

Victoria talks to Nellie about her witnessing talk with Father Holli. Nellie is certain that with Victoria's and the witnessing of others that he will come around. She hopes Nellie is right.

She arrives home around 11:00 A.M. feeling as though nothing was accomplished; pain still terrible on into the afternoon. She decides to spend the rest of the time in prayer of silence and Spiritual reading. While spending the time in prayerful study she feels no need to go to the Charismatic Convention. It would serve no purpose.

Jack arrives home having been drinking and it continues. He has had his dinner and then says he had another meeting with Gerald. She doesn't quite know what to believe but she does know he is drinking. She is so happy she stayed home and didn't go to the Convention. She continues to pray in silence.

"Oh dear Father, how much farther do we descend? We sure need help."

A great peace fills her. "Let Your Will not mine be done. Thank you Jesus, for hearing my prayer."

Been so restless all day, but did have a good sharing in her Mantra prayer time this afternoon at the Anglican Sisters. She felt His Presence in a very powerful way. As silly as it sounds she felt as if her prayer was heard.

Jack must have been out late again as Victoria finds him sleeping in the living room when she gets up this morning. When he wakes up he is quite hung over. He's not able to get to work till the afternoon.

"Why is he still going to work," she asks. "There is so little going on at the office. Is there is something he is not telling her?"

Since he is prone on the couch and in such a humble and weakening state, she uses the opportunity to talk with him about their lives, their marriage together and as a family. She tells him that before his life can be turned around and be happy he is going to have to forgive and be forgiven. He agrees with her that he must forgive and be forgiven but he is not ready to accept the "Faith" part. He really didn't believe her. They take a walk to the park and the subject is dropped.

She prays for her sons tonight. They are in the midst of all this confusion but for whatever reason, she and Jack never sit down with them and discuss the situation. They are so busy doing their own thing they never stop to consider their sons and their feelings.

Therefore they shouldn't be surprised when Matthew comes home with the news that he is going to quit school. He has one more year to go, but he has other ideas about how he wants to spend it. It's a blow to Jack and Victoria, to say the least. Jack, especially who has such high ideals when it comes to an education. What can Victoria say? She did the same thing herself. And who can blame him considering all that's been going on here. It seems fighting and arguing is the order of the day. He says he will be going to Holland in October for six months with a friend from Brae na Beith they know well.

Jack returns from another trip to South America to try and salvage what is left of the company. She trembles in fear knowing he is in one of his vile moods. When Matt tells him he is quitting school, Jack goes on a rampage.

He rants and raves, "What have you done now, Victoria, while I've been away. F—ck, J.C. Can't I depend on you at all? Can't I leave without everything falling apart?"

With tears of frustration, like raindrops that fall like rivulets down her screwed-up face, Victoria tries defending herself but only ends up being attacked even more. She runs to her bedroom to sit in silence, trying to cope with the tears of confusion as the Rosary beads fly through her fingers. A great peace fills her whole body as she feels herself relax. She is calm and at peace, again, for now. She recalls when James also did the same thing, leaving school to travel and nothing was said.

The next morning while cleaning up the kitchen, she remembers it is her sister-in-law, Pearl's daughter's wedding day. She had forgotten about it. Just as well; it's almost as if she was deliberately stopped from going because she would have moved out for good. Yes, she is intending to leave Jack! She can no longer live with so much stress, rejection and depression. You name it!

Her thoughts are on a rampage and although she can't put it into words, there are times when she has vague thoughts of taking her own life; because of this she would have moved out for good. How can she live with someone who hates her so much? Because of the way he treats her, she feels she must make him terribly unhappy. She must be a terrible person as he so clearly and firmly tells her in so many words. It's just the way he talks to her, making her feel inferior with his insulting remarks about her background. She can no longer live with so much stress, rejection and depression.

But, you know, for all of her down times, she still has her good relationships with the people of the churches she attends. She still goes to the Tuesday morning meditation gatherings at the Sisters of the Anglican Convent across the street. She has good friends in her own church and the Catholic Charismatic and Pentecost Groups on the other end of town. She is not alone. Being around them she feels more like herself; a good woman in her own right. Her prayer life is growing as well. She has much to be thankful for.

------------------        --------------------        -------------

*"Thoughts, dancing through her mind, keep her buoyed up as she sails in her little red sailboat to the next unknown harbor. She is not ready to give up the rudder yet. So, where is her next harbour to sail into? Who will be there to greet her?"*

------------------        --------------------        -------------

Tuesday arrives and she prepares to go to her meditation hour at the convent. As she stands at her door before walking over to the convent, she prays to herself,

"Blessed Lord, what is it you want me to do with my life. There seems to be so little I can do to help others."

With a feeling of helplessness, she prays, "there seems to be so little I can to do. With all the unhappy people in the world what can I, in my small way in my small world do to help? Surely, there must be some way I can be of some use to others."

The thought drifts off with the breezes as she walks across the street to join her friends and the Sisters in this powerful form of meditative prayer.

After their meditation time they go to the dining room for coffee and a snack. Victoria finds herself sitting with one of the Sisters; before she knows it she is discussing, in private, the financial problems she is having in her life without a salary coming in.

She says to the Sister, "I wish there were something I could do to help us through this difficult time." What do you think I could do to help out, Sister?"

The sister, in her long gray habit, which swallows up her petite frame, looks at her wide- eyed and says, "How about I come to visit? I might have a solution to your problem. Have you ever thought of taking in boarders?"

No! The thought never even entered Victoria's mind.

"But," she exclaims to the Sister, "Come to think of it, I do have a room in my basement that I would like you to see." Her heart skips a beat!!

The next day the Anglican Sister arrives at her door and Victoria invites her in. They go down to the lower level, (it's almost as if Sister is familiar with the place), where there is a huge room that contains a small kitchenette surrounded by a long bar on one end. Behind the bar, lined with four stools, there is a sink, a small apartment fridge and a stove with four small burners. A couch and two comfortable chairs face a generous fireplace. There is quite a wide space between the couch and the back wall. Sister's mind is working overtime. "You know," she says, "why not erect four little private roomettes along this wall?" Conveniently, a bathroom is situated down the hall, no shower, however.

Victoria's mind is working overtime but says nothing. What can she say? With her feelings of joy bubbling up and spilling over, she exuberantly thanks Sister as she walks her to the door. Victoria is sure this is something good. Once Matt sets off on his quest, there will be two more bedrooms on the main floor that will be empty. She doesn't say anything to Jack when he comes home. He'd only have a temper tantrum, anyway. Best keep quiet about this.

The next day she hears from her sister-in-law, Pearl to tell her they will be in Toronto in January and hopes they can get together.

"Oh dear, Victoria says to herself as she reads the letter, "I didn't send Pearl her daughter's wedding present. I must get it ready for mailing." She writes a note to send with the package.

Dear Pearl:

Well, finally, I have Katie's wedding gift ready to go. I am sorry it is not gift-wrapped but since it is so nicely boxed for mailing I didn't like to change it. So sorry we missed the wedding. Your sister said she looked beautiful.

Nice seeing everyone at the funeral and wake for old granddad!

We are looking forward to seeing you when you come to Toronto.

Love to all,

Victoria

---------------    --------------------    --------------------

**Oct. /83**

She writes, sharing her thoughts on paper.

I am a Born Again Christian! A Contemplative! I am not a religious; not belonging to any religious order. I am housewife and mother. This is very precious to me and brings me great joy. I have never been more secure or happier in my life and it is only the beginning. Here I am, at 48, discarding the old to begin anew. I remember the Commercial teacher at the Convent in my hometown, Sister Ellen, profoundly revealing to me years ago, that God had other plans for me other than joining a convent. So I will write the future happenings in my life that may or may not reach out to touch and speak to other souls that are crying, crying, crying, as I cried, for answers and found it in a miracle. A miracle in the birth, life, death and resurrection of our Lord, Jesus Christ, who I am finding out, is most loving. He does not want to see us suffering and in pain: physically, emotionally, mentally or spiritually. He took it upon Himself to take on our likeness so that He could relate to us as humans, but without sin and so suffered as we suffer. How could I have ever thought that I could live my life without Him: without the silence of every precious, present moment of His Love.

"Oh Father! You were here. Even when I discarded You, You were with me. Although I didn't know that in my constant tears of discouragement I cried out for you, I believe You cried out for me, your lost child. I was the lost lamb and You found me. And, like a lost lamb, I am being held in Your arms and protected from harm. I love You."

--------------- --------------------- --------------------

The next morning she wakes up very discouraged. Every day the news is full of the roles women play in the home and in society. The talk is about nothing else but freedom, liberation for women. Get out of the house and work as men are working is the loud cry. Women should be earning their own way instead of being dominated by the power of their husbands and men. Women should be free to do their own thing.

"But," she thinks, "I'm not educated enough to do anything."

Her eyes swell in the tears of the lonely as she has her little "pity party."

Where, oh where is the love, she wonders.

She thinks about the small stained glass business she had in Brae na Beith which filled some empty void and made her feel like somebody, but that didn't last long once she moved away. She had tried working part-time in a store that sold lamps and lighting fixtures. That didn't last long either. The male storeowner had other ideas at day's end after the last customers left. And she had really liked that job, too. She tried staying with a child after school while the mother worked. That didn't work out either. Victoria had to go to a funeral so the family fired her; she wasn't there when the child came home from school. Victoria felt bad she had let them down. She tried delivering papers door to door. Just wasn't her cup of tea. Anyway, she felt bad because she was taking the job away from some kid. She even tried selling Avon door-to-door. She enjoyed that because she loved meeting the women in their homes. A move took care of that, too. Nothing seemed to fit her no matter how hard she tried. Was it that she didn't want to work, or was not able?

For the rest of the day after going to Mass and having coffee at Cultures with her friends, where they also discussed "women's lib" she thinks about all these attempts to be a free woman. Society tells her she is not being fulfilled as a woman just being a housewife. Her life as a volunteer over the years in that secular society doesn't count. Certainly the volunteer work didn't bring in a paycheque. And with the state of affairs here with Jack not making a salary she feels she isn't pulling her weight. But, on the plus side she is always home for her kids at the end of the school day. Yes, it sure is a dilemma.

Like Jack says, "Get off your butt and do something useful." No point in discussing it with him; he would only laugh at her anyway.

She notices an ad in the local paper giving a rundown of the different courses for adults at the local college. Now maybe that's her answer. Yes, of course! She feels her spirits lifting.

She trots off to the college where she doesn't have to wait even a minute; the councillor can see her immediately. After some discussion she asks Victoria to fill out a set of questions to find out just what courses would be right for her. After Victoria finishes, the councillor asks her to sit in the waiting room as she evaluates the answers. Victoria is on pins and needles as the minutes go by. Finally, she is called into the office.

Then the blow hits home As Victoria sits there straight and tall in her tailored suit of beige with the red scarf, her hair done in the latest fashion, the councillor keeps staring at the results as she says:

"I'm sorry to tell you, dear, but I'm afraid you are incapable of taking any of the courses here."

"Why not," Victoria exclaims in a quizzical tone of voice as she tries to get the councillor's attention. She is very puzzled by this response.

"Well, my dear," the councillor finally lifts her head and looks smugly at Victoria.

"Since you ask, then I guess I'll have to tell you. You will never pass the courses. You are MENTALLY HANDICAPPED."

To Victoria's shocked ears it appears as though the councillor is screaming loudly those cruel and nasty words; another blow to Victoria's ego and to another already low opinion of herself. She can't believe what she just heard. She cries all the way home; hardly able to see the street ahead of her. Jack is away so she didn't have to listen to his taunting. She will never tell him, of course. It would only confirm, in his estimation, the certainty of her lack of abilities as a woman.

And it only confirms and conjures up a picture in her very jumbled mind, as her broken and sick heart sinks in despair, how societies' narrow view of women, the handicapped, the marginalized, the bedridden and sick, the elderly, children, those in the womb, and those in poverty and different Races are viewed and categorized in little boxes, although she couldn't put her thoughts into words.

As she walks across the street the next morning to go to the Sisters' meditation time at the Anglican Convent, she prays to herself:

"Lord, what is it you would have for me to do? Open the door and show me the way. I feel so powerless to help. What can I do to help?"

She opens the gate entering the Convent's beautiful garden walkway to the front entrance; opens the door and gazes at the statue of Blessed Mother, Mary facing her; and in a flash she thinks of the Sister's idea that she "open her door" to boarders.

------------------ --------------------- ---------------------

The church has arranged for the ladies of the C.W.L to volunteer for the Good Shepherds Hospice in Toronto. The Secretary, Diane called Nellie to tell Victoria. Victoria gets the call this evening and is asked to call the others and tell them about it. She calls Edna as Nellie had asked her to and finds out that Edna already knew. So there really was no reason to make the phone calls. She is a bit put out to have this important job taken away from her and a bit jealous, she has to admit.

"I guess I'm not so important after all. Why would they do that to me; ask me and then do it themselves?"

And then the words came to me as clear as day, "Let Nellie handle it."

She felt satisfied about that but could she be humble? She knows she's not very humble. She has to lead and has had to all her life.

She goes to Mass this morning expecting to say to Nellie, "You can do the calling." But, thinking about it, she was afraid that she would again be proud that she had made the sacrifice in favor of Nellie. "How noble of me", she thinks.

During mass she prayed for humility. She felt peace all through Mass. She was being prepared to handle with humility what happened next.

Nellie goes to the back of the church to get the list and then she comes to Victoria to tell her she would call the ladies herself. Because the decision had already been made within her, Victoria is given the grace to handle the situation, feels no anger, rejection or resentment and could accept with peace. She is pleased Nellie is doing it. It makes her feel good to give it up for Nellie. She prays Nellie did not call her in the first place to show superiority or gloat. Anyway, on the way home, she prays that she is sincere in her feelings toward God and that it is not her own ego. She asks for a sign; again peace fills her heart and she starts to cry. She hopes this is a sign of her sincerity.

Now, this pride of hers is working overtime again. Always wanting to be noticed, chosen, cared about and loved for the things she does. Being smarter than others and showing off. The thoughts keep torturing her. No matter what she did in the past she was always hated for what she did.

She writes; "my motives were wrong. Everything I did was to make an impression. Now, I know that what I do in the future will be for God alone; for the love of God. Only He matters. Only He cares. No one else does. No one else is important. I know I will slip back and it will be difficult but I know I will be shown a way out. I have the help of the Blessed Trinity. Praise You, Thank You. I love You!

She was invited to have coffee with a friend after Mass today. A very interesting conversation because she didn't realize her friend, Joan's interests were so close to hers. They sit for an hour over the cold coffee very much engrossed in their common interest in the spiritual life. When she gets home, she decides she should write Joan and tell her about the book, "The Cloud of Unknowing."

She writes the letter then realizes it was very pompous and patronizing. It seems she just wants to brag about her relationship with The Benedictine Monastery in Montreal. She loves the book, "Cloud of Unknowing" but who is she to assume others would!

At 3:00 this morning, she is led to this book and in the pages she finds these words;

"Chapter 17: Page 7 "That a true contemplative will not meddle in the active life nor with what goes on around him, not even to defend himself against those who criticize him."

She thinks; something for me to contemplate; I'm beginning to think I meddle too much and tend to be presumptuous. Oh dear, was I too presumptuous in my letter to Joan?

As she thinks about the results of her Sheridan visit in being refused the Courses, she realizes now that it was not because of the negative reaction of the councillor at Sheridan and her hurt pride, but she knows now, it is because she must follow the life of a true Contemplative.

She sits in thought; "that is my true Vocation. I must go to University but not for a career. I want to study. I have a real hunger for it but in a deeper vein that what Sheridan can give me. The Lord works in mysterious ways. My times of meditation are refreshing, relaxing and also can be ecstatic. It is the Love of the Holy Trinity. This love is the healing, loving touch of Jesus' healing Hand on our foreheads."

She ran into a friend, Bernadette this week and they spent the time in sharing their spiritual lives. But it didn't go so well. She wrote to her but did not send. After reading it she decided not to send it since it was no different than their conversation."

She writes; "Oh, dear Lord! I'm having a very difficult time with my newly found spiritual life. How pompous, arrogant and presumptuous I sounded in the letter."

------------------     ------------------     ----------------------

Jack takes the day off today; he and Victoria drive Matt to meet his friend. They will then take them to the airport where both boys will fly to Holland for six months. Matt is only 17 but he is determined to do this. No point in trying to stop him. Of course, James did the same thing at that age when he went to Switzerland with his school buddies one summer. Well, Matt earned his own money, as did James, only under different circumstances, so, she guesses, as parents they have no say in these matters.

After they see Matt and his friend off, she and Jack go into the city to have drinks and dinner. On the way home the conversation between them gets out of control, due to too much alcohol, with Jack accusing her of not being firm enough with Matt's decision to quit school. They end up in a big fight with Victoria being the scapegoat for the decision and the endless problems in their marriage. The guilt rises again that she can't be the kind of wife Jack wants. She knows she is trying her best and yet she is always made to feel she has failed again and again. The pain all through her body is excruciating; her head feels like there is a belt tied around it squeezing it tight. She can't wait to get home. She screams back at him in defense but what is the point; she can't possibly win anyway. She is the crazy one. He calls her every dirty name under the sun, swearing and cursing all the while. When they get home she rushes to her room crying her heart out. She grabs her rosary and begins to pray. At the third decade she is at peace and falls into a deep sleep.

--------------- -------------------- --------------------

*"On the quiet waters, with the stirrings of the breath of a night's breeze, the little red sailboat gently lulls her to sleep."*

--------------- -------------------- --------------------

Now that Matt is gone and with Jack still making his everlasting trips to heaven only knows where, trying to salvage what's left of his company, Victoria has more time on her own. That is short-lived, however, when James, who is back from Switzerland and, struggling with his university classes, fails his second year. He is now home with nothing to do but lay around watching television. At twenty, there must be something better to do than getting into her hair. She gets out the daily papers and looks through the want ads. He, of course, wants to make his own way, as well, but what! They finally find something that might suit him in an ad put out by a Toronto Insurance Co. This job lasts two months, and home he is again. This time they find an interesting ad written by the Hudson's Bay Co. in Red Deer, Alberta. They are looking for a young person they can train to run the store one day. Victoria is so excited. To her, it sounds ideal; what with his one- year university under his belt and his father's family in the same business. She persuades him to send in his resume. Sure enough; he gets the job and off he goes. In her enthusiasm, she doesn't see that she was the one that found the job for him. She just wants him to show some initiative. She is proud that he accepts the job and she is keen on the adventure for him. But who is showing the initiative? So with both boys gone and the house empty, she is free to do her own thing, whatever that is.

One morning, after Mass, the men and women are all sitting around the booth at the coffee shop very much immersed in an interesting conversation. They are talking about a very elite religious group called Opus Dei, operating under the Toronto Diocese. There is a gathering of the members coming up the following week. Would Victoria like to go? They go on to explain that it is a group that teaches the theology of the Catholic Church and the spiritual life of the soul in greater depth. Well! Since she is asked to join this exclusive, elite group, how can she say no?

--------------- --------------------- ---------------------

She writes:

"I asked Fr, Noon to spend some time with me. I felt the need to have him hear my confession. I have been receiving a very interesting scripture from the bible and I wanted to discuss it with him. The scripture, Sirach 39:1-15 is based on a Calling to write; and to make oneself available to pray with people and over them for healing. At the state I'm in right now, I can't see how that fits into my life. I have so much to learn, especially about the church and spiritual life in general. I know I need a deeper understanding of my spiritual life. Someday, perhaps, I will put this to good use. As to when, or how, I don't know. I wrote Fr. Noon a letter after seeing him but decided not to send it."

--------------- --------------------- ---------------------

Victoria has been spending some time with Nellie who is very upset about her husband leaving her. She is contemplating suicide saying that God wants this from her as a sacrifice for what is happening between her and her husband.

The following is part of the letter Victoria wrote her:

"You are becoming obsessed with what you think God wants from you. He will answer your prayers but in His own time and with what is best for you and your family. He is all mercy and Love. When He sent us His Son Jesus He showed us the Love he had for us. He doesn't want us to think of Him as angry or hurtful. Wishing your death as a martyr would not change anything and it would turn your children away from God and He doesn't want that to happen. I am sure you don't want that either.

As far as your marriage is concerned, try and accept what has happened for now. Claude may or may not be back; it will be God's

Will, not yours. You cannot force the issue or God. I would hate to think that you are doing the opposite and that is pushing Claude farther and farther away. Wait! Wait! Wait! Do nothing for now but love and praise God for the many blessings given and done for you and, there are many if you would just stop and see them around you. Your family need you and want you happy, confident in God's Word and Deeds. Patient and Loving as Mary, our Blessed Mother was. Pray for these gifts rather than destruction of yourself. These gifts will gain their rewards and God will love you the more for them and so will your family."

Your loving friend
In Christ Jesus
Victoria.

---------------- --------------- -----------------

God has brought these scriptures to Victoria: The Book of Job, Judith 8:11-28, Sirach 1:2, Wisdom 1:1-16, 1-9. Nellie's letter in answer was very disturbing; but Victoria knows the Holy Spirit will lead Nellie the way she should go.

Good news! She heard through the grape-vine Nellie has moved to Toronto and joined the Good Shepherd Society. Praise the Lord!

Victoria had an appointment at 1:00P.M., to see Sister Patty Gates at the Carmelite Sisters Convent in another city. While going up the elevator to rooms, Sister looked at her strangely and, holding her, quoted Sirach: 39 confirming what she already knew. Sister then, quoted Hosea: 2: 19-24 as she held her.

For some horrible reason, Victoria took her bible and threw it against the elevator wall. Her friend picked it up and handed it back. Sister Gates and her friend prayed over her as she cried in tears of shame; why did she do such a terrible thing? She could feel fear within her. What is happening to her? What does it all mean? Where is she heading?

SHE IS SO FRIGHTENED"
Letter to Sister Patty Gates, Carmelite Sister:

As I sit here trying to write this letter to you, I am very much in awe of this whole revelation. When am I going to wake up and find all this changed and I'll be the Victoria I was 5 years ago? When I say "revelation" I mean this Call to a vocation with the Carmelite Sisters I was telling you about in case you have forgotten. Why could I not have just a normal; "going to church once a week" relationship with God.

25

When I sat in the priest's office, being 30 years away from God and the Church, and spilling out my guts for my many sins, he said to me, "as a penance I would like you to look for God's Presence each day in everything you do and everywhere you go," I never dreamt that it (my Faith) would grow to such an extent. Right now I feel panic and fear; as if it is all out of my control and my body is somewhere else. Nothing about me is the same. I don't recognize myself at all.

I am very glad to get your phone call. I feel very lighthearted and joyful and although this can change and I can sink into the doldrums again, generally, I am joyful, knowing that Jesus is with me. Your phone call made me so happy knowing I can continue in my marriage with Jack and the boys for a while. I am so happy to put everything in His Hands and say, "Yes Lord, when the time is right, it will be right." Also, that I can listen to my Lord's Voice without feeling guilty or that I'm doing something wrong. I will not shut Him out of my life. What I would miss if I shut Him out. I thank you, Sister, for taking the time to reassure me.

Yours in Christ Jesus,
Victoria Adams

She writes: "Jack and I take a walk to the lake this evening; the winds are playing games with the waves. God is in a rough and tumble mood and although there is no rain to add to the fury, He is certainly enjoying Himself and bringing pleasure to me in His play. The Tongues of the Holy Spirit flew from my mouth in joy at His Presence.

------------------ ----------------- ------------------

When they arrive home from their walk, there is a phone call from a friend of Matt's. She is in the hospital in Toronto, very much in need of prayer. Heidi is nineteen. She can't hold food in her bowls and so needs constant hospital care. She has what is known as Clones Disease or something like that. Victoria promises Matt she will go to see her.

She visits Heidi today and finds her spirits good but under a lot of drugs. She had an attack while there and Victoria felt drawn to pray over her for healing. She prayed in tongues as well and then blessed her with the Holy Water someone had given her. She gave her the Lord's Prayer and a book of daily readings. Victoria then left. Of course, she never knew what came of the prayers over her but with the rush of the Holy Spirit flowing over her at the time, she is glad she had gone to see her.

She writes a letter to a Sister of the Carmelite Order:

"Dear Sister Mary:

I am writing you today to ask you to send me some information on Vocations in the Carmelite Order. I have been discussing this with Sister Gates of the Notre Dame Mother House and she suggested I write you. Perhaps you might, after Christmas, consider giving me an interview, as well, because I feel the need to discuss with you or with whomever you suggest.

Sincerely

Victoria Adams

Another letter to:

Benedictine Monastery, Montreal.

Dear Father Laurence.

I received your letter Friday. Thank you.

I accept your patience with me. I have a feeling you will not see my desire to become an Oblate Novice of the Missionaries of the Mary Immaculate Community. This humility helps me to realize I am not who I believe I am. I accept this decision with much joy and peace because I know that this will strengthen me. I know that the longer time spent in reviewing in prayer is a purification I would not have otherwise, considering the stressful lifestyle I am living. However, if I had not written you to become an Oblate Novice, I would not have been made aware of the situation and the changes that your decision and talk did for me and my prayer-life. I have noticed in this short space of time changes in self-discipline, perseverance, peace and a different approach to my meditation.

End of letter.

She realizes the letters are just thoughts on paper so she doesn't send them.

----------------- ------------------ -------------------

Well, here I am again trying to write. I am finding it very difficult to put into words what I want to say and how I feel. I still feel strongly about my Call. However, I am living in a very strange way. I am very much alone. My activities outside the home have been cut to a minimum and this has been happening gradually over the past six months, even longer than that, because although it is necessary for me to work to bring in some money for us to live on as Jack's income is nil, even that has been taken away from me. Desire and opportunities, including the weekly local paper for jobs has even stopped coming to the house through no prompting of my own. A few months ago I ordered the paper delivered again and again, it stopped being delivered.

I go to Mass every day and am involved with the women of the C.W.L. and parish and still I am not very often approached to help out in any way, and, if I am, something intervenes to change my plans and I do not participate. It is all very weird. I also find I am a calmer, quieter, more accepting, obedient and thoughtful person. I have also changed my ideas about myself, hopefully for the better. But, you know, I still don't know much about all this.

Do I sound as if I have humility; doesn't sound like it, does it? So this prayer life must continue in utter silence, emptiness and much more poverty to gain the graces needed to live in God's Presence in a more humble state that will lead me to a more fruitful prayer life."

---------------- -------------------- -------------------

Christmas is now taking much of Victoria's time so all her religious preoccupations appear to be put on hold for the time being. No matter the situation at home, everything is focused on preparing for the season. She and Jack take the Saturday to do the shopping for Christmas gifts; then she must wrap them and then, with the cards, write and mail out to friends and relatives. She then takes the Sunday to bake fruitcakes and to cook a variety of foods to be ready for the influx of visitors expected. Through it all, with the stress and demands upon her body she is in excruciating pain. She tries her best not to let it bother her but she can't wait to get to bed and to rest. Of course, there is no point in complaining; no one would listen or believe her anyway.

To top it off, their income is at a very low ebb right now. She and Jack are continually at each other's throats over money. She has to ask him for every cent. His ego won't release him from the responsibility of handling the finances and letting her take over; which is sad considering her secretarial, book-keeping and banking experience. He also doesn't seem to realize that her every day meals and the running of a household are her responsibilities. She needs to know what money she has to work with to run a house efficiently.

"Her mind screams; how can a body remain calm and sweet? She is such a bitch!! No matter how hard she tries, she can't seem to do anything right. Is this any way to spend Christmas?

He makes it clear one can't expect anything more from an uneducated bitch; the slanderous, hateful words spill out like hot, running lava from a volcano. She becomes vicious and tries to fight back, only proving he is right. She runs to her room again. A half hour's nap with her rosary tightly gripped in her hands calms her, but can't get rid of the pain through her whole body. When she comes to the kitchen to continue making the pies, all are calm and serene. Her rosary is nestled in her pocket. It's like it never happened; till the next time!!!

---------------   -------------------   -------------------

*"The skipper wishes she could sail away as far as the little red sailboat would take her, but it's not the time. She knows, somehow, something good must come out of this, but what?"*

---------------   -------------------   -------------------

Her spirits rise again through this Christmas season, the bright spots in her life being the relationships with the people of the many ecumenical spiritual groups to which she belongs to celebrate the season, the Birth of Christ, Jesus. And then there are the daily Masses and Christmas Midnight Mass. And finally the highlight is Christmas Day. How beautiful! So much to be thankful for!

Jack's company may not be functioning financially, but the week before Christmas Jack's partner and his wife invite them to the Bar Mitzvah for their son, taking place in the local Synagogue. It is a very solemn and beautiful ceremony leaving Victoria very touched, most honored and impressed. It is a beautiful Jewish Ceremony, which just happens to come about before the Christian Birth of Jesus Christ in the New Testament in our modern times. It is wonderful linking of both the Old and New Testaments.

Christmas Day is quiet this year with both boys away; it sure is lonely without them. She cries a lot, why, she doesn't know and the physical pain is excruciating as she stands over the hot stove making doughnuts, and preparing Christmas dinner.

A nice surprise though, Jack joins her for Midnight Mass. The stars in the clear, winter sky blink unceasingly as a bright moon shines on the lightly fallen snow. They live in such a beautiful town and the church has the gracious look of old-fashioned times long ago.

Christmas morning she and Jack open the gifts they hadn't opened the night before and feast on her home made, sugared doughnuts and a big breakfast later in the morning. She prepares the turkey with the stuffing of breadcrumbs, apples, nuts, rum. She puts it in the oven about 2:00P.M. It is their usual Christmas fare but without the boys it doesn't seem the same. Still she is sad when it is all over. She crashes into bed before the sun sinks into the horizon. It's not the same with the boys away.

--------------- -------------------- --------------------

*"She and her little red sailboat try to find a harbor to moor on the lake before winter sets in with all its fury. She is not sure where to go; it seems she is not prepared for what is in the winter storms ahead."*

--------------- -------------------- --------------------

She is suffering much pain through her whole body. She just can't stand it any longer so she goes to her doctor. He decides to put her in the hospital to take some tests. It all started a week before with pain in her chest. Her own doctor is unavailable so another Doctor replaces her. He repeated her doctor who said' "you have fibromyalgia." (The Book of Job came up in the bible.)

The pain is somewhat improved but then she has a difficult time ovulating and so decides to see Dr. Martin who directs her to an obstetrician. While in the office, Dr. Martin says she didn't have fibromyalgia, which, she thought was causing all the pain for so long a time. What he said surprised her; making her think her problems are all in her mind. She says to him, "why are you lying to me? Who can I believe, anyway?" She is very upset, but she is sent home.

She again has the pain in the chest. Thinking she is having a heart attack, she goes to emergency and who should be there but Dr. Martin, the very doctor that she had told off. She let him know, in no uncertain terms that the doctors are prejudiced against her, saying that her problems are all in her mind.

She thinks, "What do doctors call women who come to them with imaginary illnesses? Hypochondriacs I believe it's called." Is that the category they are putting me in?"

She told him she would be the one to decide when the search for the problems of her health is over. She tells him there is something else going on besides stress. He then puts her in the hospital. As it happens the visit to the hospital is very providential; she goes through embarrassment and humiliation because, somehow, the nurses got the information or assumed she is stressful, or CRAZY? MORE LIKE CRAZY!!! She soon finds out why she needed to be put into the hospital.

Mrs. McGraw from Montreal, in the next bed, says that the Holy Spirit works miracles through prayer to help heal stressful pain and emotional illness. She gives Victoria a book on the life of St. Theresa, who had been cured through prayer. She tells Victoria to pray to the Blessed Mother; telling her troubles to her and she would help her. Sure enough, as they pray the Rosary, she feels a healing of something but of what only God knows.

Amazingly, she senses changes in the whole atmosphere of the surrounding beds as she lies in her bed. Is it her imagination or is there more laughter amongst the patients and nurses? Is there a true healing Spirit falling in one-way or another?

Then, a patient, Mrs. Least and one of the nurses tells Victoria about the dreams they had. She tells them the story of her own experience with dreams and the example she had as a child:

"When I was a young girl, I had a frightening dream that I was going to have a baby. Sure enough, that is exactly what happened. At age 19 I was raped by a young man and became pregnant. If I had only believed in the power of God then, I would have lifted up the dream to God and He may have given me the insight to know what to expect and divert it. The knowledge and wisdom would have come from somewhere."

She then interprets their dreams for them. She prays it helps.

Her stay in the hospital is coming to an end. She knows now why she had to be here. It is God's Work, not hers. She has received another healing, healed with the Grace of self-respect. She knows she will not chase after anyone any longer, trying to have them like her. It doesn't matter whether they like her or not. Isaiah 1:16-20 – 38:1-8. She believes that is what happens when she listens, hears and does God's Will and not her own.

As to whether others believe, it doesn't matter.

While in the hospital, the doctor suggests she take lithium for Manic Depression and PTS. She must be monitored at the hospital once a week to make sure everything is under control. Healing comes about in many different ways through prayer.

--------------- --------------------- --------------------

*"Sailing into the unknown in her little red sailboat has its rewards."*

--------------- --------------------- --------------------

1984 and winter passes. Jack is still without work. What about their savings? Well, she doesn't know if there is any, he doesn't confide in her. They're still eating so there must be money coming from somewhere. Money or no money, life goes on and they get a call. One of Jack's relatives has passed away and they must go to N.B to attend the Wake and Funeral. A niece is to arrive on the bus from Toronto, as she will be travelling by car, with them. When Victoria opens the door to Jessie, what to her surprise, she finds a young man standing there with her. He speaks very little English but enough to get by. Jessie laughs as she tells how he sat next to her on the bus and in broken English, tells her he is moving to Canada from Italy.

She sweetly pleads, "He needs a place to stay until he finds a permanent place. Would you know where Leonardo could stay?"

Why Jessie brings him here, Victoria is at a loss to know. They are planning on leaving for N.B. the next day, for heaven sakes! What to do with him? Well, there is only one thing to do, let him stay in the house while they are away. He can look after the place and do his thing as well.

Victoria asks him, "we will be away a week so would you mind looking after the place while we are away?" Her mind is in turmoil. She can't believe what she's saying?

He is overjoyed. The language barrier doesn't seem to be a problem. Imagine! A complete stranger from another country finds a roost in a strange home and, without questions asked, is made to feel welcome.

So away they all go the next morning, taking off at 6:00 A.M., never doubting for a moment that the place would be looked after.

At her in-laws' home where the Wake is being held, she paces, with blurred eyes, the upstairs hallway. Holding on to the railing, she gazes on the people below; as she silently cries. Her sister-in-law sees her and comes upstairs. There is no one around except them. Millicent starts to tease her, calling her the "town-crier." Victoria can't help but laugh, which breaks the ice.

Her sister-in–law leaves, Victoria again looks over the railing to those below. She sees a couple she knew back home when she was young. Seeing them brings the memories flooding back. The young doctor had visited her family regularly. She recognizes the woman with him; the nurse who looked after her when Victoria, at 19, was in the hospital having her baby. The couple are now married but, as a single couple, had come to visit her when she was living in the Unwed Mother's Home.

Victoria joins the family line-up. They are greeting the many people bringing their condolences and well-wishes to the Adam's family. As the young couple and Victoria shake hands, they pretend they don't know each other. The faces of the young couple, except for their eyes, which soften at the sight of her, show no recognition. She loves them very much for keeping her secret. She knows instinctively they are happy that she is married into such a good family, as they wish her well.

While in N.B., she gets in touch with her brothers and sister. This year is their mother and father's 50$^{th}$ Anniversary. So they make plans to celebrate at Musquash in the old Adam's family cottage. In discussing it with Jack's family they are happy to let them use the family cottages. So in the next few months they discuss the plans to get together during the summer.

They return home and, they find everything in good order; their silver still in the buffet drawer. No, the young Italian hadn't let them down. She is happy he has found a place to live.

Life slowly gets back to normal, and yet, she is not prepared for the phone call she gets from a friend she knew in the last town where they lived. Victoria had met her through the Teen Center she had set up and ran there. Mary is in a panic. She needs to talk to someone and somehow, she remembers Victoria. They meet at the coffee shop where they discuss her marriage, having just separated from her husband, and her daughter, Debbie who has been giving her trouble.

"Victoria, do you suppose you would mind if Debbie moves in with you for a while?"

Victoria is stunned. How do these things get started anyhow? She had never told anyone about her thoughts to take in boarders! She doesn't know what to say off the top of her head! First there is the young Italian and now Debbie. GEEZ!!!

With desperate tears Mary pleads for help. She can't handle her daughter's behavior right now. And Victoria, being the obliging vulnerable victim, says, "maybe, for a week." I'll let you know. She decides to pray about it.

That Thursday she goes to the Charismatic prayer meeting at St Matthews. During the prayer time she asks for prayers about taking in boarders; Debbie and, perhaps others as the Anglican Sister had suggested, to help their income. They all join together to pray for her and others' needs.

She sees an ad in the local paper. Students, from the local college are looking for rooms to rent for the coming school year. Another possibility raises its head.

Jack is still making his trips for his company to Latin America, hoping to get them to pay up what they owe but with no success. Since there is no money in the company, he doesn't get paid for these trips. Who pays for those trips? He also continues to look for other work, but prospects aren't good.

On top of all this there seems to be something happening in their marriage. He doesn't seem to want her sexually any more. The verbal rejection still continues but now this. She doesn't understand what is wrong. She is scared to bring up the subject sensing he may say something to hurt her.

She turns to her prayer life more and more often; her scripture readings, meditation times, her rosary once a day or night, her Mass and Notre Dame Sisters contact at St Andrews every day, Opus Dei once a month, her meditation time with the Anglican sisters once a week and her Charismatic and Pentecostal Prayer Group meetings once a week. Life would be unbearable without these and her friends.

What is the matter? Something seems to be wrong. What has she done now? He is becoming cooler and cooler toward her. Not only is his behavior a barrier to her affections for him but he is also adding injury to the insults toward her.

Her morning's meditation with the scriptures brings up an interesting thought:

"And now I am going to break the yoke of his that weighs you down,

And I will burst your chains.

For you, here is Yahweh's decree:

There will be no more offspring to bear your name" Nahum 1:13-14

This scriptural reading is very interesting. She must keep meditating on it every time it comes up. What does it mean?

He can't make love to her anymore! After seeing a doctor about some pain and bleeding he has been having, Jack finally explains to her why he can't make love to her any more. Or is it that he doesn't want to?

The same scripture comes up again. Nahum 1: 13-14. What does it mean? Does it mean she must live a life of chastity? Before too long they are sleeping in separate beds in the same room. That suits her just fine. He was smothering her anyway. She is glad to get rid of the grasp of power he has over her.

In her inner spirit, in silence, she takes a vow of chastity not telling anyone.

--------------- --------------------- ---------------------
*"Now she understands why she is the one lone person in her little red sailboat."*

--------------- --------------------- ---------------------

Matt returns home, humbled, exhausted and broke, after 6 months in Holland. He has learnt much; especially the hardships that people on the other side of the world have to live with. His travels abroad have given him much food for thought including his goals in life. A better experience he could not have had.

Debbie's mother phones again. She is in a panic about her daughter's behavior. Victoria takes a drive up to visit them and gets a better idea of the situation. She agrees to take Debbie in as a boarder at the beginning of the school year.

Then, who should arrive home from out West but James? He has come down with a terrible virus which he has picked up, heaven only knows, where. Sadly, he blames Victoria for his sickness, saying that she forced him to take the job out west when he didn't want to go. Of course, he couldn't say "no," could he? He didn't say he didn't want to go. Anyway, with treatment he is back to normal except for the humiliation and the sense of failure.

In the long run, though, like Matt, this did him a lot of good and taught him a lesson. With the experience under his belt and determination to better his life he decides to go back to University.

Life goes on and now she has her two sons home for the summer.

--------------- --------------------- ---------------------
*"She is steering her little red sailboat in the direction the wind blows; where it goes no one knows."*

--------------- --------------------- ---------------------

Jack arrives home and they sit with a cocktail before dinner. After two or three he is in a good mood. So she takes advantage of this and after dinner she brings up the plans she is making to help with the income. She says she needs his approval before she goes ahead. She knows, deep down in her heart, she must go ahead anyway.

His initial reaction is a loud one. "There is no way I'm having a bunch of losers running around in my house." His swearing is strong enough to melt snow in the Arctic.

Victoria then says, in her firmest voice, "they are not losers; they are students attending the local college. And will pay rent for the rooms. God only knows, we can sure use the money right now until you get a full time job." She sounds angry to her own ears.

She attends the last meeting of the year before summer and asks the Charismatic Group for prayer to help her in her decision to take in boarders.

Their plans to go celebrate her mother and father's Fiftieth Anniversary are finally finished and they take off for N.B. the 2$^{nd}$ week in August.

February 1934 was a banner year for Dad and Mum Diamond. Fifty years later, in Aug. 84, they and the descendants of this marriage are now all together to celebrate at Musquash, the Adams summer compound, and this memorable occasion. It is a glorious and happy occasion for all. Jack's family cottages and the main cottage are full to the rafters with family from all over Canada. With all unhappy and negative happenings put aside for the time being, the families enjoy fully the companionship, surroundings and ambiance of life on the seashore and the good memories that go part and parcel with such a "once in a lifetime" occasion. They hated to see it end and promised to meet again some other year.

--------------- --------------------- --------------------

*"She, as the lone sailor in her little red sailboat, is going to have to take a firm hold on the rudder to control the difficult winds and tides ahead. Is she prepared to submit to a more powerful force within and around her?"*

--------------- --------------------- --------------------

She writes her thoughts: "Is my suffering making me more like Him? Are my physical and emotional pain at not having any money to live on and no bills paid? Is it the difficulty of looking after teenagers before 8:A.M. and after midnight? Is it the pain of Matt's rudeness? Is it the pain of seeing the suffering of others? Is it the pain of rejection? Everyone suffers; the rich, the poor, the good and the not so good. How blessed it is to have a purpose in suffering. Am I, in some small way, beginning to recognize the suffering of Jesus?"

Preparing dinner for Jack one evening, she keeps it warm till they have their "happy hour." Today he arrives home in a good mood. He succeeds in getting a job with a computer company in sales. However, he doesn't get paid until he sells computers.

"It's a very competitive business, Victoria. I'm going to need your support. I hope I won't have any trouble with you and those students."

Sitting in silence she tries not to get upset with his thoughtless remarks. Has she not, over the years always supported him, and, "for heaven sakes, what does he think she's doing now? Thank God, he finally has a job; she must try and think positively."

He stresses, "I'm still going to have to continue to work for my company as well, to keep it above water. I have to get my investment back. I invested a lot of money in this company; I can't afford to just write it off. I'll still be traveling to the Latin American companies and we're going to try China."

She can't question his remarks about his business, but it is so difficult to trust him to know what he is doing. He must have a nest egg somewhere! We are living beyond our means in an expensive community and still must keep up with the Joneses. What more can she do to please him? She must put dinner on the table. He complains that dinner is cold. His tongue-lashings continue. She wishes she could keep her mouth shut but she never seems to succeed very well. The battle begins. Because of the new job prospect it is not as bad as it usually is. She cleans up my kitchen and goes to the bed-room with the single beds. He goes off to the den to his television and papers. The rest of the evening is quiet. Matt is off somewhere with his friends.

--------------   --------------------   --------------------

*"The little red sailboat is now sailing into a very beautiful harbor."*

--------------   --------------------   --------------------

She writes:

"Can you believe it? It is an answer to prayer. A miracle! Pope John Paul 2 is coming to Canada and especially, to Toronto. I just can't believe it.

The miracle, to me, is that I, as a Catholic Women's League and Opus Dei member through my church, am included amongst those who will attend the Special Mass for the Priests of the Arch Diocese of Toronto with Pope John Paul 2 as Celebrant. What an honor! One I will never forget. A real blessing!!

Another blessing; I have received an invitation to attend the Papal Mass at Downsview, North York, where again, the Pope is the

Celebrant. Jack and I will have good seats; Row C, Block 4, Section 8, Sept 15. How is it possible that I, Victoria Adams, from the backwoods of N.B. be so blessed? Also, after the Priests Mass, I was almost able to touch the Pope Mobile as it went by where I was standing. My imagination led me to believe he even looked right at me, and why not!!"

For weeks after, she and her friends gather at the coffee shop and reminisce over the glorious experience of those beautiful few days. Victoria is so affected by Pope John Paul's visit, that she makes the effort, on the first Friday of every month, to take the Go train into St Michaels's Cathedral, Toronto. The Mass and Exposition of the Blessed Sacrament usually takes place at noon so the visits don't interfere with her routine at home.

This one day, she is sitting in the pew praying her rosary when a group of children come into the church with their leader. They head for the front of the church and move to the altar. She just can't believe what happens next. There are the children running around the altar before the Sacristy, that holds the Eucharist, the Blessed Lord Jesus. Victoria bursts into tears. She can't seem to control herself. As she sits there with tears streaming down her face, an older gentleman comes up to her and asks her, "are you all right," with a worried expression on his face. She continues to cry and with trembling words, she tells him what she is witnessing on the altar.

"Thoossse chchchildren, rrrrunning around the altar, are ddddesecrating and are ddddisrrrespectful to ourrr bbbbeautiful Lord. How cccan they dddo ttthat?"

The man sits next to her and says soothingly, "My dear child, you have been given a great gift." He makes the sign of the cross on her forehead, kisses her face and hands and gives her a big hug. Then he left, returned and said his name is Gerry. Then he leaves. She is stunned; that is so strange. Who was he, really?

On the way home, on the Go train she hears, sounding in her heart, the words:

**"Blessed Holy Spirit, give me a double portion of Your power." 2 Kings 1:9**

The words never seem to leave her. The mantra repeats itself over and over again. "Blessed Holy Spirit, give me a double portion of your Power." She has no control; the words seem to give her strength to deal with her life; Jack and the goings on in the household.

Thanksgiving and Christmas holidays arrive and James comes home from University for the holiday. The students have all gone home to their families to leave Victoria and family to have a quiet time through the holidays, for a change, with no arguments to speak of.

"We have much to be thankful for," she thinks as she sits in the church with her family, waiting for the Mass to start.

After getting home, she finishes the preparations and serves the huge dinner of turkey, chestnut dressing, roasted potatoes and dumplings, fiddleheads, pumpkin pie and ice cream for dessert. Stuffed, like the turkey, she and Jack decide they had better walk it off. They stride along to the park, following the lake, where there are many strollers out to enjoy the beautiful weather. They have a peaceful walk, and for a change, no arguing.

--------------- --------------------- ---------------------

In Feb. she offers her services at a school at another parish in the area. It is a small job; just supervising the children during the noon hour. They certainly are a noisy bunch of kids. She is paid a pittance but every little bit helps.

Around two in the afternoon, two weeks later, on the way home from her volunteering, Victoria decides to visit the church to pray the Rosary. The church is empty. As she sits there running the beads through her fingers, she hears whispers behind her. She hadn't heard the door open or close so she is surprised to hear the soft voices. She finishes her rosary, rises and turns to leave the church. She glances around to find out where the whispering is coming from. About the middle of the right isle, seated in one of the pews is a young couple in serious conversation.

Victoria, in her usual concern for others, decides to go over and speak to them. She sits in the pew in front of them, not wanting to appear aggressive and, turning around she tells them her name.

She quietly says, "Is there anything I can do for you?" never thinking that she is leaving herself wide open to whatever might happen next. Innocently, she plays her vulnerability role with them.

The girl pipes up, "his parents turned the hose on him and kicked him out. They don't want to have anything to do with him."

He just sits there staring, letting her do the talking. Without asking any more questions, into Victoria's mind comes the thought that her visit to the church to pray the rosary at just that time has to be for a reason. She knows she has a room and that her mandate is to help others, though she doesn't put her thoughts into those exact words.

Actually, she would rather not think about it. If she did she may not go through with this. She must trust but she is so new at this "trust" thing and who would believe her, anyway?

She discusses her offer with them but, she says, "You will have to pay room and board."

He doesn't seem to have any trouble with this and says he will go home and discuss the payment of the rent with his parents. After getting their names, Victoria gives them her phone number and continues on home.

"Oh, God, What am I getting myself into," as she finally faces what she has just done. She can't believe she did this.

That evening the phone rings. It is Gerald's father. He doesn't waste any time; he says, "I'll pay the rent, no problem. It is very nice of you to do this for my son."

"That's all right," Victoria says, "I have other boarders as well."

"Thank you! Here is my phone number should you need us for anything. Is it all right if Gerald moves in tomorrow?"

Before answering she wants to know about the relationship between Gerald and the girl, Diane. He says they have a close relationship. Victoria tells him that Diane will not be able to move in with Gerald.

He says, "you are setting the rules but I would rather she didn't either."

So it was agreed. But was Victoria prepared for the result of this decision to give Gerald a place to live? Only time would tell. And who would be there to help? She, of course, can't see the future.

--------------- ---------------------  ---------------------

*"Where is her little red sailboat taking her now? Where, oh, where is the Love?"*

--------------- ---------------------  ---------------------

She now has three boarders downstairs with Debbie and Gerald upstairs. Her family, Matt, James and Jack are getting angrier and angrier by the day. What's the matter with her, anyway, to have all these people in their house? And who can blame them?

There is a force, larger and more powerful than she driving her, which no one can understand.

The church is preparing for Easter, which is coming up in a week or so. Victoria comes home Friday morning and, walking into the house, she notices a strong and strange odor in the house. She walks down the hall toward her bedroom and she realizes that the smell is coming from Gerald's room. It smells like something burning. She knocks at his door and then enters to find him sitting cross-legged in the middle of the floor with a small fire burning in a bowl at his feet. He is chanting something out loud. She says nothing, turns and closes the door and rushes to her bedroom where she crashes down on her bed and grabs her Rosary. She is terrified. What can she do? She certainly doesn't want to make him angry. So she continues to pray. All of a sudden the phone rings. She picks it up and sobs into the phone, "hello."

To Victoria's great surprise it is none other than 100 Huntley St., a Christian T.V. Ministry. The woman on the other end of the line says she was prompted to call this number as prayers were needed. Victoria is astounded. She is speechless for a moment. Just when she needed them the most! She finally finds her tongue and tells the woman what is going on in her house. The woman then begins to pray for Victoria, Gerald and the situation. A great peace fills her soul and her body relaxes, confident she will receive the help she needs. The power of the Holy Spirit in the Name of Jesus destroys the evil forces in the house.

Debbie, also living with them, is showing rebellion and lack of discipline. What to do? Victoria sits over a cup of coffee early in the morning the next day and thinks about a way to handle the rules in the household with so many young people running around. She sits quietly, meditating in silence then says to herself," I think I had better write out some rules for them to follow; maybe that would be a way to handle it.

After saying her usual morning prayers Victoria and Jack go to Mass. House is so quiet when they arrive home. After getting home she begins to prepare dinner for Jack's boss and his wife. They are coming to dinner around 6:00 P.M. Diane phones to talk to Gerald. He did not answer phone. She arrived to pick him up for the 12:00 Mass. He did not answer the knock when she went to his door. So she goes home leaving him a note saying there was evil in the house. He does not read note. He calls her to pick him up for Mass. Diane knew we were having company for dinner and she had to go home before they arrived. She and Gerald arrived back about 2:30 when Victoria got a call from Diane's mother saying she is very worried about her. Gerald has been acting up. Diane calls Fr Noon, the priest at the church. Gerald wants Diane to stay for tea. Victoria wanted her to go home. Gerald would not let her go. Jack is getting angrier and angrier. I finally call Gerald's father and Diane's father and mother. They all come. Jack calls the police and police calls ambulance. Gerald will be taken away to the hospital where he will get the help he needs.

She prays to Jesus, the Healer, for Gerald through the whole ordeal:

"Blessed Holy Spirit, give me a double portion of Your Power." I feel the Holy Spirit was directing the whole scenario. I Praise and thank You, thank You, thank You, thank You Jesus, our Savior."

They take the poor guy away on a stretcher and everyone leaves around 5:30; Jack's boss and wife arrive at promptly 6:00 for dinner. The Holy Spirit keeps her going through the whole dinner.

She prays: "Blessed Holy Spirit, without Your power I can do nothing."

Jack's boss seems to be more positive about the company. She doesn't know for sure about that. He asks her to make a stained glass window for the Synagogue.

--------------- --------------------  --------------------

What a day yesterday! She's exhausted but wants to write David of 100 Huntley St. to tell him what had happened to this young man in her home and of the work of the Holy Spirit in bringing her help from them when she needed it most. She is still in awe of the whole episode. They continue to correspond and Victoria feels very blessed by his attention.

It is a very important link in her spiritual life in that she now sees that God can use all faiths; Pentecostal, Catholic, Protestant, Hindu or Islam, including Media, and those who have a meditative form of religion that she is being taught by the Benedictines in Montreal through the Anglican Church, if one has a strong enough faith to believe in Ecumenism.

--------------- --------------------  --------------------

The next morning Victoria prays her morning prayers and meditates. She goes to Mass at 9:a.m and suggests to the people if they might be interested in praying the rosary before Mass. She picks up James at the train station, drops him off home, and then goes to school. The children are acting like wild animals during lunch hour. Best keep quiet. On the way home she stops at St Andrews to make the way of the cross. She and James go to lunch at Cultures. After his dental appointment, she and James go home. She makes dinner. Matt wants pork chops and also had chicken for James and Jack. Matt's friend, Lane, didn't get job with the firemen. She is so sorry. He was so looking forward to this challenge.

Gerald, who is still in the hospital call her for medals. He said she could visit him in the hospital. She is cautious about that. However, she is happy he asked her.

The Jewish Passover is being celebrated through the Catholic Charismatic group in one of the local churches. A friend calls and asks if she would like to go with her. How could Victoria refuse? It was a most enlightening and beautiful ceremony. The Passover took on a whole new meaning for her. She knows it wasn't like it really happened on those days long ago but, it was a tiny stirring replay.

------------------ ------------------ ------------------

*"Her voyage in her little red sailboat takes on a whole new vision."*

------------------ ------------------ ----------------

### Easter Weekend

She started her Thursday morning in silence with her prayers. After getting a few things done around the house to prepare for Easter, she calls the hospital to ask to see Gerald. She is surprised they released him. Found out he was let out to attend Diane's preparation classes and her Baptism. She really doesn't know what to think of that. Anyway, they must know what they are doing, but she wouldn't be surprised if he was trying to get out and stay out. Is what came to her in her readings in the bible about Gerald?

Introduction to the Prophets: Isaiah 38: speak Lord, your servant listens. Kings 3: lay hands on him, Isaiah 38 again. She decides she will do nothing until her prayer in silence directs.

Now she must go to the Anglican Church Convent for meditation; then to the bank where she runs into Yvonne. Victoria was going to call her and there she is. They go to the coffee shop where she talks about her brother who is an alcoholic. She suggests Yvonne offer up her mother's Mass for him. Pixie is also there. They discuss what needs to be done at the church for Easter and Victoria offers to help.

After the coffee break, she goes off to the school to supervise during lunch hour. Boy, they sure are a bunch of noisy kids. The teachers hate it so why don't they do something about it? What to do now?

Victoria will stop at the church to make the Way of the Cross, Mass and Exposition of the Blessed Sacrament at 7:30 this evening. She decides she will read Breviary and meditate in the church.

She arrives home to prepare dinner; Matt's dinner wasn't ready and he blew up at her. He's always angry with her. Well, at least all the boarders have gone home for Easter.

### Good Friday+

Before making breakfast for James, Matt and Jack, She prays her Office of Prayers and meditates. She will spend the rest of the morning cleaning the house for Easter. Although she is suffering a lot of pain today she will go to the Home Show with Jack. She is glad she did as she really enjoyed it. So many different Ethnic Groups with their booths of wares. She and Jack have lunch in a fine restaurant; he is treating her much better. They have had the full day together. She missed Mass but that's ok! When they got home she phoned Diane. There is a change in her attitude toward Gerald. She is much firmer with him and is determined he won't leave the hospital. Praise the Lord!!

### Holy Saturday

Victoria is not functioning very well this morning. She asks Jack to go shopping without her. He also got the boys' breakfast. She got into a couple of arguments with Jack and then something prompted her not to argue. Jack then left and she was glad to have a chance to rest.

She took advantage of the time alone to pray, meditate and fast. She feels sick with excruciating pain through her whole body. She is beginning to realize the reason for her family's persecution of her and always angry with her. She knows her spiritual life is probably one reason and also giving a place for street-kids to live; disrupting their home-life. She lifts it all up for their salvation, as she believes that is what she must do. She prays to be given the strength to accept it if that is why she suffers so much pain.

According to the scriptures, Jesus died on the cross at mid-afternoon and at 3:00 the church is full, to pray the Way of the Cross. It is very beautiful. The choir sang the Seven Quotes Jesus cried out as He hung on the Cross, Book of John, Chapter 19.

This beautiful ceremony is over and she rushes home to finish her baking and cleaning for Easter, but still not feeling well. She starts to bake a pie but she is in too much pain to continue. Jack finally arrives home. She can't finish the work so she lies down for a while. She contemplates the Way of the Cross and Jesus' Crucifixion. She likes to think her illness, the pain relates in some way to Jesus' agony. Is this pain part of her cross? She is feeling much better so she gets up and continues her preparations. Her evening is a peaceful one. Thank God.

**Easter Sunday+**

Victoria wakes up at 6:00 this morning, praying her usual morning prayers and silent meditation, praising God, thanking, blessing Him and glorifying His Holy Name. She calls Mum to wish her and Dad a happy Easter. She tells her Dad went to church with her. Alleluia!

She prepares breakfast and sits over her coffee; finally gets dressed to go to the church for Diane's Baptism. When she gets there she is shocked and humiliated to find out the baptism was last evening. Being new at this thing she didn't know. She didn't stay but drove away only to decide to go back. Her mind begins to have odd feelings thinking Diane doesn't like her. "How could Diane do such a thing since she is just baptized? She must hate me terribly."

The church is full. As she stands through the whole Easter Mass a great peace overwhelms her when the priest walks by her and blesses her with the Holy Water. She is able to overcome the crazy thoughts. She arrives home and stupidly tells the family. Matt and James say nothing; Jack said, "I guess they didn't want you there." What a terrible thing for Jack to say. She should not have shared with them.

"Do not throw your pearls before dogs lest they trample upon them with their paws and turn and tear you to pieces." Matthew 7: 6. Yes, it would not make much sense to anyone else, that's true.

------------------- ------------------- ----------------------

*"She, in her little red sailboat, senses her loneliness as she drifts along with the tides. She knows not where they will be taking her. Will she be able to cope? Tears fall and there is no one with whom she can share."*

-------------------- -------------------- ---------------------

Easter now being over, the C.W.L. spring meetings begin. An executive meeting is held at the home of one of the members. The meeting doesn't go over very well. As Vice President you'd think she'd have a say in what is discussed, wouldn't you? They are

45

discussing memberships and the upcoming parish picnic. The members slam her down when she mentions they do something in a religious vein. She feels humiliated. It served no purpose. "What did she do wrong?" Again she berates herself.

Victoria wakes up about 3:00 A. M., very distressed. She feels she's not doing properly, the work God is asking her to do. With Gerald, her silence worked. As long as she was silent, the Holy Spirit was able to work through her to others to get Gerald to the hospital, but she has not been silent at the school; speaking loudly, in a worldly way and doing her own thing; not letting the Holy Spirit work through her. Only the work of the Holy Spirit matters in solving problems and situations. This was proven again at the C.W.L. meeting.

The following is the result. "He spoke to me through His Word: Isaiah 30: 19-26, Haggai 2: 4-9"

The last three days have been most successful at the school.

Tuesday: the Holy Spirit, through me got very angry with the children. They quieted down beautifully.

Wednesday: again, much quieter in the lunchroom. They are doing well.

Thursday: Again, they are doing very well. However, Dave Young seems to think that the system I am trying won't work. He doesn't know it's the Holy Spirit doing the work through me. Praise the Lord!! I suggested we try some music during the lunch hour. He will provide the music.

After telling the principal of the school she will not be supervising the lunch hour any longer because he is neglecting to improve the children's behaviour, she resigns. She knows through God's Word, she must leave even though she loves the children. So getting home from the school she prepares herself a small lunch, then taking her bible she goes to her bedroom to rest and opens her bible.

The following scriptures give her reason to pause; Isaiah 42: 5-9, Baruch 6:11-72,

Isaiah 35: 1-10, Isaiah 30: 8

Why? Time will tell. These are prophecies. She spends an hour praying: "Jesus, Mary and Joseph, all the Saints in heaven and earth, help me.

Victoria's niece will be getting married in Montreal. It comes to Victoria through prayer that she will be taking that trip to Montreal to go to the wedding and to visit their parents. She talks to her brother about it but they end up in a terrible argument on the phone. She doesn't know why they argue but she senses her brother doesn't want her to go.

She prays: "Blessed Sweet Jesus, I pray You give me the courage to do what I must do. Your Name is all-powerful. I pray with confidence and love knowing, in faith, that you will help me. Thank You, Praise You, Bless You!!!"

--------------- ----------------- ---------------

Victoria writes a letter to her friend, Nellie, but after reading it through, decides not to send it. It is far too arrogant, judgmental, patronizing, egotistic, vain and, more. She surely would hurt her. Certainly not the way Jesus would have talked to her. Is it a lesson for her to learn? It's almost as if she is writing about herself. "Egotism" means vanity, self- exaltation and self –conceit. Humility means, amongst other things, to feel small in the presence of others; to be nothing. To know that whatever God has chosen for her, in His mercy, she is nothing and can do nothing without Him.

She writes; "I, Victoria Adams, am nothing. I am dust, I am small, meek, unworthy to wash His feet. He has chosen me because I am nothing. Because I am nothing He can do His work through me. I praise you, thank you and bless you, my sweet and wonderful Father in heaven. I love you, I need you, I adore you and I am humble before you, Sweet Jesus and the Blessed Holy Spirit. Without You I can do nothing."

--------------- ----------------- --------------------

Victoria's mum is going through a very distressing time with Dad; she writes to say she will be moving to be near her son. Victoria doesn't know why but she's very concerned about this decision for some reason. Perhaps she should write and tell her not to make this move; she is best to stay where she is. After writing the letter to her, Victoria decides not to send it.

As it happens, Mum goes to Montreal to attend her granddaughter's wedding. After the big argument on the phone with her brother about going to his daughter's wedding, here he is phoning Victoria to come because Mum is in the hospital in Montreal having had a stroke and he wants his sister there with her. She is thankful and grateful she had "listened" to the Word of God in those scriptures. His Will be done.

Can you believe it? She would have had to leave her job at the school anyway. She would have lost the opportunity to tell the principal she is resigning because of his neglect of the children.

And now she writes, as she travels on this train to Montreal.

Through His Word: Isaiah 42:9, "See how former prediction came true. Fresh things I now foretell. Before they appear I will tell you of them." In Hosea: 2 He tells me how much He loves me. He tells me in Isaiah: 35; I must travel His Sacred Way if I am to do His Will; the Sacred Way of Love."

----------------  ---------------  ------------------

*"The tiny sailor in her little red sailboat must sail this Sacred Way without a compass or chart to guide her; only the sails of Faith will take her in the right direction."*

----------------  ---------------  ----------------

Victoria sits with her mother in her hospital room. It's been a week and Victoria has seen some improvement but she still can't speak or is able to sit for very long as she is paralyzed on one side. Victoria is staying at her niece's apartment, which is just around the corner. This is a harrowing experience, to say the least. The darn doorbell keeps ringing; the first time she rushes to the door and finds no one there. The next five times she doesn't answer, saying to herself, "the heck with it. I'm glad I went the first time, at least I know there is no-one there and I just won't keep running to that stupid door!" The nights are long in a strange city, an unfamiliar apartment, which is ten flights up, and her mother so sick. Through all this, she gets a phone call from Matt asking her when she is coming home, as he will be graduating from high school next week.

--------------  --------------------  --------------------

**Dear Matt**

As I write this letter to you, I am sitting in a chair opposite your grandmother's bed. She is 76 years old today. She can't swallow or walk at this time but, hopefully will be able to soon. We are heading for her home tomorrow morning. The ambulance will take us both to the plane where we will have four seats reserved for the flight; three for her because she can't sit up too long, and one for me. I am sure she is nervous about the trip but she will be sedated and so will sleep. I am very glad to be with her during this difficult time. She needs to know she is loved and is not alone which she would be if I were not here. She is in a strange place and, because of her illness, does not need the extra stress of travelling alone.

Once I drop her off at the hospital at home, I will then have to tend to your grandfather who is alone. I don't know how long all this will be. We are going to have to make arrangements for both our parents to be looked after, as they are unable to look after themselves any longer.

I know that, for you, it is a difficult time as you have so many responsibilities, what with your school work, your job, and having to make your own meals, etc. I know it is also difficult for you to accept the fact that I'm not there to make things easier for you. However, I do appreciate your patience and the sacrifice you are making for your grandparents' sake. Through our lifetimes there will be periods when there must be sacrifices and love demanded from us which may inconvenience us. This will, I hope, bring us satisfaction and joy in knowing we contributed our share for the love and comfort of others, especially those who are unable to look after themselves.

Matt, I am sorry I can't make your graduation or your birthday. I know these are important events in your life and you worked hard to graduate. I'm afraid, parents, at one time or another will disappoint their children and, sadly, this is one of those times. I know you will understand because you are much more loving than you pretend. I will be home soon.

I send you my love, my joy at your coming celebration which I hate to miss and my thoughts and prayers.

All my love,
Mum

--------------          --------------          --------------

Victoria finally gets her mother home and into the hospital. After she gets to her parents' apartment, she sits down and writes a letter to the airlines about the way they had handled their flight home.

After being told that her mother would be placed on a stretcher and taken to the plane by flight attendants, she just can't believe what happened next. She finds her mother being shoved roughly around by two burly airport attendants as they put her in a wheelchair. She, with the tubes still attached to her arm and nose, is then carried bodily onto the plane, where she must sit up all the way home. And for this disgusting treatment her brother had paid $600.00 for the flight from Montreal to N.B. Victoria was so angry she didn't mince words to tell them how she felt.

Her mother, of course, in her sweet way, says, "there now, Victoria, don't get upset. They have rules to follow."

"Yes, ain't it the truth!" Victoria is furious. When they land at the airport in N.B., there is no ambulance waiting as promised. The ambulance being 10 minutes late, and because no passengers can get onto the plane for the flight out until all passengers are off the plane they bodily remove her mother from the plane to a wheelchair without any thought to her condition.

She writes, "I can tell you, if it had been a man who was sick and a man to look after him, we would have been treated a lot better and differently."

Tears roll down her cheeks as she recalls the terrible injustice of it all.

She gives her letter to the airport attendants where they had landed. Hopefully, the next sick person will have a better flight experience.

What flashes back to her is the scripture, Isaiah 42:9.

She writes her brother to tell him what happened with the flight home, and to tell him what has taken place concerning the plans for their parents. He writes back with the news that he and Jane have been asked to go to S.A. for his company. Victoria does much praying and searching for answers through the scriptures to confirm this move.

This morning her thoughts are confusing and upsetting. Later, at 1:P M, she sits here in this bedroom left vacant since Gerald left and she is aware of the miracles around her; the warm sun, the roses so beautiful and healthy, the clothes line Jack has put up for her, holding the blanket that waves in the breeze, the birds singing God's praises, the wind, so cool, sounding it's voice through the trees, the hum of the traffic which tells her she's not alone, the view her seeing eyes behold of majestic trees reaching to the heavens above and around. Her heart sings with joy at being a miniscule part of this miracle around her.

And she writes:

"How can I not believe that it is God's calling me when He is so good to me? In the three and a half years, since I heard God's Voice through the scriptures, Saints, in heaven and on earth, showing me the Way and speaking to me in silent prayer, telling me I must stay with my marriage, nothing but good has happened to my life. I obeyed Him and stayed. Jack has been healed of his alcoholism through the laying on of hands with the Power of the Holy Spirit. My soul has taken on a healing too with the Love of Jesus Christ. The year that it took for my healing to come about has been a beautiful year in that I found peace, joy, excitement, friendship, with God, and the people around me.

My friendships, through the inspiration of the Holy Spirit, led me through the dark tunnel toward the Light of God's presence with wisdom, patience and love. I began to sense a change coming over me. I was able to cope with no salary coming in; no money at all for three years, even though there is much excruciating pain through my whole body. Praise the Lord for blessings bestowed upon me. My soul was gradually finding peace. Surely only God in His Mercy and Love could bring about such peace in the midst of such burdens for such a sinner. How could I possibly doubt? I begin to sing in tongues in my joy and thanksgiving.

Then, for some strange reason, sadness fills my heart. Hiding my face in my hands, I cry, knowing it is all so hopeless because so many harden their hearts against God and His Word of Love for them. It breaks my heart. Oh! If only they could "Hear" His Words. He is so patient and so merciful with His little children. How can seeds grow in such hard soil? My heart aches because I can only do so little and it takes such a long time and I'm so anxious for everyone to know Him and I'm so inadequate.

As the tears flow, I realize, with the Grace of our patient, loving and merciful Father within us what we, as women, are called to do.

We, as women are loving, self-sacrificing, patient children of God who are made in the image of Mary, our Mother. The gifts He has bestowed upon us, as women, are the very gifts that could save the souls of ourselves, our families first of all and the souls of the people He chooses to bring to us every day. It is so simple.

All He asks of us, as women, is to accept His call to a deeper spiritual life, as we become closer to Him in our contemplative way of life of meditation. In our prayer, thankfulness and praises, he will speak to us, gently prodding, patiently, his desires for the people around us. If we are silent in our prayer life we will be able to hear Him and, in obeying Him, do His Will and accomplish great things.

We are continually striving, in our unhappy lives to find answers about the many diseases of our times; to bring about answers to abortion, the empty souls and minds of the young, our children, the fatalistic attitude toward the elderly, the evils of crime and pornography, the lack of morals in society, the deterioration of the role of women's place in the home, the necessary desire for equality within women and the domination and abuse of men toward women and children. We are caught up in a spinning, spinning wheel as around and around we go, frustrated, angry and restless because we see no answers.

All the activities and meetings we attend, the role we play in society as workers and as volunteers, the raising of our children and the care of our homes, will go nowhere if we are not led by the Voice of God by the Power of the Spirit within us.

We are all good women, anxious to do what we can to make a difference, but so many of us would rather "do" than "be" what our Creator wants us to be; loving people, who will listen in silent meditation to what He wants us to do.

I am a secular, layperson living a spiritual life in silence in a secular world. In my silence He directs my day. He brings me joy, peace and contentment but he has shown me how to use sadness, unhappiness and compassion for Him who is suffering because of our neglect of Him who is so lonely and also for those who are also sad, lonely and hurting. I know I am a sinner and I need His mercy "to be, not just to do." Luke 10: 38-42

The tears flow in my sadness for what is happening around me. I cry because I know that what God has shown me, He will also show us, but we are not ready to stop and listen to hear His Word, are we, my dear women?

For twenty- five years I shut my soul and senses off from Him who was calling me. How cold was my heart and how sick I was. However, I thought I had to do something with my life; I thought it was wrong to sit around doing what I thought was nothing worthwhile. Since I didn't have a University Degree, I started a heavy routine of volunteering, trying to help those I felt were the lost in society. I worked with women in trouble with the law, the Children's Aid Society, opening my doors to street kids, volunteer at my children's school to set up library and a youth center. Busy, busy, business was the by-word, but I was still discontented. I felt that all these so-called accomplishments led nowhere and accomplished nothing for the people I was trying to help, or so it seemed to me. My husband was also busy as Vice President and manager of his companies and his traveling for said companies. We entertained, spent money and I became unhappier and unhappier. All seemed so useless to me.

What was missing? Was I not busy enough? Then Society told me that I was not fulfilled because I did not have a full time job. I was told I must upgrade myself because I was not qualified to do anything worthwhile. That led nowhere and only made me feel worse. My husband berated me because I was not working. He stressed continually by his words and actions that we were not equal and so he had a right to dominate and bully me. This was not stated in so many words but that was how he made me feel. I did not question this because I believed he was right. I began to feel a rebellion against what he and society said I must do to fulfill myself. He was becoming more and more impatient and angry with me because of my tears of frustration, my feeling s of inadequacy. My anger grew and so did hatred. He was never home, finding solace in bars, his clubs and his business companions.

And then, I took a couple of courses in stained glass and set up a little business. This beautiful art form brought joy, pride and pleasure and seeing the reaction in my customers brought me joy as well. Working in this medium was a blessing in disguise as I worked with the different colors of glass my eyes opened up to beauty and the peace in silence as I cut away and placed the beautiful colors together to bring about glorious patterns. However my heart was still cold and hard so I really did not suspect or understand what was happening to me."

--------------- --------------------- ---------------------

One morning, as she is hanging out clothes on the line, she can hear a strong voice within her, saying: "WAIT FOR MY CALL. WAIT FOR MY CALL. WAIT FOR MY CALL. DO NOTHING BUT REMAIN IN INNER PEACE UNTIL I TELL YOU WHAT I WANT FROM YOU.

After hearing those powerful words loud and clear, she rushes to her room very perplexed and fearful. She opens her bible. Isaiah 35: 1 – 10: The Judgment of God.

She has no choice but to listen. What is He telling her? She is in a quandary as to what the Judgement of God, Isaiah, is telling her:

"The glory and the judgment of God at this time are coming again to the people today as it did in Jesus' day. The people must first know Jesus who loves us, forgives us our sins and then brings us to His Father to know Him, love Him and serve Him with our whole hearts and our whole souls and our whole minds. Jesus who is our Redeemer, shines out to us from the people around us and He shines out from us to others as the Holy Spirit who guides us, comforts us and speaks to us God's Word and Will for us.

But for us to hear his Will we must be open to His Word through meditation and prayer. We must become silent. As I become more contemplative and aware of God's wisdom working in me, He shows me His Love for His people in many ways. We must become more like little children. As Jesus said: "Let the little children come to Me." Luke 18: 15-17."

--------------- ---------------------  ---------------------

*"What is happening to the lone sailor in the little red sailboat? She is so alone. No, she is not alone; creation, the fish of the sea, the birds of the air, the calming waters and the twinkling stars at night are always with her."*

--------------------- ----------------- -----------------------

Through prayer and silence she will know, in His Time, what God's Call is for her.  She decides to walk to the park by the lake with her writing tablet.

"Jesus, you are so much a part of my life that I know You will answer me. You are my Friend and I believe in You. You know my thoughts better than I know them myself. Please, don't think me vain or sure of myself if I talk to You in this way. What fascinates me about the spiritual life is that we need not think about one little thing. The Will of our Father is within each minute according to His Will. My thoughts are His thoughts, so no matter what I do, where I go or who I see it is what He wants done, it is where he wants me to go and who He wants me to see. None of it is difficult, or what I would not want, most times, although I probably would not have thought of it myself. I may have gone elsewhere, seen different people and done what I wanted to do. In the past that was the way it was and I know I would not have chosen this way of life for me. However, I sense that this way of life suits me. It makes me happy, peaceful and content. I am pleased to do His Will. You have given me these few beautiful times knowing it would make me happy. I know that the trials must come, but I also know Your Spirit is with me to see me through them. The trials are an inevitable part of life whether or not I know it, however they are so much easier to accept and deal with when my spiritual life has become my life.

54

Gradually it is becoming easier to accept it as being in me and being me. It is becoming less strange and more normal. "Keep it simple," a priest once said, and it surely is. Nothing is simpler."

She continues to write:

As I gaze around me in this park I see so many people enjoying so much the peace and relaxation, the balmy summer days. How many of them know it comes from our Creator, or if they know, do they acknowledge the fact to themselves or out loud. I'm sure some do. How do people express their love and gratitude for their lives? Are there many ways? When they love a child do they realize it gives love to their Maker or do they think in those terms? When their boat skims along and their sails hold taunt in the wind do they know that it is a spiritual power? Do they think in those terms?

My heart aches! How alone I am. Yes, it is easy for me to feel happy and good when He condescends to come to bring me consolation. I can feel it when He fills me with His presence. It is not the same when He seems far away from me and I am on my own. Then I am the same old irritable Victoria. I am impossible to live with. When He is not near I can't even pray.

Oh! Lord! WHAT DO YOU WANT FROM ME?

Victoria is prompted to write the memories of the past but thinks better of it.

-------------------- ------------------ ---------------

*"As the little female skipper settles down in her little red sailboat for the night, she wishes she could forget the terrible memories of the past."*

-------------------- ------------------ ---------------

One Saturday morning, while praying and meditating in her "prayer closet," (She is now using one of the bedrooms facing the street as a place of prayer.) she hears a noise outside her window. She opens her eyes and sees a stern face with two piercing eyes staring in at her. It is Jack. He has walked across the front of the house on the planter and looks into her window, spying on her to see what she is up to. She screams. She can't believe what she sees. He is disgusted with her.

"What in H___LL do you think you are doing," as he rushes in and pounds on her door. She tries to explain, but, of course, he doesn't understand.

He yells, "Have you gone crazy?"

55

So what's new? She decides to write him, hoping that the explanation will help him to recognize that what is happening to her is not a negative but a positive way of life for her and her family.

Dear Jack:

This letter I'm writing you is to help you understand that what I am involved in is to bring stability into our family way of life. I would appreciate it if you would read it with an open mind.

I know you don't understand what is happening. I think it is time I frankly shared it with you because you are my husband, assume you are my friend and you are a very important part of what is happening. In spite of what you have put me through I still love you.

Before we were married, I believed you when you said we did not need God in our lives, that our minds and brains were all we needed to give us the good life. How wrong I was; but I was so in love with you that I believed anything you told me. Now I know I love God, in the Name of Jesus Christ very much because He has forgiven me, His lost lamb, for turning my back on Him and hurting Him. Because He has forgiven me, I know I have no choice but to obey Him. Through my prayer life, my meditation, bible readings, my church and support of other Christians, I know He speaks to me His Will for me and I cannot deny Him. He has opened my eyes and my ears to hear and see His Will for me. I praise and thank Him. I have done what He has asked of me four years ago and I will continue as long as God Wills. The connections I have made with others are only small examples of the work He is asking me to do. If you and others wish to continue to be angry with me that is entirely up to you; I have no intention of backing down or retracting my words to any of you. God's Will must be done no matter what happens to me. I have faith I am being given His strength to handle anything that comes my way and I will receive peace and joy through it all, even your anger. I see beauty in His world around me and I see love in the people he brings me and sends me to. Most of this is very difficult but the rewards are tremendous. I have seen changes in all with whom He has touched through me, including the students in our house, Jacques and others.

Thanks to the Sisters at the Anglican Convent across the street who were prompted by the Holy Spirit who suggested we have street kids, who have no home, and college students move in with us to help our financial situation. But it is not just the money; we are doing God's Will here in this gesture to help others. We are being well rewarded; I was not without a cent for the month and a half I was away with my mother. He never sees me in need. I know that what I am doing is right but it is not easy.

Jack, I hope this letter helps you understand a little better my need to pray and go to mass. It is my lifeline and anchor to Him who speaks to me and whom, I know, loves you, the boys and me very much. He is looking after us. What I am doing is the least I can do. It is a commitment, a Calling I cannot ignore. I love you and the boys very much.

Love, Always.

Whether she likes it or not she is prompted again to write to her brother in S.A. where his company has sent him.

Dear Daniel

This letter, Daniel, is very difficult for me to write. I love you, Jane and your little ones very much. I am sad to see you so far away from those who love you. The letter I wrote you before you left I don't know if you received or not. It was also very difficult to write. But because I believe in God our Father Almighty, who is all merciful and loving I am committed to write no matter how difficult the task. And so I must write you again.

When you have had the spiritual experiences I have had through prayer of the scriptures, fasting, the Rosary, Mass, His saints on earth and functions of all churches, No matter denomination, etc. you begin to realize that your relationship with God is not imaginary. He really does exist through Faith and there is no ignoring the fact because He will not permit you to ignore Him once you are called to follow Him.

And so now we come to the reason why I am writing you.

Daniel, it came to me as clear as could be in a dream the other night about three weeks ago that your position in S.A. with your company will be shortened. Now I will explain to you the confirmation I received concerning this because I did not intend to write you about this until He had made it clear to me that this was His Word and His Will and not mine. This is how I approach anything I hear. I must get confirmation two or three times and then I begin to pray. First of all it had been coming up in scripture the following words that had revealed to you in the letter I sent you re S.A.

Isaiah 42: "They carry out plans that are not mine, and make alliances not inspired by me. They have left for Egypt without consulting me."

This has come up for the last three or four months and more frequently lately so I knew it had to do with you. He was calling you to my attention with dreams and words." I continued to pray for confirmation but I knew what I must do. Then, about a week ago I was praying my rosary round three in the morning, just about the time I meditate. All was quiet again. As the beads were running through my fingers one by one a picture of you came into my mind and the Holy Spirit rushed through me. Your company also flashed through my mind. The Holy Spirit stayed with me until your face vanished. Still I did nothing. I wanted one more confirmation.

This morning at Mass, the reading came across to me loud and clear:

Jeremiah 1:10: go now to those whom I send you, and say whatever I command you.

It is Yahweh who speaks. I am putting My Words in your mouth.

I knew I was attracted to that reading because it is the same scripture He brings to me when He asks me to do His work and, amazingly, what I wrote in the last letter I sent you. Then, this evening, as I scanned the T.V. Guide, I came across a play put on by the company you work for "-----Presents."

It was a play about a woman who has an insight into the coming death of her employer and she must tell him about it. I knew, then, without a doubt, that I received the last confirmation.

And so this letter is written because our Father in Heaven demands that I write it.

He in His Love and Mercy will reach out as He did in the past to His chosen ones to save their souls from destruction. He chose Jesus Christ, His Son to die on the Cross to save us from our sins and still we close our eyes to this reality and go our merry way ignoring our responsibilities to Him and our fellowmen, women and children.

Daniel, I hope and pray that you will not choose to ignore again His Will for you and harden your heart to His Will.

Your loving sister
Victoria

She prays: Oh! Lord! You always tell me to get up early to say my prayers, and I don't listen. Am I frightened as to what I might hear? Will I send the above letter? Is it Daniel or is it Jack?

**"What do you want from me?"**

--------------- -------------------- ----------------

She prays again for Jack and his company: Holy and blessed Father in heaven, you know the situation with Jack's company better than I do. You know the trouble Jack and his partner are having. We need your help, Blessed Father, according to your Holy and Blessed Will. Should we invest into the company again? Please help us to come to a decision. Should we keep the company alive? I ask this through Your Blessed Son, Jesus Christ and the Holy Spirit, one and only God on High. Lord, what is your judgment on the company? We will do Your Will. Thank you, Praise You and Bless You. Without You we can do nothing.

Give me the wisdom; Proverbs 1:1-7 to know Your Will for the company. Proverbs 10: 22, Isaiah 38.

She tells Jack but his response is unbelieving and doubting when she told him about the answer to her prayer to God concerning his company. Somehow, she is not surprised. She prays in the Name of Jesus Christ by the Power of the Holy Spirit. Isaiah 42: 5-9. That's all she can do.

She writes and prays. Oh! Such pain you put me through. Oh, such love I feel for you in all humility. You speak to me in the depth of my soul in tongues and I know not what You say to me, but I do know that I strongly feel that I want to give myself to you to do with what You Will. I want to spend all my time in prayer but I know I must not. Please let my tears help. What can I say to explain what is happening to me? I cannot explain!

--------------- ----------------- -----------------

Victoria must prepare to go with Mary to Opus Dei for the Recollection in Toronto.

After doing some spiritual reading, she confesses to the Opus Dei Priest her weakness in temptation.

He said, "Why are you confessing that, it is not a sin to confess." She said, "I know. It's my thoughts I am confessing. I can't handle my thoughts of temptation without having God's Graces to overcome them."

He told her she must use mortification such as rising earlier in the morning to pray, giving up things that please her, etc. Strange that she should be thinking of doing the same thing; walking to church instead of getting a drive, giving up coffee, etc.

However, in thinking about this "mortification" thing, she believes that is why their bathrooms are not being repaired. It is menial and humiliating work to scrub bathrooms after the six kids in the house use them. Must she do it for mortification? That word "mortification" sounds terrible, doesn't it? Seems she suffers enough already. And, you know, walking to church can be such a pleasure.

And, she says out loud: "and I'm not giving up coffee I repeat, I think I'm mortified enough as it is."

The next day she writes: Oh! Joy is filling my heart this morning. Obviously these past few days of blues were caused because I was not heeding His word for me. The image of our Sweet Jesus now, not only still contains the image of His Sacred Heart with the flame but the image now has the Host, the Eucharist, the body of Him who is our Savior. This vision of the Host was added two weeks ago at Mass. Fr. Louis was discussing the Eucharist in his Homily and then the vision came to me. Oh! Praise Him, thank Him and bless His Holy Name. I could see it on the wall in the sanctuary.

**Afternoon of the same day she continues to write:**

What has come over me? I feel the love of Jesus in my soul, the beautiful love of Jesus in my soul. Who could possibly know what pain He suffered unless one has been through His agony on the cross? I answered His invitation that He was giving to me from the image of Him and the Eucharist. How else can I help others unless I know His Pain? The Pain He suffered for us when He died on the Cross. Of course how could I possibly know; I who am the worst of sinners who closed my mind and heart to Him for so long; how could I possibly know? But how will I ever be able to go through what He is asking me to go through?

"Oh Blessed Virgin Mary in the blue cloak, I need you. Pray for me to your Son, Jesus. I need your protection and strength. Oh! Blessed Sweet Jesus, in your mercy, I pray that whatever pain I suffer for You, You will protect me. Give me the courage and the strength to handle whatever You desire for me. In Your Holy Name, Lord, I ask this as I am very weak and incapable on my own to do Your Will without Your help.

---------------- ------------ ----------------

The next morning she wakes up very spiritually dry and not in a very good mood. She is very grouchy with Jack and very impatient.

He is leaving for Seattle today. She asks for the car to go to Mass and he said, "No," so she phones Mary and she said she will be busy so Victoria said she would not go. Jack finally gives her the car. Anyway, all this is beside the point.

She invites Mary for the afternoon to witness to her the happenings of her spiritual life but is not satisfied it is the right thing to do until she receives confirmation from the scriptures. What finally comes up is Proverbs 1: 1-7, Isaiah 37: The prophet is consulted and Isaiah 41: 9-16. Yes, she was helped wonderfully because her discussion with Mary was, I believe, very profitable. Praise the Lord.

Why is she dry, feeling down and depressed? She senses that dryness always comes before good things happen. And then after all is accomplished, she receives much consolation. Thank You, Praise You and Bless You My Lord Jesus, in Your Holy and Blessed Name.

She had a disagreement with Matt who wanted the car. He finally agreed to wait to use it tomorrow. Later they go to a restaurant for lunch and then to the harbour for an ice cream.

The next day she goes to Mass where wonderful and joyous uplifting comes to her and she feels God's presence surrounding her. What can she say to explain the peace and joy that she feels during this hour?

Silently she prays: "Oh! My Father in heaven, nothing I will ever do, have ever done or am doing deserves this joy of consolation. I cannot find the words to explain what has come over me. Again the image of Jesus holding the Eucharist appeared to me. This time I am kneeling at the foot of the altar and He is extending the Eucharist to me. This comes back to me time and time again. Thank You, Blessed Sweet Jesus, my Saviour, my Friend. What does it all mean?

Dear Sweet Jesus. I hear you speaking to me. You hear my desire for you. You would like me happy and content in darkness as in light. You will come to me and tell me what it is I must do, answer, Book III Chapter 27, self-love. She thinks to herself, "yes, I cannot resist what I have known in the past; what I have grown used to. It is difficult to break old habits of self-love."

She prays, "Blessed Sweet Jesus, I need Your protection from myself. Dear Blessed Mother, Mary, Let me know that you are with me to help me, in the Name of your Blessed Son, Jesus, I ask this. Do not leave me alone in my struggle in dying to self."

She picks up the phone and calls Nellie to tell her that this is the last phone call she will be making to her. Nellie abruptly says, in response, "It's about time, it should have happened two months ago. I need my freedom at home and at work." She sounded peeved.

And so now Victoria has her freedom, the answer she finds in book "Imitation of Christ".

She prays, "Dear sweet Mary, let Nellie know I did not necessarily want to hurt her. I appreciate what she has done for me in the past. I am sorry if I hurt her but it is God's Will that the relationship end as she has already stated.

She writes a letter to Nellie apologizing but decides not to send it after reading "Imitation of Christ" Book III, Chapter 45, All men are not to be believed." Our peace reigns.

Her peace and clear conscience comes from God, not a letter to Nellie.

------------------ ------------ --------------------

Jacques, one of the street kids living with them, is giving her much trouble. He has many unresolved issues; he would not listen as she tries to help him. She is sitting in the garden chair drinking tea and reading "Imitation of Christ, Hidden Judgments of God, Book III" and, as she reads, a soft and kind voice says to her:

"Victoria, you must love no matter how difficult it is, you must love. Love even the ones who hurt you. Even as Jesus loved the ones who hurt Him even the ones who killed Him, He loved them all. You must learn to love like that, Victoria. Love the way you loved your sister when she was angry with you. Learn to love like that."

"But how can I learn to love like that?" An inner voice speaks to her: "Pray to Mary to help you."

Later, when the hydro man comes to the door to read the meter, she is able, (even after his anger and impatience toward her when the garage door was locked), to offer him a glass of water. Usually, she is so impatient and nasty with them for bothering her. This time it is different. She now knows that, without God's graces she would have been her old, hateful self again. She feels that the glass of water is a symbol of the Living Water being given to that poor, hot and tired hydro man who, no matter where he goes is treated terribly because no one wants to be bothered with him. "After all, she thinks, "he costs us money for a service we need, doesn't he?" No, he's only doing his job.

On Saturday, they get Matt off on the train to the university. What a struggle getting him off. It's been a long haul for him over the years but he finally now has his independence. After coming home, having something to eat, Victoria then has a chat with Kim, Matt's girlfriend. She came to the train station with them to see Matt off. She has her problems but is not willing to use faith to rectify or change her outlook on life which the church offers as one way for those who need help. Victoria had suggested she join the charismatic group in her church. Kim admits to not having any church participation. There is obviously no more she can do for her. Anyway, she is sure the relationship between Matt and her is over since he is out of the picture now.

--------------- --------------------- --------------------

*"She feels the loneliness in her little red sailboat. Where, oh, where is the love?"*

--------------- --------------------- --------------------

Today, after Mass she takes a drive to the harbor. It was quite a task getting Matt off to University so she can use the break. It's her favorite spot to relax when she is uptight. When she gets there, all of a sudden, she notices the headlines in the Globe and Mail at the corner box. The words scream out at her, "hurricane heading toward Florida Coast." Now she doesn't usually pay much attention to newspaper boxes but somehow her gaze fell on this particular headline. A thought plays around in her mind for a short minute; she thinks she should pray about it. The thought disappears as quickly as it comes with her mind still dwelling on Matt leaving to go to University. They will miss him; he can be a rascal sometimes but a pleasure to have around.

As the morning wears on, she walks over to buy ice cream and again notices the headline. Again thinks nothing of it; only thinking that she should use self- control and give up the ice cream. She throws caution to winds. "No way, I've earned it." She walks to the bench nearest the water, a place where she never sits but it is a beautiful spot, out of the wind.

As she sits there relishing her ice cream, a young Chinese couple walk toward her. Her companion leaves for another direction but she asks if she can join her. Victoria said, "of course" and she moves over to give her room. She said she is from Ottawa and that she hopes the weather will improve for the Labour Day weekend. She then begins to discuss the hurricane heading toward Florida. She seems very concerned about it. They chat for a little while longer and then she gets up and goes to sit with her companion. Now, with this contact, Victoria knows, without a doubt, that she must pray, in tongues, for that hurricane to go out to sea away from land. And so she begins to pray, first of all in English that the hurricane will go back out to the Gulf of Mexico, gradually become weaker and die out. Then, without any effort on her part, the prayer in tongues, the language of the Holy Spirit begins.

She thinks about the book she had read by Agnes Sanford, "Creation Waits." Agnes had written about her Gift from God to do His Will and pray for the control of the dangerous volcanic eruptions of mountains in California. Victoria feels drawn, as she sits here, to do the same thing for this hurricane.

The spiritual prayer in tongues ( Scriptural, Acts 1) erupting from her inner being is at first, loud and vocal and then recedes inwardly as a mantra so that she can pray without speaking. It started about 2:30 or so in the afternoon. She thought about nothing except what she must do. About 6 PM. she, tunes in on the radio to hear that the hurricane has stalled about 75 miles off the coast of Florida, with all the people evacuated. The hurricane has been stalled about the time she started her prayer in tongues. She did not want to interrupt her prayer so did not meditate. But she did pray her evening prayers.

She thinks, "Should I stay up all night?" And then thinks, "No need to do that, this mantra will continue all night while I sleep, anyway."

She wakes up during the night and could still hear the tongues sounding in her inner being. She does not get up to pray as usual; she is determined nothing is going to interrupt the mantra. She is very pleased she has been chosen for such an important task. It is 4:00 AM., turns on the news and hears the storm is still stalled 75 miles out. She can't believe, that through the power of prayer such a phenomena. Imagine! Her prayer is doing this. WOW!! Praise you, Thank You and Bless You, I pray to my Blessed Father in Heaven.

She gets up about 8:00 A.M., turns on the radio to hear the hurricane is still stalled. And then, what happens! Human thoughts take hold and invade her being. "This is only prolonging the agony for these people," She thinks. "My Faith is wavering!" By 3:00 the hurricane is wavering too, not quite decided as to which direction to take. By 8:00 news, the newscaster said it is the craziest and the most erratic hurricane ever known.

"Oh! God, help me, I don't want all this responsibility on my shoulders."

It didn't enter her egotistical mind that, of course, there would be others that God would have prompted to pray, as well. By now the hurricane is taking a definite course down the panhandle and would arrive on land with all its fury and destruction about 4:00 A.M. People who had moved back began to move toward shelter again.

Her prayer in tongues continues. It becomes very erratic on the surface. Whether it continues without her hearing it, she doesn't know. It's 10:00 PM. She's in a terrible state; her thoughts by now are on her weaknesses, frailty; on her own personal feelings and guilt for these people. I'm sure I'm being attacked and the devil is having a heyday with me.

"YIKES!!! Please help me, what am I going to do?" she cries out in fear. She gets down on her knees, praying as if her life depended on it.

The answer comes in a flash. "Call 100 Huntley St." They had helped her before so she is sure they would help her again. When the phone is answered, Victoria tells her that, through confirmation, God has asked her to pray for the hurricane in Florida, that things were going wrong and would she help her.

The woman on the other end of the line said she was not asked to pray and that only those that God had asked could pray. And Victoria admits, "Well, I think I am the one who needs prayer because of my pride, vanity and my lack of faith."

And so, as she spoke it all came clear to her what had happened. She began to see that He had allowed all this to happen to her so that she, in her weakness, vanity and not having died to self would realize that when she began to take the credit for the stalling of the hurricane, even though she had praised and thanked Him, He knew she was not humble enough to place the whole thing in His Hands and had unconsciously begun to take responsibility for this herself. Evil then took over her thoughts and although she meant well, everything fell apart. Victoria puts down the phone, her mind clears and she thinks of nothing but her prayer in tongues. She is at peace.

It is Monday morning. Listening to the news she hears the hurricane still had not touched land. By the afternoon, however it takes over and slams land at 125 miles per hour in its full fury. Thankfully the people have all evacuated so there are no deaths. It finally dies out by evening and is over.

Thinking this whole episode over, She realizes she is so full of pride and vanity, that she thought she was the only one God had called on to pray for this hurricane; that the whole responsibility was hers alone.

--------------- --------------------- --------------------

She writes: a death to self. Sounds weird, doesn't it. Unless I die to self I will never be able to do the work He is asking me to do without the interference of me as I am. I must become a new person, completely shed of all the old me that is not Him; to take on a new me that is in Him.

She continues writing: my vision at Mass this morning is of Jesus and His Sacred heart at the altar. He is holding the Eucharist. I am at the foot of the altar and I am old; this I now know, is the old me that must die so that I can be made into a new me.

"Oh, dear, this is all so weird!! Sometimes I think I'm going bonkers."

The Reading is: "God Himself will help you." I feel so much better. Our Father in heaven has shown me joy and consolation these last three years since I first knew Him. He has given me a taste, be it ever so small, of a life with Him. With this knowledge and the desire to want to do His Will I know that no matter how difficult it will be, what trials he puts me through, that I will go through them so that I may die to self.

"Blessed Father in Heaven, I thank you for your patience in bearing with your child who is so weak and silly. I dash around like a bat in half-light unable to see the right way to go. But, unlike the bat, I need light to know my way and only my Lord can provide me with that light. Oh! Light of Light, shine upon me, your blind child, and bring me the Graces I need to follow the path You Will me to walk and do as Time moves on." Thank You, Blessed and Loving Father, Praises upon You, Your angels and Your Saints. Imitation of Christ: Self Love, Book 1V Ch. 27.

-------------------- -------------------- ------------------

*"The little skipper gazes at the morning sun as it lights up the sky after her night of darkness."*

--------------- -------------------- --------------------

This morning after mass she goes to a little coffee party for Mrs. Petre. She so loves those times with her friends. However, this evening there is a Reception for the Parish Priest, and for some reason she hesitates about going.

She phones Jack when she gets home to say hello, and suggests they go to the mall to pick up the groceries. It then came to her that it is strange that she would give up the C.W.L. Parish evening to go shopping. So she picks up her bible for confirmation, and what should come up but "Obedience to the example of Christ." This upset me. Was she not obeying Him by staying home? Was not that His Will for her? And so then the Holy Spirit brings her Exodus: "the Levites chosen by God to test the tabernacle of God," Haggai 2: 13 "The prophet consults the priests," and then, Imitation of Christ, chap. 15 bk. 1, "works done in charity."

She decides to phone a friend to tell her she won't be going to the Reception. Her friend says, "Victoria, the reception is on the 11th not this evening."

Lo and behold! She was obeying Him by staying home. After all this, she got the wrong date. Thank God! She laughs and laughs. She can't help but believe He is laughing too, with glee.

Mary has been persisting in picking Victoria up the last day or two for Mass and this morning she succeeded. Nothing was said on the way but at the end of the mass she came to where Victoria was sitting in the church to ask if she wanted a drive home. On the way she related to me that on Thursday the rosary recitation was in reparation for the films that is now being shown on "Women in the Church" and "Life, Faith and Family" with October being set aside for this particular purpose. Women are badly maligned and ignored for their many roles in the church and this is being ignored by the Bishop of the Diocese. They, as a group must pray; she will pray in tongues, and the scriptures that are revealed to her for confirmation.

For the past few weeks she has been running into Winnie and Bridget of the Prayer Group. She senses there is a reason but she didn't know what. She and Bridget meet at the church and they begin to chat. She prays over Bridget's heel, who said it became worse. Victoria is happy Bridget, who is also suffering a sore back, has begun attending the meditation group at the Anglican Sisters of the Church. For some reason, after prayer when she is with Bridget, Victoria tells her she is going to continue suffering great pain if she did not give up her idea of going to school to finish her education. Victoria is very frustrated. Bridget hears her but did not listen.

Victoria wonders impatiently, "why in heaven's name do I even bother."

Bridget wanted to go to meditation so they go. While meditating it came to Victoria again that Bridget must not go to school and tells her. Bridget got very angry with her and told her she might be right, but that it had to be confirmed to her specifically. Victoria, very cool, said, "running into you this many times confirms it." She tells Bridget she wants to do her own will, not God's. Bridget blasted back in anger and told her to mind her own business. Victoria prayed to the Holy Spirit again to confirm this. She prayed for the Gift of Discernment. Now, each time she sees Bridget, Winnie is always with her. She is prompted to speak to Winnie but does not know why. This morning, in answer to prayer she picks up the book "Elijah Task." It came to her clearly that her task was ended; she was now to tell Winnie about Bridget and Winnie would take over from here.

--------------- --------------------- ---------------------

**Still concerned about Daniel, Victoria writes the following letter.**

Dear Daniel and Jane:

Your letter arrived today and it was with much joy that I read it.

We are all well here. Matt started University this Sept. and seems quite content, but lonely. He is such a homebody that being away from home overnight upsets him although he has had a few escapades in that category. He is like Jack's brother, Colin. He is finding the work easy as he has grade 13 which is considered first Year University.

Because Jack has not received a salary for two years Matt was given a grant and a gift from his brother James who received money after his bike accident, so with the money he had earned this past year he was able to make his year financially. I am happy for him for he has finally grown up after five years of confusion and unhappiness. He is taking Computer Sciences and has a job at the school. James has finally graduated from university this past June and is now working in downtown Toronto. He is just finishing up his first week. Having to get up at 6:00AM every morning to catch the bus from here is not sitting well with him, but I'm sure he'll get used to it as he adjusts to a new schedule. He would like to join the Roy Thompson Hall Theatre group and get into some theatre work. He was active in this area through the job he had at the university and so hopes he can get involved more actively here. It is a pleasure having him home.

Jack is very involved with his new job at Boeing Computer Services and is finding out he is a born salesman. He is still trying to keep his old company above water but he had to close his office so I don't know what will come of this. However he still maintains his contacts and he and his partner are still making trips to fulfill the remaining obligations. They are still discussing China but nothing will be decided for a while. He is well and happy even if we are still struggling financially. Praise God, at least he is not drinking.

I, for my part, have rented out the three bedrooms to students from the local college to bring in some extra income. James, of course, still has his room. They certainly are a diversified group of young people. One is a girl, 16, who is still going to high school. She decided to bring home a kitten the day before yesterday. So now we have to contend with that. Luckily the kitten is house broken if Debbie can bring herself to put him outside. However, during the night, I guess Debbie forgot because the next morning she met with a mess in the cat's bed. Since Debbie has a hard time going to bed at night and a hard time getting up in the morning, the cat will have to adjust his needs to hers. If not, then there is a lesson to be learned here. Since she also has a hard time obeying anyone, never mind the needs of the cat, it will be interesting to see what evolves from this episode with the cat because I have no intention of doing Debbie's job for her. Anyway, we shall see.

I am enjoying all the young people around. They all have problems one way or another. Two of them are street kids and one, Jean Jacques, who comes from Montreal, although quiet and stays out of trouble, is a workaholic and will stay at school from 6 in the morning till midnight. A car ran into him the other night and now he is in bed for a couple of days with a sick stomach. I have a feeling his late hours are not spent at the school. He is interested in communism. I'm afraid he sees nothing but work in his life. However, he has fallen in love with the cat this past day. The other young man downstairs comes from Owen Sound. He has decided that his main objective in life is to make lots of money since what else is more important. His father is an alcoholic and I'm afraid I see the same problem in Terry. He is a very nice boy though so I'm sure, with prayer and time he will be all right. He is taking accounting at the college. Since the rest of his family are labourers this is quite an accomplishment. He also has a nice girlfriend who is majoring in music. She will be a good influence on him.

69

Both Mum and Dad are like two lovebirds chirping away at each other with Dad now having taken over the responsibilities of the little love-nest. Never have I seen two people so happy. They are, in their old age, learning to love one another and to share their good fortune at being alive for a few more years under God's care. They love their little place with its beautiful view, protected from the outside world. They have a tough, loving woman who comes in every day to feed them and tell dirty stories in her kind and generous way. Mum is getting around with a walker and also uses a cane. She performed her one joy the other day when Mary took her to one of the malls.

Love to all.
Your sister
Victoria

She didn't send the letter not knowing where they were. She finally receives Jane's letter saying that they had arrived safely in S.A.

"She is so glad she didn't send the above letter, but she should not have put off sending the letter telling them not to go to S.A. Did she listen to God's silent Word showing her the way?

She berates herself; "I never seem to do anything right. Oh, well, maybe my letter wouldn't have stopped them anyway."

Jane's letter arrived a few days after she wrote the one telling them not to go to S.A. She had put off sending it and has done nothing but suffer in anguish and pain, Ezekiel 13:16-21. She can't put off sending the letter telling him it is not God's Will he go to S.A. She must do what she is called to do, no matter if it is too late.

--------------- --------------------- ---------------------

*"Tears of confusion from her closed eyes flow like falling rain as she bows her head letting the little red sailboat take its own tack."*

--------------- --------------------- ---------------------

Saturday she went to the church to talk to Fr. R.; instead who should come in but Gerald and Diane. Considering her past experiences with them the sight of them confuses her so much she panics and could not speak to the priest. She waits in front of the church so they wouldn't see her. Fr. R. goes down the opposite isle and she calls out to him to ask him if he would see her sometime.

He said, "yes, how about Monday after Mass?" Sunday afternoon she phones the Rectory to tell him she can't see him.

Imitation of Christ: The reading tells her she is afraid to do God's Will. She must learn not to let other people's opinions bother her.

This morning she comes into the church and Fr. R. is the priest in attendance. She feels a strong urge to go to him which she does with much humiliation and embarrassment although she laughs at the uncomfortable feeling. It is important that she share with her Spiritual Director, Fr. R, everything that is taking place in her spiritual life so that she is being given help and confirmation.

After seeing Fr. R. and telling him what was bothering her spiritually, she leaves the church and goes for a drive to think about what he had said.

Sitting on a bench overlooking the calm waters she picks up her book "Imitation of Christ"; all that comes to her is "self- love." She tries to rationalize it and make excuses for herself; but then it all comes pouring out of her. The books "Imitation of Christ" and the "Elijah Task" makes it clear to her that she would never be able to do God's Will if she continues the way she is going. She knows she must face her faults of arrogance and self-love. And then the tears start to flow and she prays for forgiveness. And still, even now, she thinks she did a great thing. Nothing she does or says is ever going to be enough of a humiliation to satisfy her for the haughty way she's been acting. How can she be so arrogant and proud? She believes she deserves what is happening to her and more. After what she has done in the past, how can she possibly think that she is something special?

She prays; "were my actions with Fr. R., self-love and patronizing as Fr. R. heard my comments of the priesthood and their work as priests?

I am praying for wisdom and love to accept, with humility, how I am acting in my conceit, pride and arrogance. Help me, I pray, to see myself as others see me in every way. I know it will be difficult to accept but with strength and the necessary Graces with prayer, I know I will be able to cope with the truth about myself."

In my arrogance I deserve, Nahum: 1-14. In my humiliation in dying to- self, I pray that He, in His Mercy will allow Isaiah 8:3 to come about. Isaiah 37, The prophet is consulted. Hosea, Isaiah 54: 4-10 Isaiah 35, Isaiah 38: 5-6

So many scriptures come to teach me as I read the bible, I can't quote them all."

-------------- -------------------- --------------------

Jacques, one of the young street kids who moved in a while back is giving her some trouble. It seems, in one way or another she is finding him difficult to handle. Why, Oh why are these kids so hard to handle? She sure can't do it without prayer. She writes the following letter to Jacques hoping that he will hear what she is saying.

Dear Jacques:

These words came to me today loud and clear through scriptures from the bible, Psalm 95, and in my prayer time, since you have told me you are staying another month.

"If only you would hear His words today. Do not harden your heart as your fathers did in the wilderness when they challenged Me and tested Me although they had seen all my works. They were a people whose hearts went astray for 40 years in the days of Moses. That was why I was angry with that generation and said, "How unreliable are these people who refuse to grasp my ways, and so, in my anger, I swore that they shall not enter into the place of rest that I have for them."

These words could not be more clear, Jacques. You are to go home immediately, on Friday, as planned. If you don't go, I cannot guarantee an easy ride. You are listening to the world around you, Jacques. It is not for you. If you choose to go ahead with your plans, do not come to this house again or try and get in touch with us.

--------------- -------------------- --------------------

They are having some new counters laid in the bathroom. So the workmen turned on the water after laying the counter and the water flooded all over the bathroom floor. They began to repair the job as part of the price but Victoria, in a huff, stopped them saying their job was finished. She wasn't thinking that their job was not finished if they didn't have the water turned on. They would have fixed it with no trouble but she told them to leave. She was so upset she did not think. Now Jack has to go through the trouble of getting them back again or calling a plumber, which will cost a lot. Oh! When will she ever learn? She is devastated at her mistake. She again brings her spiritual thinking into her mind and sees it as all part of her dying-to-self. She has to admit she will have to accept the chastisement, which she deserves.

"Now Jack will be angry with me because I didn't keep them here," she weeps. "And we will have to go through all this tonight with no water. I should have listened to them and said nothing."

She hates herself. "I should have said nothing and minded my own business, keeping my mind and eyes on Him at all times." She feels like crying. After all, with two young people in the house now, as well as another one moving in she can't believe she did such a stupid thing.

---------------  ---------------------  ---------------------

*"Her little red sailboat is very difficult to handle; the waves are tossing her about. She can't seem to hold on the tiller to steer it against the power of the wind. She feels so alone. However, she takes a firm grip on the tiller and prays; going she knows not where."*

---------------  ---------------------  ---------------------

Terry, A young man, has moved into the extra empty bedroom now that Gerald and Jacques are gone. She is worried about him since he seems to be working such long hours,

She writes some thoughts about Terry.

"When you came home this morning after working the night shift, I looked at you so tired and unshaven, and I prayed, "Ok, Lord, what this person could not do for you, one whom you chose to free from his burdens and cares. He is such a strong young man in that he has so much character and discipline. He works long hours and plays long hours and I ask myself, "what for?" He spends all his hard-earned money for things that "go up in smoke." He is wrecking his mind and his body on things that are "gone with the wind." He believes that his way of life is the free-way because he is using his own free will, without a thought to a life he appears to want to destroy."

She hopes he has come to this house to find a chance to see something different than what he was used to. Hopefully, with the kindness, mercy and love through prayer for him, there might be a change and freedom from all the things that make him what he is today that seem so important to him.

She was going to write to him but changed her mind after reading it. The letter is so preachy, arrogant and patronizing.

Debbie has been living with them now since the first week of September and up to today she has been trying to understand Debbie and think only the best of her. By revealing a little at a time; she will only draw the conclusions necessary.

As Victoria sits here at the kitchen table with a soup boiling on the stove, her kitchen a mess, Jack reading in the living room, Matt, who is home for the Christmas holidays, doing a laundry and watching T.V. and Debbie endlessly on the phone, She thinks of the suffering she is enduring for Debbie's sake. All of a sudden, a vision flashes in her mind of the Lord's suffering on the cross and His Passion endured in silence for all sins. She is humbled and prays that she will always be able to see His suffering on the cross when something is bothering her. Her ministry! Is it to endure pain in silence? The last mantras that have come to her are: "endure the pain for me, Victoria" and "help comes with God's Word."

Debbie is constantly on the phone: she doesn't finish her laundry; she stays out too late or is in bed too long. These habits irk Victoria and she feels like speaking up and saying something to her. I must look toward the cross; always toward the cross and Jesus suffering on the cross. ±

She felt such joy at the Benedictine Retreat, feeling like bubbling over in laughter where she was to be silent. Fr. Gerald said to the group, "What hymns shall we sing for the Mass, "Keep your mind on the Cross?" She felt as if he were speaking directly to her. Her joy didn't end as she thought about that message but she was able to control her laughter.

She wonders, *What else will happen if I keep my mind on the Cross.*

As long as she has the Cross in her thoughts that will be all that her mind will have to concentrate on. He will solve the problems happening around her in His good time, as her mind will be empty to receive His Word.

--------------- -------------------- --------------------

Victoria writes the following: Debbie's girlfriend, Elaine arrives. But that is another story. I decide not to go into the details of it at the moment but will write a very interesting truth about lying which the scriptures have just revealed to me.

Lying takes on many different forms:

The one that is commonly known is the denial lie. No, I did not do it when it was very obvious they did it.

Another lie is the following example:

Elaine takes the phone to talk to a former boyfriend of Debbie's whose name is Chris. After the phone call Debbie and Elaine sit at the kitchen table and discuss the phone call. Elaine said that Chris asked her if she was living away from home now and Elaine told him "yes, for some time; and of course, she wasn't. Chris says: "Oh I didn't know that" and of course, believes her. Both girls giggle over Chris's gullibility in believing everything he hears. Is it right that Elaine lie to him? Why should she want to make him look ridiculous?

"Where, oh, where is the love"?

In Debbie's case this is what I must deal with amongst other problems. The lies to make others and, in particular me, look ridiculous.

For example: Debbie and Cam, her boyfriend, went to Buffalo to shop on Boxing Day.

Or---they said they were going to Buffalo to shop. So off they go five minutes after telling me they were going. She phoned late evening to say she would be staying over at friends of Cams. In the meantime, the next morning Elaine, the friend, comes by bus from Cambridge to stay the night. I had not been told of her visit ahead of time. Debbie arrives home around 3 PM with Elaine here.

She said to Elaine, "oh! Just remembered on the way home about you coming"

Needless to say I was a bit peeved. I have an argument with Debbie concerning Elaine's visit. She should have asked me ahead of time whether she could have a guest or not. I felt this argument came about through prayer but if I had kept my mind on the Cross, what would have happened? Anyway, Debbie's gone again and around midnight she phones and asks if Elaine could spend the night.

I said, yes, if you come home now."

She said on the phone, "We are on our way to a party at a girlfriend's."

I then asked her, "What is Elaine going to do if she doesn't come here?"

She said, "Elaine will go home and I will go to her place after the party.

She then asked me if I would be mad when she got home. I said, in no uncertain terms, "of course I will be very angry if you disobey me. Either you come home when I say or go to the party and then Elaine's, and don't come back, that's your choice."

Twenty minutes later she arrived home without Elaine.

Now we come to the lies. Was there really a party? Would she have gone to Elaine's, and how were they going to get to Elaine's since she didn't have a car?

All I know is that, Blessed Mary, as I hang up the phone I begin to pray the Rosary and I know, without a doubt, through your intercession, Blessed Mother, Debbie came home.

This morning Elaine arrives. She had stayed in the next city overnight with friends. She did not go home as Debbie said she would.

--------------- --------------------- --------------------

*"Victoria sails into a cove where she and her little red sailboat will settle to rest. She is contemplating. She has to reach the peace she needs to continue her voyage."*

--------------- --------------------- --------------------

Victoria sits at the kitchen table trying to think of the words to write to Debbie. She is trying very hard to understand her, so the words don't come easy. She has taken on this role to have these street-kids in their home to help with the financial situation they are dealing with but she certainly didn't expect to get involved with their personalities, etc. Is it more than she can handle? It certainly is a learning experience. Is there more to this than just helping with the finances?

--------------- --------------------- --------------------

### Jan 1st/86

A new year and what is ahead; and is she prepared? She must make a cake for New Years' Dinner but first of all she wants to write this down:

When I think about yesterday, I am confused and yet, overjoyed. I haven't in the last few weeks been very dedicated to the ritual of reading my Breviary or my prayers. Either I have been too busy, too lazy or too tired. Only God knows, what is going on within. All I know is I was "brought through the coals, brought to the lowest" and I know now how necessary that was. I have been "playing god" and that was made very clear to me through a little Grimms Fairy Tale I heard on the radio last weekend.

I referred to the little tale when I sat in the chair in the living room yesterday afternoon feeling exhausted over my "set-to" with Debbie concerning her use of the washer and dryer and Elaine, who spends too much time here, using the shower at the same time. After this very draining episode between us and about other burdensome problems like Jack, etc., I sat in the chair and thought how exhausted I am carrying the burdens of all these people on my shoulders in the past few months

76

And then, I continue to write:

"If it's a burden for me with these few people to deal with, how could Jesus have coped with the burdens on His shoulders of all the sins of all the people in the world, and then to die on the Cross for these sins including mine?" I am exhausted thinking about it.

Then, "I don't have to carry anyone's burdens as such. It is not necessary for me to be concerned for them; in whatever way they displease me. He had done that part of it when He died on the Cross. All I have to do is focus my attention on Him and He will take care of the rest." Wow! What a revelation!!

I had been feeling very deserted as if Jesus didn't love me, and then I remembered that on the 20th of Dec. at a Healing Mass, He came to me with the words "I Love you, Victoria" when the priest said out loud to the audience, "I Love You" out loud and wished us all peace. I was given the gift of Jesus's love, of course, in so many ways over the years but it seemed important to me to hear the words spoken out loud. And then, again, as I picked up my missal that a friend gave me, I opened it to the words "I Love You," again and I felt my heart leap. Over and over again I ask myself, how can He love me; I who, in the past two years or more have been so egotistic. To think I thought to do God's Work for Him being so ignorant of God's Ways. However, I assumed that way was the right way. Someday I will write it all out but, as of now, I know that all I must do is to only love Him and not worry about anyone or anything else.

"Love Me more, Victoria, because I Love you" is the meditation that keeps coming to me. What more do I need? That and the words that the priest said at the Retreat, "Keep in mind the Cross." I know that He will look after everyone else who comes in my path in His own way. Praise You, Bless You and Thank You, Blessed Holy Trinity; Father, Son and Holy Spirit, Amen!

-------------- -------------------- --------------------

Last night she got up with much pain through her whole body, which isn't unusual. While praying for healing, the words come to her very clearly, in meditation, "Endure the pain for Me, Victoria, the pain in your body, endure for Me."

She is able to accept those words very peacefully and happily, now that she knows. Strangely, She knows now for certain what pain she must endure; Jack's criticism for one thing; always putting her down with a litany of her faults.

-------------- -------------------- --------------------

Victoria writes on paper her feelings about Debbie, the street-kid:

As I sit here trying to think of what words to write to you, I am also trying to understand you. Heaven only know, I'm trying. You have been told very firmly and as strongly as I can tell you to do your laundry, to get washed and dressed. Other than going downstairs and pushing the button into the washing machine, you did nothing else but go back to the bed. You have been on a continual holiday since your mother dropped you off, bag and baggage, on my doorstep four months ago.

Victoria writes about the boys that come and go to visit, late hours and failing in her school work. Victoria's mind is boggled, "I have been patiently waiting to see what I am dealing with here. Is Debbie just plain stupid or is she pretending to be stupid? Or does she think she is smart? Does she really believe she is putting something over on us?"

Victoria finishes her thoughts about Debbie.

Jack arrives home late in the evening after visiting a pub, to bedlam in the house with the extra kids invading his privacy. It's impossible to make him understand the reasoning behind all this. Does she really know, herself, why she is going through this? He yells and screams at her once they reach the bedroom. What can she say that he would understand or believe?

--------------- --------------------- --------------------

Victoria writes her spiritual thoughts:

Today is beautiful. I know I'm not alone because the Holy Spirit has come to me again after leaving me feeling unhappy for so long. I asked our Blessed Mother, Mary to help me to know in what way He would have me answer the meditation; "Help with the Word of God."

A half an hour later a great peace came over me and such joy as I realized I must pray unceasingly, in silence. To pray in the marketplace or wherever I am Called to pray. In my Contemplation He again comes to me and I could so strongly feel His Presence. It is so hard to explain what came over me; as if I were in another world. My body lightens up and I reach out to Him and prayed a prayer of the Holy Spirit in tongues. I then curled up in a small ball and felt like a small child in His strong Hands, to pray and sing in tongues as I felt the tears of joy stream down my face. This had not happened to me for quite some time. I felt as if He had left me on my own for a number of months and was again returning to me, filling me with consolation. For an hour, unhappiness, loneliness and pain had left me. The pain is back again now though, although I feel happier and closer to Him than I have in a long time. Praise Him, bless Him, and thank Him; Glory to God on high. I love Him, even though it seems, at times, I don't. I have so much self-love that I must conquer.

The fact that I had to send those letters to my brother, Daniel still haunts me. Through the promptings of the Holy Spirit it was necessary for me to write Daniel and tell him he was not doing God's Will by being in S.A. and it still haunts me. Then, as I feel remorse, such joy I feel as I am prompted to read the book, "Elijah Task." "I know your suffering and the work you have wrought in your heart."

Such peace overwhelms me and such joy as I read those words. I know now I did the right thing. Praise You, Jesus. Bless the Holy Trinity. Thank You, Praise You and Bless your Holy Name.

--------------- --------------------- --------------------

*"The little red sailboat seems to be sailing on its own tack now. The skipper has nothing to say anymore. She reaches out in prayer; whether in silence or with the sounds of the litany of the rosary beads. Whatever it is, the aloneness, not having to make any decisions as to which way to sail, brings peace."*

--------------- --------------------- --------------------

Christmas and New Years' are over and all the boarders are back. Jack is at the end of his tether. He just can't understand why this invasion upon his life has to be. Sometimes she wonders where all this is leading to. Is she doing God's Will or her own? The quarrelling between them never seems to end. He controls and manipulates her mind and she can't help but scream in defense, making her cry. Off she runs to her room. Where, OH! Where is the love?

She goes to church early to say her Breviary and morning prayers. She likes it much better this way. Fewer distractions and she has to go to Mass anyway, so might as well take the extra hour to make her visit to Him during that quiet time in the morning. She likes to think He is happy with her effort.

As secretary she is all prepared to go to the C.W.L. Executive Meeting later but she realizes she did not have a pen with her. It's too late to go back home to get one and so she goes to the drugstore after Mass to buy one and to pick up the book she left there. She was delayed there as they couldn't find her book. She decided she would not go to the meeting.

She arrives home around 10:00. Debbie's boyfriend's car is in the driveway. Victoria is fit to be tied. She goes to Debbie's room to see whether she was still in bed. Sure enough, she finds Cam, her boyfriend, in her room; now she knows why she missed the meeting. She gives the two of them a real tongue-lashing. Debbie gets angry, huffs and puffs, grabs her books and she and Cam take off for school. After she leaves, Victoria writes another letter; helps to release the stress. There are a lot of changes coming about in Debbie, though. Perhaps she is finally beginning to see some light; spoke too soon, though.

Its 3:00 in the morning and something wakes Victoria up. She notices the light in the hall is still on. Debbie is not in yet. Fifteen minutes later she hears Debbie come in. Victoria gets up to greet her at the door. In her anger she says to her, "Debbie, this has gone far enough. If this continues I am going to have to ask you to leave." She rants on a little longer; Debbie looks at her bleary-eyed. Drunk, I suppose.

Victoria grabs her booklet and pen to write some spiritual thoughts:

I know I must not hate her, that I must love her no matter what she does. It's her actions and attitude I hate. "Please help me to love her, please help me to see her unhappiness, her rebellion. Please help me. Please help her. Forgive her and let her know Your Love. I lay her burdens and sins at the foot of the cross, Sweet Jesus. I give them to You. She is so confused and lost. I know you will help her, Lord and so I come to You in faith, hope, love and confidence knowing she is safe in Your Loving Hands. How fortunate we are to have You to guide us every step of the way. How good it makes me feel that I only have to turn to You, and Your Holy Family, angels and saints for the answers I need. According to Your Holy and Blessed Will, You will be there to help. Thank You, Praise You and Bless You!

--------------- -------------------- --------------------

Yesterday Victoria writes Debbie a letter saying that she has an alternative to leaving, that she could stay if she prayed to Jesus to forgive her for her sins much like the heroine in the book "Carmen," a story about a rebellious teen-ager I had given her. This time Victoria gives her the letter.

Victoria becomes quite light-hearted and gay almost happy; almost affectionate toward Debbie. Again with her personality, she manages to worm her way around and talk her out of it, but Victoria told her she was serious about what she had written in the letter. She has no idea if she even read it. Probably not!!!

Again, Debbie did as she pleased even after Victoria's angry attitude toward her. She went off to the boat show and in the evening said she was going out for coffee. She goes to bed about 10:30 and still Debbie is not in. Victoria is very concerned with the bible readings she has been getting. She feels as though she is being disciplined and told off for her attitude. Victoria muses; "my attitude, of all things; what about Debbie's? Am I on a guilt trip?"

-------------- -------------------- --------------------

### The next day: Jan 13, Victoria's Birthday

After Mass a group of women from the church stop at the café for coffee. She left the cafe to go home quite unhappy as she really felt a couple of the women did not make her feel too welcome; my Birthday, too.

Returning home there was Cam's car in the driveway again. She realizes she should not have been at the cafe after all. She walks into the house, goes to Debbie's room and of course, there is Cam her boyfriend; Debbie in her bathrobe getting ready to go to school.

She writes:

After disciplining Debbie and Cam I feel so downhearted; turning to my bible and books for some direction from the Holy Spirit, it comes to me very strongly that as long as I carry the burden of my own past sins I cannot possibly help Debbie. My life, in the past was even worse than Debbie's. My anger at her was a reflection of my own guilt and anger. How could I expect to help Debbie under these circumstances? In despair and humility I feel the need to kneel and ask forgiveness for my own past sins. How can I help anyone when I myself was so sinful? I so badly need healing. Only time will tell if He has forgiven me. I asked our Blessed Mother, Mary to intercede for me. My feelings of guilt and anger, I know won't be changed overnight but I hope and pray for the love, patience and understanding I need to help those who come into my life now and in the future. In Jesus Name, I pray! One day at a time.

-------------- -------------------- --------------------

Just as she stops her prayers and meditation, Victoria gets a call from a friend to ask how she is. Jan said hadn't seen her at the

Sisters of the Church for meditation in a while. This is true. She hadn't gone since the meditation Retreat directed by a Benedictine Monk. While praying at the Retreat, it came to Victoria very strongly to "lay hands" for healing on Jan for the pinched nerve in her hip. Since then, Jan phoned her to say she has not been suffering with the pain and can walk without any trouble since. Our Blessed Sweet Jesus healed her using me as an instrument. Praise Him, Thank Him and Bless His Holy Name, the Healer.

As it so happened Victoria had no drive to go to that Retreat and two other women were to have gone with Jan. They asked her to go with Jan and they would find another way. She is sure it was God's Will that she go with Jan alone otherwise the other women would have been chattering away and she would never have found out about Jan's bad leg and would not have thought to lay hands on her. Providential?

And now, this letter to Fr. Burrows copied from blue notepaper, concerning Victoria's request to become a nun with the hopes of becoming an Oblate.

Dear Fr. Burrows:

In the beginning of this New Year, my prayer for you is one of solace and peace in your work and in your prayer life. For this I pray to the Lord.

Victoria stops and contemplates the words written on the blue writing paper. Her mind flashes back in memory to the words the Sister at the Sacred Heart Convent in her home town said to her when she wanted to become a nun.

"Dear, No, You are not to become a Nun. God has other plans for you."

She thinks, "Perhaps she was right. Maybe I'm not to become a novice or an Oblate, but must live my life as a layperson, whatever that means?"

She didn't send the letter.

--------------- -------------------- --------------------

She prays:

"Blessed Holy Father in Heaven, in the Name of Jesus, I approach You in all humility to ask You to explain to me what it is You are trying to tell me. I am so confused. Please help me. I want to know and do Your Will but I am having a hard time understanding. Give me the wisdom I need to do Your Will. I am nothing but a poor soul who can't do a thing without Your help. I know You are telling me something but I can't pray about it unless you reveal to me, in your patience and mercy what You want me to pray for. Thank You and Praise Your Holy and Blessed Name. Are You asking me to pray for Jack? Or is it for me?"

---------------------    -------------------    -------------------

*"She sits in her little red sailboat in the silence of the night to listen to His instructions; what He will say and what answer He will give to her complaint?" Then, still in silence, she hears: Quote scriptures, Habbakuk 2: 1-3, Hebrews 10:36-37*
*"Write down the Vision clearly upon the tablets, so that it can be easily read. For the Vision still has it's Time, pressing on to fulfillment and will not disappoint. If it is late, wait for it. It will surely come, it will not be late." She, lulled by the silent stirrings of the waves, falls asleep."*

---------------------    -------------------    -------------------

She must keep on writing and praying. Soon all will be revealed. Victoria can't believe these scriptures she's getting. She sits in utter silence, "what is happening to me," flies through her mind?

Her Spirit soars!!! But she must come back to reality, or is what she is experiencing the real reality? Being very tired she crawls into bed and falls into a deep sleep.

The next day:

She is very upset today because she has to tell Debbie she is lazy. She believes they think terribly of her for the things that she must say. She prays that it is God's Will, Jeremiah 1:19 confirms. She praises and gives thanks. She knows that she is loved and that in the end it will be for the best because if she fights the good fight with courage, she will be rewarded with everlasting life with her Father in Heaven.

She thinks:

"I am a housewife, 51 years old. My goal in life is to be a contemplative. Yes, that's right. I want to be a contemplative, not an engineer, a doctor, a nurse, a fashion designer, a secretary or a store clerk; but a contemplative, (one who lives a life of prayer). There are people who spend years and thousands of dollars learning how to heal the sick, store clerks who help customers, engineers who build, fashion designers who dress people, and secretaries who manage managers. They are all worth-while professions and occupations that help others; so why not contemplatives that help others?

This came to her like a flash as she strained to open the garage door this morning so that she could drive Debbie to school and then, go to Swift Sure Couriers to have Jack's name-tags sent off to him in Washington.

This realization came about because of her hateful response to Jack's call from Washington this morning. It was not the initial call that caused the problem. Oh No!! She didn't mind that he called her at 7:30 A.M.; wake her up to tell her to have his name-tag, which he had forgotten to take with him on his trip, sent out to him as quickly as possible.

"Sure Jack," she sweetly said, "I will get it away to you immediately."

Her idea was to go to mass and then to the courier's office to have it sent away today. She was just about ready to go out the door at 8:30 when the phone rang again. It was Jack in Washington saying that he had taken it upon himself to call Swift Sure Couriers to tell them she was coming and to make the arrangements for the name-tags to be shipped out to him.

Well, she couldn't believe what she was hearing. After giving her the responsibility of having the name-tags sent out, he did not trust her enough to do the job. It was 5:00 A.M. in Washington. He could have been sound asleep after making the initial call if he had trusted her, and there he was in a dither because he could not be sure she would do what she was told.

What did she do? She got angry and blew up at him over the phone. Now, what she should have said, "yes, Jack, you are right. I know I would not have been able to handle the situation; getting the name-tags away to you on time or properly, so it's just as well you made the phone call to Swift Sure to make sure it is done right. Thank you for taking the responsibility off my hands, or some such unlikely and saintly response.

Instead she yelled at him "did you not give me the responsibility to see that I would get the name-tags away to you?"

"Oh!" He said in surprising innocence, "did you already phone Swift Sure?" I screamed, "of course I did." She could not believe her ears that he would have so little confidence in her.

She shouted over the phone, "now will you go back to sleep and leave me alone?" He said, "OK, and hung up the phone."

84

"Oh, why did I have to get angry with him," she asks? He always seems to upset her no matter the situation. She seems to be always on a guilt trip with him.

She is angry for a while; sleeps on it and then realizes the episode is a mild one and there is really no real damage done. Will her conscience help her see that eventually she will get over it; the bad memories will gradually recede into the depths of the unconscious to pile upon the many other stacks of bad and good memories that tend to come back to please or haunt her? She does know that it made her even more aware of her failures as a person; that because of failures and sins many other people in the past were affected. She is no saint.

Friday, Jack arrives home from Washington in a bitter mood. Victoria doesn't know the cause for his outbursts but as the weekend goes on its merry way she feels so guilty; couldn't seem to do anything right. She tries to think about what she is doing wrong, and then she remembers the name-tags, although the incident was never mentioned.

They sit over their drinks Saturday before dinner. She hopes to talk with him to find out the problem. As she talks, a string of swears words from him fill the air. She dares not say anything more. The guilt falls like a dark blanket over her heart and soul. Was his problem the name-tags?

--------------- -------------------- --------------------

She is lost in meditative contemplation:

I sit in contemplation at St Michaels in Toronto. The first image that I see is Jesus and His Sacred Heart. The first words are, "Love me more, Victoria". The second image is the Blessed Virgin Mary, side view seeing only her veil. The next image is Jesus and blood dripping from His Sacred Heart. The next words are, "I am the Lord your God, you shall have no other gods before Me." The next image is Jesus with flames coming from His Sacred Heart.

Then "Marshedelago" in tongues by the Holy Spirit, sounds within me. This is a mantra fighting against evil. The next image is a cross in the background.

Then Jesus gives me the Host at Communion. He moves to the back of the altar and I am at the rail. Jesus, still with His Sacred Heart and Mary are now facing me though not clearly.

Jesus is still behind the altar. I see an old woman at the rail and a child is with her. The cross is behind Jesus. Now the words, "I love you; love me more, Victoria because I love you. "I love you, Jesus."

An image of Jesus and His Crown of Thorns comes to me while I am reciting the rosary—the Sorrowful Mysteries. The Face of Jesus is dripping blood and His Face is in agony. It is a partial side view. I have found out since, it is to give me courage. And the words, "endure the pain for me, Victoria."

I find all this very strange because I do so little. However I do know it is for my spiritual growth. They are His Gifts and His Loving Graces to help me along my way. Without them and the gift of tongues and the overwhelming chill that envelops me I would suspect that I am mad. Praise God, Bless Him, Thank Him and Glorify His Holy Name for these gifts. I cannot express adequately what they mean to me. I am nothing but a human being, who sinned without hesitation, who discarded and turned my back on Him, my love and salvation, so long ago. "I love you, Jesus. I love you, Victoria", and then, "I love you Jesus."

Scriptures:   Baruch 6: Do not be afraid. Isaiah 62   Debbie, Ezekiel 1. Jeremiah 1: Tell them all I tell you. Jeremiah 39

All these scriptures I lift up to the Lord, Our Father in Heaven. He will use them according to His Holy and Blessed Will. I don't know what to do with them. In Jesus Name, Praise You, Thank You and Bless You.

As she rides home on the bus she is utterly in shock. What does it all mean? I am so afraid. There is no one to share these visions with. Am I going crazy?

--------------- --------------------  --------------------

*"The little red sailboat is completely out of control as the storm rips and tosses it about in the rough waves. What can the little skipper do? Fear is all within and around her as she grabs the rudder to beach her little craft."*

--------------- --------------------  --------------------

Oh! Mary, blessed Mother. I am so frightened. What is happening to me? Who can I turn to for help? OH! Sweet and Blessed Mary, everything is going out of control. I am so alone. Who can I talk to about these things that are happening to me? Please help me, Mary!!!

I deserted You, my Lord, but You didn't desert me; You took me back. What are you trying to tell me from Your Holy and Blessed Word.

Hosea 2, repeated, Jeremiah 36: Baruch 6: Do not be afraid; they are not gods, Isaiah 50, Book of Jonah who disobeys, Habbakuk.

--------------- --------------------  --------------------

Daniel and family have been on Victoria's mind lately; wondering how they are in S.A. She knows she must pray for their safety, as she has not heard from them. Perhaps they didn't get the letters she sent them. One never knows what happens with the mail in these strange countries.

After praying the rosary early this morning clear words spoke to her soul,

"You must make the way of the cross for Daniel in tongues every day through the remainder of Lent beginning today until Easter Sunday."

And so she begins by going to her own church. The doors of the church are locked. She decides to go to St Michaels in Toronto by subway. There is a baptism going on; she feels Jesus touches these children. She goes to the first Station of the Cross; strange feelings came over her; very weak and her heart feels as if it would burst. After she finishes, the priest arrives at the church and she feels compelled to share with him what happened and about her prayers for Daniel.

He said, "You are praying the Stations of the Cross to protect Daniel and his family in the terrible country of S.A., which is so unchristian."

Half way through the two weeks joy begins to fill her heart as she prays the Way of The Cross in tongues for Daniel, her brother and family. She knows, without a doubt, that whatever way is God's Will her prayer is being answered for Daniel. Praise His Mighty Name. Thank and Bless Him!!

A friend takes her to see a Carmelite Sister today.

--------------- -------------------- --------------------

*"She sits in her little red sailboat and her heart sings: This is the day the Lord has made, let us rejoice and be glad in it. It is the end of her search and the continuation of her voyage; a voyage where she is ready to sail into the unknown."*

--------------- -------------------- --------------------

She writes:
Malachi 2: "The triumph of the virtuous on the day of Yahweh," I am far from being virtuous but it seems appropriate as to what I have committed myself to. I feel at peace, that I have come to the conclusion knowing my search is over. I am giving up the desire and the luxury of belonging to any Order, whether it is the Notre Dame

Sisters, Carmelite Sisters, Benedictines or any other, anything that will stop me from doing His Will for me. It is not for me.

As well as all the other spiritual readings I have been doing with such joy, I have just finished a book given to me by a friend, written by Catherine DeHuek Doherty called "Poustinia".

"Poustinia" is a way of life, living in silence and I know that this is what I have been doing, albeit haphazardly, in the past year and in my future, what I am being called to do, "Poustinia in the marketplace." How beautiful it sounds and how joyful the idea makes me feel.

--------------- --------------------- ---------------------

*"The search is over and my voyage as a little poustinik sailor begins, my voyage in the Poustinia, my voyage in silence in the marketplace as her little red sailboat stops at each port along the way."*

--------------- --------------------- ---------------------

She continues to write her thoughts:

With the repetition of this Prayer, I know He will help me. The Holy Spirit will guide me console me; instruct me with His Words of Wisdom. I am not alone in this secular world where I find it so difficult to live a spiritual life.

Sister Maria said that I must stay in this world. That is God's Will for me so that I can help bring souls to Him who loves them so; Jack and others who don't know Him or love Him. I know that I want nothing more. I am content in His Will for me.

I must give up the thought of a convent life or an enclosed life. Live a life of chastity and fasting. Take up the cross of my life here in the world where God seems not to exist and follow Him through His Word and in silence to the people to whom He brings me. It is really very simple; He will speak to them in my silence as He has done in the past year.

Take up my cross! It's strange; a cross is very heavy, very difficult to carry, it is painful, it weighs us down. We want to run away from it and perhaps hurt others because we have to carry it for them. Maybe others are to blame for the cross we have to bear and so we want to hurt them, make them suffer the way we are suffering. That is the way it is when we are a non-believer. We are human, after all. Life is hopeless, cold, burdensome and cruel. The cross is so heavy we want to end it all.

And then, we find God, the Father, God, the Son and God, the Holy Spirit. All the Glory be given to the Holy Trinity. Suddenly the cross is not so heavy; love fills our lives; and those for whom we carry the cross. Love makes us realize that we don't know how to help, but the Blessed Trinity helps us. The cross is heavy and burdensome but not for us because we don't have to carry it alone. We are following Him who loves us and died for us and the cross becomes so much lighter. It is very strange until we begin life with God as our Father, knowing we are loved and protected; as we hold His hand like a child unable to walk alone.

My visit to the Carmelites made me realize I don't need them or the Benedictines or anyone because I have Him. He told me from the beginning when He said He would show me the way and he would teach me Himself" and the words "I am the Lord Your God, you shall have no other gods before me," the first of the 10 commandments. Praise God! What more do I need? I love you, Jesus!

The book, "Poustinia" confirmed for me my spiritual life is going in the right direction. All of a sudden it all seems very right and no one can tell me otherwise. God's Word is revealed to me in the Poustinia, (in silence) for people for whom He has a message, to those He has brought to me for help as in the past. Gerald and Diane, Mum and Dad, Daniel, those street-kids who are living with us, and so many others that He has placed in my path in one way or another. I must tell them what He has revealed to me for them and others as the years go by. I must write.

--------------- --------------------- --------------------

Delores, one of the Executive members of the CWL came to Victoria one day after mass and invited her to have lunch with her and her daughter. Victoria was so pleased to say yes; Dolores has very strong spiritual leanings and she and Victoria have a lot in common. She thoroughly enjoyed a lovely lunch and meeting Katie, who has just arrived home from Europe where she has been a student at a Music Conservatory in a convent there. She had been given a scholarship to attend this very prestigious school. Katie began to chat as they ate saying she didn't want to go back to continue her studies. Her mother looked at Victoria shaking her head. She seemed very disturbed. Victoria felt a strong premonition there was a reason why she was invited to this home today.

After Mass the next morning, Katie comes to her in tears. She is so upset that she had to go back to Europe. She asks Victoria what she should do.

As Katie listens to the answer, the expression on her face changes and she looks at her startled at Victoria's words to her,

"Katie, if you feel so strongly about not going back I'm sure you know what you are doing but, how will you pay back the scholarship you received for this excellent opportunity?"

Victoria gets a letter from her today. She is now back at the Conservatory prepared to continue her music studies. Praise the Lord! She is beginning to walk her own road.

--------------- --------------------- ---------------------

### Easter weekend writings:

Before I got up this morning, it came to me that I must pray the rosary. While praying to Mary she leads me to the book I was reading about Fr. Damian who sacrificed his life for Lepers in a Leper Colony. It came to me, "sacrifice, Victoria. Carry your cross."

Then it came clear to me by the filling of the Holy Spirit that went through me that I must provide a home for kids with no home. It will come about in spite of Jack. Having students is just a trial run to teach me how to handle having young people in the house but it will not be students forever. Is this right? I won't know until all this comes about. I am His to do with as He plans. We shall see.

I prayed the Rosary again. I must read about Fr. Damien. Fr. Damien was a servant. Today, Easter Monday, offered myself up as a servant like Fr Damien.

The next morning, off to Easter Mass then home to prepare dinner. I just can't get the Damien Story out of my mind.

--------------- --------------------- ---------------------

### Victoria writes:

"The following is how the Poustinia works in my life. I am brought to silence (Poustinia) at any time, day or night. He spiritually uses me and then everything slowly takes place in His time, not mine. It is a lesson to learn the hard way.

As Victoria wakes up at 12:30 A.M. she believes she is being told something. Is it a word of Knowledge in the Poustinia? She can't get back to sleep. As she lays there resting she thinks about Mary who had sprained her ankle. Perhaps she needs help to drive her son to work, her husband to the train and pick up Jessie, an Elder on the way back and take her to church. She thought, "I can pray over

Mary's son while driving him and then ask her husband about taking in kids since he is on the Board of the Children's Aid Society. All well and good!

She begins to pray her rosary and Jessie's face comes to her and a great spiritual rush fills her. She then falls asleep. The same thoughts are with her when she wakes up. She phones Mary at 7:20 who says, "No, thanks I have made other arrangements.

Then Jack wakes up and wants her to drive him to work. She is very confused; nothing is working out as she planned. She goes on to Mass.

After mass Mary asks her if she would drive Jessie home and pick her up for Mass the next day. Victoria told her she couldn't.

Mary asks, why not? Victoria answered, "I don't always have the car." She then offered to take Jessie home. Mary said she would ask Peter, thanks, anyway.

She is so perplexed. How come it didn't work out as she had planned at 7:30 that morning? Perhaps it wasn't God's plan after all. Mary must think I'm nuts.

Even though nothing worked out as she planned she still thanks and praises the Holy Name of Jesus. She had still made the offer to help.

The next morning she gets a call from Mary asking her to take Jessie to Mass. All is confusion again; she had to say no, as Jack wants her to drive him to work for 8:00. Then she gets the bright idea that Jack stay home since he isn't feeling well anyway. It means she can pick Jessie up. She immediately phones Mary. Mary is relieved because she has a meeting at 10:00 and couldn't take Jessie home after Mass.

Veronica sits with the phone in her hand; so that was the plan all along. Holy Moly!

After driving Jessie home she goes to the café; there she runs into a friend, Elizabeth. Victoria is brought to a complete stop when Elizabeth says she needs help. They go to the car and Victoria prays over her with the laying on of hands. Elizabeth then goes to St James to see the Healing Team. Praise God!! They prayed over her and this brought about the healing she needed, in the Name of Jesus! Alleluia!

--------------- -------------------- --------------------

She is so hard on herself:

How can I be a servant like Fr. Damien who lived amongst lepers? How could Mary have a child not having known a man? Nothing is impossible with God. He will let me know in His Time. He will protect me from all trials and tribulations as He protected Michak, Shadrak and Obendigo from the fiery furnace. Dan 31: 91-97.

"When two or three are gathered in My Name I will hear and answer," Jesus said.

I keep thinking. "Why can't others see Your Works? Why are they so blind?"

Oh, forgive me Lord, Forgive me the things that I say or think about others. Who am I that I should be so judgmental when I have so little Faith? Give me patience, love and strength. I am so little myself. Thank You for the graces I have received. I love You, Jesus.

Oh, what must I do with the gift I have been given, the Gift of Faith? I know I am being asked something, without a doubt.

Yes, life must go on and be lived because we do exist here on this earth, in this time and place and all these needs must be met while we are here. I am not in a convent where life is a continual prayer and contemplation. No, I am here and I must stay here and do whatever is expected of me no matter how difficult it is. What am I being Called to do? How can my life be like Fr. Damien who served lepers?

Here it is a half an hour later. I put my clothes in the dryer and I see how down to earth I am. Then I am sitting with the men and women after mass, having coffee with them; talking about the upcoming church meeting on Pornography. Is this what is meant by being in the Poustinia, everyday living?

Like picking up a phone, I pick up my rosary and pray to Mary, the Mother of Jesus. I pray she will intercede for me in my trouble and for the troubles of others. "Sweet Mary, so many times my prayers have been answered. I praise and thank You, Jesus.

--------------- --------------------- ---------------------

Victoria is supposed to go to the Meeting put on by the churches in the area but decides against it. She feels strongly that staying home and praying in her Poustinia in silence will do more good. She feels she will be doing God's bidding in this way so that His Will is done in this case. As she washes and cleans up her kitchen after dinner she is left in a quandary. She starts questioning herself. What to do! What to do? She picks up her bible and starts flipping through the pages. She closes it and then opens it. It falls to:

Habakuk: 1-5, "For I am doing something in your own day, that you would not believe if you were told it."

She makes the decision to stay home. During the time of the meeting she prays in silence until she feels herself going inward and the words become His Words not hers. The Holy Spirit takes over and she believes the meditation is taken to the meeting. She can hear a woman speak and can see the people in the room. In faith she knows that the Holy Spirit has taken over the meeting and the speaker. His work was being done in the people. She knows, without question, that by staying home and letting the Holy Spirit work through her in silence, the work of prayer has more effect than if she had gone to the meeting.

However, she becomes unnecessarily hard on herself, (not unusual for her), thinking the women from her church will talk about her for not going. But, it really doesn't matter what they think! At the expense of her feelings His work must be done. Even if they hate her for not going, she really doesn't care. She is being healed of the fear of disrespect. I must remain hidden. No one must know about these Gifts He has given His humble servant. Daniel 3: 24-50, 51-90.

Victoria woke up this early Monday morning knowing that she must not go to Mass. She is drawn into her Poustinia after her morning prayers. In her closet of silence she is aware of a small voice within her saying, "You must be silent. You must come into your Poustinia more often. You must pray.

She begins to think about the bible study she wants to have with the young people every Thursday.

She hears within: "You must bring them to the leader, and all you must do is pray. I will work through you; you will be in your prayer closet. You must remain silent. No one must know the work is being done through you and the work will be done. The children will be brought to our Lord, Jesus."

It is arranged by the priest that Michelle will be the leader of the Bible Study. Victoria finally realizes her position has been taken over. In spite of this, Victoria goes to the Bible Study on Thursday evening. The bible study begins and is on the "Beatitudes"

Without being asked, she stands up and starts talking about the Scripture. Everyone stares at her with mouths wide open, like fish in a tank of water. The room is silent. She slowly stops talking, realizing what she is doing. She sits down and as Michelle continues her teaching, Victoria quietly walks out of the room and cries all the way home. She knows she hated relinquishing her self-righteous position over to Michelle. She is jealous. She wants something important to do so people will look up to her instead of just having to pray in silence with no one knowing what she is doing. There she is, humiliated again. In her closet of silence, she was told to just pray, not participate. When will she ever learn?

--------------- --------------------- ---------------------

*"She sits in her little red sailboat. The tears, like falling rain, stream down her face from a broken and lonely heart. "Where, oh, where is the love? No one loves her."*

--------------- --------------------- ---------------------

As she lies in her bed this early morning she still wishes she were involved in a religious community. She so needs the friendship, the stimulation of spiritual discussions. She thinks about the book she has just finished reading, "Poustinia." The writer of the book, Catherine De Heuk Doherty, was chosen by her Bishop to set up Madonna House, A place in Combermere, Ontario, for priests and lay people to live, following her way of life.

Victoria muses to herself, "What I wouldn't give to live with them and live the kind of life Catherine explains in her book."

She gets a strong feeling she should write them, explain to them her spiritual life and then go and visit them. She thinks, "I will go the two weeks Jack is away."

She phones Audrey but she doesn't sound too keen. She hadn't finished "Poustinia," the book that Victoria had lent her. She gave it back to her unfinished.

Victoria thinks, "Perhaps I should go alone,"

--------------- --------------------- ---------------------

She receives a spiritual revelation:

I am meditating in silence this morning; a prayer, deep down into my soul. Then a revelation fills my thoughts. "I am going to suffer. Everything I am reading in the bible points to this; the sufferings of Jeremiah, The book of Daniel and the three men in the furnace, being protected by the Angel of God, St Michael the Archangel, Hosea, which refers to a Calling. Then, my prayer of silence in the Poustinia yesterday, the words, "do not be afraid, we will help you. Do not be afraid, we are with you."

What is going to happen that I will be given protection, that I mustn't be afraid?

--------------- --------------------- --------------------

*"She and her little red sailboat are sailing somewhere, but she doesn't know where."*

--------------- --------------------- --------------------

**Back down to earth:**

Victoria gets a phone call from a worker who is with an organization that helps street kids and youth in trouble. The worker asks her if she would see a young mother and child who need a place to live.

"How did they get my name," she wonders. She tells the worker she will see the mother.

She attends Word, Faith, Christian Church Bible Study that evening after running into Michele Sims in a store. The scripture being preached is on Habakuk 2:24

"Write the vision down, inscribe it on tablets to be easily read,

This vision is for this time, eager for its own fulfillment,

It does not deceive if it comes slowly.

Wait, for it will come without fail"

This is absolute confirmation of what has been coming to her for some time. So now she must do what she is told and write down at all times in her journal what her Father in Heaven wants from her. She can't believe it!!!

Victoria meets Michele's husband, Debbie's father, who had suggested she be Debbie's guardian, at the bible study. Debbie is one of the street-kids.

The next day, having heard from Debbie's math teacher, Victoria brings Debbie together with her mother, the school and Debbie's father. These meetings go a long way to helping Debbie's relationship with her father. Since her relationship with the Word, Faith Christian Church, Victoria is beginning to realize that what is happening to her is real, that she is not crazy. Thank you, Jesus!

--------------- --------------------- --------------------

**Victoria is so frightened:**

With all the weird things that have been happening to me at the Legion of Mary meetings that I have been attending on Tuesdays for the past month, I am certain I am going bonkers. The last three times I went to the meetings, as we begin the third decade of the Sorrowful mysteries, "the crowning of thorns" I find myself with a complete physical change; heart beating faster, pulse climbing, weakness and then I begin to shake. At the last meeting I shook twice. I ended falling out of my chair and landing on the floor. It is so embarrassing! What is the matter with me? I had received an image of Jesus with the crown of thorns sometime during Lent of this year. Perhaps I am letting my imagination run away with me. I'm frightened! Only time will tell whether it is from me, our Father in Heaven or the devil?

I have a healing appointment Monday. Twice with Fr. Peters who is the priest at the Legion of Mary Rosary meetings. Twice he did not want to keep the appointment with me. The last time I stubbornly waited it out until he showed up. He saw me all right and I ended up making a fool of myself. Blessed Lord, why am I going through these terrible things? The only answer I can come up is that I am persisting in doing my own will and not waiting it out until His appointed Time, and so I suffer.

Part of the learning process, as Pastor Henry put it in his sermon tonight at the Bible Study. Again I saw his remark as a confirmation of the terrible things I am going through.

And so today during this month of May, Mary's month, I am glad that the shaking I suffer happens at the Legion of Mary's Rosary meetings and with Fr Peters. It has taught me humility. Oh, how humiliating.

"Best it happens in front of spiritual people who know what I'm going through.

Why am I going through this terrible shaking at the Legion of Mary Rosary Meetings? What is God trying to tell me? I am a sinner. I disobeyed Him. I discarded Him. I have sinned so terribly in the past, why should I be chosen for unusual things and happenings, spiritually? He should choose people more saintly than me. I am far from being a saint and no matter how I strive I will never be one, with the ego I have. I can only be thankful for these humiliations and grateful for these lessons for my own good. I pray for the strength to endure.

--------------- -------------------- --------------------

Victoria decides to write a note to Fr. Peters to apologize for her behaviour when she imposed herself on him to meet with her. She also writes that she is going to go to a Healing Mass to receive the healing she needs to overcome the shaking she goes through in the Legion of Mary meetings.

She says, in her note, "I hope and pray my healing comes about as I really need it"

Victoria sits in the front pew during the Healing Mass. A few friends from the Legion of Mary are there and sit with her. As the Mass continues, all of a sudden she begins to shake again. She doesn't say a thing, just hangs her head and deals with it silently, hoping no one notices. Or does she want someone to notice? Is this her ego, the devil or some other reason for this? She is so frightened, not understanding what is happening. She has been getting scriptures on Daniel and the interpretation of dreams, and so I bought a book on dreams. Scripture: 4:16-25. Another scripture comes to me; Daniel 3: 49-50, Shadrack, Michack and Abendigo in the furnace, protected by an angel. What does this all mean? My mind flashes back to the time, as a child, I dreamt about being pregnant and that's exactly what happened. All dreams must be lifted up to our Creator to solve the message.

--------------- -------------------- --------------------

*"She and her little red sailboat drift into a small alcove, hidden away from fierce attacks, as she tries to deal in silence with the storm surrounding her."*

--------------- -------------------- --------------------

Victoria and Matt go to the airport to pick up Jack. While waiting, she notices a sign where they are sitting. It reads, "Tunnel to Terminal 1 upstairs." She didn't see any significance to this except to think how convenient if Jack ever had to use that terminal. They go inside where the passengers were coming off the planes. Two women come over to her and ask her where the tunnel to Terminal 1 is. Victoria is able to tell them. How amazing! The wisdom of the Holy Spirit is continually working to help everyone no matter how insignificant the need. WOW!

She is praying the Rosary before Mass at St. Andrews this morning and as she sits in the pew, she's shaking again. Her mind goes blank. She feels someone sitting down next to her. It's Diane. She says nothing about the shaking. Victoria is very uncomfortable.

"Please Lord," I pray, "is this Your Will? If not, please, please, take this away from me. But let Your Will, not mine be done."

She feels her whole face and body burning up. She hears Diane's voice saying she is going to visit a friend who is sick. She asks if Victoria would go with her. She turns to Diane and agrees to go. She chats with Diane's friend for a while, and to her surprise, finds out she is Niki's mother, her son, James' friend. Amazing! She is so happy to lay hands on her for healing. Thank you, Jesus, for bringing this about.

---------------  --------------------   --------------------

*"She's in a daze as her little red sailboat seems to sail on toward its own direction. Where is she going; where is she heading? She would rather not know."*

---------------  --------------------   --------------------

Victoria goes to a Charismatic inner healing Mass at St James. Perhaps some answers will come out of this. She knows she needs a healing of some sort. She is just not feeling very well, much physical pain. While sitting through the Mass she goes through the shaking again. Fr. Steve is preaching: "We must not be afraid to go as far as God wishes us to go. It is important to be open to God's Will."

She can't believe her ears. She almost feels like laughing out loud in joy. A confirmation!

As they all gather for lunch in the basement of the church, Leonard comes up to her to chat. Since he knows her spiritual life she feels free to share with him what happened.

"You know, Victoria, this is how I see it."

He goes on to say that the shaking is being used spiritually to shake away the chains to heal Jack, you and your marriage.

"You mustn't be concerned about the shaking. It probably comes from your emotions. Your emotions from some subconscious problems in the past causing the shaking. It is probably necessary for healing."

He smiles as she looks at him. She gives him a hug in thanks. Whether he is right or wrong, I am thankful for those kind words.

They go back for an afternoon of song, prayer and healing. The leader calls people up to the front for the laying on of hands. Victoria is the first to go. Leonard, Mauvereen and Janet pray over her. She is slain in the Spirit and sways with Leonard catching her and gently lowering her to the floor. There she lies for a few minutes allowing the Holy Spirit to fill her and heal her. She feels the pain leaving her body and she is at peace. She rises, with Leonard helping her and then goes to her seat.

The priest and prayer group then pray the rosary; again Victoria goes through the shaking.

"Oh my Lord," silently, she prays. You know how I suffer through this very humiliating spiritual experience. I know that the healing team thinks that it is for my marriage, Jack and mine but I can't believe that our marriage, in particular, is so special that it warrants these actions. I also can't believe that we, Jack and I are so special when there are so many better people in this parish and other parishes. I must wait it out. You are all Wise and Perfect; only You know the reason for all this, my Lord and my God."

--------------- --------------------- ---------------------

*"She cries as she sits in silence in her little red sailboat. Raindrops fall on her face mixing with her tears."*

--------------- --------------------- ---------------------

### May/86

She sits in the garden, meditating in silence. She picks up her bible and it opens to the Book of the prophet Jeremiah. She reads that Jeremiah is made a prisoner in chains. She begins in this silence to reflect the goings on in her own life. Of course she knows she's not literally a prisoner, but is she? Are the chains of the unknown world of her spirituality holding her? Going through all of this there has to be a reason. Something tells her, all who do not have faith in a Creator will treat her despicably. She will go through many trials and much suffering but she has faith her Creator, God will protect her. Daniel 3: 49-50. Scripture: the fiery furnace.

Her faith is not strong enough yet, she who is a sinner. She prays the answers will be revealed.

--------------- --------------------- ---------------------

*"Yes, she prays that with faith, she is made secure in her little red sailboat to sail these uncharted waters. She knows she will be able to grip the rudder; steering and sailing to where, to whom and to what He is asking of her. She knows though, she has a long voyage ahead; she and the little boat are so fragile"*

--------------- --------------------- ---------------------

### My own personal thoughts on a Spiritual Life.

When Jesus, the Son of God, as a human, came to live His life on earth, He came to train the apostles and others; to make His Father known. This training took 3 years. They, at first didn't believe who He was even after the miracles He performed. On the 3$^{rd}$ day after His death on the cross, He rose and ascended to His Father. He revealed Himself to them when He returned proving to those who doubted his identity. They all believed with much joy and happiness. Before rising again to the Father He promised them the Gifts of the Holy Spirit to guide and protect them. The Holy Spirit descended upon them and they were wondrously blessed and equipped for the mission they were chosen to do. This can only be accomplished in the Name of Jesus Christ.

And so it is today. If we believe, the same could happen to us; training, guiding and protecting us with His Mother, Mary as the intercessor to her Son, Jesus.

There are many times when I doubt. Being a sinner, I need to be healed over and over again, but the Power of the Holy Spirit, in the Name of Jesus is always there through prayer, meditation and silence. My relationship with the fellowship of others in prayer and worship, receiving the Eucharist, the Body and Blood of our Lord Jesus Christ which Jesus demonstrated to the Disciples at the Last Supper before His death on the Cross in the scriptures, gives me the strength I need to continue. I fail many times and will until I die, but I know I'm not alone.

Am I ready for whatever is demanded of me? Not knowing yet what that will be, God help me; I hope and pray I'm ready. What is it You want from me? Please help me know what You want me to do. In Jesus Name, I ask this according to Your Holy and Blessed Will. Thank You, Praise You, Bless You.

Hosea 1, Isaiah 59:21: Macabees 1:18: Daniel 3 24-29, Jeremiah 31:32: Habbakuk, Jeremiah 4.

I cry for help and I am given it through prayer and the scriptures where I will receive interpretation.

--------------- -------------------- --------------------

Victoria walks across the road to the Anglican Sisters Convent to join the ecumenical group for meditation. Her friend Elizabeth sits next to her. As she listens to the meditation tape she feels strongly, God's Presence. After the tape they begin to meditate. Her thoughts turn to Debbie, her teen-age boarder. It is so difficult to concentrate on Jesus in meditation.

"It is so easy for the mind to wander," she thinks. Twenty minutes is such a long time. She continues her mantra, "Maranatha, Come, Lord Jesus!

Hail Mary, full of Grace the Lord is with you. Blessed are you amongst women and blessed is the fruit of your womb, Jesus.

Holy Mary Mother of God, pray for us sinners, now and at the hour of our death. Amen.

The Rosary sounds again within her. Twice more, when she feels her heart speeding up. She begins to breathe very hard and begins to shake all over. Elizabeth comes to her rescue and allows Victoria to lean on her.

Half way through this shaking she asks, "Victoria, is it the Holy Spirit? Victoria whispers "Yes. I hope so."

Again someone else notices and mentions this frightening, physical shaking. She tells Elizabeth it has happened four times at the Legion of Mary Prayer Group and once at the Charismatic Prayer meeting.

She prays in fear and trembling:

"Oh my Lord, I love You. I am Your servant. Do with me as You Will. According to Your Holy and Blessed Will, let me glorify Your Holy Name. Blessed Sweet Jesus, if this is not from You, this shaking while praying Mary's Prayer, then take it away from me, because if it is not You, Jesus, it is my ego and vanity. Take it away from me, I pray, if it is not from You, take it away from me, however, let Your Will be done. Thank You, Praise You and Bless You for the suffering and the pain I am going through in Your Name. Blessed Sweet Jesus, let me Glorify You. That is all I desire, that Your Name be Glorified. I know You are here. I feel Your Presence and Your Love. I pray You are using my weakness to help others through me. There is strength in weakness, Lord. 11 Corinthians 12: 6 - 10. Thank You, Praise You and Bless You; Glorify Your Holy and Blessed Name."

--------------- -------------------- --------------------

*"Something or someone is helping the female skipper in her little red sailboat. She is too small, frail and weak to handle the rudder, as the little craft seems to lose control, sailing through those strong winds."*

--------------- -------------------- --------------------

I realize now it is not for others that I am going through this humbling, shaking experience during the Rosary. Let's face the truth, I am a sinner. Not just now, but all of these past 50 years. All those sins must be destroyed and healed if I am to carry on the mission that God is calling me to. Dear Blessed Sweet Jesus. I am healed. Yes, healed of all those disgusting sins, self- importance, sexual sins and so many other destroying inner sins of the past. Thank You, Praise You, Bless You, Glorify Your Holy and Blessed Name.

On Friday, I phoned Elizabeth and she met me at the church. I went through the embarrassing shaking again, so needed her support.

After it was over, she suggested I go and talk to a monk in Orangeville, which we did. He believed everything I told him about the shaking, about the images of Mary and Jesus. He said he had heard this "shaking phenomena" is happening more and more often. I know that I was meant to talk to him. Praise God. It was a lovely day. On the way home I listened to Elizabeth and the problems she is having in her own life it is the least I could do for her.

Sunday, Jack and I go to Mass.

I start to shake again and manage to control it though, as I'm sure Jack would be disgusted. What is the matter with me? I'm being irrational again. What is all this for? Surely there is a reason for it. I can't think straight. I must be going crazy.

Went to the Prayer Group meeting the next evening and joined the group praying the rosary. They were all at the back of the church but I went up to the second row; changed my mind and went to the back row. As the rosary began I started the shaking again. The man sitting next to me didn't seem to notice. Neither did those around me, I assumed. Was I disappointed? I was going to grab the arm of the man to help me but, would I be trying to draw attention to myself? I stopped shaking and then Anne asked me to pray a decade of the Rosary. My mind was buzzing around and round. As I prayed I mentioned I could see our Blessed Mother crying in sadness. Tears started streaming down my face. One of the women said to me Pray these words:

**"LORD, JESUS CHRIST SON OF GOD, HAVE MERCY ON ME A SINNER!"**

I repeated the Jesus Prayer again:

**"LORD, JESUS CHRIST, SON OF GOD, HAVE MERCY ON ME A SINNER."**

Then the Mass began.

I felt such joy fill my heart as the realization came to me of a great healing within me; of years and years of living a life of the sin of Pride and other sins being wiped away. Now I know why I have been going through this very humiliating experience of the shaking during the Rosary. Mary has been interceding for me to Her Son, Jesus to pray for me to our Father in heaven to heal me. God allowed me to go through this shaking to make me realize my weaknesses without even realizing it. Tears came to my eyes. Thanks to God, my Saviour, Jesus Christ by the power of the Holy Spirit and our Blessed Mother Mary for her intercession. At the end of the Mass the priest came to the back of the church and I asked him to hear my confession. Since I wasn't fully aware of the healings, I only confessed to him the shaking and wanted spiritual direction. He seemed disgusted with my confession, not seeing my words as a true confession. He said I did not hurt anyone and did nothing wrong. It came to me after that he would not take me seriously, not understand what I was confessing or wanting help with my spiritual life.

When I went home a picked up a book for some spiritual reading and I read that some things and words we must not share. They are just between God and us.

Matt 7:6. "Do not throw your pearls out to the swine lest they trample on them."

Most certainly, this "shaking" was viewed by everyone, but not everyone would see it as spiritual, would they. God's Word is only for those that have "eyes" to see and "ears" to "hear."

Reading Scriptural Prophecies: Shaking: Concordance, Amplified Bible Explanation: the "shaking" was a means to frighten me away from my firm belief in my faith. I lived through it, did not run away in fear, stuck with my Faith and now I know, nothing will "shake" me from my firm belief in a Higher Power." Scripture, Book of Job.

Tuesday I take the bus over to the Legion of Mary meeting. I know, without a doubt, I'm healed. The shaking is over. I didn't shake through the whole Rosary this time. My friends at the meeting knew what was happening and all gave me a hug. I could feel their joy. The priest joined them at the final decade of the Rosary; he kept staring at me as if I were crazy. Heaven only knows what he expected me to do but I sure felt like laughing out loud. As the healing team has said; "the chains will be broken", and so they are. I am going to the Charismatic Prayer and Healing Mass this evening.

I can only sit quietly. A lot of people are being slain in the Spirit. But, Lord, Jesus, You come to me in a different way. The Holy Spirit Fire falls upon me and sets me on fire as I sit in my seat. I feel as if my heart were burning and would burst out of my chest.

The spiritual songs fill my heart and I feel such joy!!

--------------- -------------------- --------------------

*"The lone skipper in her little red sailboat sailed on into the red skies of the sunset, moored into a cove to spend the night in prayer, peace and security."*

--------------- -------------------- --------------------

No more writings for now:

Victoria wakes up in the middle of the night, and is unable to get back to sleep.

A scripture reading comes to her mind and speaks softly. "Speak Lord, your servant listens" 1 Sam: 3. That's all she hears, nothing more.

She begins to pray in tongues for some reason. She does so until she falls asleep.

She wakes up 7:00 AM and finds Jack has gone to work. Sitting on the side of her bed, she picks up a book "The Prophet Listens." The section she reads is about the prophet praying and being brought to the mountain. This answers her prayer meditation, "Come to My Mountain, Victoria."

She gets up, makes a cup of coffee and, sitting at the kitchen table, she makes a spiritual Holy Communion by the promptings of the Holy Spirit. Such joy fills her heart.

"She whispers, Oh! He is so good to me."

This activity tells her she is not to go to Mass this morning. With her coffee she then goes to the living room to pray her Brevery and morning prayers. She feels His Presence; and joy filled her heart as she prays.

What happens next as the morning wore on, tells her why she wasn't to go to Mass. She had obeyed His silent Word in her heart. Such joy spills over like a fountain of water.

After she finishes her prayers, she has some breakfast and starts her housework. Around 11:00 she feels a strong urge to go into her closet of silence. As she did so she begins speaking in tongues within her as a meditation. This continues for some time and then, without her realizing it, it changes to the words as she hears them, "Marsh de la go! Over and over again it spilled out deep down in her spirit. "Marsh de la go! Marsh de la go!" With experience, she knows this is a prayer to rebuke evil spirits. Praise God. She now realizes she must Fast as a prayer. It's a prayer too.

She glorifies as she prays thanking and praising God for His many blessings. She doesn't know why all this happens, but she obeys anyway.

That afternoon Victoria visits one of Jack's cousins whose husband is dying. She goes to pray over him with the laying on of hands. Although they both didn't show very much enthusiasm with what she is doing; praying in both English and in tongues, Victoria did it anyway. Tears of joy come to her eyes as she does this.

She prays on the way back home, "Let Your Will be done, Lord not mine, but I truly believe he will be saved."

She talks out loud, "OH! That must be why I went through those prayers in my closet this morning." She laughs as she dwells on the thoughts. Thank God, she had obeyed.

--------------- -------------------- --------------------

### Matt's Birthday/86

Jack and Victoria were not home to celebrate Matt's birthday as they were in N.B, a funeral for one of Jack's family. It was a tragic death and very sad. They also spent some time in Victoria's hometown. It was a happy time with her parents and sister. She silently prayed for their health and happiness; even laying hands on her sister. I doubt it was appreciated but no matter.

They then return home.

They, Victoria, Jack, boys with daughter-in –law Janet, James new wife, go to Mass, as a family this Sunday morning. We then celebrate Matt's birthday. She is so happy that they were all there on a Sunday other than Christmas or Easter. The Readings were 1 Kings 17:17-24, Galatians 1:11-19, and the Gospel Luke 7: 11 –17.

She was led to pray for James and Matt as she listened to the first Reading: "Ezekiel heals the son of the widow."

She goes into her prayer closet after James and Janet leave. She receives the Word that Debbie, a street-kid, would spend the summer with her father. She began her Rosary for Debbie. Then Musquash comes into her mind. The phone rings. It is Joel, Jack's brother from Musquash, giving us our nephew, Sam's phone number. Jack calls and it was arranged that Victoria would go to Musquash July 1$^{st}$ to stay with Alex's kids, as planned. Victoria is pleased that it was already arranged Debbie would stay with her father for the summer. Victoria doesn't want her here with Matt alone in the house. After all, there's no point in tempting Matt or her. Victoria knows how strong the sexual urges can be and if they are left without her around, God only knows what would happen.

They got their financial Rights from the sale of Jack's family store. They surely needed it. Victoria was a tad upset she wasn't given a chance to state her opinion as to how it should be used. She can only trust that Jack knows what he is doing. He had decided he wanted to build a deck with glass doors. She didn't see this as very practical but what's the point of saying anything. All she can do is pray.

Victoria prays:

"Blessed Sweet Jesus, when You leave me, I am desolate. I didn't know I could feel so sad. St John of the Cross, in his writings, calls it a dryness of Spirit. Although I know You are still here within me I feel you want me to struggle on and grow in my Spiritual Life by leaving me alone and growing in Faith."

I went to Mass this morning. Thank you for Your Powerful Presence in the Body and Blood of this the Holy Eucharist. I know, without seeing, You are this Eucharist.

With the prayers of the Rosary I prayed for my friends. I know You come to them without my going near them as I pray in my Poustinia in silence. Thank you for using me even in silence. When I am drawn to pray over people I find my body going through such a strange sensation. My whole body goes limp and I can hardly breathe. I can't explain it. I know that when I'm in my Poustinia, I believe no one notices. It is all according to Your Holy and Blessed Will.

Did I do something wrong when I went to the Children's Aid Society? I guess not.

The next day they sent Jennifer and her daughter Kimberly to me to give her a place to live for a short time. It is a confirmation of the thought I have that I should convert my basement into a home for unwed mothers. I can see now why You, Lord, put me through that rape and pregnancy as a young girl. Or, not that You, Lord, put me through it but that You allowed it to happen. Thank you and Praise You for being with me through the difficult ordeal. I love You!

Blessed Lord, is it Your Will that I still go to Musquash Bay on the first of July to be with Alex's children as planned?

This coming weekend I'm going on a Retreat at the Holy Spirit Centre in Hamilton. Fr. Gerald will be the priest.

Our Retreat: first evening, I meditated and prayed the rosary after dinner. Another woman joined me and we said it together. I turned in early. The next morning we spent time in silence and prayer. Confession is included in the program this morning. Felt drawn to do so. Always pride that is so much a part of me; always thinking I'm better than others. Thank You, Lord for Your forgiveness through the priest.

I set up an appointment with the Head Sister here who is giving the Retreat. She belongs to the Order of Social Services and so I knew that somehow, she would be able to help me with my desire to set up rooms in my home for Unwed Mothers. She became negative saying that so many people have these zealous ideas but so many of them never become realities. I said that I understood and felt my back going up in anger. Pride! Blessed Holy Spirit You stepped in and she and I began to talk about Jack and his drinking. She made me see that this was an important barrier in the accomplishing what I felt I was Called to do. Dear Jesus, my God! I burst into tears, feeling, without a doubt that this was the problem. As long as Jack was not going to help he would not accept what I wanted to do. Yes, it became so clear to me that my crying of sadness turned to joy.

Time for Mass and the Priest in his Homily, confirmed what the Sister and I had discussed. He said that one must listen to God by using common sense and by obeying anyone who is sent by Him to help us. Such peace flowed through me as I listened.

She had asked me if I wanted to talk to the Alanon Sister here before the Retreat is over. Oh! The tears flowed with joy, love and relief knowing that Your Will can be done no matter what may stand in the way. I was able to be humble enough to listen to her, thanks to You, Lord, for sending me to the Priest for confession. Without that forgiveness and the intercession of Mary, our blessed Mother in the Rosary, I know, without a doubt, that none of this would have worked out as I would have gotten angry and walked out.

"Oh, Lord Jesus, I love You. Thank You for Your Blessed Body and Blood in the Eucharist today, my strength, my hope, love and faith, my courage, my Friend. Without You I can do nothing. Lord, I know that what You want me to do will not be easy. Jack is only the beginning of the obstacles, but I do know You will help me meet them one by one and they will be overcome."

Evening and we all meet for dinner in the dining room. I start to eat and then fall into my spiritual Poustinia of silence, sitting right there at the table with all my friends as well as strangers. One stranger, who is sitting across the table, keeps staring at me. I sit there in silence not able to move or eat, for quite some time. They all ask if there was something wrong with me. As they get up, Elizabeth comes to me, asking if I'm all right. My three friends knew what was happening as they had seen this in me before. I get up and start to walk out hardly able to walk or see; every part of my body goes limp, muscles, bones, etc. My breathing comes fast and my heart feels as though it is going to break out of my chest. I make it to the chapel and someone approaches, sits next to me and asks, "Are you all right? I whisper, "I'm fine, thanks." What could I say?

"Oh blessed Sweet Jesus, How could they understand what is happening if I told them. It is so hard to explain. I stayed in the chapel about 45 minutes having the feeling come and go; one minute ready to go then another minute back into my Poustinia again. What is it all for? Who am I praying for? Only my Blessed Father in heaven knows. Oh Lord, although my feelings about this spiritual experience is mixed; joyful, embarrassing, panic, humiliation and even exaltation, I believe "humility" is the main feeling knowing that You are present within this soul as light, energy, mystical, and love. Am I being used in some way or is it my imagination? This I will endure because I know that You, Lord, are Love.

Yes, Lord, they go to churches, to Mass and prayer meetings but they only give you lip-service. They do not believe Your presence is real within them. They don't realize that they can reach out and be touched spiritually if they believed. You are reaching out to them and are so unhappy that they ignore You. They really don't know that You truly exist. I'm sorry, Lord."

--------------- -------------------- --------------------

*"As she sails along in her little red sailboat, a misty rain falls, as do the tears of fear and confusion."*

--------------- -------------------- --------------------

"Oh Lord, why me? Why do You choose me for the beautiful happenings of each day? When I think of myself and what I have been in the past, nothing but hate, anger, confusion and mind always on sex, and so many other despicable behaviors I wonder how You can love me. Why was I not aware of Your Presence earlier so that I could have given myself to You a long time ago? Why did You not want me when I asked the Sister if I could join her Order and become a nun? You knew me and chose me long before I was born. Somehow for whatever reason, I had to go through what was my life till I found You. Even now, I am still nothing and still You love me. I'm still in terrible physical pain. Is it because I am not doing Your Will very well? At times, I can't understand if Your Word in the scriptures and in meditation, are for me. Oh! Lord, I do need help!"

--------------- -------------------- --------------------

Victoria comes back down to earth:

She talked to Jack today about finishing the Rec room downstairs as a home for unwed mothers. How angry he looked and he blasted her.

He emphatically said, NO!

Matt got upset with her as well. In her scripture readings she finds a justification in faith coming up in her decision.

Victoria reads in the newspapers and media, Doctors are on strike and closing hospitals. They want to see pregnant women who want abortions to use abortion clinics instead of the hospitals. She is very concerned and upset. Victoria's mind flashes back to when she had a child at 19. The pain through her body is excruciating. The rape, reaction from the small town she grew up in; stories like these seem to find their way out and spread like wildfire being fed by more falsehoods and innuendos and her confinement in a Catholic unwed mother's home. Memories keep flashing, flashing through her. Did she ever consider an abortion through those difficult months? No, not once; never.

These articles stating the beliefs of the baby-killer and confirmed by the doctors who are approving the killing of babies, makes her nauseated. Thinking back, she remembers the family who wanted a child and couldn't have one and had adopted her baby boy.

"Oh! My God," she thinks, "where are we heading as a country?"

Her heart is breaking with disgust and anger. "Where are we heading as a people?" she asks herself. "How much worse is it going to get? Is there no turning back? The doctors are condoning the killing of babies. It isn't as if women were really in danger; this is the 21st century."

Her thoughts become more and more angry. "(I can't call them mothers, these actions are desecrating the title, mother). They just want their freedom, to do their own thing no matter the cost, at the cost of their own souls. Will we be so immune to killing that there will be no holds barred? We just kill because someone stands in our way, never mind the innocent in the womb. Oh, my heart is breaking. Oh Lord have mercy on our souls, I plead with you."

She thinks about the Blessed Mother Mary who, by the Power of the Holy Spirit, was given a child to carry in her womb without being married. She gave her "Fiat," yes, even though she didn't understand. Matthew 1: 18-25, this Child, Jesus Christ, who was born to the world to save the world. How many of those aborted unborn babies could have spectacular futures if allowed to live?

Matt and Jack are sitting in the living room listening with disgust to her words. They make it quite clear how they stand on the issue. Jack yells at her saying she is putting them on a guilt trip because they don't agree with her. Matt's words leave her upset and angry. She answers back, saying that maybe more people should be put on guilt trips. Perhaps they might care about what is happening around them, because as it is right now, there is no such thing as a conscience or sin any more. She tells them that an abortion, the killing of babies, must be one of the worse sins against God, if not THE worst. Jack, being a non-believer, tells her, in no uncertain terms what he thinks and Matt goes along with him.

"Blessed Lord, Your Light shines in the darkest corners of a soul to help them see, but sadly some are so blind they will never see."

The next day when Leonard, her friend from the Charismatic Group, and Casey, his son, come over to discuss the renovations of the rooms downstairs, she asks Casey if he would take some of them to the abortion clinic in Toronto to join the march against the killing of babies.

Friday, at breakfast, Victoria asks Debbie if she would like to clean house for her; that she would pay her. She would start today. Well, it's almost 1:00 and she hasn't shown her nose except to answer the phone. Victoria decides she will give her a few days and see what happens.

Monday, Debbie again doesn't show up to do the work in the morning. No sound from her room. Victoria is just about ready to raise the roof. She sits at the kitchen table to have her lunch and around 1:00 who should waltz in but Debbie. She had gone to school leaving before Victoria had come from her room. She had something to eat and got to work.

"Thank God, I hadn't said anything to her" Victoria thinks. "We're so quick to judge aren't we? Only God knows the thoughts and hearts of others. Scripture: Daniel: Suzanna. Prayer and the reading of scriptures are so important so that we don't go wrong judging others."

--------------- -------------------- --------------------

*"She sits in her little red sailboat. A few Canada Geese swim around as she eats her lunch. She shares with them. How trusting they are in their Creator. They neither reap nor sow and yet He provides them with all their needs. They know Him in their silence."*

--------------- -------------------- --------------------

When Leonard said he loved her, at first she is thrilled. And then she begins to realize that she loves Jesus more than anyone, even Jack. She loves Jack, of course, he is her husband but, yes, she loves Jesus, spiritually and only Him. What can she say that hasn't already been said and so she says nothing more; except to repeat, "I love You, Blessed Trinity, Three in One, Father, Son and Holy Spirit."

--------------- --------------------- --------------------

She writes her thoughts about Leonard who offered to finish rec room for street-kids:

How upset I am about Leonard and his desire to kiss and hug me all the time. It upsets me because I know it's wrong. It causes feelings in me I did not like in the past and still do not like. These feelings only caused trouble for me in the past. What is it about me that men are so attracted to me? Am I doing something wrong? Am I leading them on and don't realize it?

When I want to give my whole life to Jesus how can I possibly want to do or be close to anyone else? How can I deal with it?

Jack hasn't wanted me sexually since 1970, then, in the 1980's I vowed to give my body over to a life of Chastity. Hebrews 13: 12, Nahum 1:13-14. How difficult it is to have to kiss and hug Leonard. I don't want to hurt him because I know he wants me; saying he loves me, but I know the Lord has work for him to do here in this house. Surely God doesn't expect me to reward Leonard with sex. No, not God; Leonard, or the devil tempting me. Is this why Leonard said he would do the work for nothing?

"Blessed sweet Jesus, I love You. Thank You for coming to me while praying my Rosary during the night. I could see an image of myself hugging You, Jesus. Although You are not hugging me, as yet, I hope and pray that in time You will hug me too. I have been given this vision of hugging Jesus to help me cope with Leonard and his sexual advances. Thank You, Jesus. I love You!! No one else is important to me but You, my Blessed Sweet Jesus. Thank You, Mary, for interceding for me to your Son in my agony. I know you heard my prayer for help. Thank You, Sweet Jesus, for being with me. Thank You for filling me with Your Peace instead of letting me lose self-control.

"Oh Jesus, I love You! I give you my life. I know You have a reason for allowing me to go through this with Leonard. Thank you for giving me the strength to say "no." Just keeping it innocent; just hugs as I would hug a friend and no sex. Praise God.

I pray I will continue to be given the Graces I need to deal with this relationship with Leonard in a loving way, as a friend."

The thought came to me during the night. Perhaps I will use this experience I am having with Leonard, to help women. It is to show them that we can have a friendship with male friends without sex. Praise God. Use my suffering, Lord. Put it to good use. I could let Leonard hold me without feeling anything. Praise God. Thank You for coming to my rescue. I pray for Leonard, now that I am being given the Faith to deal with the problem. I pray for Leonard and all men who think women are just good for one thing, sex, and to be used by them. How sad. Scripture, Luke 8:2

--------------- -------------------- --------------------

*"The tiller of her little red sailboat is becoming less cumbersome in her hand, but she doesn't know if her faith is strong enough to allow the weak grip she has to lead her she knows not where."*

--------------- -------------------- --------------------

Victoria takes a relaxing walk through the mall gazing at all the shop windows; enjoying listening to the music over the loudspeakers. A piece of music she recognizes fills the mall. "Daniel." She loves that song and sings it to herself as she strolls along. It stays with her as she drives home and on into the next day.

Thursday the phone rings and it is Birth-Right, an organization available to women who need advice about how to deal with sex, preventing pregnancies, abortions and other complicated issues such as sexual diseases, etc. She tries to figure out how they got her phone number and then remembers; Barb, one of her friends through the church, is a board member. Barb says she is looking for a place for a pregnant client, and her child. Yes, Victoria is willing to, at least, meet and talk with her. The girl doesn't have a car so Victoria drives over to the office. Victoria is shocked by the woman's appearance but pretends not to notice. She is very bedraggled, emaciated, tired and very unhappy. The child, a boy, is sitting on her knee. They chat for a while and decide that Victoria will pick her up and take her to her place tomorrow and then drive her to where she was living. Her name is Carol; the boy's name is Daniel. When she heard his name she immediately thinks of the song "Daniel" she had heard at the mall yesterday. She knows then, without a doubt, that this is Providential. Scriptures --"Book of Daniel."

--------------- -------------------- --------------------

As she is driving today to the church, she thinks about Leonard. Her relationship with him seems to be a battle she must endure and suffer again and again against sexual harassment, in the future, with other men, but she knows, with Faith, she is never alone. There will never be another rape. With this knowledge, she will be able to help unwed mothers and those who want to abort their babies.

Victoria meets Leonard at the church and she tells him exactly where she stands with their relationship. He admits he wants to have sex with her but Victoria emphatically says "no," that it isn't right, that they are both married, they are Christian, that the action is immoral and wrong. He said that he would respect her feelings and leave her alone.

After Victoria gets home she hears from Carol to tell her she would take the place with Daniel. She then phones Leonard to make plans to get the little roomettes built.

--------------- -------------------- --------------------

## July/86

Victoria is supposed to fly to New Brunswick and so, takes a look at her flight ticket to confirm flight times. She is supposed to be with her brother-in-law's children at the cottage in Musquash Bay. The ticket says, July 3. Darn, delayed again another day. She gets the feeling she's not to go."

She decides to phone Jack's brother, Jim and Marni to tell them she will be delayed. Marni tells her the children are leaving Friday. Since Victoria was going down to be with them at that time there really is no point in her going then, is there? Is there a reason she must stay home?

"Yes, well, again, Lord, Your message is "My Plans are not your plans and your plans are not My Plans."

Well, I think it matters not one way or the other whether she goes to be with them. Perhaps she's just giving herself a big ego-trip in thinking that she's doing something great by being with kids, whose father just died, who are seen as rebellious and difficult. Somehow, just the fact that she's willing to go could be enough.

She goes anyway, arriving on the 3rd, the kids are still there. She is still able to spend some time with them as they weren't leaving until Friday. She knows she is not alone in this time with them. She feels The Creator is all around her as she senses the beauty of Musquash Bay and the Spirituality it has to offer. Inwardly she knows He is present with her and these youngsters. One or two Indian children arrive to join the kids while Victoria is there.

---------------- --------------------- --------------------

As she sits on the breakwater overlooking the Bay, Victoria meditates:

It is wonderful that these young people, native and non-native, have a close relationship. "Thank You, Jesus."

They seem to love one another as brothers and sisters rather than hate their fellowman just because they are a different color and race. In time I pray we will all be bound together in Love, in spite of the wrath of the families and people on this Bay. It has gone on far too long and must change. Alex and his family have opened their hearts and their homes, in spite of the community, toward reconciliation with the Native children. Love breeds Love and Love will conquer hate. Jesus is Love! Oh! If they could only see that He truly exists and wants the best for us. I love, praise, bless and give thanks, in Jesus Name.

This Land is Your land, Lord, our Father in heaven, the Creator. It doesn't belong to the white man or the Indian because we are all Your children in Christ Jesus. We are all Your children and You very generously, with love for us, gave us this land and we must learn to love one another and live in harmony, being grateful and thankful for Your goodness to us, placing it all in Your Loving Hands and in Your Care. The smallest blade of grass, smallest insect, and smallest fish in the sea are Yours and without You they would not exist. How could we, as a people, be so proud and egotistic as to think that we could possibly be clever or intelligent enough to bring about all this glory and magnificence? Without Your Word, we, as Your Creation would not "BE." Your Word in the scriptures brought about, Book of Genesis and John 1:1-5.

Oh Lord, my God as I continue my visit to Musquash, You revealed Yourself to me today. How can I possibly explain it? Such love, power and magnificence poured all around me as the rain clouds covered the sky. Oh! Holy Spirit, please help me explain this phenomena.

I feel drawn out to the rocks on the breakwater of the Bay around 7:30 A.M. again. I wash my face, hands, brush my teeth and prepare my coffee. The sky looks ominous, rain-clouds coming from all directions. In spite of the weather, I go to my favorite rock. I take with me my coffee, rosary and Breviary to pray. I stay an hour and the clouds are moving in except over my head. A light with rays of warmth covers me right over my head, with the dark clouds very close all around. I finish my prayers and go back into the cottage to get my toast and more coffee. I come out again with a favorite book Carlo Carreto's "Love is for the Living." As I sit on the veranda I notice it is still very bright over my head and I look to see if it is still bright over the cottage. Sure enough, dark clouds everywhere except over the cottage. Joys fills my heart as I realize You are here at the very place with the sun shining down; the black clouds being held back. I begin to cry, the tears streaming down my face. I pray to give thanks for this Vision, I see as You hold me, Your little child, in Your large, protective Hand. You show me Your glory in Your Creation. The sun is so bright, I cannot look up; the wind is blowing. I feel Your Power, Light, Love and Your warmth pouring down upon me. Suddenly I hear a rooster crowing repeatedly in the distance. A scripture from the bible flashes in my mind. "Peter denies knowing the Lord, Jesus, as He is taken to His death on the Cross." John 18: 16-27. OH! Lord, I denied You once before; I pray I never deny You again. I love You. In my weakness and frailty, perhaps I will again as I did in the past, but I pray not. You forbid it, Lord, according to Your Holy and blessed Will.

As I write this, the rain clouds now cover the sky completely except for a light glow over Musquash Bay. Praise You, Bless and thank your Holy and Blessed Name, my Lord and my God. You shine Your healing light over these communities because they are special to You. Peoples of all races I don't even know are special to You as the Creator of the universe. May they learn to know You, Love You and serve You in this world and be with You in the next.

I love You, Jesus as I, in my weakness, can possibly love anyone.

--------------- --------------------- ---------------------

*"The tiny sailor in her little red sailboat is overwhelmed as she sails; feeling the warm sunlight peeping through the dark rainclouds all around her."*

--------------- --------------------- ---------------------

It is late morning and Victoria hears a car drive up to the cottage. In walks her sister-in-law, Nadine, from Musquash City, where the river that flows into the Bay. She has come down to invite her to lunch at the Golf Club in the city. Victoria is thrilled.

"Yes, love to." Victoria spills over in happiness. They take off for the city after a swim in the salty waters of the Bay. This is Nadine's

115

second home, as much as is her home in the city of Musquash, having spent her summers here with Jack and her brothers.

As they drive through the streets of Musquash, Nadine tells her about the criminal case that's going on in the courts at this very moment. A criminal has terrorized the town by killing people at random, a priest, a storeowner and family members just in the past few months. As they pass the Courthouse, people are lined up for miles. Nadine doesn't stop but Victoria knows she has been led to this very spot at this very time; not just to go to lunch at the golf club. She goes into her prayer closet of silence of prayer as they drive by. They then have a fabulous meal at the Golf Club, with Nadine introducing her to many of the local Musquash members and visitors. It is a grand social hour.

Nadine is a reporter of the local paper and is always in search of a story. On the drive back to Musquash Bay they discuss some of her writing interests, one being the First Nations who, as she says, are a much-maligned peoples in this country Canada. Victoria admits she doesn't know or understand much, just what she hears being discussed, and not in very positive language. She does know they live on Reserves, a number around where she grew up. Nadine chats on, saying she is going to be visiting one of the families on the Musquash Reserve to interview them that afternoon. She asks Victoria if she would like to go along with her. Never one to say no to new experiences, Victoria says she would love to.

They both arrive and are taken upstairs to the living room. There must be about six boys and three or four girls, including mother and father, all sitting in a circle. Victoria recognizes the youngest girl as the little one who came and sat with her in the ancient Reserve Church the Sunday before; putting her arms around Victoria and asking her if she is a nurse.

While Nadine is doing the interviewing, the mother tells Victoria her daughter is sick and one of the daughters tells her she has epilepsy. Victoria asks them if they would like her to pray over her daughter. They go into another room where she prays over her little daughter. The mother then brings in another daughter for prayer and the Laying on of hands. The prayer in tongues that comes from Victoria's mouth did not seem to bother them. Victoria, however, feels her breathing speeding up and she shakes as she prays over the both of them and the mother. It is a very joyful prayer time with no fear. They are one in their Faith in the Lord, Jesus Christ. It is almost as if they expected her.

Nadine and Victoria leave them with smiles and hugs all around. They then go to one of the local restaurants in the nearby Acadian village.

Is Nadine aware of what had taken place with the family they visited and Victoria's role in it?

Before flying back home, she talks with a couple of carpenters to give her an estimate on the refurbishing of the Adams summer cottage. It sure needs work and no-one is putting any money into it. She wants to see it kept for her sons, Matt and James. Jack and she certainly don't have the money to put into this old place with so many projects on the go at home: the family room for young people being one of them. Lord only knows what the future holds.

--------------- --------------------- ---------------------

*"She now knows, that in time, with the power of the winds, tides and an Unseen Hand steering the tiller of her little red sailboat, she will find her heritage on this isolated bay."*

--------------- --------------------- ---------------------

She is left alone on Musquash Bay in her in-law's cottage, immersed in the beauty of it all, enjoying the silence creation has to offer her. While she gazes over the Bay the sun sparkles like jewels on the waters. She feels such a strong pull to these surroundings. Somehow she feels very strongly as she sits on the breakwater that she and Jack are not to live together; a break in their marriage.

A scripture, Hosea 1-2, comes to her. When the Sister from the Notre Dame Convent, who is her spiritual mentor, first directed her, she brought Victoria to these biblical passages: "He, Jesus, is my Husband and I am His wife. Such love I have never known all my life. I want only His Love. He is my Love. He brings me joy. He takes away my loneliness. He gives me a taste of heaven and so I want more and so I do His Will to make Him happy. Why did I ever leave Him so long ago? Why did I listen to others who wanted me to deny His existence? Jesus wants me to be happy and joyous, helping me through the down times."

She must write:

He wants us all to be happy and joyous. Not as the world knows happiness and joy but as He gives it in His Way, which cannot possibly be compared. The earth is His creation to be used for our needs, and happiness, but it is not even a miniscule of the happiness our Father within us provides if we only let Him.

He is weeping while hanging on the Cross, in the garden of Gethsemane, and in His time of prayer on the hillside. His sadness, because of our stubbornness and our lack of love for Him is something we can't imagine. How can we hurt Him so? How could I have hurt Him by my ignorance? How can I possible return that love? Only by obedience and thanksgiving, praising and Blessing His Holy Name as an offering, can I show my love. My obedience makes Him happy; that is only the beginning. But still our little minds and bodies will balk when He takes all and asks too much. When will I be able to give myself completely?

Oh Lord, my mind darts from one subject to another like a butterfly on the wing who cannot settle. My life is like that, like the butterfly. I depend on my heavenly Father to direct and guide me, to keep me from harm. I know nothing other than what He wants me to know. My mind is blank so that He can plant His Word into mine. Wisdom and knowledge; just right for me in the way that He sees is right for me as His servant. And so He gives me His Holy Spirit, (Acts 1) which dwells within my soul with His Graces and Gifts. He allowed me to go to the lowest point in my life so that I would turn to Him for help. Without Him I can do nothing as I was so aptly shown. He sent His Son, Jesus Christ into my life to bring me to Him by the Power of the Holy Spirit. It is through baptism with water as an infant and then Baptism of the Holy Spirit. He brought me His chosen one, Mary, the mother Of Jesus, to intercede for me, as she turns to her Son to answer my prayers for those whom I pray. He has brought me His angels and saints to be by my side to also intercede for me and to protect me from harm. His saints teach me about Him and open my eyes to His Glory, His Love for me. Even strangers, friends and family; saints around us every day who are His children, and have been saved by Jesus Christ, His Son, through His Grace and Love for us, are brought together to help one another."

--------------- --------------------- ---------------------

She is praying her Rosary sitting on her favorite rock early this morning of July 16, 1986:

Oh Sweet Mary, this is what speaks deep into my heart and soul at this present moment in Time:

Repeat the ROSARY PRAYER this way; no more "thee's" and "thou's", only repeat "you" and "your."

Hail Mary, Full of Grace, the Lord is with you.

Blessed are you amongst women and blessed is the fruit of your womb, Jesus.

Holy Mary! Mother of God, pray for us, sinners, now and at the hour of our death. Amen!

IT COMES AS NATURALLY AS BREATHING!!

--------------- --------------------- --------------------

*"The next day she takes the tiller of her little red sailboat and sails home. She has obeyed her mystical skipper. She sings as she sails along: "Come, let us sing to the Lord and shout with joy to the Rock that saves us. Let us approach Him with praise and thanksgiving, singing joyful songs to the Lord" Psalm 95"*

--------------- --------------------- --------------------

She is now home and it begins all over again. Oh! What will she do? Leonard is her cross with his flatbed in her driveway, no room to park cars and his desire to hug and kiss her all the time. He says it is normal to want to want sex and we should do it but she finds it difficult since she doesn't believe it is right to have sex outside marriage and they are both married. She believes in the sanctity of marriage.

She prays: Prayer to the Holy Spirit.

"Blessed Holy Spirit, beloved of my soul, I adore You. Strengthen and guide, enlighten and console me. Tell me what to do. Give me your orders. I promise to submit myself to all that You desire of me and I accept all that you permit to happen to me. Only let me know Your Will. Amen"

--------------- --------------------- --------------------

Since her body is the temple of the Holy Spirit, She is the bride of God, the Creator in the Name of Jesus Christ, our Saviour. Does that mean that she is also Leonard's bride, and any others who want to have sex with her? She emphatically says NO! Oh! If only she had known this so many years ago. In those days she had no strength or knowledge to fight. So naive was she, an innocent child.

She doesn't want to hurt Leonard's feelings; she likes him as a friend, nothing more. She must go through this suffering. There is a reason. Why? Where, Oh where is the love? She can only thank God for preparing her for whatever reason. Mark 9: 48-50.

She prays her Rosary, thanking Mary, her blessed Mother for interceding for her. She knows she has been given the gift of strength, being able to overcome Leonard's approaches, and any others. Daniel 3: 49-50, Timothy 1: 12-17. She can overcome her weaknesses. Her Faith is becoming stronger. Like Saint Paul of the scriptures, who wrote," it is when I am weak that I am strongest," that she is sure she can conquer.

What will she do about the place downstairs? She is in a quandary. Maybe she is not to do any work downstairs. No tenants, no money; and she sure won't get tenants if the place is not finished. She doesn't blame Jennifer, a street-kid, for being upset even if she didn't show it.

She prays her rosary for patience with Leonard. He has had three weeks now and still he is no farther ahead in finishing the roomettes.

--------------- --------------------- ---------------------

This early morning while praying:

I have been revealed the word "Love." Love that is God's kind of Love, a Spiritual Love which is love, not of the flesh, of the world, 2 Corinthians 5:14-17, but a new kind of Love. Love of the inner person as he or she is with all the faults, weaknesses and failings, as You, Lord, who is within us all, loves us with all our faults, failings and weaknesses. Whether we are fat or thin, short or tall, no teeth, lazy, dirty, boring, talks too much or not enough, cries or laughs, slow or fast, workaholic, or alcoholic, prostitute or gambler, drug addict, or criminal, even murderers like abortionists, and the mothers they prey on to kill babies in the womb, those who use abortion as birth control, men who use and abuse women for their own sexual satisfaction and other ways of abuse; all religions, races and faiths. You love us all. I search for You in the Marketplace and in the streets to find whom my heart loves: Scripture: "Song of Songs" 3, and "Poustinia," by Catherine DeHeuk Doherty. I find Him in my fellowman. Thank You for these gifts and blessings. I love You.

Thank You for giving me Jack and Leonard for it is because of them I know You.

--------------- --------------------- ---------------------

*"She is never alone in her little red sailboat; she feels a Presence in the wind, the waves and creation around her. A mystical presence she cannot see or explain but knows, in her heart, mind and soul, is there."*

--------------- --------------------- ---------------------

Before leaving for Musquash, Victoria receives a call from Birthright about a 23 year old woman and her child who needed a place to stay. She said she would see her. Victoria then gets a call asking her to pick the woman up at the transit Go Station. She is shocked at the girl's appearance; hollow, sunken eyes, very thin and pale, she seems undernourished as well. She has a child with her. Victoria thinks about the baby this woman is carrying. It is a very sad state of affairs, to be sure.

As they sit out on the swing Glenda talks on and on about her first husband having beaten her up all the time. She says she is now living with another man, but when Victoria tells her she doesn't allow boyfriends in her home she said she wasn't living with him. As the visit progresses, the story gets even more gruesome. She tells Victoria she has cancer of the cervix. She hangs her head and begins to cry. Victoria puts her arms around her and holds her; telling her she is very brave to have another child.

"My dear," Victoria says, comforting her, "this is surely a miracle that you can have this baby."

She tells Victoria she is late in her 8$^{th}$ month and that the baby is due any time.

It never enters Victoria's mind she probably shouldn't have a person in her home that is just about to have a baby and in such terrible straits. Victoria decides to lay hands and pray over her. Nothing happens. Victoria doesn't feel any stirrings of the Holy Spirit. When she finishes Glenda begins to laugh, saying her baby is tickling her, making her laugh. Victoria then prays over her son, Michael.

Glenda finally decides to leave. Other than giving her a cup of coffee, Victoria offers her nothing more even though she is preparing dinner. Glenda says she will take the place and would pay 150.00 down and 150.00 for the first and last week.

Victoria doesn't offer to drive her to where she was going. This bothers her terribly. "How could I not offer to take her in this hot weather, one who is pregnant and has cancer, to where she had to go?" She chastises herself and prays for forgiveness.

It is 4 in the morning; Victoria gets up to go to the bathroom and then, like a bolt of lightning, in the silence of the night, comes the words,

"She is lying to you. She doesn't have cancer. She is using that story to get your sympathy. She wanted you to drive her but I wouldn't let you."

"Oh! So that's the reason why I didn't drive her." Joy fills her heart. Going back to bed, Victoria thought and thought about

Glenda. She couldn't fall back to sleep; she remembered Maureen's remarks; "Birthright knows that she tries to use them."

Victoria can't believe it. She prays, "Thank You, my Lord and Saviour, for keeping me from driving her." And then she thinks about Leonard. She begins to realize what he is doing, as well. He is playing games too. He is trying to take advantage of her for sex. He has no intention of putting in the door nor will he finish the rooms except in his good old time, if at all. She is determined to call his bluff. She thinks, "when he comes today, I must get angry, tell him I'm too busy to sit with him and if he doesn't finish the work I am paying him to do, then I will tell the Prayer Group what I know about him and that he is a farce."

"Oh Lord, You let me go through this scenario with Leonard so that, through Glenda's example, I would see Leonard for what he is and what he is doing.

She realizes it is the *Gifts of the Holy Spirit; wisdom and knowledge. I must not believe and trust everyone. A great lesson learned. I am so happy I waited it out before opening my eyes to see Leonard for who he is."

--------------- --------------------- ---------------------

*"She in her little red sailboat need not be afraid. She is not alone."*

--------------- --------------------- ---------------------

Victoria continues her prayer:

Blessed, Lord, You know them better than I do. You see their souls. You know that inside we are good so we must look beyond the surface. And so we have Love. Loving the person no matter what he or she does or how they look. And so I must be hard on Leonard for his good. We need not like their actions but can love them in spite of them.

"Thank you, Father in heaven, for revealing this to me this night. And so, as she lies in her bed trying to sleep, this is what she hears in the silence of her heart:

"Be not afraid. I go before you always. Come follow Me and I will give you rest." Isaiah 41: 10. She feels at peace now and joy fills her heart. She is glad she waited it out and did not get angry with Leonard. There is always a right time. She knows that if she had, God's Will would not have been done through her.

--------------- --------------------- ---------------------

Leonard arrives early this morning. He says he'll do what is necessary to finish the work he started; the rooms downstairs and the

122

door. Praise God. She didn't have to say the things she was going to say to him.

To thank him, she gives him a big hug. His face breaks out in a big smile and hugs her back. Victoria felt as if she were hugging Jesus. She and Leonard discuss the shaking she goes through during the Rosary. Leonard tells her she doesn't have to go through it. She has a free will. She thought she was free of the shaking, but she guesses she isn't. OOHH!

The Book of Jonah, in the bible comes to her mind.

"Oh no," she says to Leonard, quoting scripture, "I don't want to be like Jonah. By disobeying, I could end up in trouble. Abraham could have disobeyed too; he could have said I will sacrifice my son another time or said no, period." Genesis, 15.

She goes to her bible after Leonard leaves.

She exclaims, "I can't believe it! What should come up but the Book of Jonah, Wow!! Confirms my belief, for whatever reason my Father in heaven has in mind. I must obey. The Reading during the Mass this morning was also on Jonah." WOW!

--------------- --------------------- ---------------------

*"As she sails her little red sailboat through the wind and rain, she is wracked in pain. Where, oh, where is the love?"*

--------------- --------------------- ---------------------

Yes, she is wracked with pain. She is trying to understand why. Is she doing something wrong that she suffers so? Like the Book of Jonah, is she disobeying?

She prays: "Oh Lord, I am so afraid. I don't understand. The Mystical Energy is so strong within me. Either I'm slain in the Spirit sitting up or I go into a trance. I thought the shaking was over, Lord, but still there is the spasm of shaking during the Rosary or during a prayer meeting when prophesying is going on. What's going on? I am frightened. I can't pretend to know anymore. I can imagine I am being used in some way to help others but is that only my ego, the devil torturing me?"

She continues to pray, "We need money badly. I have to have an exterminator in tomorrow and we are overdrawn in the bank. Please, hear my plea for help.

Even with her doubting, She is being given a gift today. A friend, Clifford E. brings her a Pugo Pine tree. It is a sign of peace. Her soul is lifted up in joy and love. Cliff could easily have planted it in his own property, but still, he gives it to them.

She prays for Clifford and places him at the foot of the Cross. "I ask that You wrap Your Redeeming Blood around him, Lord Jesus, to protect him from the evil one. Amen!! Thank You, Jesus, the Healer."

Victoria is going to meet with Fr. Coolie at 3:00. Fr. G Reggie, the Benedictine Monk who was the Speaker at our Retreat, told her to see him concerning her spiritual life.

She will never do anything extraordinary; she must remain simple as a little child, staying in the background. This shaking during the praying of the Rosary is not simple. It is not staying out of the limelight; it is out of the ordinary. Is she being attacked? Let this be so. Victoria knows she will be given the strength to handle whatever might be, but she needs help to overcome the fear that she feels. She shares these thoughts with Fr. Coolie; it was most interesting. When she told him about the shaking, he said,

"I was wondering when it would come to Canada. I am going to an Assembly of the Charismatic Movement in October. That very thing will be discussed." He said he would know more about what is going on after the Assembly.

Fr Coolie certainly put her mind at ease. She also shared with him about her receiving a "Word of Knowledge that she was to accept the cup of suffering while making the Way of the Cross, and being drawn to a stained glass window of Jesus and the Cross in the church.

Fr Coolie said, "Yes, it is the cup of suffering; you will suffer."

Victoria then went on to tell him about her dream of being stabbed in the back.

"Yes, my dear, he said, "there is no doubt in my mind that you will suffer." Revelations 2:10. "Do not fear your suffering. Give the Glory to the Father, Son and Holy Spirit, as it was in the beginning is now and ever shall be world without end. Amen!" There are things happening today you would not believe if you saw it. Habbakuk 1, Alleluia!"

Fr. Coulie believes God's Presence will be revealed. He tells her, "your eyes and ears will be opened to His Word in the Scriptures for teaching and knowledge," and then he prays over her. She is humbled, she knows she is an unworthy servant.

--------------- --------------------- ---------------------

*"In her little red sailboat, she is sailing through another exciting day not knowing where she will be led on this mystical voyage."*

--------------- --------------------  ---------------------

So many things happening to Victoria; so many words revealed to her heart and soul, Words of wisdom that she would never have thought of herself. She prays that all things are happening one by one in sequence for the good and happiness of all. She knows if she did everything on her own as in the past before she found what is offered her through prayer and meditation, everything would be in turmoil. Left on her own she is lost. Hymn: "Amazing Grace."

Had lunch with a friend today; she listened as Victoria shared with her the vision to have a place for unwed mothers and street kids. She immediately told her that the church would help her. They would have fund raising for her help in this Work. She also suggested Victoria talk to the town for approval and approach Children's Aid Society. However, Victoria believes Sister Ellie of the Sisters of Notre Dame, will help her get a sponsor. Praise God!

She goes through the spasms again. When will it all be over? Such physical pain she suffers.

She prays, "Is it Your Will, Lord, as I continue on this voyage into the unknown?"

--------------- --------------------  ---------------------

A knock on the door and who should it be but Leonard. Victoria is very upset. She says clearly to him without hesitation, "you are using me, Leonard and I hate it." It is finally sinking into her dull brain; he only wants one thing from her. Sex!

Her reaction to Leonard's return and his response, even after her past anger, means only one thing, she is being healed of her fear of men, their insinuations and come-ons toward her. Very strange! The words that come to her heart are that she can accept men and their attentions without sex. She laughs out loud in joy and gives him a big hug. Praise, Thanks and Glory to God, she prays.

Jack has joined his brother sailing on the Atlantic. She has just been informed that a 60 mile an hour gale has hit the area where they are sailing. She will be helping Sister with the Bingo at the church today. With this dangerous sailing in P.E.I. on her mind, she arrives and begins her walk around the tables.

Oh my! What's happening? She gets an urge to stop. She leans against the wall in the bingo hall and goes into her (closet) of silence. It happens three times and then she begins to pray in tongues. She prays on and on as she stands there. Is this prayer for Jack, his brother and the crew? One never knows, does one!! Sister comes over to see if she is all right. Victoria smiles her "Yes." Finally the feeling passes and she continues her walk around the tables in the bingo hall.

Her prayer is heard, she is confident. Thank God, Amen!!"

--------------- --------------------- --------------------

As Victoria sits here on the docks at West River Rd. watching the dogs scurrying, and sea birds flying for food, the people, in their boats, the old and young, walking and talking, holding hands and eating ice cream, she thinks of all God's Gifts available to all:

Do they give a thought to the feeling of pleasure and love bestowed upon them at this moment in Time? Many who are burdened with illness, stress, depression, poverty or too much wealth, will they ever know until it's too late that He is the answer? Will they ever know that all they have to do is lift all up to the Powerful Holy Spirit in the Name of Jesus in thanksgiving for the good things given to them, hearing them and helping them through bad times? It's so very sad.

"Oh Lord, God, I pray my prayers will be heard for them. I lift them all in thanksgiving for the good and the bad because it is only with the downs in life that we will search for and finally find He who is Love. I love You, Jesus."

--------------- --------------------- --------------------

*"Docked with the other boats in the harbor, she sits in silence in her little red sailboat praying for those around her."*

--------------- --------------------- --------------------

Victoria gets a phone call from Birthright, in the next town. They tell her that Glenda will not be staying with her. She is in the hospital having her baby.

"Victoria," the woman says," she sounds very happy so don't worry about her. She is fine."

Oh! I'm so glad to hear that news." Victoria exclaims. Does she have a place when she gets out?"

"Yes," she is told, "with a friend." She doesn't say whether it's a man or woman friend.

All is well in Glenda's world at present. Victoria truly believes that in prayer to the Higher Power, she was touched when she laid hands on her.

Leonard came to visit her today. They sat and talked about the healing she had received. While they sat there she felt herself sink into Silence. He showed no reaction so she couldn't tell what he

126

thought, but he did say it didn't bother him whether she talked to God or whether God talked to her. She then told him what had come to her in silence.

A little voice said, "I want Leonard to work with you."

He said, "I have to hear this for myself." She said quietly to him, "Yes, Leonard, you are right, you must listen, not just pray, listen. The Holy Spirit is trying to tell you that He wants something special from you, not just what you're doing here. Not just building roomettes for street-kids but in other ways. We are to be a team. She told him she needed a male friend to help over the hard times because it will be difficult. He then got up to leave.

As he did so, she grabbed his hand and said, "I love you." Not the love of the flesh or of the world, but the love of Jesus" He said, "I love you, too." He hung his head, not looking at her.

The next day Victoria has to go to the bank and then decides to go to the church. "Don't feel much like making the Way of the Cross," she says to herself as she walks along, but she feels a strong pull to do so.

As she starts the Stations of the Cross she gets very hot, the sweat pouring off her in rivers. She gets through the first 4 Stations when, all of a sudden the church bells start chiming. It is 10 minutes to 3 in the afternoon. It is not even on the hour. She is in spiritual ecstasy, hearing beautiful songs of praise, glorifying His Holy Name. She starts to laugh and listens. She begins to sing in tongues to the music of the bells. Such joy fills her heart. She stops walking the Stations of the Cross and goes back to her seat still singing. "You are so beautiful to me, You are so beautiful to me, Jesus."

--------------- --------------------- --------------------

**Early morning prayer:**

Oh Mary, my Mother! There is no way I will ever be able to go through this shaking without fear when I pray the Rosary. Please help me! I am going to go to the Legion of Mary Prayer Group this morning and I know I will go through the shaking again. Be with me. Hold my hand. I love you, Mary! With your help, I will go through it.

I went through a little shaking and then it stopped. Thank you, Jesus, the Healer, through Mother, Mary's intercession. I saw the healing Power of the Holy Spirit working in Margo today. For the first time I saw this mystical energy go from me to her and the transformation was beautiful. She was healed of her anguish, her illness. I was in my Poustinia of silence at her house today. She was open and accepting of what was revealed to her, because she has Faith. She has been praying for her family and she knows her prayer was heard. "I love You, Lord." She and I praised Your Holy Name in prayer.

After reading my book on fasting I will fast today until my lunch with Vida tomorrow.

"Oh, Lord, my God, I am so unhappy; we have so little Faith. Please, dear Father, please be patient with us. There are so many who do love you and will obey. Please be patient because we love you and ask for mercy upon us who are sinners. I am unhappy as I read the Scriptures. Please, don't give up on us foolish children. Please forgive us. We know not what we do. Praise and bless Your Holy and Blessed Name."

--------------- ---------------------- ---------------------

*"She, in her little red sailboat, contemplates nature around her. She can only keep on praying in silence as she searches to find answers."*

--------------- ---------------------- ---------------------

Fr. Louis of the Portuegese Church, where she helps out with bingos, invites her to go and sit in the chapel to pray in front of the Blessed Sacrament. As she kneels there, nothing comes to her mind; for the moment, not even a prayer. The minutes tick by and then she is drawn into her Silence. She then falls into a strange trance and begins to shake. She is the only one in this little chapel. She feels a powerful Presence. She knows Jesus is present in the Blessed Sacrament on the altar. She wants to believe He is with her. She takes out her Rosary and begins to pray.

"Oh, Mary I don't know what is right or wrong or whether what I am doing is right or wrong. I don't know if it is You, Lord, who manifests Himself to me. Could it be Satan, who prowls around like a roaring lion to capture souls?

She is suffering so much pain as she kneels here.

--------------- ---------------------- ---------------------

She and Matt are at Swiss Chalet for lunch today and while sitting there, she goes through the trance of silence. Again, yesterday with Vida at the luncheon Victoria had for her. It also happened with Margo. Is it all, supposedly, the manifestations of a Powerful Spiritual Presence. But, she doesn't believe she would be used, a terrible sinner, in that way. Why would she be used in that way? She thinks she is just making a fool of herself. It must end.

"Satan must go, Lord, now!! Begone, Satan, in the Name of Jesus." Amen!

Everything is wrong. Matt, James and Jack are unhappy with her. Vida is her friend and she should not be put through something that would upset her. It should make her happy. However, it did make Margo happy and my cousin, Joan.

She prays: "Help me, Mary, to understand, to know the truth. What is it God wants from me? I can't believe anything anymore. Everything is getting out of hand."

She prays the Exorcism Prayer to St Michael the Archangel, the Rosary to her Blessed Mother, Mary; making the sign of the Cross to banish the devil, believing all is well as she thanks and praises the Holy Name of Jesus.

--------------- -------------------- --------------------

As she sits on the toilet in this moldy bathroom which is so dirty, she think about uninstalled patio doors which aren't needed and unfinished roomettes for the young street-kids in the family room.

Jack is away for a month; no help there. She feels like crying.

She cries! She read Book of Job in the Bible. Is her Faith being tested? She prays for peace and Joy; to be given the strength to cope with what-ever life has to offer, good or bad.

At Mass this morning she prayed the Rosary before it began. Everything is controlled with no manifestations. She will wait it out and see what is in the future but she believes her visit to the Blessed Sacrament and her prayer to St Michael the Archangel was right. She is looking forward to going to the Charismatic Conference this weekend. Maybe answers will come to her there. She will fast today according to God's Holy and Blessed Will.

--------------- -------------------- --------------------

*"She is praying for help as she sails her little red sailboat she knows not where. She is frightened and feels she is losing control of the rudder; the sails are not taut, they flap out of control in the fierce winds."*

--------------- -------------------- --------------------

Sister E, after telling Victoria she would go with her to see the Mayor about the Home for Street Kids Victoria is planning, changes her mind. Well, Victoria doesn't let it bother her. She knows she can do it herself having had experience in doing this sort of thing in Brae na Beith. She had set up a Youth Centre in the nearest town so she is well prepared.

A few weeks have gone by and Jack arrives home today from his sail with his brother. Seems quite fit and not in too bad a mood.

Then, without thinking (as usual) she drops the bomb. While they are having a glass of wine before dinner, she tells him again that she wants to finish the basement for homeless street kids. She tells him that Sister E, Birthright and others would help me financially if I got permission from the Mayor of the town. Well, Jack blew up, getting angry again. She sits silently as he walks away sulking with another definite "NO."

"What else did you expect, Victoria?" Her thoughts are firm:

"Well that's not going to stop me. I know what I must do."

She knows now why she was brought to the book on Fasting. She whispers to herself, "I must fast, no matter how long it takes, one week, two weeks or three weeks, I don't care. It's going to be a form of prayer. I must also witness this to everyone who knows what my plans are. However, I can't do this without Spiritual help. I must pray to know when to start. Who is prompting me to do this?"

--------------- --------------------- --------------------

She writes her thoughts:

Well I sure made a fool of myself. I am so quick to jump into my own ideas, to come to my own conclusions. Whose idea was it that I fast? Am I ever going to learn to wait until the time is right? As Fr. G says, "if it isn't your idea, Victoria, you just sweep it under the rug." I must go into my prayer closet, Poustinia and pray first.

"The Elijah Task," is a book on the discipline and training of a prophet; to bring me to the lowest point of dying to self. So much humiliation I must endure in front of these people; my shaking, going into a trance in my silence in prayer. I must go through the worst of training. I am clay to be shaped in the potter's wheel, Isaiah 64. I suffer so much pain; physical, emotional, mental, it hurts.

Yes, Mavis is right. I am to be silent. I know now that I will never want to make myself obvious in a group again. I am a sinner and I must go through this to die to my ego. It is a hard lesson.

"Thank You, My Father, our Creator, for giving us Your Son, Jesus, the Blessed Holy Spirit, St Michael and Your Guardian Angels, and the Communion of Saints in the Spirit world and on earth. Amen!"

I'm so upset! I'm crying with frustration and tears. When am I going to get those roomettes finished downstairs? It has been over a month now since Leonard said he would do that work for me; building them for those young street kids who need a place to live.

"Oh, Lord, Mary, our blessed Mother, the communion of saints, to whom do I call for help?"

Glenda wrote me today saying she needs a place to live with her new baby. I would like her to stay here but how can I ask her to stay in a place that is such a mess. No walls, leaking water, cold and damp; it is not a place for a baby. Why doesn't anyone care? What can I do by myself?

"Please help me! Please help me! I am desperate! What am I doing wrong? Lord, God Almighty! You are all I have. You are all that I have to call on. It is all in Your Hands, but how long must I wait? I feel so helpless. Please help me. In Jesus Name, according to Your Holy and Blessed Will, please, I pray my roomettes will be finished. I am trying to be patient but I'm very upset. I can't wait much longer. Praise and thank You,

Jesus. I love You. Let Your Will not mine be done as far as the roomettes are to be finished. I am finally at peace with this conclusion that comes to me through prayer. You are my Love. I can accept this because only Your Will is best. What do I do about Glenda, though?"

--------------- --------------------- ---------------------

*"The little sailor in her little red sailboat is praying the storm will end."*

--------------- --------------------- ---------------------

Alleluia!! Leonard comes over to tell Victoria the wall- boards will be delivered on Monday. He will be able to finish the roomettes next week. Wow! She knows her prayer was answered. She prays and thanks God in the Name of Jesus Christ, by the Power of the Holy Spirit.

As they sit before dinner sipping their cocktails, she tells Jack the latest with Leonard and the roomettes and shares Glenda's letter. He vehemently says, "No, I don't want her and a crying baby here." It's bad enough we have all these brats living with us now."

She says, in return, "How else are we going to bring in some money to live on? Nothing stops you from going sailing for a month while I'm here looking after things," she screams. With martinis to feed the flame of anger the quarrel between them gets ugly. Dinner is another flop as she runs to the bedroom in despair and tears. She falls asleep and dreams she sees a newspaper, the headlines saying, "God is your Master." She wakes abruptly. What does it mean? The questions keep pounding in her mind. Must I allow Glenda to come here against Jack's Will?

The next morning she gently said to Jack, "I'm not going to have Glenda here until you give permission to have her move in. Jack then said, "Yes" to Glenda coming." She raises her voice in Praise and thanksgiving. Tears are running down her face in joy.

He said, "Well, she and the baby can come if the baby stays downstairs."

"The baby is only 2 weeks old."

Jack said, "She is to stay downstairs and not use the bedrooms upstairs."

"Yes, I promise."

Then, he said, "She can come if the rooms downstairs are finished."

Now to get the roomettes finished.

She continues to praise and thank God in silence.

--------------- --------------------- ---------------------

Victoria can't understand why Leonard is taking so long to finish his work here. A gaping hole in the wall with no patio doors, roomettes not finished and other odds and ends to do and yet for some reason all is postponed. What's the point of saying anything to him; he won't listen to them anyway. It's as if he's trying to show his authority or something. Or is it sex he wants? She just doesn't know.

She prays, "Oh Lord, If it's sex, well, no matter what he might think, I will not give my body to him. I'll do without the unfinished work first."

She thanks her heavenly Father for hearing her cries. She knows she is nothing. If it makes Leonard feel good to punish for withholding sex; then so be it.

"Thank you, Jesus", she prays, "for this humiliation and for the love You show us through Your Word. I love Leonard and I hate to see him in pain. I don't care about the door. I just don't want to see Leonard hurt. On her second prayer thought, "Is he being hurt? Or am I?"

--------------- --------------------- ---------------------

Then this morning her trip to Toronto was cancelled. Vida drove her to Mass and, on the way, Victoria told her about the hole in the wall of her house; not having a door installed.

She was asked to read the 1$^{st}$ Reading at Mass. The scripture Reading was Ezekiel 12:1-16. Ezekiel was told by God to exit through the hole in the wall with his baggage. Did Vida hear and remember the scripture and what she told her?

The most interesting thing happened on Victoria's way to Cultures Restaurant after Mass. As she was walking along she happened to look down and, on the sidewalk, she noticed a piece of paper. As she picked it up, somehow she knew spiritual work needed to be done. She sat and read it as she drank her coffee. The letter was from Julie to Lynn. They had had a lesbian relationship a few years back. Lynn was upset because Julie was not paying attention to her 12 years later. Lynn was now into another relationship with Shirley. As Victoria waited for the bus, Lynn came over and told her she had her note. How she knew that, Victoria didn't know but, anyway she gave the note to Lynn and said, "I will pray for you, love."

She said, "I will pray for you, too." Victoria answered, "Thank you, I need that."

Lynn left then and as she walked away it came to Victoria that she must give her the pamphlet she picked up at the church called, "How to see the good in others."

She went back into the restaurant to give it to her but she wasn't there. Victoria then went to wait for her bus and who should come along but Lynn. She gave her the pamphlet.

She said, "Is this religious?"

Victoria said, "No" she put her arms around her, kissed her and Lynn laughs, "what is that for?"

She said, "because I love you. Jesus is Love and lives Love. I love you no matter what you do or no matter your life-style.

Victoria prays Lynn is touched and that she will come to know and believe. Praise God. I love You. Jesus loves His children so.

This is what is known as doing the Lord's Work in the Marketplace as Catherine DeHeuk Doherty wrote about in her book "Poustinia!"

If that hole in the wall of her den had been fixed the Reading at Mass would not have made an impression on Victoria. Arriving home she got a phone call from Vida who did not zero in on the reading.

Victoria thinks, perhaps this was just for her ears alone.

She has been in pain and agony all day long. Victoria chastises herself; how arrogant and prideful she is thinking, "I would discipline Vida in the Lord's Name? How conceited and hateful can I get? How I hate myself for my sins!"

Victoria prays her rosary in tears, then, goes to see old Kathleen at the hospital, realizing what true humiliation it is as she sees Kathleen ready to die. Victoria continues to chastise herself because she believes she is nothing. What is she going through all this for? She remembers a book she read, "The Dark Night of the Soul" by John of the Cross.

--------------- -------------------- --------------------

*"As she sails along through the dark night in her little red sailboat, she shouts out loud, "where am I heading? Where is this little boat taking me?" No one hears her. She feels fear and is in much pain."*

--------------- -------------------- --------------------

## August 86
She writes:

All I know is that Jesus died on the cross for my sins, that He loves me. I am starting over again like a new – born baby, as the image I have, reveals---a brand new vision, a new book and a clean page. Is what happened in the past, spiritually, true or not, whether it really happened, I don't know. I would like to think it did because most of it was good and beautiful.

I feel that a lot of it that happened was "love," love for God and my neighbour. Whether it was done with forceful, tough love, wishing the best for the people I encountered during the past three years and in the future, or whether the power given was fanciful and came from me or out of a spiritual power, I don't know. Was it providential, coincidence, imagination? My small weak faith as a new-born baby tells me that most things that happened were good things and in most cases, made people happy. I believe, without seeing, the Holy Trinity's Presence through it all. Some of it wasn't so good; like the letters I wrote my brother, when he was in S.A., the embarrassing shaking that happened with my friends at the church, my relationship with Jack and the boys.

Please, I pray, help me to know the truth. I am a sinner. I need to know the truth and so I start over again. I place myself, a brand-new Baby in the (8) cup of Your Hands and I pray being there that I am protected. I know, Lord, that in Your mercy and love, You will be patient and kind as I am disciplined. I have so much cleansing and purifying that needs to be done; I am such a sinner. I want to be shiny and new. I am grateful for all I am being taught, so take away the knowledge that I do not need and give me a mind filled with what is best for me to know; wisdom, silence in prayer, unceasing prayer. I want to do Your Will in all humility and submission; as it is only when I am weak that I am strong to be a servant in the Name of Jesus Christ. Quote scripture. St Paul, in the Book of Acts.

--------------- -------------------- --------------------

She sits in a restaurant for lunch after she finishes her volunteering day with the E. Fry Society at the prison for women. All of a sudden, these words come to her:

"Sit, rest, wait, study, write, listen for My Word and look after those children I send you. And, pray, always pray."

She prays, as tears run down her cheeks, "I love you Jesus. Thank You for sending me these words of confirmation today. She repeats the Mantra echoing within her, Lord Jesus Christ, Son of God, have mercy on me, a sinner." She hopes no one in the restaurant notices.

The next morning and as she sits in the sun, a cup of coffee and the scriptures on her lap before her, she prays, "I claim victory over satan and all evil spirits who roam through the world for the ruin of souls, in the Name of the Father, His Son, Jesus Christ and the Holy Spirit. Amen"

Tonight Victoria will be going to the Charismatic Prayer Meeting, standing up before the group and telling them what she is claiming. It is important that she do this as a witness to what happened during the shaking she endured. She knew she was going to go through something serious because she was warned ahead of time.

"Do not be afraid, do not be afraid," keeps coming to her through the shaking when she prays the Rosary; "Oh, what is it I must do? Tell me what I must do".

A few dogs trained to lead the blind, walked by her today. Yes, in silence, they obey their masters and so she knows she also must, or like them, she will be gently chastised.

--------------- -------------------- --------------------

As she does her housework today it comes to her what she must do:

Will I go to Mass, Legion of Mary, Prayer meetings or stay at home, write my book, and help souls either here or elsewhere, and pray, pray, pray, pray, mostly pray? You wish me to live a contemplative life in silence in and around the house, doing housework, being with the young people who live here, when and if they need me and to be with Jack. If silence it is to be, then silence it will be. And through it all, I must thank, give Praise and Bless His Holy Name. The Saint, Father Damien of the Lepers just came to my mind. How do lepers fit into my life?

--------------- --------------------- ---------------------

*"As he sleeps in her little red sailboat through the night, she dreams"*

--------------- --------------------- ---------------------

Jack resigned from his job as salesman for Boeing Computer Services. So now what happens! She knows their income will be from the street-kids living with them. It will not be easy; they are going to need all the help they can get with faith in prayer.

Having discussed the situation with the Notre Dame Sister, Victoria knows what she says is true; Jack will be brought about as low as he can go.

Boeing builds planes! Is there any connection between Jack's losing his job with Boeing and the dream she had where there are planes flying overhead attacking and Jack trying to help? In the dream, Betty Ann, his secretary, takes her to the office. They go up the elevators to the floor where Jack is. Victoria finds him lying on the floor. She goes to him and places his head on her lap. As the dream ends she wakes up in a cold sweat and shaking. She picks up and starts praying her Rosary, lifting up this dream to find out its meaning.

Ok! Is this is what the dream means? Boeing Computers fires Jack and he is trying to stay to continue the job. But no good! He rushes away. His job is dead and finished and Jack is devastated. She's trying to help but there is nothing she can do, except sympathize.

--------------- --------------------- ---------------------

*"What is going to hold this little red sailboat steady with the howling, terrifying winds causing all this shaking?"*

--------------- --------------------- ---------------------

She writes:
The spiritual shaking has again come back, especially when I pray the rosary in silence. It came upon me again when I was with Sister Ellie and Sister Stan, Notre Dame Convent, yesterday morning. Sister was talking about her niece who, she thinks, is being attacked

by the devil. I went through a terrible shaking and then broke down crying. In fear, or what? Is God using this shaking to help Sister's niece?

"Oh Blessed Lord, is this real, is my imagination going wild, or is the devil attacking me? I'm scared"

Again the shaking at the Legion of Mary meeting; this time a friend asks one of the ladies to pray over me with holy oil. Then at the prayer meeting last evening, he came to me and said, "Victoria, you must be careful about this shaking. You must try and stop it. Just empty your mind and say to yourself, I am nothing. Repeat this over and over again."

Of course he is right. I am nothing. He told me to pray from the heart and so I did with my rosary this morning. I repeated the rosary just a few minutes ago and tried my best not to let myself go too deeply into prayer. I tried praying with a whisper instead of going too deeply within. Somehow it just didn't seem right.

"Oh my Blessed, Mother Mary, what does He want from me? What is His Will? Please help me know His Will. Is Fernando right or is my way the right way? Help me to know the truth. I really don't want to shake in public."

--------------- -------------------- --------------------

*"The hurricane winds have died down, the little red sailboat has stopped its shaking. All is calm on the waters. The fearful, little sailor can now sleep in peace."*

--------------- -------------------- --------------------

Praise the Lord, for He knows when we do all things. He made all things possible. Nothing is impossible with God, the Almighty. Because we are all unique, we are special in His eyes. It is these unique gifts and graces we have been given that he wants us to put to work. If we ignore these gifts and graces we are like missing pieces of a jig-saw puzzle. The puzzle that can never be completed and so we, as God's children, are never completed or fulfilled. The gifts and graces lie dormant within us. We can never be that special something He intended us to be. A part of us is dead; the soul lies dormant and lifeless. No wonder He is sad. Are we not sad when a child is missing? We are incomplete as a family. The one we loved has gone and we feel empty within ourselves. Everything within us and around us is dark and depressing. We walk around like dead people; even when we have plenty of riches and goods, we are lifeless within ourselves. We are keeping God out of our lives and we wonder why we are so lonely, sad and depressed. Our uniqueness, which would make us happy, is not brought to the surface. It is stifled; that special something that makes us one with our Creator. That child within us is not allowed to grow.

Jesus said, "Let the little children come to me. Do not stop them for it is such as these that the Kingdom of God belongs. For I tell you solemnly, anyone who does not welcome the Kingdom of God like a little child will never enter it." Mark 10: 14-15.

Let us be like little children. Let our uniqueness come to the surface and shine as a child, without a blemish or a tarnished spot. Then we can let that special-being shine through and be what He intended us to be; having grown from a child to a unique and distinctive individual.

--------------- --------------------- --------------------

Victoria is still that little child, not having found herself yet. She cannot hide from the eyes of those around her who are judging her, seeing her go through every humiliating thing happening to her and defenseless to fight back. She is exposed to the eyes of God and man at this very important time in her life. It seems to her this past summer has been the most difficult in her existence and she knows how difficult her life has been in the past. The most humiliating, embarrassing and difficult has been the shaking; especially when those around her could not possibly understand.

And yet, she knows, as Bill, of the prayer group said, it is being allowed to happen for a reason. The pain is excruciating; all through her body. She has to lie down and she prays her Rosary. In this prayer time, Victoria understands that this is so; to expose, humiliate and bring her to her knees so that she would come to realize that she is nothing, nothing.

At this moment she feels she is nothing. She has no friends, Jack has no job; he and she are so far apart and have not much in common, including a sexual life. The doors and rooms downstairs are still not finished. The young people living here ignore her completely. Even her activities outside the home have been taken from her. Others are accomplishing and being recognized; she is nothing.

As a secular person, if she didn't know that all this was happening for a reason; that she is being trained for something, she is sure, but knows not what, she could end up in an insane asylum.

In spite of these negative thoughts and feelings, she knows she is loved, more than she has ever been loved in her life. She feels His love for her in a most special and unique way. She feels His Presence and His closeness, needing nothing more. It is a Love that is warm, peaceful and calming; one that allows her to love others around her. Even people whom she doesn't even know and would ignore before her special relationship with the knowledge of the mystical world.

In spite of that difficult "shaking" experience this summer, there were also wonderful and joyful things happening. Like finding God at Musquash in the bursting sun through the rain-clouds that covered the sky, going into her Pousitinia and the laying-on-of-hands for Nora, Margo, Philomena and others who were all healed in some special way.

Then there was the praying with the little Indian girl, who through the laying on of hands, in the Name of Jesus, healing the little one in His blessed and special Way when Nadine brought her to their home on the MicMac Reservation on Musquash Bay. Nadine was writing an article about this Indian family. Also feeling the Holy Spirit go through her as she and Nadine passed the Court House where a man was on trial for murder.

Mary's Son, Jesus' Presence when she needed them most when she was going through the "shaking." Several times the Holy Spirit filled her as the chill went through her. Words that came to her while reading the bible and spiritual books that spoke to her and taught her about satan and evil spirits.

Also, the healing she received at the St Joseph's Portuguese Church while helping with the bingo; angels and saints daily surrounding her.

These were the words that came to her at the time: "Leave your family and follow Me." She was preparing to visit her Mum and Dad in N.B. The scripture words were confirmed when Mum phoned and said she could not afford to pay her way to go down and Jack lost his job.

She I also healed of the sexual advances of men after Leonard's continual harassment of her. She is healed of her fear of men. There are so many glorious and wonderful things that have proven His Presence to her and especially His Love and mercy. She feels she will never love Him enough. So now she waits; waits to see what He has in mind for her next. It never seems to amaze her that she does not have to be a nun, a minister or priest. She can live her everyday secular life doing what normal people do but still follow, with conviction, her Faith as a Lay Christian." All praises and thanksgiving for prayers answered.

--------------- --------------------- ---------------------
*"She sails on in her little red sailboat in confidence and faith, knowing all will be well."*
--------------- --------------------- ---------------------

Well, again Victoria asks Debbie to leave. She had been away all week. So she goes over to Cam's mother to see what is going on since Debbie phoned in at 10:00 PM the night before to say she was sick and was staying at Cam's. Debbie got very angry that Victoria had gone to see her.

"How dare you interfere in my life," she screams at her. They end up in a stupid argument. Victoria really believes it's time for her to leave. She is as ready as she will ever be. She doesn't need this house and what it has to offer any longer. Her time is finished here. She can teach her nothing more. Is she right? Only Time will tell.

Katicka is fine for now. She is one of the young people Victoria is counseling. They sit in the pew of the church after Mass. Katicka tells her she isn't pregnant after all. What a relief for her as her face reveals a big sigh and smile of relief. Victoria knows she found much more, not just by going to church; she so happy for her. She gives her the prayer against satan and rebellious angels. This revelation of knowing that our Lord, Jesus Christ really exists within us is what she wishes and prays for all the young people and others she shares her faith with.

--------------- --------------------- ---------------------
*She smiles as she lets the sails of her little red sailboat take her to calm waters."*
--------------- --------------------- ---------------------

She writes in her Poustina:

It is the birth-date, the Nativity of the Blessed Virgin Mary; the Birth of Jesus. As the scriptures relate, she is the daughter of Saints Anne and Joachim, and they are His grandparents.

Please, you who read this; don't think me presumptuous that I would know God's thoughts through the scriptures but this is what I believe.

Our blessed Father, God knew we, as a people, needed a lowly person, Jesus, His Son, to represent Him on earth so it would be easier to relate to Him, God our Father. His Son needed to be someone who is like us in every way but sin so that we would feel at home with Him. Mary was not married and knew no man sexually when she became pregnant by the Spiritual Power of the Great and Holy Spirit, Third Person of the Trinity, Father, Son and Holy Spirit, although she was promised or engaged to Joseph.

Jesus is not superior to us because we can never relate with someone who thinks he is or tries to be better than we are. We could never like or respect them. And so Jesus allowed Himself to be lowly and gentle so that He could reach out to mankind. People today, as in Jesus Time, who think they are superior, hate the weak, the gentle, and the lowly. He was and is today, the King, and in His submissiveness, lowliness and humility is still hated.

--------------- --------------------- --------------------

Jack will finally have a job after a year without work. This will take him away from home more and more. Then Victoria will no longer have him. Never will it be plainer to her then the fact that she will only have her Spiritual life. She is completely and utterly alone. Silence in a mystical Presence; that is what being alone means.

Silence with her God. "Be still and know that I am God" Psalm 46-10, words she remembers seeing and reading at the Al-a-Non meeting in the dingy church basement when she lived in Brae na Beith. (1st Volume, Allegory) She is beginning to hate the noise, the chatter, but still she is lonely.

She prays:

"Lordy, Lordy where am I being led? What do you have in mind for me? Every time I try to do something; reach out to someone other than Sister Eleanor, I am stopped; phone lines are busy, I am stopped?"

Words that I must meditate on keep coming to me: Life of eternal damnation, Treasure, Famine, Jacob wrestles with God, Genesis 32. Console my people.

Oh! Blessed sweet Jesus, here I am making so many plans; visiting my brother and his family, going to Niagara on the Lake if we didn't go to see my brother, but here I am down with a dastardly cold which has put me to bed. Jack and I end up in a battle. Did all this happen so we would just stay home? (Book of Job) And so we stay home.

As I lay in my bed I have a strong feeling I am staying home for a reason, and so it proves to be.

As Victoria lay dozing Jack decides to go see his partner, Gerald and leaves her alone. She receives through prayer, by the Power of the Holy Spirit, Words of Knowledge. Some of them she can't understand but she does understand the message "5331." She knows it is a telephone number and that it is given to her for a reason. She gets out of bed and rings up "845-5331" and there is no such number. She finds the telephone book in the kitchen; it opens up at the "m's" so she starts looking for the "845's. Nothing comes to her and so then she decides to look for "5331." Sure enough, "844-5331," with the name "K Martin." Something tells her not to call the number. She goes back to bed and falls asleep. As she sleeps the word "crossroads" comes to her; 100 Huntley St.; the Pentecostal TV program and prayer line.

Victoria jumps out of bed, calls them and tells them what happened. At first the person answering said she couldn't or wouldn't intercede with her because, she said, "I don't know the reason for the intercession and whether it is for a man or a woman." She sounds frightened and unsure.

Victoria then tells her that she had just received a Word of Knowledge that she was to call 100 Huntley St. Finally the person agrees and lifts up in prayer K Martin. Victoria prays, along with her, in the tongues of the Holy Spirit. A great, strong force goes through her whole body. She continues to pray and a great peace fills her. She knows, without question their prayers have been heard and Victoria knows that K Martin is being helped. She begins to cry as she puts down the phone. The words from a psalm come to her, "Those who sow in tears shall reap in joy." Another Word of Knowledge comes to her that whoever it is had been contemplating suicide and had been diverted.

Such Joy fills her heart. She is so thankful that they didn't go anywhere today. If they had she would not have gone into contemplative prayer and this person K Martin would not have been helped. She lifts up in praise and thanksgiving to the Healing Powers, in the Name of Jesus that made this possible. Amen!

--------------- -------------------- --------------------

*"The little red sailboat takes her to a small harbour where she moors, disembarks and walks along the breakwater path."*

--------------- -------------------- --------------------

Victoria plans on going to the harbour but decides to go first to Mass at St James. She prays the Rosary with the prayer group and then receives the Eucharist. She lifts praise and thanks to God for this Gift of the Body of our Lord, Jesus Christ our Saviour. After Mass she picks up some groceries and then goes on to the harbour as planned. She walks along the breakwater following the path. It's beautiful along the harbour this evening. All is quiet. She walks to sit on a bench when she notices a woman sitting there so she sits further on. For some reason she is drawn to her, watching her closely and feels more and more strongly drawn to her.

Victoria watches her and thinks, "How would she react if I, a perfect stranger, go to her?" Especially if there was nothing wrong? What a fool I would be! A fool for Christ! As she watches, the woman lies down on the bench for a while.

She thinks, "I'll just time her and if she stays down too long I'll go to her. I don't think it's normal that someone should be lying there at this time of the evening."

Finally the woman sits up. Victoria decides to go over to her. She takes her hand and asks her if she is all right. She says nothing and keeps her head down. She is probably a woman in her forties or fifties. She could smell her breath and it is very sweet. She can't tell if the woman is ill, whether she had been drinking or what, but she just knows something is wrong with her. She holds on to Victoria's arm and hand. It is now very dark. All of a sudden she starts to cry and cries as if her heart is breaking. She cries and cries. She keeps asking Victoria who she is, where she had come from and what she was doing here.

She said, "I can't believe this is happening."

Victoria knows in her heart that this is Jesus here putting His arms around her, giving her the love she needed. How can this be said to her without frightening her?

The woman keeps saying over and over, "I can't believe this is happening." Usually I'm the one who is helping others." She cries and cries. She keeps saying how ashamed she is. She then asks where her friend is.

Victoria sees a man standing in the shadows of the twilight. He seems to be interested in what is going on. He bothers her. She feels he is being nosy and curious. She tells the woman about him. It turns out he is a friend and has been for forty years. Victoria goes over to speak to him. He tells her that this has happened before. She didn't ask what happened to bring this about. She just knew that Jesus knew and that was all that was necessary. The man and woman go back to her and they both thank her. Victoria knows the woman is all right and she is being helped. She knows that in some way she is healed.

Victoria sits quietly and continues to pray, lifting up in tongues, thanksgiving and praise.

**Oct./86**

She can see more and more clearly that her life now is in her closet of silence. She doesn't know how, when, where or what; it is all so strange, when she called into the closet of silence, she suffers such physical pain. This afternoon was very extra-ordinary and overwhelming to her as a secular person but to the spiritual her it was beautiful.

While she was at the Legion of Mary meeting, the members mentioned the names of the two people that Edna and she had visited at the hospital. Bill Ulmer, Marg's friend, and Mr. Palmer. After hearing those names, nothing came to her but sitting in the restaurant having coffee, the words came to her that she must go to these two men. She came home but could not work. She felt the silence and felt drawn to prayer in tongues. While sitting on the swing; the phone rang and she went to answer it. It stopped ringing. She picked up her bible and scripture numbers came to her mind. First of all, it came to her she must not talk to anyone on the phone. This was confirmed with James 3: 1-12, Ezekiel 3: 22-27.

She finally goes to the hospital and after seeing Bill she visits Ellie, who is also in the hospital. She then leaves the hospital and goes to a little lakeside village where there is a small, old-fashioned market-place to buy some groceries. She loves to shop there even if it takes her out of her way.

On the way home she inwardly hears these words, "Go back to Ellie and lay hands on her."

This put her in a panic because she could imagine Ellie's surprise when she approaches her about this. Victoria goes back to the lake to pray about it and the scripture, Mark 13:13 comes to her. Also the words, "You are my servant, heal my people." And the Book of Luke, the physician and Healer. Then the words of this song:

"Be not afraid
I go before you always
Come follow Me and I will give you Strength."

The Book of Daniel; "the fiery furnace".

So she goes to the hospital. She knows she is not alone so, what did she have to be afraid of.

She parks her car and goes to Ellie's room. Ellie is not there as she had to see the doctor. Victoria decides to wait. She sits down and the nurse said she is taking a bath. Victoria waits and waits. There is a woman in the other bed. The nurse comes to check her once, examining her neck. There was arthritis in her neck. She was also having an operation on her foot. After the nurse left, Victoria knows that this woman was the one she was to lay hands on and not Ellie. She goes to her bed and tells her just that, not knowing what her response would be. She asks her what her name is. She said, "Dorothy."

And so she prays in English and in tongues for healing in whatever way the Lord wanted her healed. As Victoria prays her body shakes. It was very powerful.

"Oh, she exclaims.

Victoria doesn't know how Dorothy has been healed but praise God it is done, according to His Holy and Blessed Will, Amen!

Was Victoria also used to help Bill even though she didn't visit him? She prays:

"Lord, give me the Grace to be humble; nothing in the eyes of others and to see this as a blessing. To be nothing in the eyes of the world around me is to be something in Your Eyes, Blessed sweet Jesus. You are doing powerful things in my life; powerful and miraculous things in the lives of others. What can I say? Bill Ulmer died last night at 10:00P.M. RIP Bill.

--------------   --------------------   --------------------

The door of their home is always open to more street kids and others. She hopes and prays these kids will be made aware in so many ways of a loving Presence.

She is supposed to go to the funeral for Bill U. for 11:00 AM., but goes to meditation gathering at the Anglican Sisters' Convent across the street. She is late getting out of there, so she would be late for the funeral. She decides not to go to the funeral.

When she gets home, she feels terrible that she hadn't gone. For two hours she prayed about it. She picked up a book, "Poustinia," where she read: "we have a free will and can do as we please." She did what she pleased and stayed home from the funeral. In this instance, she feels she had put her will over the Will of God, rightly or wrongly. She has that Right.

She begins to think of the funeral. How beautiful it would have been. They are so close to one another; these Charismatics, "The Servants of the Light." She begins to feel sorry she hadn't gone but she made her choice and didn't go.

It is evening, and she goes to the Healing Mass at St Michaels with the Servants of the Light Group. During the healing with the Holy Oils and laying on of hands, she is slain by the Power of the Holy Spirit, falling to the floor. Someone of the team stands behind her to help her fall.

While she lies there she senses a small voice speaking to her, "you do have a free will, Victoria, but remember I love you."

Yes, she can do as she wishes but only in obeying that still, small voice makes her happy. And, she knows that, in making others happy, it makes her happy. How could she disobey after all the things, the beautiful things that have been done for her in the past.

--------------- -------------------- --------------------

*"She, in her little red sailboat, must trust that the good Spirits in the winds around her will sail the little craft where it must go without any help from her."*

--------------- -------------------- --------------------

Victoria receives a phone call from the Adolescent Social Services. They want her to give a room to a Native girl from the correctional centre. She said she would. She knows nothing about the Native peoples. She has no preconceived ideas or judgments.

She prays: "Blessed Mother, Mary, please help me. I am weak. Give me strength. Intercede for me to Your Son, Jesus Christ, my Saviour. I know I will only be given as much as I can bear. 1 Corinthians 10:13. Praises and thanks I lift up in prayer to God and my Spiritual Family in the Name of Jesus."

On Friday she will be going to visit a Drop-in Center in the nearest town with Mark, the Administrator of the Adolescent Social Services.

Yesterday was a strange day. She went to Mass at 8:30 AM; prayed the Rosary for souls in Purgatory and the Our Father, Hail Mary, Glory be to the Father, five times and then added: "Oh! My Jesus, forgive us our sins, save us from the fires of hell. Lead all souls to heaven, especially those most in need of your mercy."

After Mass who should she run into but Ellianor. She was supposed to be in the hospital. She did not look like someone who had had an operation on her nose.

Victoria greeted her, "Oh, hello Ellianor! What are you doing here? I thought you were still in the hospital."

"Oh!" she said, "the doctor sent me home the same day. He said that I had taken water."

Victoria just about keeled over. She couldn't believe it. She remembers saying to herself and then telling her, when visiting her, "you don't need this operation, Ellianor," Nothing is impossible with God! Still don't know whether Ellie's nose is healed, though. No matter! I give all the Glory to God, the Healer, Jesus Christ, by the Power of the Holy Spirit.

After talking to Ellianor, Victoria then drove with Mark to their appointment at the Drop-in Center. As they drove along it came to her stronger and stronger that she must tell him her story. Tell him about her spiritual life, through prayer and the laying on of hands, bringing about healings in the young people who live with them. How would he accept it? She had to take the chance. If he didn't like it or approve she would just not work with them anymore. The Lord's Light must shine. The Glory of the Lord must be made known. It is time for this to happen. And so she tells him. Amazingly he accepts it very well although he said he doesn't believe in God.

He said that whatever works; it was not up to him to judge. She tells him, after she had laid hands on him and prayed in tongues, that if he wanted to think about whether he wanted her to work with him or not, she would understand.

She told him frankly, that it didn't matter what he thought, she is going to continue doing what she has to do whether the Adolescent Support Services approves or not. She suggests he tell them what happened today and he could let me know what they decide.

She tells him that she intends to continue letting her prayer-life guide her as part of the healing treatment.

"I am being up-front and honest with you, Mark. If you want me to work with you and the organization it is necessary to accept me in those terms."

They had their photo taken as a group and were silent on the drive home.

Mark D and Eileen O, from the Adolescent Support Services, were here this morning. Victoria witnessed to them that she will be praying with the street-kids for healing. They are worried that if she witnessed about her Faith in a Spiritual Life, the Support Services will get a bad name. Oh! This breaks her heart but she is not surprised. She guesses it's the way of the world, today.

So with this in mind, she doesn't know what connection she will have with this organization and their plans to arrange a group of private homes to take in young homeless young instead of using group homes.

She prays for the young homeless living in their home and she prays the Name of God will be glorified, that healings will come about and that their eyes will be opened to the truth.

The following are the young people who are living in their home:

Ron, a 25 year old from the psychiatric ward of the Toronto hospital, is a schizophrenic, alcoholic, and drug addict.

Linda is a Sheridan student and is living as a boarder.

Joe is from the Adolescent Support Services.

Ron has been with them for two months; the first three weeks he slept quite a bit. He drank heavily but was not on drugs during that time. The day before he was to go into Rehab in Toronto, Victoria laid hands on him and because of the Healing Power of Jesus Christ and the Holy Spirit, his desire for healing and his faith, he was healed of the alcoholism and, she is sure in many other ways that she knows not what. Amazingly he has not touched a drop since. Praise God.

Linda, a Street-kid hates herself, is angry at the world, wanting people to be angry with her. She is a reasonably good Catholic. She kept saying things to make Victoria and others angry, so that she could cause trouble. Did she want to be punished for something? Victoria didn't mince words, telling her exactly what her problem was in no uncertain terms. Victoria could feel the joy go through her and she knew Linda was being healed. She went to church and has been well since. She now has a job near her mother's home and stays with her overnight. Victoria hopes she lives at home with her mother.

Ron is seeing his father and brother this weekend. She prays he will move back with his father.

Terry, at the moment, Victoria has not been able to reach so she will leave him alone. He says he doesn't believe in God. His appearance is not good, very thin with dark circles around his eyes. Victoria gets the feeling he is not too well. However, he is a positive young man and seems happy enough. Perhaps he is good at hiding his true feelings. He also comes from a broken home.

Joe is 18 but seems about 14 or 15. He has a learning disability. He came to them angry with himself, the school and his parents. After praying with the laying on of hands, he now seems happier, enthusiastic about improving and learning living skills. She has a feeling he will be with them for a while as Debbie was.

Happily, Debbie she is now on her own and spending more time with her mother. Victoria is so happy for her.

She had a visit from Campaign Life workers today asking her to contribute to the Cause of unborn children. She certainly believes in this Cause, Anti-abortion, but she had to tell them she couldn't help as she was planning on going down to N.B. to see her mother who is dying and needs the money. They said they would pray for her. She will be going on Sunday and will ask a priest to give her mother the Last Rites of the church.

Victoria prays and gives thanks having her life controlled by a Higher Power. When she surrenders to that the love of the Spiritual Power within, she knows that everything will work out for the best. It all seems so right, as if she had made the decision on her own.

The other day Victoria tried to get Edie on the phone to ask her if she wanted her to get someone to replace her to do hospital visiting. There was no answer when she called. Calling again around 6, Edie said someone else had taken it over but she wondered if Victoria wanted to go to the Palliative Care meeting. She agreed so all worked out as planned.

Yesterday Sister Ellie, Notre Dame Sister, called her to talk. She asked her if they could spend some time together as she wanted to discuss the work that Mark wanted Victoria to do with Street-kids. She knew that she must get some spiritual direction concerning whether she should witness my Spiritual life in the lives of the young people who live here.

Sister Ellie said she was going to go to the Notre Dame Mother House. Victoria asked her if she could go with her. Sister said she might be able to set up an appointment with one of the Spiritual Counselors, Sister Bernice.

Victoria was thrilled to hear this. Sister phoned her back the next day and said

Sister would not be able to see her; it would have to be counseling through prayer. Victoria said she would like to go anyway.

Victoria offered to drive but Sister said, "No, I don't want you to spend the money on gas." This upset Victoria but tried not to show it. OK, she said, I'll drive your car."

After she got off the phone she got a call from Margaret who wanted her to go to the Meditation Group with her. Since she was upset with Sister, Victoria thought it might do her some good so she agreed. Still thinking she would like to go to N.D. Mother House, she went to Mass. She just couldn't make up her mind.

She thought that if Sister didn't come to Mass she would go to the Meditation with M. However, when she left the church to go with M, she thought she would check to see it Sister's car was still there. Sure enough, it was, so after talking with Sister who said she was still going, Victoria knew she wanted to go. Thank God, she did. She feels so at home with those Sisters, and so happy there. Not only that, Sister B said she could see her after all.

Victoria told her about Mark and the Adolescent Home. She told her that she had witnessed to him about the young people who were living with them and that she must go public. She told Sister she had to know that what she was doing was from God, whether it was her ego or a source of evil.

Sister said," You are wise to question your motives because it is so easy to make the wrong decision and will regret it later if it doesn't work out the way you envisioned it." She listens to Victoria's story about her conversion, her experience with the shaking at the Legion of Mary Meetings and the Charismatic meetings.

After listening patiently to her, Sister said, "I would like to work with you. I would like you to take on the Ignatius Prayer Program." She then asks her if she ever prayed with scripture, whether words ever came to her, and Victoria mentioned a couple, "stone and light." She seems pleased.

She asked her to write a Journal, to write all the scripture lines that came to her through prayer as there is a pattern that shows itself. She said she would like to see her once a week after she gets back from N.B. They will arrange something.

Victoria feels comfortable now that she has the Notre Dame Mother House and Sister B in her life.

She now feels that what has happened to her has really happened and that she didn't imagine it.

Words that speak to me with the praying of the scriptures:

"Your plans are not My Plans
My Plans not your plans,
Your will is not My Will,
MY Will is not your will."

Yes, that is becoming clearer to her as she lies here. Her sleep is peaceful this night.

--------------- -------------------- --------------------

*"The little red sailboat is taking on its own tack; the female skipper on board has released her hold. All is peaceful round her. She prays; He leads me to the still waters"*

--------------- -------------------- --------------------

The next day, the pains in her stomach are so bad she decides to go to the Emergency. The doctor tells her she shouldn't go to N.B. There go her plans down the drain. She was going to leave tomorrow, stay a week with her Mother and Dad; then go on to visit some of her in-laws. One of her sisters-in-law has a drinking problem and she wanted to pray over her. Then take a flight out for home on the 16th.

The best laid plans of mice and men when they aren't God's plans.

She knows she is being put through a preparation for some reason. The words come to her, "Surrender to Me." OK! I hear loud and clear from within. A great Spiritual flash!

Fr. S. has given her some advice about Jack not wanting boarders in the house.

These scriptures: John 2:19, "destroy this Temple and in three days I will raise it up again." Daniel 13: "innocence"

It's been three years now since the Anglican Sister from Meditation Group, gave her the idea that she and Jack provide a home for young people.

At first Jack shouted, in anger, "No, I don't want us to rent out rooms to people we don't know and can't trust."

She believed that Jack was wrong; that she must answer the Call. And so, before they realized it, a young man moving here from Italy, came off the bus with our niece who was coming to visit. He stayed the summer looking after the house for a week when she and Jack had gone to N.B. That was the beginning. College students came next and then the kids and young adults off the street, hospitals, etc.

Victoria prays: "Blessed Sweet Lord, please help me. Here I am in the midst of the secular world of the urbanite Province of Ontario;

unbelievably, living within my Christian spiritual world of prayer and silence. This is very difficult; so easy to be steered away from this form of prayer life."

She is sitting in Cultures with friends after Mass this morning; a really nice social time. Someone mentions Ellianor is going back into the hospital again to try and have the operation on her nose. Like a bolt of lightning it comes to Victoria the experience she had the last time Ellianor was in the hospital for this very same thing. Victoria waits until everyone else is gone and then mentions to Ellianor what occurred the last time she was in the hospital. Victoria shares that she was not surprised to find her at Mass the next day not having had the operation.

Victoria said; "I feel that God does not want you to have the operation, Ellianor."

Ellianor looks very upset. Victoria tells her how God uses her in her spiritual life. Ellianor says nervously, "what would He have me do? You will have to come up with a better explanation than that. My sister is Charismatic and has brought nothing but trouble upon her family since this happened. I don't see any real good coming from this."

She is defensive.

Victoria quietly tells her that God does not want her to have the operation but wants her healed with the laying of hands with prayer.

She said, sounding upset, "I have had the laying on of hands before and I don't want the operation on my nose. You're frightening me. How could you do that? God wants the best for me."

Ellianor gets up to leave and Victoria says she will pray for her. She says, in a whisper, "thank you," and leaves.

She prays:

Oh Lord, please help me. How odd and frightening all this must seem to someone who doesn't believe. I know how odd I must seem to them. I know I had no choice but to say what I said to Ellianor. So many doubts fly around in my brain. "Lord, I believe, help my unbelief that all I say and do comes to me, a contemplative, in the silence of the present moment.

--------------- -------------------- --------------------

Thoughts keep spinning around and around in her head.

It is one thing to be a Christian and following the Christian way by obeying the 10 commandments, going to Mass, doing charity work and taking in the Sacraments that the Catholic Church teaches;

it's another thing to actually obey the Voice of the Holy Spirit within, using those Gifts such as healings, doing prophetic works and witnessing to others, speaking and doing in word and action, His Will in a concrete, deliberate fashion literally.

Can she be mistaken? Their reaction is usually very negative and unbelieving.

"Is what she is doing what is wanted from her?

She questions:

I have to know that what I'm doing is not my will or the will of the devil, the evil one that can come upon us so subtly and make us think the wrong way. Or could it be my ego? Please answer my request. Am I being given a Calling? I know this is all quite normal in the Spiritual world but not very normal in the secular world. I feel so alone.

Every once in a while someone comes to me who confirms my thinking, but I find most people who believe do not actually believe a Spiritual Power exists amongst us, sending out rays of Light through us and around us; energy and Mystical Power, working miracles as a real existing Force from our Creator, God, through creation around us and in peoples who are so in need of that Light, Love, Mercy and Graces, but, sadly, are blinded by the world around them.

It is truly happening today as was promised in the scriptures when the Holy Spirit descended upon them to help them continue Your Work; Book of Acts.

Oh! Lord! I believe! Help my unbelief. I have seen Your Work and Your Power so many times since I accepted You as my Saviour, Jesus, and the Holy Spirit was released in me. I am Born Again! Thank You Jesus, I love You.

I must write my book.

-------------- -------------------- --------------------

*"The little sack, at the bottom of her little red sailboat holds all her treasures, rosary, food, water, bible, a prayer book, a medical kit, flashlight with extra batteries and pages of writings."*

-------------- -------------------- --------------------

Well, wonderful and not so wonderful happenings with the young people. She writes her thoughts and prays for healing in some way. Surprisingly, they were most willing to tolerate her.

Linda is planning on changing courses at Sheridan in January and will go into Liberal Arts instead. She is very clever and would be wasted in the Business Major she was taking. She seems so much happier with her decision.

Joe's mother's male partner came to see him yesterday. How wonderful that was. I'm so happy they made the first move toward him. It is their responsibility as we can't expect young people to act like responsible adults. Also this makes Joe feel wanted. I'm so happy for Joe. I am thankful he is finally getting his head together as far as his school work is concerned too.

Joe finally realizes how he was hurting himself by acting as a con-artist, fooling us, parents and teachers into thinking he had disabilities. Amazingly, he agreed with this about himself and is ready to do something about his laziness and is working hard to prove he has no disabilities as he pretended.

Ron came to me a couple of months ago in very bad shape. He had been in the psychiatric Ward of the hospital for schizophrenia, drug and alcohol addiction. I prayed over him for healing and he hasn't been drinking since. He seems to be coming along slowly. He is working one day a week and still on employment insurance. He has a girlfriend who stays at Grace House; I don't know her problems but sense they help each other. He is trying to get some training from Manpower so that he can work steadily. Everything takes such a long time; I will not ask him to leave, though.

Maria, a Native girl, came to me two weeks ago. Certainly isn't having a very good time of it. She came to me from Syl Apps Correctional Centre with the positive attitude of wanting to change her negative past. The first day she moved in we had a bad start. The police picked her up in Toronto, drunk and passed out on the street that night. The police phoned me from the police station after she gave them my name and asked me to go and pick her up, which I did.

I really don't know how she expected me to react but, with prayer, I am able to come across in a loving, patient way with her. I am beginning to wonder if my approach is bothering her. She came home another night with a cut on her arm. She said she had slashed herself with a razor blade. If it had happened the night before it would not have been healed so well. She would have had bandages on the cut, as well. I prayed with the laying on of hands for her healing in whatever way is God's Holy and Blessed Will.

Another morning, she came home and told me she had sex with a guy who took advantage of her while she was drunk and then he took all her money. Again she came home very unfriendly; most times she has been friendly, and didn't want to talk. I coaxed her until she opened up and she told me someone stole her 26 beers she was trying to sell and then stole all her money.

She told me, angrily, "I want to move out. I can find my own place and live on my own."

I said, with as much patience as I could, "dear, I don't think you can live on your own. It'll take time. Why don't you try to start enjoying it here?"

I suggested that I pick her up at work and that she have a good meal with us each day.

She huffed and puffed, "don't treat me like a 9 years old; I can do as I please."

I got angry, and said she is acting like a 9 year old by her behaviour. I keep telling her that I love her as a friend, that she has a chance to make a good life for herself here. She pounced out of the room with her coat on, (10:30 PM). I went to the front door with her and told her again, I loved her.

Her eyes flash, "how can you love me when you don't know me?"

Yes, true! "But only You, Lord, can teach us to love even our enemies and our neighbors as ourselves".

She stayed out all night, coming home around 8:00 AM. (She was supposed to be at Tim Horton's for work at 7:00) She then grabbed her bag and took off again without a word to anyone. I really don't know what to make of her. Time will tell. Is she trying to shock me? Is she telling me the truth? I'm tempted to call Syl Apps Correctional Services and talk to her counselors but, somehow, I don't think it's time. I have to deal with her as I see her. I pray for patience. It's all answered through prayer. How easy it is when the burden is lifted to the cross.

Twenty minutes later Kay Bow of the Adolescent Services called. She is Maria's counselor on the outside. She said she wanted to talk to me about Maria. Praise the Lord! You are with me always. I love you. I guess Maria must have contacted her.

Kay comes at 4:00 P.M, arriving with Maria and a counselor from Syl Apps. Correctional Centre. We all sit down and I tell them that Maria is hurting herself by the kind of life she is leading, keeping bad hours, not eating properly, drinking, drugs and sleeping around. I told them that if she wants to live here, she must change her life-style, she must eat one meal a day, either with us or downstairs with the others, change her friends and keep reasonably good hours.

Looking straight at Maria, I said "You must try and live in this household as you would in any normal household and family." I clearly said to her, "I can't have this, your behaviour here, because it is not a good example to the others who live here. You have a choice, Maria. You can either follow the normal pattern and rules here or find another place to live. We want the best for you, we are willing to help you make a new start in life but you will have to do it on our terms, not yours. You have until the weekend to decide. It is our way or out the door."

I felt strongly, I am speaking the words by the Power of the Holy Spirit, 2 Kings 2:9. I must not ask Maria to forgive me. I am right, I'm sure of it. When will I ever learn to "Let Go and Let God? Please help me, Blessed Mother, Mary".

She left and it is now Thursday afternoon; she didn't come back and not working today. For the last two days I have been chastising myself, feeling that I had sent her to her doom. I had no right to tell her to leave. As long as she was in this house, at least, she had a good place to live. In time she would change, where, living elsewhere she would not do as well. I'm being inundated with fears, regrets and worry about Maria, blaming myself.

I received a beautiful, book, written by Dan George, an Indian Chief and spiritual leader. Since Maria is Native, I decided I'd give it to her. I got this book from a friend, Edith, who told me that no matter what Maria decided it would be her own decision and I was not to feel guilty. She made me feel better but I still feel guilty. I decided to give Maria the book today with a card asking her forgiveness. I went to the coffee shop where she works to give it to her but she wasn't there. So I brought it home in case she showed up there. When I got home I got to thinking and praying with the scriptures. It was revealed to me that what happened to Maria was God's Will allowing it to happen, or, perhaps her own choice.

--------------- --------------------- ---------------------

After finishing her writings on the street-kids Victoria takes off for the afternoon, shopping and to Cultures for lunch. While there she meets a very nice man and his wife. Alan is head of the organization called "Christian Friends." They are working with Christians in Israel to bring the Jewish peoples to Christianity. His wife, Raymonde is a member of Women Aglow.

It was through this W.A that Victoria's Christianity was confirmed by the Great and Holy Spirit in her life after having attended a Retreat with them on May/82. Raymonde has a bible study at her place sponsored by WA. She asked Victoria if she wanted to join them.

The Women Aglow Christian Group is teaching "Spiritual Warfare." The Study uses the scriptures to teach how to banish satan and his evil followers in the Name of Jesus Christ. Ephesians 6: 10-18. This is very important because satan has certainly been playing havoc in the world. She did not attend, however; it was not the right time.

Victoria has also finished two books called "Vision" and "Racing Toward Judgment," by David Wilkerson. Written in the 70's he is predicting that God, who is not happy, will allow destruction to come upon the world until people, find Him in their lives.

--------------- --------------------- ---------------------

### New Years Day /87

Jack goes to bed, Matt and his girlfriend are away and here Victoria is all alone to recite her prayers as they go into 1987. She is at peace in her beautiful silence. She feels His Presence within and around her.

1986 has seen a very powerful spiritual growth within her.

She prays: "My God, My Father, I know You love me. I feel Your Presence. No more confusion. I hear Your Word to lead me, Your lamb, to safety. I trust, I believe, I have faith in You will do with me as You please. I want to do Your Will because I know Your Will is the best thing for me and for those around me.

The Lord is my Shepherd, I shall not want.

He lets me lie down in green pastures

He leads me beside the still waters

He restores my soul.

Yea, though I walk through the valley of death, I fear no evil. Psalm 26

--------------- --------------------- ---------------------

Life comes back with a bang as Victoria, having to discipline Joe this morning in a very firm and not a too pleasant way because he was rude and disrespectful, is interrupted as Jack comes into the kitchen to interfere and undermine her. She rattles on and tries to solve the problem and settle the quarrel herself. Deeper and deeper she gets into the argument and angrier and angrier Jack gets. Then

Matt gets into the argument too and terrible things are said. By this time she is so upset she puts on her coat and goes for a walk, feeling that everyone is against her. Tears run down her face in anger and frustration.

--------------- -------------------- --------------------

*"Trying to control her little red sailboat on her own, the frail skipper is just about ready to sink, as the high turbulent winds batter it."*

--------------- -------------------- --------------------

Arriving at the park and sitting beside the still waters of the lake, she begins to pray, "Lord, have mercy, Christ, have mercy," keeps repeating within her.

As she walks home, the words come to her, "You did not turn to Me," over and over again, "you did not turn to Me."

A great peace fills her as she realizes it's true. She had tried to solve the problem herself and she couldn't do it. She sank deeper and deeper; deeper and deeper into the turbulent waters almost over her head.

She opens her bible when she gets home and Ezekiel 43 and 47: 1-12 came to her. She had walked into deep waters and did not call on the Holy Spirit to help her. Such joy fills her heart at the realization that she must learn from this lesson; she has only to turn to Him in silent prayer when she gets into any kind of trouble. Praises, blessings and thanks be to God for His goodness. He had directed her and sat her down beside the still waters at the park. Peace came into her soul when she thought she was alone. He restored her soul to peace with love. He does not want to see her unhappy. Now if she can only continue in this way, turning to Him when anything goes wrong.

She prays: "Lord, I am not worthy that You should enter into my house, only say the Word and I shall be healed." Luke 7:2-10.

This scripture has been repeating itself over and over again for the past month or so, at the Eucharist of the Mass and now the Holy Spirit is repeating it at other times as well. This morning she is lying down and it begins again; "Lord, I am not worthy to have You enter into my house, only say the Word and I shall be healed."

And then a friend, Mary MacKenzie, comes into her mind. Victoria phones her to ask her how she is and how she spent Christmas. Mary interrupted her to talk about the Healing Mass she is having for her family tree. Isaiah 25:6-8 and again Luke 7:2-10 came to her. Mary suggests she phone Maureen and she agreed that Victoria phone the priest and set it up. And so Victoria will. She feels that generations and ancestors long past can be healed of evils and illnesses that have passed down from generation to generation to now. She will pray that future generations will know God's healing power and love, in the Name of Jesus, in their lives.

She will pray they will be healed, so that they will turn to their Faith.

For this she prays in Jesus Name. She asks this as a humble servant. "Let the battle end, Lord, for my families, against the evil one." In Jesus Name, I pray. Amen!"

The Healing Mass for her Family Tree is on January 26/87 at 8:00 PM. She hopes Jack comes with her and they pray together for their families. I know Maureen, a disabled young friend will. Praise God!

--------------- -------------------- --------------------

### January 13th/ 87 Victoria's birthday. She is 52 years old.

A new birth-day as her old life is over and she is living a new life in Jesus Christ. She has been given through Faith, the Gift of the Grace of Love, through our Father God, who is Love, by the Power of the Great and Holy Spirit. She raises prayers of thanks and praise. Another gift she receives through prayer and readings are the words from the prayer, "Our Father---Forgive us our trespasses as we forgive those who trespass against us. These are repeated over and over again within her. They began as she was praying the Rosary in silence during the night. So unsure, always unsure, she questions again, "Am I saying it the right way?" But the Rosary continues to the end. What are the words telling her?

Victoria decides to talk with her Spiritual Director, Sr. Bernie. She said, "Pray about it, dear, but, first, let me tell you a little story.

"She was a little child and her father asked her to do a job she didn't want to do. She did it though grudgingly. When she finished she said, "thank You," to her father. Her father said, "you are just as welcome," the meaning being that she was getting back only the welcome that she was giving in thanks, very grudgingly."

Victoria got to thinking about this and began to realize that she was only being forgiven the amount that she was able to forgive, which, in thinking about it, was not very much.

"Actually," she said to herself, "I am not able to forgive at all when I truly think about the situation." She decides to go to confession. For some reason tears began to flow as she begins her sharing. He said to her when she finished. "Forgive us our trespasses as we forgive those who trespass against us." Those are the very words that came to her in prayer on the day of her birthday. An amazing confirmation of the Holy Spirit, she believes. God, in His love and mercy will help her deal with her lack of forgiveness. He said to her that very few people know when they must forgive someone. He said that God, through the power of the Holy Spirit, has given her the Grace to know. She has been given a Word of Knowledge.

She prays. "So from now on, if there is someone I can't forgive, I will pray the prayer Jesus taught the disciples, the Lord's Prayer." Luke 11: 1-5. I believe Him and trust His Word."

As she continues meditating there is a knock on the door. Leonard, the man who is helping her, is standing at the door. Then she gets a phone call. It is Sister Bernie Victoria had called earlier. Somehow she feels that Sister's call was delayed until Leonard was here. On the phone she tells her, "Leonard is here visiting."

Oh, Blessed Lord! Without the Grace of the Holy Spirit, Victoria knows she would have given in to Leonard for sex. With her abrupt "NO" he left as quickly as he came, saying, "If you don't want me to come, I won't."

Before Christmas, Leonard had asked her to go to a weekend Charismatic Retreat with him. She told him she would like to go. Victoria then had a visit with Sr. Bernie and she had told her about Leonard and his wanting her to go on the Retreat with him.

Sister Bernie said, "There are four reasons why you should not go."

1 Leonard's sexual advances
2 No money
3 Did not get your husband's approval
4 No drive; you must not go with Leonard.

So she decided not to go. Sister also said that satan has taken over Leonard's spirit who wanted nothing more than to see you fall into sin. Sister's words were enough reason for Victoria, considering the confusion and unhappiness she suffered with Leonard this past summer. She doesn't know what she's going to do about Leonard.

She thinks, "I hate to say it but he is bad news; and he's supposed to be a Charismatic Christian and Catholic? Lord, have mercy! Wish he'd leave me alone. Who does he think I am, anyway? What is it about me that this always happens to me around men?"

The doorbell rings and she goes to answer it. Who should be standing there again but Leonard. She's washing floors and could not have looked worse. He tries to put his arms around her and tells her she's beautiful; that he wants to hug and kiss her and can't live without her.

Balderdash!! She pushes him off and quietly asks, "How is your wife?"

He said, "I don't know, I haven't seen her."

How sad. Well, maybe that's his trouble, she thinks.

"Maybe, Leonard, you should see your wife more often."

He stares at me and steps back. She then tells him she has no intention of going to the Retreat with him, saying that it wasn't a good idea. She told him that she had told Sister Bernie about them, and her wise remark that they are better apart. She tells Leonard;

"Leonard, she told me that we were being attacked by satan, and I believe her."

He said he didn't believe that because he has Jesus on his side.

She said, "Leonard, we have free wills, Jesus is not going to stop us from fornicating unless we ask Him. It would be very dangerous for us at the Retreat. He is protecting us now by my refusal to go with you."

He left the house angry and disgusted. He didn't sit down the whole time he was here, prancing like a caged lion.

--------------- -------------------- --------------------

**She writes:**

"Oh, I surely have been protected in the past; so many times I have been given the wisdom to know what to say to guys who have tried to seduce me. Your Army of Guardian Angels watching over me and protecting me and I didn't even know it. His love for me is without bounds. It stretches to eternity and beyond. It is here and now cloaking me with velvet wings and enveloping me like a cocoon. As I went my merry and sad way as a child, teenager in trouble and as an adult, so sure I could handle everything myself and still He was with me. How can my thanks be enough? How can my love be enough? I could never be grateful enough because my little mind could never imagine the love my Lord and Saviour deserves.

You ask me to live in chastity. It is only Your Grace that makes this possible. I know the immensity of what has been given me over the years. I know that if I said right now that I didn't want to live in chastity any longer I would not have the self-control to stop. Nothing in my past life could hold a candle to what has been given me the last four years through the Power of the Holy Spirit. I never want to do my own will again. What has the world got to offer that has brought me nothing but heartache and suffering? Nothing!! Nothing!! Absolutely nothing!! However, I know I must live out the rest of my life with all the world has to offer but I know I would never be able to function without the Gifts of Grace: Love, Wisdom, Gifts of the Holy Spirit. Galatians 5."

--------------- -------------------- --------------------

She begins to work around the house, her thoughts still on Leonard:

Leonard will go on denying that satan is always on the prowl waiting for unsuspecting prey. He thinks he is immune to such evil. She knows what she must do.

So she phones him and suggests, "Leonard, the only way I would go to the Retreat with you is if we go to someone for healing and the banishing of satan from our relationship." His answer was: "would we not just stay away from each other?" He stubbornly believed that it would not be necessary. Perhaps she can't trust herself?

She hung up the phone.

She then went to her bible and these were the scriptures that came up. John 3:19-21:

"On these grounds is sentence pronounced that, though the Light has come into the world, men have shown they prefer darkness to the Light because his deeds are evil. And indeed, everybody who does wrong hates the Light and avoids it, for fear his actions should be exposed; but the man who lives by the Truth comes out into the Light, so that it may be plainly seen that what he does is done in God."

Yes, Leonard wishes to ignore God's Word for him as a Catholic Christian Charismatic.

She prays with all her heart that he will see the Light before it's too late. "Blessed Father in Heaven, I pray for him. Please, hear my prayer, I wish him no harm." Does he love me or does he just want sex. It's so hard to know, eh, so just say "NO."

--------------- -------------------- --------------------

*"The tiny sailor in her little red sailboat, cries out, is swallowed up by the pounding of the waves against the sails, but fights the roar of the winds. She must find a place to moor her tiny craft."*

--------------- -------------------- --------------------

As she wanders around the house, she asks, "what does God want from me?

She is perplexed, confused and restless. In the last four years He has directed her, through meditation, scripture readings, prayer, and in so many other ways.

He has directed her to the Women Aglow Retreat and Bible Studies, back to her Catholic Church, CWL Executive, Opus Dei, Toronto, Benedictine Meditation Group of the Montreal Benedictines and the Anglican Sisters, Ecumenically. Fr. Julio lays hands on and anoints her with Holy Oils so that she receives one of the Gifts of the Holy Spirit for the spiritual healing of others, Legion of Mary and Charismatic Groups in other churches, including Pentecostal. He has directed her to enclosed Convents including Sisters of Notre Dame, the Mother House, Sister Ellie, a Notre Dame Sister, who introduced her to the Portuguese Church and parish. Then, miracles of all miracles, she receives a gift of a book called "Poustinia", written by Catherine Deheuk Doherty, which introduces her to the Russian form of prayer, Poustinia, (Russian Pilgrims) praying in silence in the "closet" and in the marketplace, and evangelization.

"What is she being Called to do with her life? Who is she that these things should take place in her life?"

After reading the scriptures, on the story of Mary the Mother of Jesus, these are the words that spoke to her, "Like Mary, listen in silence and ponder the Word."

She thinks she is going crazy. Is she dreaming or is her imagination going wild? She sees the four walls of this house and nothing seems real. She knows what she has to do; housework, but she can't do it. She wanders around in circles in devastating physical pain; too much pain to do anything. What is happening to her?

"Oh Mother of Perpetual Help, Pray for me."

She should just be content to be looking after this home, the young people living here and being the dutiful wife, but she can't help but feel there is more.

She opens her bible and it opens to Amos 3:7-8, "The prophetic call cannot be resisted. No more does the Lord do anything without revealing His plans to His servants, the prophets."

Something is being planned for her future but how and what. She knows she is unworthy. How can she, a sinner, be of any help? She knows He is cleansing and purging all that is sinful within her, but that will take until she dies if even then. She continually prays her Rosary to Mary, the Blessed Mother. Her egotistic thinking that she could ever compare herself to Mary is ridiculous. She is a sinner of the worst kind.

She prays: "Oh Mary my mother, please help me. Oh, this is what is speaking to my heart; Like Mary's yes, is that what is being asked of me? Asking of my inner soul? Fiat! Yes, come into my soul and use me, in the marketplace, my silence, a poustinik in the marketplace." But for what purpose?"

--------------- --------------------- ---------------------

Terry, the young man who has been living here for some time, has just come to her mind; she keeps thinking he might have cancer. As she sits here thinking about this a great and deep sadness overwhelms her. She knows this young man for such a short time. He is a very nice man, wears his hair long in a strange way and wears earrings. He was very thin and very pale. He looks like he is aging fast.

One day, she suggested to him, "I think you should see a doctor you seem so tired and not very well."

She has also been having trouble with Joe and Linda. Why am I judging them? The following words bring Victoria down a peg or two.

She loves the words Linda, the Native girl revealed to her today:
"Great Spirit, Help me never to judge others until
I have walked a mile in their moccasins." An Indian prayer, very prophetic!

"Lord, Jesus, let me walk a mile in their moccasins. Thanks for this lesson learned today.

Oh, Mary, intercede to your Son Jesus," she prays. "Give me the gift of wisdom to be as wise as an owl and as gentle as a lamb, to love God, our Creator, above all else because it is only in loving Him that we can love others. Keep me in the silence of the present moment."

--------------- --------------------- ---------------------

Victoria phones her Mum today who says she is very tired. Victoria suggests she get the priest to pray with her. She really sounds tired.

"Oh Lord, Victoria prays, "I lift her up in prayer. I lay her at the foot of the cross. Wrap Your Redeeming Blood around her to protect her from the evil one. Take her, Lord, into your healing arms. Use the pain she is suffering now, Lord, use it according to Your Holy and Blessed Will, in the Name of Jesus, Amen!"

Victoria then phones the priest at Mum's church and asks him to bring her healing oil and pray with her. He said he would tomorrow. She phones her Mum back, and tells her and her mum said, "you rascal." "Bless her heart!"

Another phone call; this time Jack's brother phones him. He thinks he has cancer of the throat. It's very sad news, but Jack doesn't seem to be too worried about it. So it wasn't Terry, the street-kid she was thinking about, it was Jack's brother. As she drives in from St. Michaels's Cathedral Toronto, the picture of Jon, the young Indian who is living with them, flashes into her mind. She is also thinking of Terry who she thought had cancer, as well. Somehow, she realizes there are spiritual connections with the three in her mind. It was Jack's brother, whose name is similar to Jon's that was being referred to. WOW! "Jesus writes straight lines crookedly." Acts 13: 10.

"I thank You, Jesus and the Power of the Holy Spirit for this wisdom and knowledge to see the spiritual connections amongst Terry, Jon and Jack's brother, whose name is also Jon."

Victoria reflects in silence:

You know, as I reflect on the above revelation, I see, as I walk by a chair in the hall, a little rag-doll; a gift I received. I think of her silence, her large eyes staring into the unknown in complete peace and submission; completely ignored unless a child picks it up and cuddles it. This little rag-doll would bring comfort to a child. However, she is passed by; completely ignored.

"Oh! Jesus, I pray, make me like that rag-doll; not fighting back; to be accepting and submissive, to bring comfort, peace and love. Give me the courage to be me and nothing more. Let me be an instrument of peace like the little rag-doll. My abilities are few;; use me as you see fit, Lord, wherever you send me into the marketplace, in silence like a rag-doll. As a rag-doll, I could do whatever is asked of me wherever I am sent or want me to be, in silence and prayer. I pray, Lord, take this tongue of mine and make it still. Make me say only what you want me to say. My words must be Your Words."

--------------- --------------------- ---------------------

Mary Mc, a so-called friend said some hateful remarks about her nerves. Victoria prays she be given the Grace to forgive Mary and others who judge unjustly.

Victoria also runs into Joan H today who tells her she finally had an operation on her hip. As they parted, Victoria remembered, "I was to have prayed over her last summer but was not inclined to do so. Either I was unsure of God's Will or too much of a coward. Anyway, she didn't feel comfortable that she perform such an act."

Victoria then remembered she had asked Joan if she could pray over her for healing. She had said "NO."

"Well. There you go, eh! Victoria smiles: "I was right. All God's children perform miracles one way or another."

This morning, she is in agony over one of the young people living here. Oh! Why couldn't Jon be living with his own family? His story is a sad one to begin with having been taken from his parents who live on a Reservation, adopted out and away from his own environment. He hasn't come home since yesterday morning and Victoria is worried. He has no money unless he borrowed some. Where could he be? If only he'd call her.

She pleads her rosary for his safety to the blessed Mother Mary. She, in the scriptures, Luke 2: 48- 50 knows what it is like to worry about someone you love.

Being a 12 year old, Jesus, a bit peeved, said to Mary and Joseph, when they found him in the Temple, "did you not know I must be about my Father's business."

Is Jon about his Father's business? Who am I to question?

"Please Mary, intercede for me and keep Jon safe."

--------------- --------------------- ---------------------

Victoria drops in at the Notre Dame Convent to visit Sister Bernie who is not around, so she sits in silence in the chapel for a little while.

She meditates, finding herself feeling very, very small. A vision of a lamb comes to mind; a little lamb, bleating and bleating. It seems lonely and lost even though there are other sheep around. As she meditates Victoria sees herself as that little lamb, lonely and lost. Then, all of a sudden, the shepherd is walking toward her. He picks her up and holds her in his arms, very tenderly and lovingly as he walks along. She is alone no longer.

Her vision changes; the shepherd becomes Jesus who was chosen by His Father to become a Sacrificial Lamb on the cross to save all the little lost lambs. He then becomes, in her vision, the kind and gentle shepherd who asks the little children to come to Him. Matthew 19: 13-15

--------------- --------------------- ---------------------

*"Her vision takes on a whole new dimension as she sits in her little red sailboat. She becomes the lamb He is carrying. She knows she is a sinner and will stray far and wide on this long voyage as she goes through the storms and harsh winds. She is lonely in her little red sailboat, lost and afraid if she chooses to go her own way. Doing His Will can be so difficult."*

--------------- --------------------- ---------------------

These words come to her as she sleeps:

"If you don't approach God first it will not be done."

In what way must she approach God and for what reason? She guesses she must approach God through prayer in silence to hear his Word. The thought about something is not a prayer. It doesn't matter what the thought is "Seek first the Kingdom of God and His Righteousness and all else will be added unto you." Matthew 6:33.

So many words, sentences are coming to her. It would take another book to write them all down. Just don't know what to do.

She prays: "However do, Lord, with me as You Will. I am sitting on the potter's wheel; the potter is at work within me, molding and shaping me into a new and better person, sinner though I am. God, our Creator is the Potter. Isaiah 64:8.

How exciting; she can't wait to see the result.

Sitting here writing these words, she sees out her window the silent snow falling. All is calm and still. The world is somewhere out there, rushing into frenzy and into more and more tragic trouble. But her world, within and all around her is silent and calm. Each little flake trusts in our Creator's Will knowing where it will fall. This soft snow- fall is not a raging one like her life up to now. She'd like to think that the white scene before her is reflecting this new change within her.

--------------- --------------------- ---------------------

Last year, Maria, a girl from the Correctional Centre, moved in to join the other young people who live here. She stands out in

Victoria's mind because of an article Victoria had read in one of the weekend newspapers.

A young man, also Native, who had supposedly killed someone, was sent to a Mental Institution. Victoria mentioned having read the article to Maria while she was here, since she also is Native. She stated that he is a good friend of hers and that they are in touch with each other. Victoria somehow felt she must meet him as she believed he is innocent of the crime. She suggested to Maria they go to see him. He phoned Maria collect at Christmas but by this time she had left to live at Grace House for Women. After New Year's Day Maria phoned Victoria and told her she was going to go and see him on Tuesday. Victoria told her she would take her if she could get the car. She was to come here the night before but didn't come.

That same day, Tuesday, Victoria's son Matt and his girlfriend went into the city with Jack. They phoned during the morning and asked her to meet them for lunch. At the bus station on arrival, she saw a bus going to the city where the hospital is.

"Should she take it; was it God's Will?" It just didn't seem to be the right thing to do, so she didn't go. The timing was just not right. However she began to have scruples and felt bad about it.

"What if it was God's Will and I disobeyed Him," she berated herself.

She met Jack and Matt for lunch. Although she worried about it she remembered she had no way home. Her Faith in a higher Power sustained her.

A letter arrived for Maria and Victoria phoned to tell her. Again there was a discussion about going to the hospital. A storm came up so I mailed her the letter. Many opportunities arose but always a good reason for not going.

Then like a bolt of lightning it hit Victoria. She wasn't to go. No! She was just to pray for him, not go to him physically, but spiritually. Matt 11: 28-30 was the scripture that came to her at Mass. A great burden was lifted.

Someone at the Mass gave her an Exorcist Prayer. She privately prayed it for some time. This reminded her of the scripture of the man who met Jesus on the road and asked Him to pray for his servant who was dying. The man said, "I am not worthy that you should enter under my roof, only say the word and my servant shall be healed." Matt 8:8, 10, 13. Jesus said, "Oh you, of great Faith, your servant is healed."

She never heard from Maria again. "God works in mysterious ways, His wonders to behold."

Victoria attends Servants of the Light prayer meeting at the church. Two priests, Frs. Kough and Pucci are in attendance. Without permission or plan from the priests she walks to the podium and begins to speak.

She believes the following words she speaks are from the Holy Spirit:

"My children, come to the base of the mountain. Stay at the base of the mountain and do not be afraid. Climb up the mountain to the top; then sound the trumpet. Sound the trumpet into the cement jungle, into the streets, into the market-place. Bring the lost teen-agers into your homes. Tell them about Me. Tell the elderly who are so sad because they do not hear about me anymore. Do not be afraid. I love you very much. I need you now more than ever"

The priest comes to the stage after Victoria goes to her seat and said loudly to the full church.

"Victoria Adams, these words you just spoke are not for these people; they are not ready to hear them yet. They are for your ears alone."

She gets up from her seat and runs from the church, crying. She just can't stop crying. For a few days she is very despondent. Then the words come to her:

"May the Peace of the Lord be with you always and with your Spirit."

The comforting words keep repeating over and over in her heart.

A friend who was in the church at the time comes to visit her and listens as she still cries.

Thank You, Praise You and Bless Your Holy Name, Sweet Jesus."

--------------- --------------------- --------------------

*"What would she do without her little red sailboat to take her to the land of wherever? As she sits she begins to meditate on a scripture Luke 5:1-11. She is aware of all the water around her, it looks so inviting."*

--------------- --------------------- --------------------

She meditates:

I am being brought back to the time at the beginning of my spiritual voyage when I had just gone through a terrible argument with my son Matt and Jack. I left the house in tears and ran to the water's edge along the lake. I sat down in agony of tears over the quarrel. As I sat there with the tears streaming down my face, I stared out over the waters before me. I could see the figure of a man walking on the water, closer and closer, then climbing over the rocks toward me. He then sat down bedside me.

I stuttered, through my tears, "Ppplleasse, dddoon't lllleeeaave mme tttooo ssssoon. YYoou jjjust gggot hhhere. She calmed down and spoke quietly, "Sit a while with me.

He spoke in a whisper, "Victoria, do not be afraid, I will never leave you. I will always be by your side."

We sat and said nothing for a few minutes and then He got up and began to walk back the way He came; down the rocks, walking across the waters and disappearing from sight far out over the lake. She sat dazed, overwhelmed, unable to move.

--------------- --------------------- ---------------------

*"With the rhythm of the little red sailboat and the spirit of the winds wrestling with the sails, the little sailor takes on a life and a mind of her own, captivated and memorized. Her spirit lifts. She is buoyed along with the powerful movement of the tides as the sails finally take control. She moves to the bow of the little sailboat. Holding on to the mainsail she stands with legs apart, the winds pushing against her body. Her heart soars and sings an "Ode to Joy."(Excerpt taken from 1st Book of Trilogy, Page 101)*

--------------- --------------------- ---------------------

While attending the 20th anniversary of the Charismatic Movement in the Catholic Church, (very similar to the Pentecostal Church), Fr. Peter invites them to come to the altar to accept a wooden witness cross. It must be worn everywhere and at all times to witness to Jesus in their lives. She could not wait to go up to receive it. It so reminds her of her mental meditation hugging Jesus as he carries his cross along the road to His death. She thinks about His tired and bloody Face with the crown of thorns on His Head. And so, she sees this cross she is about to wear as a symbol of that cross, confirming the Words she heard, "Yes Victoria, you must climb the cross if you wish to hug Me."

Leonard walks up with her and accepts the cross, as well. Such joy she feels as she receives it. She will wear the cross for the love of God.

--------------- --------------------- ---------------------

Victoria has a set-to with Matt about the cross she is wearing. He says she is crazy and that she is breaking up the family. Then she goes through the same thing with Jack this past week-end only a lot worse. He swears at her, calls her names, throws her books and bible against the wall, says he is going to divorce her, saying she is crazy and needs a head-doctor.

As he yells at her, a song pours out and keeps repeating itself in her:

"Peace is flowing like a river, flowing out to you and me,

Flowing out into the desert, setting all the captives free."

Love is flowing like a river......"

Again, Matt attacks her verbally in anger. She understands how they feel because they don't understand what is happening any more than she does. They are afraid of what is happening, she doesn't know.

Leonard came to visit yesterday. He said he had to give the cross back to the priest because he couldn't face the questions and what it meant to wear it.

--------------- --------------------- ---------------------

She prays for the strength and courage she needs to go through whatever she is called to do; wherever she is called to go. It's so very difficult.

She opens her bible and prays her rosary; meditating:

"And so I must continue; I must prove them wrong. My Faith is being tested now and I can't give up. May the peace of the Lord be with you and with your Spirit." These are the words which keep repeating themselves over and over again. I am being given the gift of peace during this trying time of the testing of my faith.

--------------- --------------------- ---------------------

### April /87
Her sister, Mary, in another month, will be a University Grad. WOW!

This reminds her of her strong desire that she and Jack must move to N.B. Perhaps fasting would help. They could look for a house while they are in the Maritimes or wherever God chooses to bring them. She believes Jack will find a job and they will be happy.

After much prayer, she decides to go to a priest and be advised about the fasting. He suggests she only fast at the promptings of the Holy Spirit. With this she stops fasting. Thank God she stops fasting for she ends up with a bout of pneumonia.

This is what came to her as she lay in bed listening in my poustinia of silence.

"So Lord, what will I write? I wait for inspiration, listening and unsure about what I am being told through the Holy Spirit."

Her prayers keep taking her back to the word "Lepers," the book she read about lepers and Fr. Damien a year or two ago, the story about St Francis of Assisi and his reference to a church called Damien. Her mind is in a whirl. She thinks about the talk she had on Thursday morning with Sr. Bernie and Agatha, and Sister's friend, Paul who had worked with the lepers. While there, Agatha, asked her to send money to the Leper Colonies. Is this what it is all about?

What am I being told? Am I imagining that if Jack doesn't move to N.B. and we stay here he could become very sick? Sweet Mary, what would Jesus have me do?"

Somehow, Victoria knows their old life is over and they must move on. Now what must she do? Should she share her fears with Jack??

One of the street kids comes to see her in her room as she lay sick.

She asks him if she should tell Jack and he said, "No, it would only frighten him and he would not believe it, anyway." So she felt at peace. It is only in silence that she can help Jack, her sons and others around her. She must be strong.

Victoria ponders a scripture story on the death of Jesus: "Mary, our Blessed Mother knew about her Son's death on the cross and she pondered it in her heart in peace and acceptance even though she as not joyous, of course, as she carried Him in her womb."

Victoria knows she is a sinner and, if she, as a sinner, must do God's Will, she too must remain silent and carry His Words from the Holy Spirit in her heart until the Truth of His Plan is revealed to her.

--------------- -------------------- --------------------

**May 3/87:**
She has been in her poustinia because of illness now since Friday May 1st. It is the first time she has spent more than a day in prayer. Although as yet this has not been confirmed by a priest, she knows that this is the Mission God is calling her to. She did not deliberately go into her closet of prayer as Catherine DeHeuk Doherty suggests in her book "Poustinia" but she knows that this is where she must be.

On Friday Victoria has a hard time settling down; she keeps jumping up and out of bed going here and there talking to this or that street- kid boarder.

Then a church member, Marg comes to tell her about the farmhouse for sale in N. B.

Jack comes to bed early and she takes advantage of the time and is inspired to tell him she wants them to move to N.B., and that she wanted to go to her sister's graduation on the 8$^{th}$. He calls her every name under the sun seeming to hate her more and more all the time. She then tells him she intends to take her share of the sale of the house and go down to live in New Brunswick even if he didn't go with her. They went to sleep hating each other but she was feeling very righteous about her decision.

"After all," she thinks, "I'm sure I'll make out all right by myself. I could open up a home for a number of reasons. I'm sure that is what my Mission is, anyway."

--------------- -------------------- --------------------

As she lies in bed still sick, the scripture revealed to her: 2 Corinthians 12: 7-10. There she is again, thinking she is worthless, nothing; just Victoria, the child from humble roots. She will make an effort to get through this life as simply as possible. She will never do anything great or even good except keep a home for Jack; just a simple housewife. She finds out who she truly is. The pressure is off; she need not try to be what she is not equipped for; to move to N.B. and start a home for whatever reason as she has been thinking and praying about. No! She must start over again. All the plans and desires of the past are swept away. She can begin anew, a clean slate. Praise God.

Now mind, there is much of the old Victoria still within her, but, through prayer and silence each day, she will be able to let her spiritual life clear away a little deeper into the pit of her soul and cleanse her even more.

The beautiful part about the past few days, as she lay in bed with this illness is, even with the onslaught of evil spirits buffeting, she is well cared for in such a peaceful way that she didn't even feel upset or running away. Many thoughts and imaginations sent to test her; silent thoughts coming and going and like the disciples on the road to Emmaus, Luke 24:13, the answers come to her. They explain each happening so she would know in what way they were being used to change her; with the use of the bible, silent prayer, the book "Poustinia and other spiritual readings.

So many thoughts causing havoc; lies about Jack, and his job problems since she is kept in the dark, illnesses like cancer, her mind telling her to leave Jack, unhappy about Leonard, and the street-kids she thinks she isn't treating right, who don't visit her while she's sick, all but one.

During all the time she spent sick in bed, though, Jack takes care of her and the household of kids even though he isn't feeling the best. Sometimes he surprises her.

She uses the quiet time to meditate on the lowliness and meekness of Jesus:

We could not relate to Him if He were superior to us, or better than we are. He was born in a manger and died on a cross. He still exists today within us after a thousand years if we only ask Him into our hearts. He is lowliness, simplicity and meekness; nothing to be afraid of.

As she reads this meditation and Scripture, 2 Corinthians 9-10 again, peace and joy fills her as it also explains what is happening to her.

She has just finished reading "St Theresa of the Little Flower." This book teaches humility." No one will have anything to do with us if we are superior to others. We must take the last place so that we can be invited to the best place. St Paul, in the scriptures, says that we must be weak because it is when we are weakest we can be made strong. We must be "fools for Christ" he says."

So now, her feelings change from inadequacy and inferiority to feelings of peace and joy, knowing that whatever is said against her is necessary so that she may become strong through her humiliation, weakness and embarrassment.

At this time Jack and she have five young people living with them, kids without a place to live. Feeling much better the next morning she goes out to the garden swing to pick up Jack's book. She is shocked and sickened to find cat turd between the book's pages; then anger takes over. That's showing real appreciation for all that she and Jack do for these young people. Then her heart softens and she can only feel sadness.

"Yesterday, with Sheryl taking Susan's clothes and $10.00, the things that Marg said to her that hurt so and the one who placed the cat turd into Jack's book; all these things she lifts up in prayer, asking that they be touched and healed; using her pain and suffering to heal them. Our Father; forgive us our trespasses as we forgive those who trespass against us. And lead us not into temptation but deliver us from evil. Amen." I love you Lord."

It is all clear now. All these evil things happen to teach, test and to bring about healing.

--------------- --------------------- ---------------------

*"She, in her little red sailboat drifts along in the soft breeze and meditates in silence, sad, tearful; not quite sure what's happening. Where, Oh! Where is the love?"*

--------------- --------------------- ---------------------

Feeling better this evening she and Jack take a walk to the lake. On the way Jack remembers he has to make a phone call. He returns home and she continues her walk. She is in a tearful mood. Is this why Jack leaves?

When she gets home she lies down for a rest and all she can do is cry.

What is the matter with her? What's the matter with her? She thinks she is going crazy? She is in so much pain. Memories of visits to doctors over the years are flashing in her mind; doctors saying there is nothing wrong. "It's all in your mind, dear." Is it all in her mind? So why is she in so much pain? The doctors had made her so upset by that diagnoses. It seemed the Dr. wouldn't look any farther into possible physical illness. Victoria wants to go and tell her how upset she is.

She begins to pray the rosary and falls asleep. When she wakes up, she decides to phone the doctor for an appointment. She feels a great chill go through her confirming it. She feels a great relief knowing she would like to forgive all the other doctors of her past; those who never believed there was anything wrong; just that it was all in her mind.

"Perhaps," she thinks, "that's what my Lord and Saviour wants for my healing."

--------------- --------------------- ---------------------

Good news! The doctor finally listens and recommends Lithium for Manic Depression. Even though she has to be monitored once a week at the hospital for as long as she is on this drug, she feels much better with the decision. She also makes an appointment with a nutritionist who does some testing, and finds out she has a chemical imbalance problem, and recommends Swift Herbal Multivitamins and Minerals.

Victoria believes, in Faith, all these recommendations are necessary for the healings within her body, mind and spirit, but she must be patient. It does take time for all these methods and drugs to work, after all. God works in wondrous ways, His wonders to behold!

With all this happening to help her she must stop this crying and feeling sorry for herself. She realizes it must be very hard on Jack, her boys and the street-kids.

The cleansing of the soul is forgiveness. It's another step in her spiritual growth. More sinful faults revealed in love. Sure takes courage to face them. This time it still hurts but not as much. It did not grate as much on her sensitive nature. His Grace is sufficient to ease the pain, the pain of criticism of the truth about her, good or bad. She is thankful her faults are not revealed all at once. It would surely kill her. The veil is removed like an onion peel, piece by piece, and like an onion, the tears flow. However, there are fewer and fewer tears all the time. "Those who sow in tears reap in joy" the scripture says, and so let the tears flow as long as they are of the Holy Spirit.

--------------- -------------------- --------------------

*"She is thankful she is alone in her little red sailboat where no one will see her tears."*

--------------- -------------------- --------------------

## May/87

She writes her spiritual visions, meditations and thoughts while in her Poustinia:

I am still wearing the wooden cross. When Jack and the boys see me, they become very angry. So, when I take it off and lay it on the table, Jack picks it up and throws it away. I pick it up and put it on again.

As I think about it, all that is necessary in the wearing of the cross is to allow me to have the following powerful meditations; first of all, because it is a witness to Jesus Christ and my love for the Blessed Trinity, Father, Son and Holy Spirit. It represents, to me, not just a symbol, but all the other symbols of death that kill, by those who have no respect for life. One example; the wood of the cross was used by those who killed Jesus Christ.

A few days before I was given this cross, the meditation I had was Jesus carrying the cross and, as he crawled along toward Calvary I imagined running to Him and giving Him a big hug. He was dirty, sweaty and bloody but that didn't matter, I still wanted to hug Him. I even saw this woman climbing the cross to hug Him there.

"Oh my glorious Father in Heaven, my Jesus, the beautiful Sacred Heart of Jesus and blessed Holy Spirit, consoler and comforter, stay with me always. Blessed Trinity, have mercy on me, a sinner. Hail, Holy Mary, Daughter of God, Mother of Jesus, Spouse of the Holy Spirit, Pray for me."

This is the same month and time, May /82, she attended a Women Aglow Pentecostal Retreat that changed her life.

--------------- --------------------- --------------------

*"She, in her little red sailboat begins her mystical voyage with, God the Father, Jesus Christ, the Son, the infilling of the Holy Spirit within her mind, heart and soul and she is "born again.""*

--------------- --------------------- --------------------

She meditates in silence this morning with powerful words speaking loudly to her: "reveal in writings how biblical scriptures affect our lives and speak to us even today".

And so the following:

In the New Testament, quoting the scriptures, if we follow those teachings of the ministerial life of Jesus; in the second year His Ministry, after His battle and temptation with satan in the mountains, He went to where John the Baptiste, his cousin, was baptizing with the waters of the River Jordan. The Holy Spirit descended upon Him in the form of a dove and John baptized Him with the waters of the Jordan, Book of Acts, Chapter 1. And so it is even today.

He, as we are, was tempted by the devil to follow him instead of God, His Father and ours. Matt. 34:4. After He chose His followers, they also had to be baptized and ask repentance for their sins. Unlike Jesus, they, as we, are sinners because of original sin and so must repent until the end of our lives.

It is when we repent and humbly ask Jesus for forgiveness He becomes one with us allowing the Holy Spirit to be released in us. It is then we receive the Gifts of the Holy Spirit to be put to His use as He Wills.

Like Jesus' Apostles at the River Jordan, we too were baptized in our many church denominations. But we, as babies were not aware of this happening. Because we were babies, we were not able to make a personal commitment to Jesus as the Apostles did. There are millions of people out there who were baptized, received their 1st Communion Host and confirmed through their church but have not accepted or believe in the Blessed Trinity, Father, Son and Holy Spirit, in the true sense of the word.

Blessed Trinity, what are You trying to tell me that my thick skull cannot grasp? What is the matter with me? Am I being disloyal to the Catholic Church? What are you trying to tell me? Is this what my life is all about; my life's story? Is this my theme? How, as a child, I was baptized and brought up in the Catholic Church but their theoretical teachings drove me and so many others away rather than doing the work that Jesus intended; to bring us to Him and our Father, as He did when He ascended into heaven after dying on the Cross. While He was on earth he taught the Apostles this prayer, "Our Father, Luke 11:2-5." This also we were taught to pray but, tell me, who believes in Faith, that this is true?

She repeats: In the Catholic Church at the age of 6 or 7 we make our first communion so that we can receive the Eucharist. We study the catechism, then, at the age of 12 are confirmed to join the church. Where does it go from there as far as our souls are concerned, may I ask? What happens along the way? What is the church not doing that it should be doing to save souls? Oh! Will I be excommunicated?

--------------- --------------------- ---------------------

Victoria and Jack go for a walk along the lake. She again finds herself saying to him, as he talks about finding a job;

"You won't find a job until we do what God is asking of us."

As he starts to walk away from her he tells her to shut up. Then he turns around and asks her, "What is God's Will?

"Jack," she says, "we have the house on the market, you don't have a job even though you are trying to find one in the Manufacturing Sector or wherever you can get one, but over and over again I feel so strongly we must sell the house and move back to New Brunswick. I know we will be looked after. We must go on Faith."

He yells, "why should I believe that rot?"

Yes, that's true. Since he doesn't believe in God, why should he believe? His eyes and ears are closed to the spiritual world of faith. Anyway, isn't she crazy, as he accuses? Perhaps she is!

Why does it keep coming back to her, "move to N.B. in faith" if it's not true? She knows that, through the scriptures she is justified, in faith, to believe.

How joyous she feels as she repeats again to Jack what they must do; sell everything and go to N.B. in faith! He calls her crazy, she's dreaming and imagining things. He tells her to come down to earth and start doing something constructive with her life instead of going around in a dream-world all the time.

He screams, "I have no intention of going back to N.B.; I hate it there and I know what's best." He curses and swears at her.

She persisted, "what is planned for us there is what's best for us."

He, in no uncertain terms, tells her to shut up. He did not want to hear such stupidity.

Through all the terrible things he is screaming she could not have felt happier. Such joy fills her heart knowing she is right. She runs from flower to flower through the garden by the Lake in her joy knowing without a doubt that what she is saying is true. He could choose to think what he pleased. In her heart she knows she is right.

--------------- --------------------- ---------------------

*"She has that joy, joy, joy, joy down deep in her heart as she sails along in her little red sailboat knowing not where she is going but trusting in faith all will be well."*

--------------- --------------------- ---------------------

Arriving home she writes:

All our married life Jack has made me feel persecuted and hated; has physically abused me and has insulted my intelligence with his actions and tongue, and it gets worse if I try to defend myself. Is it all my imagination? Somehow, I hope and pray the truth will be revealed and I am healed of my fear of him, male intimidation and sexual harassment.

Last night Jack took off for his club and a strong urge to pray came over me. I could hardly prepare dinner it was so strong. I could not even talk with Frank, one of the kids living with us. I just had to be left alone. However I did get through dinner and all the boarders went out for the night. Left alone I went to pray in silent meditation.

While praying, biblical scriptures come to mind; doubting Thomas had to see the nail marks on Jesus' hands and feet before he would believe, the unbelieving Pharisees and Jonah swallowed up by the whale for not obeying his Calling. Then the words, "when two or three are gathered in My name, Jesus promised, prayers will be heard."

She calls Rhonda and Alan to pray for them. I thought for sure something was going to happen to Jack that night. He arrived home none the worse for wear; a bit drunk but I expected that. I continued to pray.

--------------- --------------------- ---------------------

She and Jack go to Mass the next morning and all of a sudden, she gets the same urge to shake she had suffered through the Legion of Mary meetings a year ago. She again goes through the stupid ego trip when she thinks healings are going to happen. However, she knows, through prayer and the prayerful people in the Church she will gain the strength to get through this. As she walks down the aisle to receive the Eucharist a great desire comes over her to shake again. She begins to pray the Exorcist prayer:

"St Michael the Archangel, defend us in battle, be our safeguard against the wickedness and snares of the devil." Thank and Praise God, in the Name of Jesus, she is able to get through the rest of the Mass in peace.

After Mass they have breakfast at a restaurant and then drive into Toronto. Strangely they are able to converse without attacking each other. He even listens to her and answers without insulting her intelligence, as she discusses the news of the day. This harmony lasts for some time except when he is drinking. She would like to think that whatever evil that is attacking her, has been sent to the depths of hell that Sunday morning as she controls the shaking through prayer. Alleluia!

"Maranatha, Come Lord Jesus." Her mantra sounds within her as she prays. "Jesus, I'm filled with the burning of Your Love, sensing Your Presence within me as I meditate on the scripture; Luke 24: 13-18; the disciples meeting Jesus on the road to Emmaus, sharing with them what was important to know."

The words of the scriptures are always revealed to her; giving her the Graces to open her spiritual eyes to see. Praise the Lord.

--------------- --------------------- ---------------------

*"She has more control over her little red sailboat with the calmer winds and tides, as she contemplates the scriptures in her Holy Book. She lets the winds whistle through her sails, taking her, in Faith, she knows not where."*

--------------- --------------------- ---------------------

180

More trouble with Cheryl again; she comes home for her things and Victoria tells her she could stay but under certain conditions. Jack interferes and tells her what he expects of her; he let her know he is unhappy with her behaviour, her late hours, not paying her rent and so on. He tells her he would give her a two week trial period. She says nothing. Victoria goes to her door to pick up the rent money. She said she didn't have it until tomorrow. She then said she was going to go out to a pub for the evening. No sign of repentance at all even though she said she wants to try again. She says she has no place to live. She still makes plans to go out for the evening.

"How can you go to pub if you are broke? The decision is yours whether you stay or go."

Victoria hears the front door close as she goes to the kitchen. Cheryl quietly leaves never to be seen again. Victoria is left very depressed about the whole scenario.

Then, there are their own problems; money is becoming scarce, bills piling high and collectors hounding her since Jack is never home to answer the phone.

She prays, "my suffering, Lord, brings me closer to You. I want to suffer to become weak so I can become stronger."

She gets the feeling that they must live in poverty; sell everything, furniture and all. Is that what they must do? They must sell all and move to N.B. in faith. The feeling continues within her that they will be brought very low and, that is exactly what seems to be happening.

Praise God. Jack has no job and having a hard time finding one. Money is scarce and when that is gone all they will have is what the kids are bringing in.

She prays, "Oh Lord, such joy fills my heart when I think of what is in store for us. I am praying unceasingly, Lord, a prayer of the Holy Spirit in tongues deep in my soul. I still don't know whether you want me to Fast, Lord or when. I'm still waiting for Your Word."

Victoria wonders how she can be so happy when things look so hopeless. She is being led to begin a Fast. It will be one full meal a day for now. She takes some time off to go to the bookstore to buy a book, "Journey to the Lonely Christ," written by Catherine DeHeuk Doherty. She is the author of "Poustinia," a prayer life of meditation. She believes she is being Called to follow this spiritual way of life according to God's Holy and Blessed Will.

She was given a wooden cross from a priest and has been faithfully wearing it but, for some reason, it is now becoming heavier since she added beads. In the beginning she was exalted to wear it, now it is feels a penance.

She prays, "Jesus, what are you trying to tell me?" "Speak, Lord, your servant listens." 1 Samuel: 10. "Oh Lord, my mind is not working very well. No meditation sounds in my soul. I am a small child, a rag doll; tossing me around. I never know what will happen next. Oh! Mary, help me. Help me to place myself without fear in His protective, trusting Hands.

A prayer continues to our blessed Mother Mary.

"Remember, Oh most blessed Virgin Mary, never was it known that anyone who fled to your protection, implored your help or sought your intercession was left unaided. Inspired by this confidence I fly to you Oh, virgin of virgins, my Mother; to you, I come, before you I stand, sinful and sorrowful. Oh, Mother, of the Word Incarnate, despise not my petitions, but in your mercy, hear and answer me. Amen!"

--------------- --------------------- ---------------------

This evening she got really angry with Jack. He just will not listen when she tells him they must move back to N.B. since this is God's Will for them. Again she is called to a Fast. Is the Fast to bring about a change of heart in Jack or is there another reason?

She prays: Oh Holy Spirit, I pray you will help me. Answer; "The Holy Spirit will teach you all things and remind you of all I have said." "Blessed Holy Spirit give me a double portion of your Power," sounds in her heart and soul. She knows these Words from Scripture, 2 Kings 2:9 repeated as a Mantra, will give her the strength to keep going until the end.

They make plans to go to Musquash. on July 1$^{st}$ leaving her there for the summer. Jack says he will go if he finds a job. She prays they will both go, find work and a place to live there. Praise and thank God.

Why does she continue to believe their lives will be in N. B. She goes on a 3 day fast for confirmation? Why are these thoughts harassing her?

The fasting only confuses her more. She continues to wonder what it is all for. Is it for answered prayers, a job for Jack, their move to N. B.; a dying to self? She must protect herself from evil attacks;

Ephesians 6: 10-17. She thinks it might be wise to find a spiritual director to guide her through this very difficult time.

She recalls a dream she had; she is leaning against a tree very pregnant. She likes to think she is pregnant with Jesus within her womb; carrying Jesus in her heart and soul. She knows He will be with her always. No, she doesn't need a spiritual director. She believes she will be led through silent prayer, biblical readings and fasting. She had discussed this with a friend, Gary who said the saints did not have a spiritual director but were led through silent prayer. She believes this even though she knows she will never be a saint, not with her sins. It finally sinks into her stupid brain that to continually badger Jack about going to N.B. will only make him more angry, furious and obstinate. So after pondering all these things in her heart she decides to just be still and wait for God's Word for her. Psalm 46:10

Her fast ends!

--------------    ------------------    ------------------

*Her little red sailboat is stalled and stuck in a bay of seaweed not able to shift one way or another. Now what does the little skipper do?*

--------------    ------------------    ------------------

## June 87

Jon, the Indian boy, living with them, just left for school. As he left she begins to pray for him. She wonders if he should live with them should they move. "He must be here living with us for a reason, Lord Jesus".

As she went into her prayer closet today she began to feel very low. With depression taking over she is brought back over all the years in the past and it came to her that she never really succeeded in anything ever since she can remember. If she came to the point of success it was usually taken away from her. Jack has spent all their married life putting her down, insulting her, leaving her alone wherever they were, making her feel small, and humiliating her. She feels beaten. She is that old, shrivelled up woman lying at the foot of the altar; nothing left. She can't be brought any lower than she is right now; beaten, beaten, beaten. She feels she is worthless; no good for anything.

She now envisions herself standing next to the old woman, seeing the new Victoria replacing the old Victoria. She has no idea who or what the new Victoria will be or do but Jesus stands there too. The old woman disappears and the new image is now kneeling at the foot of the cross with a veil on her head as a bride. To everyone else she is a nothing. Such joy fills her heart; such a burning moves through her body like the disciples who met Jesus on the road to Emmaus after He rose from the dead. Luke 24: 13-15. She knew Jesus had more to tell her.

Another beautiful vision comes to her as she makes dinner. She sees a river flowing by, a bank and a break-water. The cottage, sitting close to the river has a gabled roofline and a lawn reaching to a peaceful bay. She see this as clear as day. She feels this is the house the Lord is going to give them to live in when they go to N.B. She feels there is a connection between this vision and what was revealed to her in her prayer closet today. Is this all her imagination? OOHH Dear!

She must keep on praying and fasting; if she does, maybe Jack will agree to their move to N.B. Scriptures brought to her while praying the bible are references to Queen Esther and her approach to the king in being able to change his mind about killing the Jews. "That's a great idea; she says to herself," I'll try to be humble with Jack and treat him so nicely he will agree to go to this beautiful cottage on the Bay.

--------------- --------------------- ---------------------

*"She, in her little red sailboat sails into a peaceful cove away from society's noises to rest. Off in the distance she sees a wharf, a little cottage with a front lawn, sitting close to the cove and reaching to the waters."*

--------------- --------------------- ---------------------

After studying the scriptures in the Old Testament and studying Moses' journey to the Promised Land with his people, "Book of Exodus," and then Joshua's commitment to continue the dangerous plight, "Book of Joshua," Victoria decides she will fast again.

She reads: Joshua blew his trumpet for seven days to knock down the walls of Jericho. Is she hearing a Word of Knowledge by the Power of the Holy Spirit to go on a fast for seven days? Is N.B. the home promised to them?

Then there is the scripture of Abraham who was asked to sacrifice his son. Abraham was determined to obey and God, in His love for him, let Abraham keep his son and gave him a ram instead. She knows she must fast and have faith.

The house is now on the market, but they have made plans with Jack's brother to use the cottage in Musquash Bay for two weeks in July. Being without work since April, Jack is not exactly enthusiastic but she's thinking positively that they will go. It is amazing to her that he is in such a good mood; so relaxed, happy and healthy. The best she has ever seen him. He is not drinking either although he could be easily swayed. They are both at peace, amazingly, considering their debts and everything going on in their lives with their sons, and the street kids who are providing a few dollars keeping them fed. Talk about the miracle of the loaves and fishes.

Waking up the next morning she is feeling groggy, weak and dizzy. She didn't even pray; and had a hard time getting out of bed but she wanted to go to Mass. She feels she must pray a Novena to St Jude, the Patron Saint of impossible cases for their situation. She must not let any doubts come in but it is so difficult. Perhaps the Fast is just for Jack to get work and not that they move to N.B. at all. "Oh Lord, I believe, help my unbelief."

Today is the Feast of Corpus Christi, representing "The Body and Blood of Christ" and very timely since she's on this 7 day Fast. His suffering and sacrifice on the Cross; Scripture; John: Chapter 19. She is overwhelmed by the vision she spiritually sees; living the scriptures in this present time; the bread and wine of life. The only guide is the "Word was made flesh and dwelt amongst us," John, chapter 1, the scriptures of the Holy Bible.

The Fast had continued for another four days and the pain through her whole body is excruciating. On the morning of the last day, a friend calls and wants her to go to an Opus Dei Recollection in Toronto. The time spent in prayer, the drive to Toronto and back is well spent.

On the way home she says to her friend; "Marlene, I can't help but feel I must move to N.B.

Their conversation seems to upset her. "No" she says, "you don't want to do that. You are to bring Jesus to the corporate world."

Victoria is left silent: the Corporate world; who does Marlene think I am?

She feels angry and discouraged. Staring in the mirror when she gets home she thinks; "no need to fast anyway and my Novena to St. Jude appears useless. I'm going to rebel and go out to a restaurant and have a feast of lobsters on Jack's income tax money. Why not? Nobody cares about me anyway."

The bonds are loosed; she now knows why she's fasting; so that Jack can find a job. She decides she'll go with him wherever, because she can witness to the Elite of the Corporate world who need Jesus in their lives. Marlene is right; Victoria must be content to remain."

But as the day wears on she begins to have doubts. She could at least have continued the Fast as God had asked her to through the promptings of the Holy Spirit. Why did she give it up? So many disastrous things can happen if we disobey. How she hated herself. It would not have hurt her to continue one more day. She turned in for the night a very sad woman; didn't even say her night's prayers. Jack, however, is proud of her.

She wakes up at 5:A.M. and it is a different story. A great joy floods her being as she lies in silence and peace. She is no longer alone. The lesson learned; we are all weak. She realizes she is weak to give up the Fast. But so is everyone else. We all fall and make errors of judgement. Oh! She praises God. She knows that in her weakness she is able to see the weakness in others, overlook them and forgive as she hopes they would forgive her. She then feels a great surge of love for God and for her fellow-man. It is in loving that forgiveness is possible. God is Love. Love is God. It comes right back to Him; one in three; the Blessed Trinity, the Father, Son and Holy Spirit who loves us. She is then brought back to the Eucharist, the Body and Blood of Jesus Christ, the Sacrificial Lamb who died on the cross for us. Love again; a sacrificial Love because love is a sacrifice, a giving of oneself. This love brings about a weakness which then allows Him to take the weakness within and brings about strength since there is strength in weakness. This strength is God; the blessed Trinity which shines like a light within and around her.

Yes, she realizes the spiritual bonds are loosed that held her to thoughts of moving to N.B. so that she can be free to accept the Will of God for Jack. Alleluia! Praise God, Bless and thank His Holy Name.

--------------- --------------------- --------------------

*"As she sails in her little red sailboat going she knows not where, she is content she is being taken care of no matter the weather she sails through."*

--------------- --------------------- --------------------

Back to the Street kids living with them!

They are always getting into trouble, it seems. Randy, and Julian, Randy's friend caused a car accident and Victoria feels she should go and talk to Julian's mother about it. Then there is Liz. Victoria asks her for permission to go and speak to her father about taking her back. She made the phone call to set up a time but the line was busy. All in good time, she guesses. So she is called to prayer and will know through the silence, what next will fall into place. She can then do as her prayers tell her or wait to see what door will open. She knows she is a servant to do God's Will without fear.

She prays; "please tell me what to do."

The words: "do not be afraid" speaks to her.

She went into her prayer closet again and prayed the Rosary.

--------------- --------------------- ---------------------

Concerning street-kids, Liz and Randy;

Liz's mother called in the afternoon and Victoria apologized for hanging up on her when she had called a week earlier. She was very angry that both her daughter, Liz and Randy, Liz's boyfriend, were living here. Ann had assumed Victoria would allow Liz and Randy to sleep together. Victoria told her she considered Ann's remarks insulting not only to both she and Jack who are looking after her daughter, but to her daughter, Liz, as well. Victoria didn't apologize but she was prompted through prayer that if she wanted to speak to Liz's father she must first apologize to Ann. So she did. Ann finally came over to see Liz. Victoria asked her if she could speak with Peter, Liz's father. He did not get in touch with her. She shall wait and see.

The day before yesterday around 5PM, no-one was doing their laundry. Since she knew the schedule; with Frank today and Susan on Saturday, she talked to Frank and asked him if he was going to do his today.

He said: "no, Jon is going to do his." "Sorry," I said, you usually do yours on Friday, please do so. Susan will do hers tomorrow"

She went downstairs and told Jon. He began to swear at her, shaking his fist at her and calling her down to the lowest. He said that she had hurt him and so many others. She said she was sorry, that she is truly a sinner and never deliberately intended to hurt him and loved him as a friend. She went upstairs quite shaken and upset and started to cry. She felt as if her heart would break. She cried and cried and cried. She could not stop. She wondered how she had hurt him as she hung her head in her arms at the kitchen table. Jack came in and saw her in her distress, crying and crying. She finally was able to tell him what happened and Jack went downstairs and told Jon off. He told him he had to be out of the house by Monday; that he wasn't going to have anyone hurt his wife.

Victoria was amazed and stopped crying thinking it was the first time Jack has defended her. Praise the Lord! She went to bed praying over Jon's behaviour. Was it the work of the Holy Spirit to help her see another side of Jack? Frank made dinner and kept coming to the bedroom to see how she was. He was so worried and concerned about her. Then Jon arrived and apologized. She smiled and said, "Bless your heart, Jon." It was such a beautiful apology.

She had gone through much pain and spiritual joy yesterday with the praying of the Rosary. Her prayers were not just for Jon, and for the two other native teens living with them, but for all Aboriginal and Metis of the Americas. She knows she is ignorant of the subject so all she can do is pray. She knows her prayer was heard. She prays again, "Lord, is it Your Will that Jon will live with us when we move; and his sister too."

--------------- --------------------- ---------------------

*"The female skipper need not feel afraid; she knows she is being protected no matter where the little red sailboat takes her. With the sounds of the wind, and the waves lapping at the sides of the boat, she sings, Be not afraid. I go before you always, come follow me and I will give you rest."*

--------------- --------------------- ---------------------

Oh Lord, "You are so beautiful to me" as the hymn goes.

In the evening twilight, the light begins to fade with all the colors becoming sharp and bright, the skies taking on a beautiful glow and splendor. It is almost ethereal, casting its own light outward. As she grows in her spiritual awareness it also takes on a sharpness, ethereal color and light in her soul which is almost too much to bear at times.

Victoria felt tempted to go to Jon and ask him if he wanted to invite his sister to dinner; as she was leaving the kitchen who should she run into but Jon. It was a spirit-led opportunity for her to ask him, and so she did. He was non-committal as usual but he didn't say no. She shall wait and see.

She then writes a letter to Liz's parents but at the present time doesn't feel drawn to give it to them. Liz met Victoria at the church for mass; she is a charming girl. After what Liz told her, Victoria knows her father is having a difficult time of it. She hopes and prays all will go well with them and she will be able to take a trip to Hawaii with him next Monday. She is unsure as to whether she should give Liz's parents the letter but, after much prayer and scripture reading she feels she must give it to them.

Jack's appointment for a job interview was supposed to be Thursday morning at 10.00A.M. She would not have had the car to go to Mass. The Readings today are scriptures, based on sacrifices to help others in the name of Love for God and neighbor. The following are the scriptures: Luke: 8- 26-39. She feels called to do a one- day fast after reading and praying on Mark 2:20, Isaiah 58 and reading "God's Chosen Fast." A Fast is a prayer form, as well. And so her Fast is for the teens living with them and that Liz moves back with her parents to love her and be patient with her as parents should.

When Liz's mother receives Victoria's letter she phones her; calling her down to the lowest for interfering and writing it. Victoria says nothing, holds her tongue, (and for her that's not easy), during Ann's tirade. A great peace fills her, giving her the courage to say what she has to say. She or Liz's father didn't like that. Yes, the truth always hurts and she is only a stranger looking after their daughter. As she talks to them a great chill goes through her and she is filled with peace. She prays the rosary after hanging up and a prayer, "St Michael the Archangel", (prayer for protection) sounds in her. Frank, a street-kid, joins her in praying for them.

Their prayer ends when she gets a phone call from the Real Estate Agent wanting to show the house and she knows all is well.

Dealing with young street kids in your home can be a challenge to say the least. Take yesterday morning for instance. Victoria wakes up to pray at around 6:00 AM, Jack got up to read his newspapers. She prays for a while longer and then decides to go with her coffee to chat with Jack. She notices one of the kids, the young Native, Jon did not get up for work. Jack goes down to see why not. Jon says he isn't feeling well. Knowing these kids and their ways to get out of working, she decides to take things in her own hands; not praying about it or anything. She goes screaming and yelling at Jon to get up for work, saying all kinds of stupid things. He very patiently and kindly said nothing and goes back to sleep.

Then there is Randy. Now he is a different story. A half an hour later she notices he isn't up either and his driver would be along any minute. He hasn't been pulling his weight around here, not working at a good steady job, nor has he paid his rent since he moved in a month ago. She is not upset he is not working; she feels there has to be another reason. He is a Born-again Christian and believes in God's Word. She doesn't know why but she feels he must take another path in life.

She suggests to him, out of the blue, "why don't you take off and hitch-hike across Canada. You won't have to listen to anyone, free as a bird, you would be."

He said "no" to Victoria, but Liz, his girlfriend, said emphatically, "Oh no, he could not do that." He gives her a funny look. The subject is dropped. Then the thought becomes stronger and stronger until it becomes a prayer. Victoria prays all afternoon and then falls asleep. When she wakes up these were the words that come to her:

Jeremiah 3:21
"Set up sign posts,
Raise landmarks.
Turn your attention to the highway, the road by which you went."

Then she goes to Mass and the Reading is Gen 28:10-22, the beautiful scripture about Jacob who had the dream about climbing the ladder to the sky to find God. He then went on a journey and after the dream he vowed he would return to Him if He protected him on the journey. This confirms her prayer in the Poustinia, (prayer closet) is right, a prayer in silence. Praise God!

This morning she has to tell Randy about her prayer reflections. He, of course, said nothing, trying to act casual and nonchalant about it all. She tells him his stay is over by the weekend. She tells him, he is not to work but hitch-hike across Canada, working as he goes. Let God's Will be done. Randy is a Born-Again Christian since he was a child so he believes in God's Word. And so she must fast. Hopefully Randy is also praying about it to confirm for himself. Who knows what will come of this.

Now getting back to Liz and her parents; she writes a letter to Liz and gives it to her. The Mass today is the Feast Day for St Elizabeth, Liz's patron saint. Liz goes to Mass with Victoria and later on in the day goes to her parents to apologize for hurting them by trying to commit suicide and other hurtful things she had done to them.

Monday, she and Jack drive to Hamilton where he signs up for French lessons for the job he hopes to get soon. The lessons are in the mornings for two weeks so Victoria must remain home to answer the phone in case there are any job interviews. This means she can't go to Mass in the mornings for now. Again, is it providential? Frank is joining her every evening for mass; this she is very happy about because Frank must come to some decisions too about his life.

Victoria also fasts on that day till the next day when son, James and daughter-in-law, Janet come to visit. She begins to have breakfast with them when she completely loses her appetite. She tells them about her spiritual and prayer life in the silence of the Poustinia or what is known as a "prayer closet". She did not feel she had to reveal any more details. She knows they wouldn't understand or believe, anyway. She just knows in her own heart the work the Blessed Trinity, Father, Son and Holy Spirit, is calling her to.

--------------- --------------------- ---------------------

*The sailing time in her little red sailboat, gives her the strength to" paddle her own canoe" with courage and strength in spite of what others may think of her."*

--------------- --------------------- ---------------------

The following thoughts she must write:

In the last day or two I have been noticing my wedding ring. It reveals to me Jesus who is my spiritual Bridegroom whom I search for in the marketplace, in the warm darkness and silence of the night. This is what He is asking this bride to do, to bring to Him, the Bridegroom, all His loved ones whom He loves with an unending love, all who would listen. And so I accept this Call, this ministry he has chosen for me no matter how difficult because He needs labourers for the harvest to grow; to harrow and prepare the soil so he can plant His Seed, His Word; street-kids; teenagers and Elders He brings to live and visit in our home to feed and nurture. They, in turn will spread His Word, I pray, in whatever way He chooses.

It is all falling into place; all the pain and darkness I had gone through, (Volume One) and when I first accepted Jesus by the release of the Holy Spirit I received in Baptism. All the difficult spiritual growth I have been through in the past 5 years with all those He has brought through my life has been a prelude to what I am now doing. During those years he fed me with consolation and joy wanting me to experience what the apostles had when He walked with them before He died on the Cross. He wanted to teach me His Word, prepare and ready me for the mystical voyage into the unknown he has planned for me. It was beautiful, exciting, challenging and well worth the pain and fear. He allowed me to go into the wilderness coming face to face with what appeared so evil during the time of physical shaking I went through with the Church Rosary Group to test and heal me of my ego; Leonard, who was building the basement rooms for the street-kids, coming on to me sexually, and many other frightening experiences which, without the help of my Saviour, God, I could not have endured. My spiritual life with our Blessed Mother, Mary, His Angels and Saints, here on earth and spiritual families who are my friends, protectors and intercessors, my breastplate and armour, ( Ephesians 6: 10 to 18) against satan and all evil spirits who roam through the world for the ruin of souls. As well, biblical, scriptural readings are always with me as a source of comfort and teaching.

Only as a humble and weak servant of Christ can I expect to win the victory of strength to conquer. It is in being smaller, weaker and more defenceless, like that discarded rag-doll, can I be a proper instrument in His Hands.

Oh Lord, I know You want me to go on a Fast starting with the evening meal. A Fast as a prayer form, for Randy, Liz, Frank, Susan and Jon, the street-kids living here, my sons, James and Matt as they continue their University lives and Jack and I. Jack needs a job, the sale of the house and I still have so far to go in all You Will for me.

"Lord, hear my prayer and let my cry come to You."

The answer I receive through my prayer: "I am the Lord, your God. You will have no other gods before Me," over and over again, the continuous prayer in my prayer closet of silence.

--------------- -------------------- --------------------

## July 8th/87

Victoria feels so sorry for these homeless kids that society has rejected. They have nothing without a Faith in a Higher Power to turn to. They are crying inwardly in fear, loneliness, emptiness and darkness all around. Like Liz in her room; no one to turn to, no one to love her. All alone, fear, anxiety, and loneliness gripping her.

Well, looks like the people who were going to put an offer on the house are now interested in another one. She is fasting and praying hard they make the decision to buy this one. She joins the community at the church in praying the Rosary before Mass with her prayer focusing on the sale of this house; that the people have a change of heart and will buy theirs. Not going to Mass the next morning, she continues the rosary just as the church community is praying.

During the rosary the chill goes through her; this, she believes is a sign her prayer was heard. She will continue to Fast. She has faith, Mary, her Spiritual Mother, interceded for her prayer request.

She prays: "Oh Lord, let this Fast be for Jack who needs to see Your Work all around him. Open his eyes and ears to Your Powerful Presence. In our activities, in the providing of food when he is not working and, except for Frank and Susan, no rent money coming in and yet, we are provided for. Jack, of course, resents having to help out and money is getting low. Praise God for His blessings because it's when we do without we become stronger as poverty builds character."

Jack, as yet, has not given anything up; still going to his fitness club and taking a two week French Course which he thinks he needs, as well, bar and pub hopping. All costs money!

Prayer-life and fasting continues. She has a feeling Jack is going to kick two of the street-kids out when he gets home. Anyway, at the moment there is a bad thunderstorm so no one goes anywhere.

Still fasting; 3$^{rd}$ day. July 10

She just hears the buyers are not going to buy the other house and have put an offer on this house. Thank You, Praise You and bless You; I exalt Your Holy Name. Joy that fills her heart; her fast is ended and she is consoled. She has a glass of orange juice, tomato juice and toast with honey.

Wonderful things have also been happening with these kids living here. After telling Randy he must not work but must hitch-hike across Canada, he phoned his mother and she agreed with Victoria. He then, on his own initiative, after missing work for 3 days gets his job back and has been working steady for 2 days. So now Victoria can tell him he can stay. She guesses the thought and prospect of traipsing across Canada, hitch-hiking all the way was too much for him. She laughs in glee. It's called reverse-psychology. And, to think she didn't even graduate from high-school. She can't stop laughing.

Continuing her writings on these "street-kids;" up to now none of them have heard about Randy's decision to go back to work and who is still going to move out on Saturday.

She goes back to bed to catch up on some badly needed sleep after her morning prayers. When she gets up, she goes downstairs to get Frank up to meet his girlfriend Maureen. She finds Jon lounging on the couch sound asleep. Coming upstairs, she tells Jack who didn't want to upset Jon. No help there. Thanks to her prayer to the

Holy Spirit who is always there to give her wisdom, she tells Jon exactly what she thinks of him; not mincing any words.

"You are nothing but a lazy bum. You show no appreciation for what people have done for you in the past. We expected more from you and you let us down. You have hurt us terribly. You will have to be out of the house with Randy by Saturday."

He said, "you won't get your 340.00"

She said, "I don't care about the money. You will leave on Saturday if you don't go to work today. Get off your ego trip, start acting like a 17 year old instead of 30 year old bum."

She then left the room, went upstairs, picked up her bible to read the scriptures and pray the rosary to have her talk with Jon established in heaven. Before she had finished the 3 decades of the Rosary, he had taken his shower and taken off for work. Now both Randy and Jon can stay with us until things are settled with the sale of the house and a job for Jack. Of course, once the house is sold we will have to move and they will all have to go anyway.

Frank is doing very well. He is going to mass with her in the evenings and has now started to take his girlfriend, Maureen. After Mass one evening she asked Victoria if she would join her in talking to her father. I was only too happy to do so. In their discussion she learned Maureen's medical history. Their faith in a Higher Power through prayer is instrumental in her healing and growth from a child who could not walk, to a young woman who can now walk. Now a conversion will hopefully, take place in that little family. She and Frank pray for them and, as a chill went through her, she knows the prayer is established in heaven. You, Lord, will play a major part in their lives from now on. Thank You, Praise You and Bless You, my Blessed Holy Trinity; Father, His Son, Jesus, the Healer by the Power of the Great and Holy Spirit. Amen!

--------------- --------------------- --------------------

*"The little skipper seems exhausted. She is weighed down with too much baggage in the little red sailboat. Does she really need all of it? She is praying she can remain buoyed up a little longer and won't sink into the depths of the deep waters. Where, Oh where is the love?"*

--------------- --------------------- --------------------

After fasting for 2 ½ day Victoria is very tired and sleeps most of the day. She is made aware through prayer she is not to say or write anything about her prayer life. It is to remain silent; just between her and her Creator, God. She continues fasting; now into her 4<sup>th</sup> day, wrestling with the strong desire for food until the end; with hopefully, the house being sold, Jack, a new job and the street-kids acting like responsible young adults or until God reveals other plans.

There is a prayer, "marsh-de-la-go" in tongues now sounding within. In the past it has sounded when her own human prayer is not working and she is given a stronger inward voice in prayer. It is a prayer in silence. She knows she is not alone and that He is with her through all of this. This promise came in scripture this morning: the judgement of God," Isaiah 35-54-55. She knows He loves her.

She feels peace flow through her and the strength to cope with the attitudes of the kids living here. She senses they don't like her. Susan left again this morning and didn't answer when Victoria wishes her a good day. She is feeling quite peaceful in spite of it all. These young people don't want to accept what she is bringing them. They think she's crazy. They talk about her behind her back, she is sure. She went to Liz on Saturday, who wasn't working, and told her,

"If you are so sick you shouldn't go to the party tonight."

She came back with, "I'm not sick, just tired."

Victoria then said, "Well, if you go to the party then you are neither sick nor tired."

"Ok", she offered, "I'll try and get a job."

So Victoria let her go to the party. He next morning she is again in bed. It is now 11:00 AM., a late night. Victoria woke her up and Liz volunteered that she has a job appointment at 1:00. She has been with them now a month and has only paid one week's rent. However, that's not what's important although it is a commitment all these young people have made. Randy is now doing well; up and working steadily, and now for Liz. She will not like what Victoria must say or do.

So continues the struggle with the street- kids. Maureen, who doesn't live here, went to Mass with her yesterday but her boyfriend, Frank, who does live here, didn't go. He is having a real struggle to follow his faith, believing he is not good enough no matter how often he sees God's goodness, mercy and forgiveness around him each day.

Victoria now has to cope with another issue with Randy. He has been stealing Jon's clothes. There are so many terrible things she must say to them when they misbehave. Trying to follow what one thinks is God's Will can be devastating. She knows God is all kind and merciful and yet here she is being anything but.

She must tell Liz she is lazy and doesn't want to work. And now there's Cheryl. What will happen to her if she kicks her out again because she isn't towing the line? She has to believe all are said to correct, chastise and teach them, to help them to grow up to be decent and productive citizens. And in the process find strong roots in their faith to help them. She needs help to discern that what she is saying to them is for their good even though it might hurt them as well as her.

She feels she is being "Called" to a Fast for 21 days as she rests this afternoon. Praying about it she realizes she is truly living some "warfare." The Fasting would be her armour. Yes, as she prays she knows something has to be done about the sale of this house, a job of Jack and agreeing to move to N.B., the street-kids; only God knows what else is going on in their lives and, last but not least, her own sinfulness. She praises and thanks Jesus for bringing this to her today.

--------------- -------------------- --------------------

*"In her little red sailboat, she has a life jacket and rubber wings to keep her afloat, a small gun to shoot flares in the sky to be seen at night, extra safety kits with dried food etc. for emergencies, a small rolled up raft, a rosary and a bible. It's home away from home.*

--------------- -------------------- --------------------

It's 9:30 A.M. and Victoria is sitting in her favorite chair in front of the patio doors that Jack, Matt and his friend installed. It is so good of them since they had never done that kind of work before. It brings the outside in and she can see nature; the green grass, trees, lush with growth and the flowers that Jack planted. It is raining and has been since she got up at 6 to say her prayers. She supposes it was raining earlier because Cruffin, their cat was soaking wet when he came to wake her up this early morning. The terrific heat-wave has been broken. Thank God.

As she sits here she's thinking about the words that jumped out at her during the readings early this morning, "endure the pain for me."

What does this mean? Yes, she does have much physical pain all through her body. As she ponders this and the sadness she feels for the kids that are living here, the phone rings and her spirits are lifted. It is a call from a friend she had met a few years ago. She goes on to tell Victoria her daughter is getting married and would like her to go to the wedding. She didn't make any promises considering their situation but did congratulate them; she sounded so happy and Victoria is happy for her.

As she continues talking with her friend she remembers they are Jehovah's Witnesses. She can't hold that against them even though she doesn't approve. Her friend was baptized in the Catholic Church. She thinks of the young bride, only 17 and thinks of all her difficult years ahead but one thing comes to mind, she hopes does have her faith and knowledge in the love of God no matter the religion, which then brings about wisdom which is her guide.

Anyway, she comes back to her chair and sitting there in silence, she ponders again the word, "pain." Her thoughts then bring her back to those words she had inwardly heard many years ago but had no idea of the meaning: "endure the pain for Me, Victoria." And so the picture reveals itself very clearly in her mind. It's the pain of these teenagers who have been living with them for the past three years and all the other goings-on in her life she endures.

She meditates:

"Endure the pain for Me, Victoria." Yes it is all falling into place. Their excruciating pain, their unbearable pain; all the pain they are suffering written on their faces, in the dullness of their eyes, on their unexpressive, unsmiling faces. All I see is fear, anger, distrust, hate, deceit; baptized pagans with dead souls; with no knowledge or feeling of the Love of Jesus Christ, their Saviour, The Son of God who is Love.

"Endure the pain for me, Victoria." Yes, Lord, now I understand what it is all about. Their pain I must endure for their sakes.

"Please, I pray, Lord, I ask You to put that pain to good use. And in the process help and teach me how to endure it, and how to help these young ones so that they will begin to find faith, hope and love.

Why am I crying? What thoughts are coming to the forefront of my conscience in thinking thoughts of enduring pain for others? I'm always crying. I am sitting quietly and sobbing quietly. So many hidden thoughts are causing anger and hatred within me. How can I help others unless I face the pain within my own hidden inner conscience? Maybe I am afraid of the pain His Love is eternally calling me to.

"Lord, Jesus, in Your Mercy, teach me to love without the fear of the pain. Give me the Grace not to be afraid of their anger, hate, deceit and fear. Give me the Grace to endure their pain with love. Is it because I must face my own pain? Is it my pain of the past? These kids want someone who can cope with their pain without judgement, with love, patience and compassion.

"Sweet Mary, intercede for me to your Son, Jesus to help me. I know what I must do and be but I can't handle it alone. Teach me, Mary. You endured much pain and suffering when your Son carried and died on the Cross. Teach me to be accepting of the pain of others as you did without fear."

--------------- --------------------- --------------------

*"Sailed out too far in her little red sailboat and appears lost. Where am I going? No food left. Waters around her look so inviting, ending it all. She hears the words, "be not afraid" echo in the winds."*

--------------- --------------------- --------------------

### Fasting, 6<sup>th</sup> day

Well, Victoria is still holding on at this 6<sup>th</sup> day of fasting. Seems like there is less physical pain then the last time she fasted this long. However, she is feeling quite weak. She knows, in faith, the blessed guardian angels will give her the strength to do the necessary housework.

She was invited to go to the Fatima Shrine in New York but for some reason everything seemed to stand in her way. She needed to be home to answer the phone in case Jack got a job interview. The sale of the house and to top it all, the weirdest thought kept coming to her mind that one of the street-kids would bring a truck in and ransack their house. With all these things on her mind she felt really guilty if she should go. Satan and his dirty tricks making her feel guilty. Was she being tested again or was it all in her mind? From the biblical Book of Job when he went through so much because he was attacked by the devil. It's a continual battle to hold on to the Truth and not to be swayed.

--------------- --------------------- --------------------

She writes:

Satan and his cohorts will do anything to stop us from embracing our Faith in God, our loving Father. We must be on the look-out continually for his subtle pranks to confuse us and lead us on the wrong path. Thank God for His army of angels and saints who protect us by surrounding us with their breastplates of armour and their shields of intercession; and especially for the redeeming Blood of Jesus Christ, in His Holy Name. In speaking the Name of Jesus in

Faith, the devil flees like the coward he is, very aware he can't stand and fight against it.

And so I went to the Fatima Shrine and spent many beautiful hours attending Mass, spending an hour in the Presence of the Blessed Sacrament where we received many blessings and graces. We then prayed the Rosary and sat through the Benediction. A very fruitful day all in all, revealed to me by the physical chills that went through me.

Oh, Lord God, You deserve our praise and love. You are so merciful and good to us sinful children. Thank you for the Blessings bestowed upon me this past few days.

--------------- -------------------- --------------------

TIME WITH STREET-KIDS:
After Victoria gets home and rests a bit, she spends an hour with Frank and his girl-friend Maureen.

Maureen has been hearing voices she says is the devil speaking to her, so Victoria and Frank pray in the Name of Jesus Christ by the Power of the Holy Spirit to cast out the voices from Maureen. Praise the Lord, Maureen did not hear the voices again. She has been set free. Victoria prays: "Glory to God, three in one, the Blessed Trinity. Thank You for saving Maureen from satan's chains".

The next day is not one of Victoria's better days; she is grateful it is a quiet one, spending the day in silence, praying, reading and doing housework as best she can in spite of the excruciating pain through her whole body. She also prayed the rosary for the soul of her deceased brother-in law Alex. She knows her prayer was heard by the chill going through her. "Thank You Mary, for your intercession," she prays. She is a bit down in spirits; still on the Fast, she has a great desire for food and takes it out on poor Jack when he gets home.

In the evening she goes to Mass with Frank and Maureen. Listening to the words of the priest she hears, "let go and let God and continue doing His Will." She keeps questioning whether she should continue fasting for the 21 days; looking for signs to tell her to stop. However it is not to be. When she gets home, she picks up the book and reads, "God's Chosen Fast" when she comes to the words; "declare the victory over every principality and power." Yes, she knows she must claim victory over satan in Jesus Name; which she did. Such a joy fills her as she realizes her prayer has been heard, confirming she has obeyed.

Earlier in the evening she had seen one of the street-kids, Liz leave with a strange man in a blue, souped-up car. Victoria began to worry. She goes to bed about 11:00 PM but can't sleep, thinking she should stay up to wait for her to come home. However she is very tired. As she lay there her legs begin to give her trouble. She gets the feeling something is telling her to get up and wait. She takes her rosary and moves to the living-room. Around 11:30 Liz and Randy arrive and Victoria is greatly relieved. Randy tells her who the man was and she feels better. She is sure she is being protected from fretting all night. Yes, our Lord, Jesus does things like that. Also she gets the idea her agony spiritually helped Liz?

--------------- --------------------- --------------------

*"What would she do without her little red sailboat to take her away into the calm waters to pray and to feel the presence and silence of creation all around her?"*

--------------- --------------------- --------------------

She prays her prayers and concerns are an intercession for these kids who live with them. They are all working now; all except Jon. Not sure about him but she suspects he is not. Randy paid her for one week of rent, Jon paid 100.00$ and Frank 140.00$. He pays up faithfully. She wishes she didn't have to ask for any rent from them. After they stopped taking the college students, most of these kids here are on welfare except for the ones where parents pay for their upkeep. When Jack gets a job she hopes we can take them in for nothing. They should work if they are not in school, however. Their lives are so unhappy because they have been kicked out of their parents' homes for one reason or another and need a stable place to live without having to pay rent; that's if they "tow the line" so to speak. Anyway, not for her to say; they are all in Your Hands, Lord.

She feels so drawn to intercede in prayer for all Indian, Metis, all aboriginal peoples. Lord, hear my prayer for them and let my cry come to you, in the Name of Jesus, by the Power of the Holy Spirit. Amen!

Victoria has stopped fasting so Jack takes her out to lunch; would have enjoyed it but Jack starts arguing with her about her desire to move to N.B. on faith. He begins to swear and anger rises up in her. She tells him, in no uncertain terms, to stop using the name of Jesus in blasphemy. She reasons to herself, that it probably was not the right time to bring the subject up but they have so little time to talk about issues or he doesn't want to talk, except about himself.

Arriving home she realizes she must continue her Fasting and pray in her Poustinia for as long as it takes to bring about what she believes is God's Will for them. She prays the scriptures from Isaiah, Wisdom, Matthew, etc. and prays the Rosary. She is more and more certain they must sell and move to Musquash where there is a winterized cottage for sale.

She coincidently happened to see the ad in the paper about the sale of this winterized cottage on the shore road in Musquash and couldn't believe it. She is convinced it is an answer to prayer. Jack can't deny it now, to moving to N.B. It is all falling into place. We will work together in Musquash. Matthew 19: 23-30. "Nothing is impossible with God."

--------------- --------------------- ---------------------

Victoria did not realize that when she gave Jack's gift of the locket for her birthday to Maureen, she would be so rewarded. Jack was furious, of course, but now Maureen is accepting Jesus in her life and will be making her First Communion starting Monday. Oh! Praise the Lord. Victoria is so happy. Maureen is retarded and ill; she really needs to know she has the love and support of Jesus in her life. The priest overlooked the fact she was raised as a Protestant and allowed her to become a member of the Catholic Faith.

Victoria let Frank know how proud she is of him that he unselfishly stayed with her as her friend, no matter how difficult it has been for him.

Sadly because of Jack's anger she had to ask Maureen to return the locket since Jack wants it back.

Praise the Lord! Later on, thank God, Jack has a change of heart. He returns the locket to Victoria, giving her permission to give it back to Maureen and this, at a time when she's feeling her worst. Oh! The unbearable physical pain she is suffering.

How she hates to say what she must say to Liz. Victoria must tell her she doesn't want her living with them any longer. She must go home to her parents. It is the best thing for her and Victoria must be firm. And all the terrible things she must say to Jack. She prays: "Oh Lord, take away this suffering. Endure the pain for me, Victoria "Yes, Lord, but give me strength."

Her pain is unendurable at the moment, but she gives thanks for the strength to endure it. The hate too she must endure. She asks herself, "do I deserve it? She prays, "Oh! Mary, Blessed Mother, I got so angry with Liz, trying to persuade her to apologize to her Dad so she can go home. Oh, Mary, my Mother, why must I have to say such terrible things? I know how much they must hurt because I know how much it hurts me to say them."

Victoria thinks Liz hates her, believing she says such terrible things about her behind her back, but she is willing to endure it if it will help Liz to listen to her conscience. Obviously she has done something terrible to make her father treat her so. She must move back home. She tells Liz that they can't afford to keep her since Jack is unemployed. She tells her she can stay here and put up with her tongue-lashing, go out on the streets or apologize to her father. "Oh, blessed Mother, I pray she will listen to her blessed angels telling her to go home."

Liz saw her mother today; a beginning. She can't look after herself. She needs her parents to look after her. Liz goes to her father today. He said he would take her back when school starts.

Alleluia! Victoria is so happy. She knows now it is God's Will that she speak to her as she did if it gets her home with her parents.

And last night she received consolation and vindication when Jack phoned the owners of the winterized cottage in Musquash, telling them he wanted to rent their place on the waters of the Bay for the summer. We have been going to Musquash almost every summer, where Jack grew up and spent his summers. It's a prophecy come true; "Your Word, Lord, is beginning to be fulfilled. We must move to N. B. in Faith."

2nd day of Fast:

A few mornings ago as she was resting, she received a Word of Knowledge, (one of the Gifts of the Holy Spirit), that the street-kids would be moving out soon. Sure enough, it is fulfilled right before her eyes, when Jack told Randy and Liz to leave. Jack is so good and patient with them; really surprising her. She did not expect it to come about this way. He sure knew how to handle them. The best way for her is to pray in silence while he did his thing with them. The house is gradually emptying so when the house is sold she and Jack can return to N.B.

Frank, who is still with us, needs a job. He hasn't worked in a week or so. Soon he will have to leave too. She has so much sorrow for the street-kids, so, as she reads the scriptures, especially the Psalms, she feels so much better. It saddens her that they don't realize that God's Word for them in their lives is their path to life's answers. Oh! If only they believed.

Well, Liz came to pick up her things today, and Victoria was not here to see it happen. She came last night to get her to change her mind but she wasn't here either. She was so upset with Liz; then she received a phone call out of the blue from a woman who owns a group home. How she got her name, she doesn't know; maybe through H.A.S. or Liz might have been talking with her. The woman told her, as they chatted, that sometimes being tough with them so that they will fall as low as possible to lift themselves up and make a move for change is necessary. Sometimes bad things have to happen before good things come about. And so, Liz is gone.

She is invited to a luncheon at Mary's, a C.W.L. member, for one of the Sisters from the Notre Dame Convent of the Parish Church where she attends. She phones Mary to tell her she would be late. Mary wanted to know why. Victoria told her she was fasting. She arrives and everyone has gone except Sister and Mary.

She stays with Mary a little longer as she wanted to talk to Mary about the fasting. She knows it is important Mary know because she has a great influence on everyone. She wants her to know she is fasting to bring about her move to N.B. She is witnessing to the power of prayer when this happens.

Arriving home, she ends her fast and she eats her dinner meal. During her prayer time later on in the evening she is blessed with a beautiful thought:

"I've received a Word of Knowledge that I need not be afraid, having to fight back, be on the defense any more. I am being looked after by my Lord and Saviour. I no longer have to be tough as I thought I had to be in the past. It is over. With the knowledge that Jesus and the Power of the Holy Spirit will fight my battles for me. He will protect me from violence, bitterness, hatred, anger; all the negatives that have been so much a part of my life. He protects me from evil. He brings me joy and beauty. I can now begin to learn how to be defenseless with His help. In my peaceful silence others can be helped one way or another. I don't have to be angry any more the Holy Spirit working through me. This is such a beautiful revelation. I know He loves me, a sinner. I believe my prayer to move to N.B. has been answered. I was filled with joy and peace. I hope and pray my penance and mortification through the fasting has brought about wonderful consolation and healing of my personality and I will be able to be that silent little rag doll.

If we accept Jesus Christ as our Saviour and Healer, He will heal us and save us from ourselves and in hurting others, as well; flaws in our psychic and personalities that we are not even aware of. In the past 5 years I have been praying I am gradually being molded in the being He wanted me to be when I was planted in my mother's womb. I must pray to be given the strength to continue to live a life of obedience and chastity; hoping and praying He will accept my offerings as His humble servant. For this I pray in Jesus Name. I also pray for others who need to know, love and serve Him.

--------------- --------------------- ---------------------

*She has been sailing in her little red sailboat for some time. She has food aplenty and stops at each harbour to use facilities. Her thoughts and prayers are being written and documented as she contemplates her life's voyage into the unknown."*

--------------- --------------------- ---------------------

She shares her silent prayers in these writings with others who may not understand these words unless their spiritual eyes are opened. But she writes them anyway; from the Scriptures, Luke 24: 13 -31; the Road to Emmaus.

"I give thankful praise for being able, in silence, to pray, talk, to share my doubts, fears and my pleasures with our beautiful heavenly and earthly families; the blessed Trinity, Father, Son and Holy Spirit, the Angels and Saints in heaven and on earth, the blessed Holy Family and through the direction and insight of the writings of the scriptures in His Word of Wisdom, the Holy Bible.

Because He loves us He wants the best for us and will never see us in need. He, of course, did not tell us we would not have difficult times to go through but he did promise, if we have Faith in His goodness, love and mercy, to give us the wisdom and strength to do His Will in our lives and in the lives of others to Eternity. I commit myself to His Will and do so with joy and peace knowing His way is the best way. We are all incapable of choosing right from wrong without His help; because of Genesis Chapter 3, the disobedience of Adam and Eve. However, He does not take away from us the right and freedom to choose.

Sadly, we do not realize that He leads us by providing the wisdom through the Gift of the Holy Spirit, bringing about intelligence and beauty, music, voice and dance, arts, sciences, business, government, the architectural marvels of the world, the use of power in every sphere and description; medicine and research, inventions, in every field of endeavor; the list goes on. All these and more He gives with His generous gifts of wisdom and love.

And so I say, Thank You, Lord for all those who, not knowing the Truth, are incapable of saying thank You. He is so good to us."

--------------- -------------------- --------------------

Victoria and Jack are supposed to go back home for a friend's daughter's wedding but they are Jehovah's Witnesses. This makes Victoria very sad considering the friend was baptized in the Catholic Church. She let them know how she felt and their answer was so upsetting.

She begins another fast and takes a drive to St Michaels Cathedral. She will take part in the Mass and an hour with the Blessed Sacrament. She receives no message during this prayer time. In the evening she prays her rosary and half way through the phone rings; a call from her friend. Her friend is so unhappy at Victoria's decision not to go to the wedding. Victoria is very blunt about her feelings that her friend and family joined the JW. As she talks to her friend on the phone the chill goes through her. She feels this is a confirmation of her beliefs. She hopes they will still be friends but, as a Christian, she believes it is important to make her feelings clear.

Her fast continues and with this she feels compelled to give thanksgiving for blessing and graces received that keep her going each day especially when she is feeling so low sometimes. She feels discouraged and prays for all her trials to end; Jack with no job, still belonging to a Club, the financial burdens, spending money on junk, taking money from the kids who are living with them. She hates taking their money but Jack says,

"No, it is good discipline for them to have to pay their way."

She hates taking their money. She would like to have them living here free until they are able to function on their own. If Jack would just agree to do God's Will by moving to N.B. she believes the house would sell and our financial troubles would be over and they could live as she believes is God's Will. She knows she is impatient and not "letting go and letting God."

Yesterday, after Victoria finished the rosary, she had a visit from the Real Estate Agent who had brought a couple through the house but who had put an offer on another house instead. Their offer was not accepted. She felt comforted by this visit and news that the couples' offer could still come through. She must still be patient.

Biblical readings keep flashing through her mind, like Jesus, dying on the Cross, praying to have this cup of suffering removed but, He knew God, His Father's Will must be done. Then she thinks about Mary who conceived without knowing a man and waited nine months for baby Jesus to be born; only to have her Son die on the Cross thirty-three years later, knowing that God's Will be done.

With these visions before her she is more confident. "Surely she can wait a while longer."

Are she and Jack unequally yoked? Before they were married, Jack had always believed that they did not need God or the church. He was adamant that all they needed were brains and intelligence; that they could think for themselves. She was so in awe of him she believed everything he said and did. However, she now knows it was not the church she was giving up, it was a belief in God, my faith in God. She believed the church and God were one and the same. This is not true. She still has her faith in God if she never goes to church. But in retrospect, the church as a family, she knows, helps to keep Faith alive. She knows now, she still has God. She has found Him, the Blessed Trinity; the Father, Jesus Christ and Holy Spirit and no one can take that away from her unless it is of her own free will. Still she knows in her heart He will always be with her. As she walks along the street these words echo in her heart and soul, "I will be with you always." This is true. He is with all believers, even those banned from worshipping in a structured building. He hears all in any way they wish to worship but they must humbly open up their hearts and souls wherever they may be; in their homes, in hospitals, on skid row, etc., anywhere at all if they just believe He is waiting at the door to let Him in. He will not impose himself on anyone, he is too polite for that but He is not deaf to the cries for help if, in silently listening in the night or day, all can hear Him calling to lay the burdens at His feet at the foot of the cross so that he can carry the burdens as He did by dying on that cross.

As she reads her past writings she begins to realize she is living with serious scruples; believing and blaming herself for all their problems, their financial state because of the lack of humility; blaming Jack, asking God to change him when really it is she who must. Considering everything she has been given since her days in poverty growing up how can she be so ungrateful! She believes she sees her faults so clearly; arrogance, aggressiveness, pride, and trying to control everything, ruling over all.

She talks to herself:

"What gives me the right to think that I'm better than everyone else; to tell Jack what to do with his life? It is so presumptuous of me to expect Jack to move to the cottage in Musquash, N. B. just because of my own strong faith in what I believe is God's Will for us. Only Your Will, Lord must be done not mine, whether it will be to go to N.B. to live or Jack get a job in his field in some part of Canada. Forgive me for being so full of pride. Teach me humility toward others. Help me to remain silent through the small, irritating happenings of daily life that irk me. Tie my tongue to the back of my mouth so that I will not utter unkind words no matter what is said to me from those around me. Holy Spirit, I pray, for the gifts of patience, mercy, humility, charity, joy, thanksgiving and especially love." Galatians 5:22

--------------- --------------------- ---------------------

*"The little red sailboat is stalled and beached; not knowing where it will go from here. It is in a waiting mode, sails lying on the sands."*

--------------- --------------------- ---------------------

She believes, in faith, our time here is coming to an end; the street-kids are all finding their own way. Frank will move to live with his grand-parents; Maureen still comes to visit as she is not aware of this. She comes on the pretense of wanting to go to mass with Frank and me. However Victoria had to tell her it was over between her and Frank. She didn't take it very well but she'll get over it. She felt let down that Frank had not said good-by. They never saw her again. But, that's OK! Good things happened during the time she spent with them. Randy goes off to live in the Teen Challenge House. Jon, the young Indian lad is still with us.

She must now prepare for the Fast on Tuesday. She doesn't know how long but she finds the headaches, without coffee, terrible. She seems to be always in a bad mood and that is not good. Fasting is a prayer and must be seen as a good thing. Perhaps I should pray about it first.

She is also considering not going to Mass since Jack doesn't approve. She must try and submit to his wishes.

Second day of Fast and she feels imprisoned. She is not going anywhere not even to church. She is enclosed in her home on Burbourne Dr. Everything is at a standstill. However, she feels a huge burden lifted knowing Matt's next university year will be looked after financially. Jack and she gets into a heated discussion about Matt paying his own way. Jack wants to use an insurance policy but she feels Matt, at 23 should pay his own way since they are broke anyway. Sure enough, after much prayer and fasting the answer comes; Matt lets us know his boss told him he could have a full time job if he wanted it. He said he thought he could also get a grant or loan. He must have told his co-workers and they went to the boss and told him Matt's situation.

She strongly feels the pain and suffering she went through with Jack, God used to help Matt. Submitting to His Will He can work miracles.

---------------  --------------------     --------------------

*"The little sailor in the little red sailboat sails on again; well aware of the mystical power steering her into the unknown."*

---------------  --------------------     --------------------

### August/87

It's been a year since I started writing and what a year it has been. If I did not believe there was a Mystical Power guiding and leading me I could not have made it.

Yes, it is true; life is difficult enough without added burdens. Lifting thanks to God. At least Jack is not drinking because if he were I would consider suicide again, but it's not to be. Without the knowledge that the mystical power of God has plans for me, I could not make it, with it I am given the grace to handle whatever is thrown at me. Every little bit of my life is in the hands of a Higher Power. However, if I forget to acknowledge this, the evil one will find a way in and then there is trouble aplenty. He will use all weaknesses to find a way in to disturb our peace.

Yes, I believe in Jesus Christ as the only answer. We will always have problems, difficulties, always be tempted and He will not take these away from us as we have a free will to choose. But he will help us deal with them even without asking, as He has proven to me so many times. We need not handle them alone as he truly loves us. He is Love. This Love is world-wide; from the streets of India, to the person and his riches, from the tavern to the slums; he is always with us in Love if we call on Him in Repentance.

Jesus will not let us down; He comes to us in Love. I thank you, blessed Mother Mary for interceding to Your Son Jesus for me.

But, how can I love and hurt at the same time? How can I love if I'm hurting?

Then the words came to me, "Love me more, Victoria," as I prayed to Mary. "Love me more."

Those are the same words that came to me 4 years ago when I started my walk with Jesus and accepted Him as my Saviour. Now I know what the words mean; I must love Him more than others, otherwise they will not be helped through me. He has given me the Gift of tough-love to help others.

Had a dream that James and Jack had set up a business in consulting in the Maritimes. That would be great. Wishful thinking, I'm sure. James is in the same line of work and owns a business.

--------------- --------------------- ---------------------

Victoria keeps hearing the words, all night long, ringing over and over again in her ears; "Move to N.B. in faith. Move to N.B. in faith? Move to N.B. in faith."

Does she go by herself? Where does she go? She has no car. How does she get there? Does she go to the Adams cottage? Does she stay until Jack comes down? Is this to convince him it must be? Does she have to force his hand?"

All these scriptures: Eclessiastes:1:11-25, Matt 6:25-34, Jeremiah 24:1-10, Isaiah 58: 1-12, Mark 11: 20-25, 1 Tim 6: 2-12.

If she must go to Musquash by herself, then she will go; she will be provided with the means to go. She will fast as of now.

It is strange that after she finishes praying the exorcist prayer to St. Michael the Archangel, Jack receives three different job interviews at the same time. What is happening? Was the exorcist prayer sounded to banish evil thoughts? She is very lonely for N.B. this morning; and so the reasons for the words, "move to N.B. in faith?"

A very nice respite; they receive an invitation to take a boat tour to Midland and the islands. They then go to the Martyrs Shrine for Mass where she prays for healings for both of them. She is compelled to make the sign of the cross on the forehead of a very retarded child that a mother is carrying. She knows in some way the child is healed through Faith.

Well, it is still persisting, "move to N. B. in faith." What does it mean? The place where she wanted to stay in Musquash is rented. She has no money to go by herself, then it must be with Jack. She will continue to fast and wait upon the Lord in silence of prayer. Isaiah 35 comes up in scriptures today. God's judgement will prevail.

Finally she thinks she has the answer. God has allowed evil thoughts to take over and inundate her with this belief that He (God) wants her to go to N. B. The exorcist and other prayers, the rosary prayer in silence and fasting are all strong weapons. Book of Job and Isaiah 35; God's judgement will prevail. Alleluia!

So Jack will get a job and perhaps they will buy the cottage. Still, she doesn't know for sure. Anyway, she won't have to persist in Jack going to N.B. in faith. God allowed her to have these terrible thoughts again and again and again. Poor Jack, he sure has had a lot of patience. Will she tell him about this? Praise God, it is over for now, but she is sure she will have to go through the same thing another time. She hopes next time she's better prepared through prayer to banish the evil thoughts attacking her mind. He uses every method possible. It is so hard to know. "Lord, I am willing to accept the scraps under the table; please keep your unworthy servant from the devil's onslaught, help me to recognize his presence. Matt 15: 21-28 according to God's Holy and Blessed Will. Amen!"

-------------- -------------------- --------------------

*"The little skipper in her little red sailboat feels very alone as she battles the storms. She must listen in silence to the words of her heart; let them speak louder the words of comfort she needs to hear."*

-------------- -------------------- --------------------

Victoria's mind is playing tricks on her as she ends her fast. She believes she is responsible for all their problems. Her arrogance and pride with Jack and probably with the street-kids in the past, and others, thinking she knows it all and, of course, Jack won't listen. So she fights back with a spiteful tongue. There are so many things wrong with her.

Jack is so much nicer to her when she fasts and when she said this to him he said, with a scowl, "that's because you're so much nicer to live with."

She rushes to her bedroom in tears believing he must be right; she is usually in a bad mood; it is only when she fasts she is nice. Then other thoughts take hold as she rests and prays her rosary. She knows she will be spiteful, arrogant and mean but she knows she will be given the necessary Graces to be able to cope so that she will be able to catch herself when she is aware of what's happening. She prays she will be given the strength and wisdom to be aware of her demons and banish them.

210

As she prays she begins to realize she must remain simple and silent; it seems to be the only way Jack is happy with her. She thinks perhaps that's the only way he will be able to control her. Why should she be the only one changing? She can't seem to help feeling some resentment. Why should she be continually punished for the problems in their lives, past and present as though she was the only one responsible? Is she responsible for the loss of his job as he is implying? She seems to be the only one being corrected, but she guesses she has the most problems. Yes, well, perhaps she's not submissive enough; always arguing with Jack. When will she ever learn?

Good news! Standard Life policy loan will be used to cover belated mortgage payment. Thank the Lord.

Matt is now angry with her because she has taken the poem he has written for his Grandparents' 50 Anniversary and made it a spiritual one. He calls from N.B U. to blast her. So what's new!

On the bright side; although the street-kids, except Jon are not here any longer, one of the street-kid's parents came to see her today, asking for healing for them and their families. Amazing, also, Frank's friend, Craig, who goes to a bible college, phoned and asked for prayers for Vickie, a friend. Lately, Victoria, who wants to rent a cottage in Musquash, has been thinking about a friend from Musquash, whose name is Vickie. A coincidence, I don't think so.

The next morning all is quiet and peaceful. She tries to get Jack to go to Mass with her today but he evades it by saying they will go in the evening. Of course there is no Mass in the evenings during the week.

Again she is getting the words sounding in her heart; "go to N.B. in faith." Why is this persisting? Why does it continue? Jack is talking about going for a couple of weeks' holiday; that's if he gets a job and not before even though the house might sell. Somehow, she believes there are other plans being worked out for them.

"Nothing is impossible with God. Blessed Lord, if this is not from You then take it away from me", she prays. "Please, blessed Mother Mary, hear my prayers in Jesus Name"

She gets a phone call from the local newspaper this morning. She had written a letter to them last spring. They want to interview her on the work Jack and she has been doing here, giving a home to street-kids. Considering this is spiritual work I am happy it is going into a secular newspaper. Praise the Lord!

Again, Jack and she get into an argument about taking a holiday in N.B. She is being snarky and hateful about it. Again, the thought comes into her mind that demons are again at work to cause an argument between them. Then, all of a sudden the words pop into her head, "Mary would not have argued with Joseph about taking baby Jesus to Egypt to get away from Herod." Matthew 2: 13-14. She then feels peace flowing through her and she is calm.

This morning Victoria is irritable again, all of a sudden, Blessed Mother Mary's image pops into her head and has been with her since. An amazing grace, for sure, to be silent and gentle. She knows it is nothing she has done. She is a sinner and has done nothing to earn it. It is a Gift from our Creator, God according to His Holy and Blessed Will. When she thinks of how she acts with Jack. OH! How can she ever be worthy?

--------------- -------------------- --------------------

*"The "sacred silence of the present moment" fills her spirit as the calming waters surrounding her little red sailboat, allows the prayers to echo from her inner being for others, and to bring her peace. She sings "Amazing Grace" into the winds."*

--------------- -------------------- --------------------

First day of Fast begins and she gets the feeling something is about to happen. She hopes the house will shortly be sold but where will they go? Is this when their move to N.B comes about? She has been hoping for so long to go to Musquash, even asking her other and James to help her out. There is a cottage there for sale and the old Adam's cottage is available next week. She feels so strongly they are to go there after house is sold. Jack though, is adamant he won't go until he has a job. So on hold again.

THE NEXT DAY

Things are not looking so good right now and could get worse, so will continue to Fast. Looks like Jack won't get the job from the latest interview or any of the others either. There is no money to pay the mortgage this month; Victoria wonders how much longer they can go on. Jack is very depressed. What if the bank doesn't cover it with the prospect of the sale of the house? Is bankruptcy inevitable? Perhaps a move to N.B. might be their only option. Since he won't believe her, in the end he may have no choice. This is how she sees it. "Lordy, Lordy", she berates herself, "I sound self -righteous.

She prays, "Please have mercy." "Give me the strength I need to cope with our situation and Jack's depression. I have a feeling he will get worse. He won't discuss anything with me. Help me to be gentle, patient, kind; to say the right things instead of harmful things. Cut out my tongue, let me be silent, Lord rather than allow me to say hurtful things."

It sure doesn't look good for the future.

Thank God for the scriptures. They always give her the answers she needs to cope; in reading them she always can find calmness and reassurance; almost as if they are speaking to her personally. She has no choice but to endure the pain, the physical and mental pain, that is so terrible, just a while longer so that He can work through her to resolve their life's decisions, 1Corinthians 10:13.

The photographer and reporter from the local newspaper will be arriving at 3:30. Victoria is hoping Jon would be willing to be interviewed. She asks him if he would, as this is his only home. Sadly he said a definite "no" but she can understand.

Society doesn't want to give teenagers a place to live. They are afraid of them or else they just don't care, too busy perhaps, or can't be bothered. Again, she understands; her experiences haven't been the best; troubles with Josh, Bill, Debbie and a couple more; there are bad apples in every barrel, don't you know it. Jon is not one of them. The successes outweigh the failures in her mind. If she were asked to take this on again she would not hesitate even though Jack, Matt and James are not exactly jumping for joy.

Jack gets very angry with her about the article the paper wrote saying it was too religious. In the early evening she gets very sick to her stomach. Jack's attitude makes her very upset; he doesn't seem to love her very much, she thinks. She decides she'll go for a walk to calm down and do a bit of praying. As she walked along the waters of the lake: Psalm 23, "The Lord is my Shepherd" came to her. She did calm down and who should come along but one of the Sisters of the Church. She stopped to chat and told Vitoria how much she liked the article in the paper, a great and much needed consolation. Thanks be to God.

--------------   --------------------   --------------------

**Sept 15/ 87**
Victoria writes her thoughts:

Today is the Feast of our Mother of Sorrows in the Catholic Church. She suffered unspeakable loneliness at the death of her Son on the Cross. I also am lonely. Am I lonely for the love of my husband, Jack, or is it a spiritual loneliness, lonely for our Father, and spiritual family? We all suffer loneliness at one time or another at the death or loss of a loved one; the loved one who may have turned his or her back on us for whatever reason.

But I have found out in my lifetime we are never alone. No, not if we have faith in a Higher Power who is always with us. After Jesus came to me by the infilling of the Holy Spirit I knew I would never be alone again. When He walked on the waters and visited me by the lakeside as I sat on a bench, He told me He would never leave me, and not to be afraid. I am drawn to my Poustinia, (closet) of silence. What for? I don't know.

My article in the local paper about "street-kids" came out a while back and received a very good response. I wonder why I didn't mention the church in the article; very strange, indeed.

I am still fasting; one meal a day, sometimes a whole day, a week or more. It is a powerful form of prayer and brings about many changes in our lives and those for whom we are praying. I credit the sale of the house to the fasting. It is also a very powerful weapon against the evil spirits who prowl around for the ruin of souls. ("Saint Michael the Archangel prayer.") Fasting, praying in silence or meditation helps us in our every-day lives and for those whom we pray to help others. An example of this is Jon, the native boy who is living with us, being given a chance, through the Courts, to be redeemed. There has been much prayer and fasting for him over the many years he has been with us as with all the young people who have lived with us. I know God in the Name of Jesus, by the Power of the Holy Spirit will look after them. Amen!

I have no car but Katicka, a young friend, offers to drive me to Mass. We pray the Rosary with the Legion of Mary members and a great joy fills my heart. Also the Words, "it is broken, it is broken" keeps repeating. The chains have been broken; the chains between Jack and me are now broken. We are unequally yoked and now changes will come about in both of us.

I am coming to the end of the beginnings of my spiritual growth. What an exciting, fearful experience. I know, Lord, You are with me and I have nothing to fear. Praise the Lord! I thank His Holy and Blessed Name!

--------------- --------------------- --------------------

*"She senses, as she grips the rudder of her little red sailboat, she is going to be sailing for some time yet. She knows she has nothing to*

--------------- --------------------- --------------------

The words keep coming to her:

"Pray more in silence for those whom you are asked to pray." This came to me after I prayed over a couple of friends today, instead of praying for them in silence, in my poustinia (closet).

Perhaps I might use the scripture: Lord, I am not worthy that You should enter under my roof, only say the Word and they shall be healed" as the soldier pleaded in faith to Jesus on the road for the healing of his daughter who was ill at home. John 4:53.

I must remain in silence; He can only work through me in silence. "Lord, heal me. Heal my desire to talk. Please help me be silent so I can listen and hear. Lord, heal me of wanting to talk all the time.

What must I do when people speak to me? The silent answer I spiritually heard, "They will speak to you and you answer them, but you must not speak to them. Speak only when spoken to otherwise remain silent." Oh! It is so mind-boggling when this happens."

--------------- --------------------- --------------------

Jack told Victoria he has written a proposal about the Adams family cottage in Musquash and has given it to his brother but he said he didn't include her because she is going to get it anyway if anything should happen to him. He has gone to his gym so she will steal a glance at it. Something stopped her; she keeps moving from one place to another, not accomplishing anything. She's very restless. She knows she must ask him to include her; not for now but for the future. His brother must deal with her if she is left alone. She has a rightful say in this matter, doesn't she?

She goes downtown to meet Jack at the café for a coffee. While there her mind flashes back to a couple she had met at this very café. He had been through a very bad plane accident as she recalls and very near death. He, in this state, had a strong urge to give his life over to follow Jesus Christ. Being Jewish he strongly felt a Call that this conversion must be put to work to convert the Jewish people.

As she sits there opposite Jack and looks at him, she thinks, "Is this what would happen to him? He would come so close to death that he would finally hear God's Word for him and convert." She decides she won't spend her time worrying about the cottage proposal.

Finally confirmed; Victoria and Jack will be going to N.B. on a holiday for two weeks. All is arranged but time of departure.

But all is not settled. She and Jack get into an argument again and, without fear she tells him exactly what she thinks of him. She tells him he is a selfish, arrogant, son-of a bitch. She threw a raw potato at him. Not very nice for a Christian to say such things but all is said calmly, without anger. She means every word of it.

He, swearing and blaspheming, yells out, "OK! We aren't going to N.B. then."

She wasn't surprised, knowing they are broke. The quarrel started, anyway, because they can't afford to help Matt pay his University year. She is sick about her son's financial dilemma. She tells herself she doesn't care whether they go back home just as long as Matt gets some help.

With his usual temper tantrum Jack runs out the door slamming it behind him.

She runs to her room in tears, sheer agony and pain. She picks up her rosary, prays and thinks, "He made over one hundred thousand on the sale of this house and he can't afford to send some to help Matt out. She can't understand it. Please Lord, hear my prayer and let my cry come unto you"

When he gets home he is still belligerent but doesn't mention the quarrel. It now being the "happy hour" they sit and drink. He tells her he had been at the bank to get a loan using the sale of the house as collateral but no luck. A bad risk, he was told.

--------------- -------------------- --------------------

*"As she sails along in her little red sailboat she prays for directions as to where she should go next. Where will the winds and tides take this little female sailor?"*

--------------- -------------------- --------------------

### Oct 9/87

Well, they do go to Musquash and it is now one week since they have arrived home. Their trip was very difficult in some ways. She prayed and fasted for two or three days in those two weeks. She had hoped these days would bring them closer together but she can't tell for sure. She was also hoping she was brought closer to her sister but it all seems so odd, as she fell apart emotionally and everyone got upset with her again. She has to believe she is being directed with the hope that, in spite of the hatefulness and anger toward her some good comes of it. In spite of these negative happenings she did have a sumptuous dinner at the Lodge, overlooking the beautiful Bay of her teen-age years.

However, Jack was angry with her in the car because of the way she acted; thank God she was given the Grace to answer soothingly which quieted him.

A sad event of this trip was the news from Jack's parents that his sister was very sick with lung cancer and would be in the hospital. She has only a short time to live. Because she had had a heart attack she could die of this instead before she suffered too much with the cancer.

"Please, Lord, I pray don't let her suffer too long. She had a very difficult life and only wanted dignity so I pray she be given this in death." A great chill went through her as she prayed.

She and Jack then went to the cottage in Musquash Bay. Matt had gone sailing with Jack's brother and had just arrived. It was good to see them; especially Matt. He looks so well.

Then began their drinking party; and as she sits there over their drinks she meditates in sadness:

"It is so difficult to give one's life up to You, Lord, when we live in a secular society. It would be so much harder if Your Presence was not so obvious to me, my Lord and God. You are everywhere. With all that is going on around me; radios blasting, all kinds of arguing and swearing; everything but spiritual sharing. I am so thankful I feel Your Presence to help me get through this."

Musquash Bay is very isolated; so easy to carry on illicit affairs, believing no one will notice. That is exactly what happened. She, in her naivety, decided she would approach him, discuss it and pray over him. Needless to say he was disgusted with her. He said she was one of those crazy religious kooks. She was able to sit through his not- so- kind words in peace and joy knowing full well he had his reasons. She had nothing to do with it. Whatever good comes of this relationship between these two is in God's hands; the not so good is from her. Only Time will reveal all.

Sunday they all went to Mass at the Musquash Mission Church on the Reserve. After getting home they all began drinking the rest of the day and on into the night. She wonders why they all went to Church.

After dinner Matt took off for University. He has turned out really well; thanks be to God for looking over him with care. He, of course doesn't want to admit God's blessings and Graces in his life; but who does? No one wants to admit God's Work, Graces, Mercy and Goodness in their lives.

Before going to Musquash, they visited her mum and dad, who are both doing well. They had happy visit. She picked up some books, one being "Joshua's People." She read it while at the cottage in Musquash Bay. It tells a biblical story about Joshua leading his people to the Promised Land through the land of Canaan with the power of fasting, prayer and listening for God's Word to direct him to the promised land; God's promise to them. She thought nothing of this book; just an interesting book to read. However, much to her surprise as they were driving back from visiting Jack's sister in the hospital, what should they drive through but a little village called New Canaan. To her amazement, after passing through New Canaan they then came to Young's Cove, where the farmhouse her friend had told her about, when Victoria was sick in bed on May 2-3.

Somehow, she felt in her heart a link to this farmhouse, New Canaan and her plans for the future.

--------------- -------------------- --------------------
*The little sailor in her little red sailboat cannot understand what is happening to her."*
--------------- -------------------- --------------------

While driving back home from N.B., she fasts for 2 meals and after the Fast she hears, inwardly, the words, "listen to My Words till death." What does this mean? The words persisted. As she continues the Fasting, the Words, "Fast for 3 days; then the Words, "study, read the old and new Testaments, the history of the Church from the beginning and write.

They are finally home. In the evening, these words come to her as she is watching TV. She is drawn into her Poustinia, (closet of silence), "Burden of Yahweh" Jeremiah 23:34. "Do not tear at the hem until the meaning is revealed. Go to your room and close the door."

She is a bit unsure about all this. "Is satan playing tricks on me again"?

"Blessed Mother, Mary, she prays, "help me to discern."

She must be careful, go slowly and wait.

Right now it is early evening and she is tired with a headache. She just wants to sleep. What is happening to her? She has no one to share these thoughts. Are all these words from God or satan? Poustinia: page 129.

An interior voice speaks: "I come to you in your silence. I will speak to you words of wisdom and you must write them down. You must write the words I tell you to write when I tell you to write them.

She has begun again her morning and evening prayers, meditation and readings. She didn't realize how much she has missed those quiet moments. Her heart is joyful and sings; as if she has opened a gift box full of treasures; songs of praise and thanksgiving; gold, silver, sparkling diamonds, rubies and sapphires; these treasury of jewels. Her spirits were empty these last three weeks without them.

Up to now she had experienced a dark, cold, ragged, sharp pain.

--------------- --------------------  --------------------

After meditating in silence, Victoria's brother flashes into her mind. He had called her to say he wanted mum to move in with them. She felt strongly this would be wrong and stated this to him emphatically. She is getting a lot of help and Mary, her sister, is there to see to her needs as well. I hope he understands and agrees.

Their son, James and Jane, their daughter-in-law, arrive for a visit. It is so great to see them. But as it is with families, a heated discussion arises over the years that street-kids were living with them in the past. Although, while giving a home to street-kids, they had articles of jewelry, money and a bike stolen, Victoria felt, no matter the negative aspect and conflicts, it was well worth it. With Faith in the Power of the Holy Trinity; Father, Son and Holy Spirit, they were doing our small bit for society and that Faith can work miracles. Since the loss of the articles we found out later, Cheryl had stolen them for money and has moved to New Brunswick.

Victoria had been invited to attend an Opus Dei meeting in Toronto but, at the time, because of James' visit she had no intention of going. James leaves the day before, so while attending mass she decides to go when one of the ladies persists. She is glad she listened to her and decided to go. She takes the bus in. While at the meeting she asks the priest to hear her confession. She has been very upset with the anger she holds against Jack and so confesses this. The priest said that if it was unintentional anger and done involuntarily, it is not a sin if one truly feels repentance.

Victoria takes the bus home from church, While sitting there she thinks about her book, Poustinia. She gets a strong feeling that somehow, she is going to be spiritually used like the "poustinik in the marketplace" as explained in the book. The feeling becomes stronger when a young man gets on the bus, goes to the back and then moves to the front and opposite to where she is sitting behind the driver.

So there he is, this blond guy of about 18, all dressed in black, pants too short, so very pale and sickly, dirty, stringy hair and very thin. He looks very tired. He keeps glancing at her but only casually as he is wearing earphones attached to a Walkman. All of a sudden he gives a great sigh.

She looks at him and quietly asked, "are you tired?"

She doesn't know whether he heard her but he seems to have had. She unbuttoned her coat to reveal the cross around her neck. Except for a glance or two when he sighed she didn't look at him so she doesn't know whether he noticed the cross. The feeling was very strong in her. She wishes she could explain the sensation of God's Powerful Presence within her.

Getting off the bus she knew she must pray for that young man, so she prayed, "Lord I am not worthy that You should enter under my roof, only say the Word and this young man will be healed." she instinctively knew he was being healed in some way. Thanks be to God.

She realizes then and there, this would be the way she must pray more often, in her poustinia, for others; in silence. In some cases it will be a vocal prayer or a prayer in silence depending on the person and whatever witnessing is necessary. She must discern with wisdom what would be appropriate for each individual. Prayer in silence is very necessary for discernment and a Gift from the Holy Spirit for those who have faith. She must not be ashamed to witness to this Grace she has been blessed with, in the Name of Jesus.

--------------- --------------------- ---------------------

*"She loves the safety of her little red sailboat as she nestles in a silent cove, wrapped in a warm blanket against the cool October night. She hears only the night sounds; crickets, night owls and waves lapping on the sands and on the side of the boat. If only she could stay within creation's womb forever.*

--------------- --------------------- ---------------------

Victoria thought she had ended her relationship with Leonard when the little roomettes he had built for the street-kids had been completed. But no, he again phones her one morning before she heads for early Mass. and asks her if she wants to go for a drive with him. She didn't want to go, feeling quite uncomfortable about the whole idea.

She hopes she ends it by saying, "no, I just got back on a long drive from N.B with Jack."

She is on pins and needles, thinking he is out to get her. In her past experiences a man has only one thing on his mind when he wants to take her for a drive. She is so glad she is able to say no. Then, for some reason, she begins to have second thoughts. What if she is being asked to witness to Leonard in some way and she is not empty enough to allow the Holy Spirit to work through her. She did some praying and spiritual reading and then felt that she must go with him.

Phoning back, she leaves a message; he calls back immediately saying, "great, wear your prettiest clothes." She answers with, "I'll see if I can find some rags," and laughs.

She goes to Mass and prays the rosary with the members of the congregation. A great peace fills her whole being.

Leonard is waiting when she leaves the church and, as she gets into the car, he commanded, "take off your coat, it's warm in the car."

That takes her by surprise. She thinks, "Why would he want me to take off my coat. It's cold out there."

As they start off she becomes more and more uncomfortable. She did not want to be in that car. He stops the car and reaches across her to find the seatbelt. She says, with a cool voice, "continue to drive, I can find it myself."

He stops often to search the map to find out his destination. She thinks, "Why does he not know where he is going. You'd think he'd be prepared."

He begins to mention her hair, mentioning she had had it cut. He then repeated, over and over again, "oh, you're so pretty." Then, he said, "but the hair cut doesn't suit you. Why are you so tense?" he keeps up the sexual talk.

She did realize she was tense; her hands cold and clammy. She is unhappy being there and he begins to sense it. "Pretend this is a date. Don't you like being told you are pretty?"

She said firmly with anger in her voice, "no, stop the nonsense. I don't want to be here. I'm only here because it's what you wanted. We are fifty years old. Let's stop playing games. You are not prepared to divorce your wife, nor I, Jack. I have no intention of having sex with you, if that's what you are after. I thought we were good friends."

221

He turns the car around and takes her home with no denial. She never sees or hears from him again.

Well, after much confusion over the whole scenario she guesses the end result was God's plan.

"Oh. Lord, I was given the protection I needed, with the joy of discernment knowing it was His Will to finally end it with Leonard. Amen!"

--------------- -------------------- --------------------

## Oct./87

Great joy fills Victoria's heart this morning as, while waking up, the vision that comes to her is the biblical scriptures about the Holy Family; Jesus, Mary and Joseph. The joy still remains with her as she lies in her bed. Jack is in the shower to prepare for his day and another vision flashes in her mind as she continues to lie there; the cottage on the banks of the waters. Will they be moving to N.B? A chill fills and goes through her. Somehow, she believes the end is near. What the end is, she doesn't know.

Jack said last night he doesn't know what he is going to do. He is having trouble finding work in his field as president of a company. He says it's best he stays working where he is now as consultant for a company. It's interesting how things are working out. So many scriptures are coming up from God's Word confirming there will be no more presidents' positions for him; jobs are few and far between.

The young Native, Jon who had moved out; a knock on the door and he is back; not finishing school and not quite able to make it on his own. Even though their own life situations are in turmoil at the moment they could not, in good conscience, not take him in again. He said, "I would like to stay with you wherever you go."

--------------- -------------------- --------------------

*"Will the exhausted little female sailor finally find a secure home to moor her little red sailboat?"*

--------------- -------------------- --------------------

# Chapter 15

## West River Road

Jack and Victoria, having sold their home on Burbourne Dr., must be out by January. Jack is discouraged and thinks they should just stay in the area where they are now living. Perhaps they should look into buying in the beautiful village near-by where housing is cheaper; West River Rd., where there is a house for sale on the corner, they noticed, when visiting the last time.

It runs along the harbor; right on the lake; reminding her of the wharf at Musquash Bay; boats and boaters, fishermen, walkers of all ages; just like home. There are lots of trails and benches for walking along the lake, an old fashioned grocery store, other shops and even her favorite hardware store within walking distance.

They make an appointment with an Agent to see the harbour front house but the information he gives is not what they want to hear. The asking price is $260,000.00, while the houses in the village sell for about $60,000.00. Also the municipality wants to split the property into three smaller ones. There is a group in the community who are interested in preserving the heritage of the village and perhaps they are worth talking to.

Is this where they are called to live and not Musquash Bay? After all, God does speak straight with crooked lines. The whole harbor and area is so like her beloved Musquash Bay but certainly not the Maritimes.

Victoria has been reading through her writings and wonders how much of the prayer life she has been experiencing is really true or her imagination. She is so confused. Are they going to move to N. B.

or not? Considering their situation as it stands; they have nowhere to live and no money coming in. Inwardly she is seething toward Jack; he is continually fighting with Matt and me, still going to his club, drinking, doesn't come home for his meals so must be eating out and still living high on the hog.

She prays, "Lord, what do You want from me? Why don't you just take me, I am useless. I'm just in the way; no good to anyone. Jack thinks I'm crazy and so does everyone else. I feel like ending it all. I'm so discouraged" Jack finally arrives home late, comes into their room; she senses a change in him. She keeps silent and pretends she is asleep.

After visiting a few houses yesterday she had persuaded him to look at some townhouses on the lake today that are selling at a much lower price. They were then supposed to view condos which were at a much higher price. Jack flew out of control over the townhouses being in a lower section of the village.

"There is no way we are going to live in those rundown shacks." He screams and swears. "How dare you. I am not going to view the condos either, so forget it."

Victoria could only praise and thank God for the outcome since neither were good investments for them. Again she uses reverse phycology and it works.

She lies in bed and prays her rosary. She feels there is something physically wrong with her. Her chest feels like a vise, a great weight pressing on it and her left arm is painful. She is so tired. She feels as if her food is a dead lump in the middle of her chest.

"Oh, dear Lord", she prays, "what is the matter with me? I have housework to do and I just don't feel like doing it," The tears flow.

--------------- -------------------- --------------------

Victoria goes to Mass this morning and then on to the coffee shop where her friends are gathered. Elleanor thinks she wants to move from here because she's unhappy. They don't know the truth, of course but, she's not unhappy no matter where her "little red sailboat" may take her. But she feels drawn to the waters; the sea, rivers, bays, streams, brooks and inlets. Why? She just doesn't know. Her Roots, she supposes, having Viking, Acadian or French, Irish; Maritime blood flowing in her veins. One never knows either what other skeletons are in the closet. She is proud of who she is and has no reason to be unhappy within.

Getting back to her conversation with Eleanor; she is of the opinion it is because of the way some of the people at the Parish Church think and talk about her, Victoria. They think she is crazy or queer because she feels drawn to pray with the laying on of hands for healing and praying in tongues. Well, she is a Born-Again Christian and Catholic and proud of it. She has been healed of self-respect; so she feels no fear of others' opinions as long as she knows she has been given and have accepted the Gifts of the Holy Spirit in the Name of Jesus Christ. Scripture: Acts, chapter 1. Alleluia!

She asks a woman at the church, who is ill, if she could pray over her and her reaction was not surprising, of course. Victoria is at peace but sad. She had prayed over the street-kids she had in her home; some accepted with such overwhelming thanksgiving; others are cautious but don't show any animosity or fear; some believe, some don't.

Even Jack and her sons think she is crazy. Well, as far as the secular world is concerned, she guesses she is, but that's all right with her.

--------------- -------------------- --------------------

These are the words that she writes, filling her spirit this night at 12:30 A.M.

"You must come to My Holy Mountain to hear the words I have for you and My people. I will speak to you and you must write what I tell you. I will wall you in so that you cannot escape. You cannot run to others, only to Me. Come to Me. Come to my Holy Mountain. For the next year you will listen to Me. Study and read what I tell you. Go to no library as you have enough books to read in your own library. I will choose the ones for you to read. Tell my people what I want you to tell them through the written word.

You will rent the cottage at Musquash and stay for 6 months to write My Word.

You have known for some time what I wanted from you. Now you are ready to begin. I love you. Do not be afraid. You will live in silence to hear My Word. I will bring to you the people I want you to help. You need not do anything. Walk, pray, study, read, write and receive me in the Eucharist. Visit me often when I am exposed. I need to know you love me, you don't give Me enough of your time. Do you really love me? Don't worry about others around you. I am looking after them. Concentrate on Me, only on Me. Discipline yourself so that you are only concentrating on Me. Your mind wanders, concentrate on Me. You must prepare yourself for a narrow, walled-in existence except when I use you to help others. I love you. As the days, weeks and months go by you will be much more aware of this love I have for you. We will grow closer. I am intimately and personally yours. Psalm 19."

Sitting here writing this in the dead of night, she is left in awe, skeptical and a bit frightened. This can't be happening. Surely she will wake up and find out it is all a dream or, is she being attacked? Is Satan trying to disturb her peace? She must Fast and pray the rosary, the Exorcist prayer and reach out to the church for help.

--------------- --------------------- ---------------------

Finally sleep and Victoria wakes to a bright, sunny day. A call comes in. It is for one of the street-kids, Randy. Jon, the native boy is still with them and will be for some time. Randy is doing very well and has been speaking with his parents. He is now ready to move back home with them. Prayer has worked miracles, she must admit. She gives Glory and Eternal Praise to the Almighty God, King and Father of these young people. It's been a tough go; 40 street-kids in 4 years, 6 at a time. Where did she get the strength to deal with it all, her own deep stress and Jack's problems too? James and Matt haven't exactly been very happy with her either. It is only the Grace of God working in her, she has no doubt.

In spite of the fact she and Jack are looking into buying a place on the harbour in the village, she still keeps hearing the words; "Go to N.B. in Faith." Her mind flashes back to her vision of the cottage on the banks of a river, and reading the biblical book, "Joshua." While in N.B., they had driven through New Canaan, the same name "Canaan" as in the bible, they had stopped there to get directions to go to the nearest city and Jack was given a card from a real estate agent. Is it all a coincidence? Time will tell, of course, she must just ignore and remain empty like a little ragdoll. She must close the wings of her intellect because she is well aware she has no idea what is being revealed to her.

Beginning days of November/87 and her fasting continues; one or two meals a day for weeks. This next Fast will be longer she believes. Many scriptures come to her as she reads her bible but still no idea what she is being told. Something is going to happen, but what and when.

As she prays about the buying of West River Rd. house on the harbour an interesting scripture comes to her; Adam and Eve in the

Garden of Eden. The temptation to eat the "apple from the tree of wisdom is strong". Now she understands what is being revealed to her.

They can't afford this lovely house on the harbour; so very like Musquash Bay, but they are so tempted. Financially are ahead of the game with Burbourne Drive finally sold. They will be debt free; they could rent an apartment rather than buy another house or move to N.B. since Jack is free to do so and could find work there. Jack, however, wants to make West River Rd. in this little village their home. It turns out someone else was going to bid on the house. The "apple" is too appealing. He will not listen to Victoria. So she trusts his judgement again, and signs the papers as co-owner. So they buy it and they are back where they were with no income. They are now owners of an expensive and elite place overlooking the harbour on West River Rd.

As she meditates on the whole scenario, she prays, "Your plan, Father within me is falling into place. We are following it step by step. This is all happening for a reason, isn't it, Lord; Providence at work. As I listen, it all becomes clear and everything falls into place. You are trying to teach a lesson here and in the process Your Word will prevail. I am not afraid."

Victoria has no idea what will come out of all this but in the long run it will be the best for them both. She is prompted to begin a two week Fast today although at the moment she's not sure she is hearing right. She is sitting on the couch in the living room and Jon, the young native, comes home after being away all week-end. He sits with her to chat about what he's been up to. She tells him about the Fasting she's planning.

"Oh," he says, "in our Native Culture you would be going on a "Vision Quest."

She is speechless. That is so true. That is exactly what she's on. She is requesting a vision of what God is asking of her. Rather than dwell on it she pushes it aside for another time as Jon is anxious to talk.

She was planning on going to Mass but he seems so anxious to talk she feels this is more important. He tells her his parents have asked him to move back home. Alleluia! She is so happy for him. He then begins to chat about this friend of his. Male or female, he didn't say and she didn't pry. Somehow she just knew she had to pray for them both. He left to clean up and she is left with her thoughts and prayers.

As the day wears on she prays the rosary and Fast one meal. She could not get those two out of her mind; a chill goes through her. She knows she was praying for them. In what way, she doesn't know but she knows her prayer has been heard. "Thank you, Lord, for allowing me as a servant, for hearing and answering my healing prayer. Praise the Lord."

It is amazing to her how she can be in a joyous disposition when she is writing and thinking spiritual thoughts but the minute she is away and in Jack's presence she is no longer happy and can't be nice to him. She complains or inwardly she's seething and cross because of his powerful demands over her. Yes, he never lets her forget she is not a very good person. He is the thorn in her side. He and the pain, the physical pain she suffers will always remind her she is not worthy and must continually die to self.

"Praise You, Jesus for helping me see this. I give thanks for Jack and the pain because without them I may have been given worse sufferings to deal with to remind me I am a sinner; to help me battle my way through life."

However there is also much joy as she contemplates the letter she has written to send to the owners of the cottage on the Musquash Bay. She prays with the biblical scriptures she has found to encourage her thoughts.

She feels she is being told something but what? She is fasting again and will continue to pray the words of the Holy Spirit in tongues. What is going to happen that they will be using the cottage? It is becoming stronger and stronger she must send the letter to rent the cottage. But why; they just bought a house on West River Rd?

--------------- -------------------- --------------------

Our Church women are attending a Saint Francis of Assis Exhibition in the next town. Again she witnesses God's work in the Marketplace in so many ways, to bring joy and healing into the hearts of many around her.

The Sunday before going to the Exhibition, Jack and Victoria decide to drive to West River Rd. to take a look at their new house and the beautiful surroundings of the harbour. She sits on a bench to watch as the men are fishing; casting their lines into the waters. They are busy chatting away when, all of a sudden, one of them catches a huge fish. The fish is struggling for air, bouncing and slapping

228

around. She could almost feel its agony. The fisherman is snipping at the line caught in its mouth. Saint Francis of Assis, the lover of all living creatures, flashes into her mind and she starts to pray. She couldn't bring herself to look at what was happening to the poor fish and what the fisherman was doing. A miracle; when she looks back at the fisherman there was no fish. She could not imagine what happened to the fish. She goes over to the fisherman to find out. He tells her he had thrown it back into the water. He had let it live. She could have cried with joy.

Now, getting back to the Saint Francis of Assis Ex. she attends the next day.

They show a film depicting the love the Saint had for all living creatures. One of the stories was how he loved life so much that he even made sure caught fish would be thrown back into the water rather than kill them. She could not believe what she was hearing. This was confirming what had happened with the fish caught by the fisherman. Saint Francis did hear her prayer for the fish.

"Oh Blessed Trinity. Thank You and Praise Your Holy Name. My joy is overwhelming; thanks to all angels and saints who give my life so much love and meaning."

She has been wearing a cross she got from one of the Charismatic priests and now she can't find it.

She thinks, "I wonder what happened to it. Perhaps my time for wearing it is over, as so much in my life seems now to be over or changing again. Five years ago I was planning on leaving my marriage and moving back home with my parents but a scripture was revealed to me, the biblical Book of Ruth. Do you really speak to me through the scriptures or am I imagining it? Because of the scripture I stayed with my marriage and heaven only knows where I would be today. Scriptures, prayer, Fasting, Rosary; is all I have to go on. I must continue to wait until all is ready to be revealed to me."

--------------- --------------------- ---------------------

*"The skipper in the little red sailboat is now sailing into new unfamiliar waters again. Will she continue to receive the visions necessary to help her sail into the next port of call?"*

--------------- --------------------- ---------------------

**Nov. /87**

Victoria gets a call her sister, Mary asking her to come home. Dad is in the hospital and mum is lonely is all that she is told presently. But as the time of her stay passes Victoria senses there is much more wrong than meets the eye. Her mother is very depressed and is talking of dying. Although Victoria was planning on going back home on Monday, she tells her sister and brother-in-law she will stay a bit longer. She doesn't have the slightest idea when mum will die but she feels it won't be very long. Her brothers are arriving the end of Nov. so she will wait and pray. She can't do much more until her prayers reveal what is best. She trusts she will be given the answers she needs.

Victoria arrives back home feeling at ease about her mother. She knows her mother is depressed, feeling sorry for herself and wishes to die. The doctor says she is well and could live another 5 to 10 years.

Victoria didn't mince any words, telling her what the Doctor said, including she is just depressed and feeling sorry for herself. Victoria knows that is the story of her mother's life; even as they were growing up. It helped Victoria to see that because her mother, Eliza, in her own coldness and unhappiness, was unable to show a mother's love for them, instilled the feelings of guilt, anxiety, rejection and fear Victoria felt while growing up, causing the kind of disruptive household they lived in. To be fair the $2^{nd}$ world war and the shack they finally ended up living in didn't help either, to their mother's disgrace and pride.

She wrote the following words intending to send them to her parents but decided not to. She felt she had no right to tell others how they should think but wanted to write them anyway.

She wrote:

"I chose this Christmas card because of the beautiful words of St Francis of Assis. He was a man of peace, love and faith in himself and in mankind. We are able to emulate what he represented for the love of all mankind only if we love ourselves, because unless we love ourselves we cannot love others. If we don't love ourselves we have the desire to die. We have nothing to live for because we don't want to or can't love ourselves. This is a sin against God's Law; you shall love God with your whole heart, your whole soul and with your whole being and you shall love your neighbour as yourself. I have asked Saint Francis of Assis to pray for you both."

Victoria knows she has received a great healing from her visit. No more does she feel guilt, anger, rejection or fear. She knows God has forgiven her and so she can forgive her parents.

"Forgive us our trespasses as we forgive those who trespass against us. The "Our Father Prayer" Yes, we can live the teachings of God through the scriptures today. That is why He sent His Son to be born in a manger, a poor carpenter's son so we will know we can live today as He lived 2000 years ago to be our strength and courage, our faith, hope and love. We need nothing more to give us the desire to live, as, it is in living we die to self so we can begin again in this life, born again now and for life eternal in His Arms when we die." After writing this card she goes to mass and begins to pray in tongues before mass started. During the Eucharist she feels great joy and knows she truly has forgiven her parents. How can she ever thank God enough for His goodness and mercy?

--------------- -------------------- --------------------

*"All is silent as she, in her little red sailboat, gives up her desire to control and just lets the sails and winds take her to ports and places unknown."*

--------------- -------------------- --------------------

**She writes:**
It is a strange day in my closet of silence today but, of course every day is a strange day when you give yourself to a Being with whom you believe truly exists within you. But today is especially strange because I have come to the realization as what is truly being asked of me. The enormity of it is very overwhelming. As I wander from room to room looking for something, I don't know what, I feel I should do some housework and, yet, I can't. Something has a hold of me; something very powerful is making me stop. I must concentrate. I must stop doing and just listen. I feel like I want to run away. I tried when I went to pick up materials for my fruit cakes but even that didn't work. I can't run away any more. I know it. I know it. I know it.

"Oh Lord, You win. I am here, I am stopped. I have been running from you all my life but, now it's over. I'm not going to run any more. You are fencing me in, putting a wall around me and planting me in an enclosed garden. You are more than I can handle but I know I will be able to flow with the power of it all. Everything around me seems as nothing, I am only aware of You within me. Nothing else is important but what You are asking of me. Lord, what are you asking of me? I read and read to find the answers but nothing satisfies. What am I being told? All is coming closer and closer to fulfilment, I am almost sure.

She continues to write:

Jack and I seem to be drifting apart more and more. He is being taken away from me. I can see it happening. He goes off to work now that he has a job; all the street-kids have gone, except Jon the young Native. I am all alone but I am not afraid. This is all happening for a reason and I am ready. I am being prepared for something when, being alone with my prayer life is all I will be able to depend upon because it will be all I'll have.

Praise His Holy and Blessed Name, the Name above all names, the Pastor preached at the Pentecostal Church that I attended with Maureen. It was a glorious evening filled with the Power of the Holy Spirit.

Some time ago, at a Charismatic Catholic Convention I was given a wooden cross to wear. I was to wear it all the time but, as I think about it I am beginning to realize that with the kind of life I have been living and, especially with Jack, I am already carrying a heavy enough cross. It is not a physical cross it is the cross of life I must carry. Why do I need a cross around my neck when I am living continually a life with more mental violence, hate, ugliness and bully tactics? Such a vile, hateful tongue and such dirty language I have never heard. Such mental cruelty and yet he pretends to be so nice to me when he wants to be. It is all a farce. Deep down inside he really hates me and always has. Even when he pretends to like me, he really doesn't. That is enough of a cross to contend with. This I know now.

I am supposed to go to a party with him tomorrow night but I hate parties.

"Lord, Jesus, this must be the cross You mean, no matter how much he hates me, help me to continue to care about this sad man because I am all he has. He has nothing and no-one else."

Why could I not have married a man who is caring, loving, compassionate, respectful, and understanding, who loved me enough to overlook my queer ways. Maybe I am crazy. I must seem very odd to him. I guess maybe he should leave me. Perhaps he just can't take any more of my crazy ways. Am I crazy? No I'm not. I'm in love with God, in the Name of Jesus Christ by the Power of the Holy Spirit, One God.

"Lord Jesus Christ, Son of God, have mercy on me a sinner. You are going to release me. You are going to release me. You are going to release me. Jack will let me go." Is that true? Such joy fills my heart.

James comes to visit on the weekend of 29th. As Providence would have it he is able to quiet Jack down. All the frustration, anger and hate Jack feels for me because of the cross I am wearing, the office party, my fasting; everything has come to a head and we can finally share how Jack and I feel about each other. Thankfully I didn't have to go to the party. As it turns out Jack said I would not have enjoyed it anyway? I felt such agony at having to go to that ridiculous party. All the praise and glory to God, the Almighty!

--------------- --------------------- --------------------

*"She can finally moor her little red sailboat in a safe harbour. It is surrounded by boats of all shapes and sizes almost like armour of protection from the winds, rains and winter snows for now."*

--------------- --------------------- --------------------

Jack and Victoria have finally moved into their new home on the harbour of West River Rd. It's not exactly N.B or Musquash Bay as she envisioned, but Victoria is by the water and, for now, it is all she can ask. Her heart sings for joy. Jack has been such a big help while getting settled. Such a healing has come over him since James's visit. Because of Victoria's physical ailment, all she is aware of is a handicap of pain. Jack has been a gem at doing all the heavy work at moving out of the old house and into here. With his help and the movers, she can take it easier during this move.

Christmas is moving closer; they have no money to send presents, cards or for baking. She is in such physical pain she can't sleep without waking up to such agony. What is the matter? What can she do to help?

She knows she would be good at selling real estate, making a contribution. Maybe then Jack would be proud of her. She should be out working, getting a job and helping out financially. What good is she? But, no, it seems God has other plans for her; for now, silence and simplicity. If that is what she is being called to, what for? What does he want from her?

--------------- --------------------- --------------------

*"She sinks into her little red sailboat letting the soft winds lull and relax her, helping her forget everything. The waves lap against the boat sending swirls of water around her. So much has happened in her life she can hardly remember everything. All she is aware of is peace finally taking over as she falls into a state of unknowing."*

I am quietly sitting overlooking the harbour having my lunch. After some meditation time, I begin to think: "You know, I don't love Jack, no wonder I'm so mean to him. Over and over in my mind the thought spins like a top! It is difficult to be nice to someone you don't love. No wonder the anger rises up in me when he says something to hurt me. I then respond with anger when I should respond with kindness. If he is angry he must have had his reasons. He is unhappy or something and if I loved him I would be able to see his side and overlook the remark. Or perhaps, I love him; I just don't like him. After all, he is my husband.

I guess I don't feel any compassion for him and his problems as a wife should, and I have no tolerance for the way he treats me. I wish I knew what I have been doing wrong all these years. Perhaps I should go to the Communal Confessional Service this evening and confess my sins for healing. Perhaps I can look on the bright side of his personality and change my attitude toward him. For this I pray, my Lord, Jesus Christ, the Healer. Amen!

As I was coming out of the church, I overheard a man talking to a couple about his sick wife. He described the illness in detail as we stood there in the foyer. They did not know I was listening. I somehow knew I must pray for her.

At 2:AM early Sunday morning, Jon, my Native street-kid wakes me up; he had forgotten his key; then around 9, Jack locks himself out while putting out the cat. I am praying, Lord for the grace to be happy under all circumstances; to see all things as a means for my spiritual growth. Give me the gift of patience with Jon when he is on the phone for hours and with Jack.

Strangely, after being awakened at 2 AM, I sat in the living room covered in a blanket and began to pray in tongues. I prayed till 4. Then the prayer in tongues changed and I was filled with joy. I knew there had to be a reason for Jon to forget his key. I knew somehow, somewhere someone was being helped. And then I remembered the husband talking about his sick wife at the church last evening.

"Lord, I am unworthy to receive You, only say the Word and she shall be healed." Amen! Yes, I received a Word of Knowledge (a Gift of the Holy Spirit) that she was healed in some way. Alleluia! Thank You, Jesus, the Healer.

We are supposed to go to a Christmas party at a cousin's home today, but Jack is not feeling well and neither am I. I have a bad back; so painful. Matt has arrived home for Christmas. Should Matt and I go to the party; no, best to stay home. Jack has a job interview tomorrow with Atomic Energy.

--------------- --------------------- ---------------------

### Dec 31/87 New Year's Eve

Christmas has come and gone and I am resting. Thinking about yesterday when Jon, the young Native who moved with us, comes to me at 10PM and asks me to drive his girlfriend, Monique, to the bus stop. I sure resented being imposed upon; why couldn't she walk to the bus stop? However, I did it this time but I will have to think about whether I will do it again. I began to think; what would Jesus do? Words fill my heart:

"He died on the cross for you, didn't He so why can't you, at the very least, carry your own without complaining?"

That is true. Why not? A great peace fills me as hear those words. I then think how dangerous it would be for a young girl to walk to a bus stop at 10PM at night. I am glad I did. A biblical scripture comes to me; "On the road to Emmaus", Luke 24:25-32, Catherine Doherty's Poustinia, Page 43.

--------------- --------------------- ---------------------

### January 3/88

Here it is a new year and Victoria still hasn't the slightest idea what God is calling her to in the future. Although she is still faithful to a spiritual prayer life, Rosary, meditation, Mass, fasting, and following the writings of Catherine Doherty of Madonna House and other saints, it doesn't seem to do much good. She feels like running away from it all today. She just wants to immerse into the secular world and pretend none of this is happening. She tries to see herself as she was before but she knows she will never be that woman again. She is trying to be like everyone else but she can't be. What is wrong with her? What is she afraid of anyway? What unseen life is ahead? Is she ready? She is running away from the silence of the prayer-life she is continually being Called to. She is so alone now that the kids are gone except for Jon the native boy. If only she had someone she could talk to; who would understand what she is going through. She is angry, frustrated and finds excuses to lash out.

Doubts and fear fill her mind but she prays it will all pass. Victoria talks to a friend on the phone and shares with her the feelings she is going through. Lo and behold, Jack hears her conversation and picks up on her unhappiness. He had not realized she was unhappy and at first had trouble relating or sympathizing but later he took her shopping for two new dresses in exchange for the two that didn't fit; then out to lunch. Back to the secular world or God's mercy and love for her?

Another blessing from the Holy Spirit yesterday, lifting her spirits. Three white doves sitting on the telephone wires; receiving a card with a dove pictured on it, beautiful doves of Peace gracing the Christmas Tree at the Church. She then thought of the blue birds she saw on her in-laws' window at Musquash last summer; blue birds of happiness.

She prays, "Oh Lord, tell me what you would have me do with those beautiful signs of Your Love. Fill me with Your Love so I can react with love to Jon the Native boy living with us. Purify my mind and heart so I can understand with patience what is going through his mind to respond properly without causing him harm. Help me to be like your Mother, Mary."

--------------- -------------------- --------------------

### Jan.6/88

Last evening Victoria was praying in her closet of silence when everything went out of control. It wasn't very nice. She cried in her pain having gotten angry at Jon over the last few days. Since last Thursday he has been going through agony because of Monique, his girlfriend. He wanted her to move into his room with him.

Victoria said, "No. it isn't that kind of a house."

She listened to him for three days crying and weeping over his love for this girl. She assumes it is a good relationship; she couldn't judge until he let her read a letter she had sent him. She really couldn't say the relationship was wrong. She just wanted time to think about their relationship. She is older at 22 than he who is 18. After reading the letter a strong feeling came over Victoria that Monique has been using him and the relationship is not a healthy one. This feeling stayed with her and is still with her. Saturday he got so angry he smashed a hole in their kitchen wall. That night he went home to his adopted mother and father and came back last night. Jon reacted when he again heard Monique wanted time for a few days and would call him when she felt it was the right time.

Today is Monday. She doesn't know for sure but she has a feeling Jon talked with Monique yesterday from his parents' home. Now Jack and she have been having misgivings about Jon staying here. Needless to say, Jack is very upset with him since the hole in the wall episode and asks him to leave. Jon has not been honest with them nor has he paid up his rent either. She knows Jack is right, but she, against Jack's wishes, said,

"You can stay as long as you stop seeing Monique."

She suspects he talked with Monique anyway even though he told Victoria he would stop seeing her; then he asks if he could take her skating.

This morning he rushes out to catch the bus at 7:30 to go to work. He arrives home around 2. Did he or did he not see Monique? He said, "no, she wasn't at work."

Jon has been living with them for almost 4 years, has never given us any trouble and is now living with them at their new home on the harbour. She has always felt she could trust him.

And so, her tears of sadness and frustration: "Dear Blessed Mother Mary, intercede for me to your Son, Jesus to relieve my mind and reveal to me the truth so I will not judge Jon wrongly. Please, help me, Mary."

Like a flash one thing comes to Victoria's mind; Jon, their Native friend; feels comfortable living with them although they are not his parents, and so feels free to release his frustrations in their midst. Although Jack got angry as any father would, they did not, in the end, kick him out. He came here of his own free will, was not placed here as an adopted child and could be himself with them.

With Victoria's very little knowledge, in a very small way, of the difficult life he and all First Nations children have lived; strange he should be connected with her.

Is it a coincidence, a prophecy, a pre-ordained mission?

--------------- -------------------- --------------------

*"The little skipper takes on a Vision Quest; fasting for two weeks. What will be revealed to her? She is both confident and cautious, but her little sailboat is yaw; steady, as she sails along in her little red sailboat, to her next port of call on her Mystical Voyage into the Unknown."*

--------------- -------------------- --------------------

# Author's Note

**H**ere the author ends the second volume, with another sequel to come of the Trilogy, written as an allegory, *Sailing Uncharted Waters, a Mystical Voyage into the Unknown.*

Does she finally find her lost love? Will this lost love be what you, as a reader, envision?

*Sailing Uncharted Waters,*
*a Mystical Voyage into the Unknown*

**Available from the author**
**and on Amazon (print and e-book)**

# About the Author

**N**an Colwell Creaghan grew up in Dalhousie, a small town in northern New Brunswick, Canada, until her marriage. She has resided in Burnt Church, Miramichi Bay, on the Acadian Peninsula for the past twenty-five years. In these environments, she has grown to appreciate the many cultures and traditions of the peoples surrounding her.

She is well educated in the school of hard knocks, humbly putting to work the trials, tribulations, and experiences she has learnt and gleaned through her own life and the lives of those around her and from her spiritual growth, the valuable gift of "love."

At age eighty, Nan faces another challenge, that of cancer. In writing this book, the second of her trilogy, she shows that living the Spiritual Life is the only way to defeat adversity and overcome life's natural evolution from which none of us are immune.

Nan has had short stories published in the Province of New Brunswick magazine, *Bread 'n Molasses*.

Nan Colwell Creaghan
399 Bayview Drive.
Burnt Church, NB, Canada
E9G 2G8
1 (506) 776-5165
Email: **ncrea@rogers.com**

239

www.ingramcontent.com/pod-product-compliance
Lightning Source LLC
Chambersburg PA
CBHW071304250626
47159CB00004B/1302